W9-CLP-002

THE REPORTER

Kelly Lange

THE REPORTER

Published by Warner Books

An AOL Time Warner Company

This book is a work of fiction. Names, characters, places, and incidents are the product of the author's imagination or are used fictitiously. Any resemblance to actual events, locales, or persons, living or dead, is coincidental.

Mysterious Press books are published by Warner Books, Inc.,
1271 Avenue of the Americas, New York, NY 10020.

Visit our Web site at www.twbookmark.com.

An AOL Time Warner Company

The Mysterious Press name and logo are registered trademarks of Warner Books, Inc.

Printed in the United States of America

First Printing: March 2002

10 9 8 7 6 5 4 3 2 1

ISBN: 0-89296-752-8
LCCN: 2001099081

DEDICATION

IN HOMAGE TO THE GREAT SUE GRAFTON

A is for
*A*LICE—my wonderful mom
&
*A*RTHUR—her kid brother
. . . *with love!*

1

Reporter Maxi Poole couldn't take her eyes off the bizarre translucent coffin, and the man lying inside on a bed of ruched white satin, with a smile on his face, and holding a set of onyx rosary beads in both hands—her ex-husband. *Rosary beads?* she thought. But he was *Jewish*. And smiling? He was *terrified* of dying. None of it made sense to Maxi, including and especially the fact that the man was, undeniably, dead.

It was a bleak fall day, one of very few in usually sunny La-La Land, as the tabloids call Los Angeles. Many of the film industry's most notable personages stood huddled against the chill—world-famous producers, directors, writers, stars—shoulder to shoulder around the spot where the transparent coffin stood on its preposterous-looking gilded bier. No matter that most of them were noteworthy for yesterday's triumphs, not today's, and certainly not tomorrow's; they were noteworthy still by virtue of illustrious past accomplishments and significant contributions to the art of cinema.

Maxi pressed her back against a pink flowering myrtle tree, literally trying to blend with the scenery. It didn't help that she was five-foot-eight and wearing a short, bright red, zip-up sweater with a red-and-white tweed miniskirt. Somehow, black hadn't seemed to suit for this occasion, but now, looking at the sea of women and men in black, she might have liked to rethink that wardrobe choice. Too late. She pushed her cropped blond hair out of her eyes, straightened her sunglasses, and folded her arms. *Just get through this,* she reminded herself.

Next to Maxi stood her producer, Wendy Harris, all of five-foot-two on platform shoes, ninety-three pounds, tawny red hair and lots of it, with notebook in hand. In muted voice, clearly getting a huge kick out of the tribal rites of old Hollywood, Wendy was doing a comedic commentary, blithely pointing out luminaries, has-beens, and hangers-on. With her face deadpan and her eyes straight ahead, Maxi gave Wendy a sharp elbow to the ribs.

"What!" Wendy blurted, making some small attempt to stifle a grin. "We're supposed to look like we're working, aren't we?"

Maxi rolled her eyes. She straightened up and forced herself to concentrate on the remains of her late ex-husband. Bad enough Wendy was having such a good time; it would be disastrous if she caught the mood herself and broke into nervous giggles. And she knew it could happen.

There was a rustling in the crowd, and Maxi saw actress Debra Angelo approaching them, her young daughter in hand. Debra caused a stir in any crowd. She was striking in a very short, very tight black Versace suit, a gold-flecked chiffon scarf wrapped loosely around tons of dark hair, and impossibly high heels that kept sinking into the soggy cemetery turf. Debra had been the wife before Maxi. At some point in Maxi's marriage to Jack Nathanson, the two women had got around to comparing notes, and became friends.

Maxi reached out to hug her. "God, this is grim," Debra murmured in her ear. "Grim, just like him."

"What, Mom?" piped up the winsome child at her side, her daughter—*his* daughter.

"I was just telling Maxi it's a dreary day for a funeral," Debra said with just a touch of a lyrical Italian accent. "But Daddy wouldn't mind that, would he, darling? He rather liked gloomy weather."

Smiling down at Gia, Maxi whispered, "How's she doing?"

"Bewildered," Debra said of her cherubic-faced ten-year-old, the child she'd been trying for a decade to bring up as a normal youngster, Maxi knew, with little success.

"Oh, there's Carlotta," Debra said. Carlotta Ricco was Jack Nathanson's housekeeper. The woman adored Gia. Seeing the girl now a few feet away, she opened her arms, and Gia scurried into her embrace. Alone for a minute, Debra breathed, "Maxi, what the hell are you doing here?"

"Working. Covering the funeral," Maxi said with a dismissive shrug and a look toward her producer, and knowing that Debra wouldn't buy it.

"Yeah, right!" Debra whooped, louder than she'd meant to. Then she glanced up quickly to see if anybody had heard. Scanning the crowd, she muttered, "Look at these dinosaurs, Maxi. And who came up with that ridiculous Lucite coffin? Even *he* had better taste than that, which is saying precious little, God knows. But the man was Gia's father, after all—"

"And the reason why she gets in fights in school, and pulls her hair out at night," Maxi put in.

"That's going to change now," Debra hissed. "Now that the sonofabitch is dead."

"*Shhhh,*" Maxi cautioned.

"Right. Damn, I am *ruining* these shoes!" Debra observed, glancing down at the fine black suede that was now coated with grassy, muddy ooze. "Fucking seven-hundred-dollar Manolo Blahniks, but it can't be helped—you never know where your next part is coming from. Shouldn't there be at least a *few* au courant movers and shakers among these turgid mourners?"

Maxi chuckled. She marveled at Debra's indomitable spirit. Debra Angelo was arguably not a brilliant actress, but she had, to date, played the parts of several memorable ladies, largely by dint of a big personality coupled with a sculpted, exotic beauty that was rendered all the more extraordinary on-screen—the camera loved her, attested many a director of photography, loved those cheekbones. And even though she had really only one act, so to speak, it was an act in sufficient demand, that of the funny, ballsy, off-the-wall, altogether endearing and thoroughly Americanized Italian jewel.

Carlotta walked Gia over to them, and with the child in the middle, all three women hugged. Kind, genial Carlotta had been with Jack Nathanson through all of his wives, and now she had tears in her eyes. "You'll come to the house after?" she asked.

"I'm sorry, Carlotta, I have to get to work," Maxi said.

"And I'm not sure Gia would be up to going to her daddy's house today," Debra put in. "But Carlotta, you'll still see her, as much as you'd like. Okay?"

"Okay." Carlotta forced a smile and gave Gia another squeeze.

Debra linked her arm through Maxi's. "Walk with me," she urged.

"Walk with you! Where?" Maxi was trying to be invisible, and walking *anywhere* with Debra Angelo was akin to walking in a blazing spotlight.

Looking toward the casket, Debra tugged on Maxi's arm. "C'mon," she said, sotto voce. "Let's give 'em a show—past wives united!" Nudging Gia ahead, she sauntered forward, pulling a reluctant Maxi along, with Wendy following behind.

Debra drew the little group up short behind a man who was talking louder than was seemly. "Jesus, what's with the see-through coffin? Is it supposed to be a symbol or something? I mean, was there some kinda glass coffin in one of his movies?"

The question was posed by a formerly famous star of a formerly famous television series, who had long since lost it all to booze and the horses. Still, he had a certain cachet that was kept alive by colorful stories of his colorful doings in the tabloid press.

"No, no," Julian Polo, who'd been the deceased's agent, replied distractedly. "I guess Janet picked it out—Jack was a big collector of contemporary art. He looks good, though, doesn't he?"

"Listen!" Debra whispered in Maxi's ear behind them, her concupiscent lips widening into a grin. Debra relished dish about their mutual ex; Maxi hoped that her higher self would one day stop being fascinated by same, but it hadn't happened yet.

"Ahh, they shoulda planted him under his star on Hollywood Boulevard, he'da liked that," the actor groused.

"He didn't *have* a star," mused the agent, who knew everything about his famous, infamous, complex, and now dead client. Mind you, Julian Polo wouldn't usually admit to anyone that movie superhero Jack Nathanson, multiple Oscar winner, didn't have a star on the world-renowned Hollywood Walk of Fame—that would be bad PR, and the deceased still had a picture coming out, from which the agency would get ten percent of his points. But this poor excuse for a man standing next to him wasn't anybody. He *used* to be James McAdam, popular star of *Doctor Bryce*, which placed in the top ten for almost a decade on NBC. Now look at him, drunk even at a morning funeral—he wouldn't remember any of this tomorrow.

"Whaddaya mean he doesn't have a star?" McAdam prattled on. "*Everybody's* got a star. Pat *Sajak* has a star. Jamie *Farr* has a star. *I* have a star, for chrissake! Jack was one of the greatest actors ever lived. '*Course* he has a star."

But Julian wasn't about to tell even this out-of-the-loop has-been the story. Years ago, when Jack's career was in its prime, Julian had confidently applied to the committee for a star to honor his client's brilliant body of work. The vote has to be unanimous, and almost always is, but the chairman subsequently reported that every one of the members threw in a thumbs-down for Jack, not a single yea, and in fact one colleague, a makeup artist who'd worked on one of his pictures, was heard to say as she tossed in her ballot, "He can eat shit and die!"

"Sorry, pal, but we knew your boy's not the most popular guy in town," the chairman had said. "Now, you can resubmit his name every other month," he'd added, "but to be honest with you, I think this whole committee would have to die and be replaced by people who didn't know him. . . ." So no star on Hollywood Boulevard for legendary actor Jack Nathanson.

Julian turned his attention to the rabbi, partly to shut McAdam up—interesting that Janet would choose a rabbi, he thought, since Jack was an admittedly bad Jew, religiously speaking.

Last month, Julian and his wife were at Spago with Jack and Janet, and the dinner conversation got onto religion. Jack remarked that ever since he made *Black Sabbat*, his Academy Award–winning period film about a witchcraft trial that echoed a high-profile contemporary case of a priest falsely accused of child abuse, he was into the whole Roman thing—the Mass, the music, the majesty. "Confessing your sins has to beat seeing a shrink," he'd said. "And how about exorcising the devil! We oughta do that one on you, Julian, roust the devil out of you," he'd said with a smirk, "and out of every goddamn agent in the business." He'd turned to Janet then and said, "When I die, darling, don't bury me in a tallis; put some rosary beads in my hands." And damned if she didn't do it, Julian thought now, gazing at his late client clutching the beads. Janet never really got the joke with Jack.

Maxi reached out and tapped Julian on the shoulder, breaking his reverie. Turning, he smiled broadly at Nathanson's two beautiful ex-wives, taking a hand from each in each of his. "Nature's noblewomen, both of you," he exclaimed. "How are you two? And Gia," he said, stooping to shake the girl's hand.

"We're fabulous, Julian." Debra smiled, blowing him a kiss. Turning then, with Gia in tow, she set off toward the rabbi standing at the head of the coffin-cum-shrine. As she wound through the crowd, an indelicate wolf whistle was heard from someone among the gathered.

"Jesus, what's she gonna do?" Julian half exclaimed.

"I have no idea," Maxi answered, her eyes also fixed on Debra. Maxi had long ago realized that there was no predicting what Debra Angelo would do, ever. This whole crowd knew that Debra had loathed Jack Nathanson, and vice versa. Seven years before, they'd all been witness to the couple's public, trashed-about, dragged-out divorce and custody battle, each sordid accusation from one prompting a topper from the other. And now she was going to give him a *eulogy?*

Wendy, too, watched Debra's languid progress toward center stage. "Sensational!" she noted in her version of a stage whisper. "Skintight black, tasteful gold jewelry, four-inch 'fuck-me' pumps . . ." Debra was somberly guiding young Gia before her, aware that every eye in the house, as it were, was on her aristocratic, wriggling fanny wrapped in quasi widow's weeds, the wind tossing voluminous hair barely contained by the diaphanous Isadora Duncan scarf wound around that perfectly made-up, exquisite face that registered grief, though *tout le monde* knew she wasn't grieving.

"Debra Angelo might not be the world's greatest actress," Wendy whispered to Maxi, "but she sure knows how to make an entrance!"

Maxi had to smile—Debra had this crowd mesmerized as she stood serenely now, hands on her child's shoulders, speaking in hushed tones. Heads craned forward, the better to hear her. She was saying that Jack had loved his daughter, and Gia wanted to say a few words in her daddy's memory.

Gia started to cry, which immediately sobered Maxi. In the five years that she had been her stepmom, Gia could always break her heart. The girl was stammering now that she loved her dad, that she was going to miss him, sobbing harder now, caught in this odd, truly scary situation for a little girl who was looking down at her smiling father lying in a see-through box. She was trying to remember the little speech that Debra had coached her on. "My daddy told me to read good books," she mumbled. "He played . . . uh . . . video games with me. . . ."

After a painful few minutes of this, Debra knelt and gathered her in a tearful embrace, then took her hand and led her away, back through the crowd, stepping carefully around headstones studding the grass toward a waiting limousine with Gia's nanny inside.

The rabbi had called the next eulogist, Sam Bloom, Jack Nathanson's business manager and closest friend, best man at all his weddings. Sam chattered the deceased's praises, telling stories about what a consummate professional he was, what a helluva guy he was.

Next, former child star Meg Davis approached the rabbi. She spoke haltingly, staring down through that peculiar casket at 230 pounds of the dead Jack Nathanson dressed in very odd burial clothes, odd, but it was the kind of outfit the man had virtually lived in lately, the kind the news photos showed he'd got shot in, and probably the only type of apparel they could find in his closet that fit him, since Jack was currently in *fat* mode: a tan safari jacket, a Rolling Stones T-shirt, and khaki pants with an elastic waist.

The speaker was tall and frail looking, with long, straggly auburn hair that seemed uncared for, and a drawn face scarred by dissipation. She was blowing her nose and talking about how Jack Nathanson had made her a star in *Black Sabbat*, she was only ten when she'd read for the part, and how wonderful he had treated her and her mother—

But something was going on, a scuffling, some sharp words, and heads began turning, Julian, McAdam, Maxi, Wendy, people all around them, the widow, the rabbi, and the rest, and what they saw completely diverted their attention from Jack Nathanson lying face up in his plastic box.

The now-grown-up *Black Sabbat* child had stopped reminiscing in midsniff, and was looking up to see what she'd lost her audience to. Wendy, ever the journalist, moved quickly toward the action. Maxi and Julian stood frozen. Four uniformed Los Angeles sheriff's deputies, one of them female, and two detectives in plainclothes, guns drawn, had positioned themselves outside Debra Angelo's limo, barking orders.

"Come out of the car, lady!"

"Hands over your head!"

"Leave the kid—you stay in the car, little girl."

Two of them began tugging at the actress, hauling her out of the limo. Debra was protesting, screaming indignantly, yanking away from them, and now and then shouting obscenities with a Romanic timbre, as the nanny looked on in horror, and Gia hung on to her mother's skirt and howled with terror.

Then Debra let out a piercing shriek and fainted while the cops were reading her rights, having just told her that she was under arrest for the gunshot murder of her former husband, Jack Nathanson.

2

Maxi punched off her cell phone and dropped it into her purse. No surprise that she didn't get any answers from the sheriff's department—it was too early. Not that she could count on information from them ever, but it was worth a try. She'd called in the arrest to the news desk at Channel Six, and told the assignment editor that the pool camera had it all on tape. Debra was her friend, but news was her job. They'd have the story in minutes anyway. The entire media would have it, and it would be every station's lead tonight.

"Well, *this* show's over," Wendy hissed. "It's anticlimax from here. Let's get back to work, Max."

"We can't leave till he's in the ground," Maxi whispered.

"Oh. Sorry. My funeral etiquette's rusty."

"I need to pay my respects to his widow," Maxi said.

"Yeah, congratulate her. She got off cheap."

"Stop it, Wendy. Someone will hear you."

"Okay, you go give your condolences to the final Mrs. Jack Nathanson, and I'll get the truck and bring it around. I'll pick you up by that tree over there," Wendy said, pointing to a purpling jacaranda up on the road.

As Wendy headed off to where they'd parked the news van,

Maxi made her way toward Janet Orson. She couldn't help wondering how Janet was feeling, as the man she'd married less than a year ago in a romantic ceremony on a moonlit beach in lush Saint Thomas was about to be laid to rest. Their nuptials had been written up everywhere, and featured on all the news and entertainment shows. Maxi remembered the night she had to voice over their wedding video on the Six O'clock News, while her coanchor sat next to her stifling snickers. It did seem weird, reporting on her ex-husband's marriage. And tonight, even more surreal, she'd be reporting on her ex-husband's funeral.

Maxi tried to remember how *she* had felt when she'd been married to Jack for less than a year. Was she still in honeymoon phase? No, she wasn't. Because fifteen minutes after the ceremony, it seemed, Jack had turned into a whole different guy. Maxi noticed it right away, maybe because she was a trained reporter. She just pretended she didn't—until she couldn't pretend anymore. But she had no idea how Janet felt today. Janet Orson was forty-three, beautiful, and highly successful. She'd made the long, steep climb in the entertainment business from studio stenographer to top talent agent, one of the first women who'd managed to break through the agency world's rugged glass ceiling. She had justly earned the respect of the industry, and had amassed a fairly sizable nest egg for herself. On the day of her marriage to Jack Nathanson, she'd told the press that it was time she focused on her personal life.

Though never married before, Janet had had hundreds of dates, escorts, one-night stands, and short-term liaisons, all chronicled in the trade columns—there had been no shortage of men on either coast who wanted to romance the stunning, powerful Janet Orson. And she'd had one very significant other, one long and well-publicized love affair with a talented, highly successful screenwriter whom she'd launched by selling his *Moondoggie*, a charming little film she had believed in that grossed an astonishing 78 million domestic.

Evidently she had believed in *him*, too. He was tall, dark, Adonis-handsome, smart, fun, attractive in every way. The two were an A-list couple for years, and they'd seemed perfectly suited and divinely happy, until he dumped her at the top of his career for a red-hot, pencil-thin blond actress half his age. The news of their surprise marriage appeared in the daily *Variety*, and, it turned out, no one was more shocked to read about it over coffee and breakfast rolls than Janet Orson.

Then she met Jack. And Maxi was sure that Janet must have felt like she'd died and gone to heaven, because Jack Nathanson got an A-plus in courtship. He was candlelight dinners and little blue boxes from Tiffany and first-class jet trips to Aspen, New York, Saint Moritz, Rome. Just six weeks after their first date, Jack and Janet soared off to the Caribbean for their divine storybook wedding, while all the bells were still ringing and the fireworks were still going off, Maxi was sure.

She saw Janet now, standing with the rabbi, talking quietly. The Debra Angelo debacle had apparently put an end to the spontaneous eulogies. "Janet," Maxi said, as she came to her and took her hand, "I'm so sorry."

"Oh, Maxi . . ." The two had known each other for years; Maxi had interviewed Janet several times. Now she could see hurt and confusion in this woman who was usually the epitome of composure.

"What was *that* about?" Janet asked Maxi. "I couldn't see what was going on. . . ."

"Debra was . . . arrested."

"For . . . for *this*?" Janet exclaimed, gesturing toward her late husband's bier.

"Yes. They read her the Miranda rights on a murder charge."

"But would she . . . *could* she . . . ?" Janet knew that Maxi and Debra were friends. Maxi knew that Janet didn't quite approve of Debra.

"I don't know anything more than you do, Janet."

"Well, Debra *hated* Jack—"

"Is there anything I can do for you?" Maxi cut in, to stop any more conversation about Debra. Maxi didn't know what to think about the rowdy arrest of Debra Angelo just minutes ago, and she certainly didn't want to speculate about it with the "final wife," as Wendy had dubbed Janet Orson.

"Well . . . you can be kind in the coverage—"

"Oh, I won't be doing it," Maxi said. "My coanchor or I will voice the story on the newscast, but I won't be writing it or putting it together. How are you holding up, Janet?"

"I'm in a daze. It's all been happening so fast—"

The rabbi was handing Janet a rose from the arrangement atop the fiberglass casket. As the two women looked down at Jack, Maxi had a great urge to ask Janet why she'd chosen that outré piece of quasi–modern art as a final resting place for the man they'd both been married to, but she thought better of it. Instead, because the bizarre presentation of Jack Nathanson in death a couple of feet in front of them was impossible to ignore, she heard herself commenting on the deceased's apparel. "In those clothes he looks so . . . so like himself," she stammered. Then wished she hadn't. But Janet didn't seem offended.

"Sam Bloom said don't buy him a suit, nobody's ever seen him in one except in the movies," she said. "And Sam knew him better than I did, certainly. But that *smile* on his face!" Janet went on, shocking Maxi with that one. "The undertaker put it there. When I asked him why, he said because your husband's wearing this funny outfit, I figure he must be a funny guy."

Maxi wasn't sure if it was appropriate to laugh. She settled for saying nothing, just looking somewhat perplexedly at the widow. Which evidently prompted Janet to go on. "And once the smile was there, the undertaker said, he couldn't take it off. Then he actually explained *why* he couldn't. Physically. Oh, God, Maxi, it's been a nightmare."

But how do you feel about your husband being dead? Maxi

wanted to ask, but didn't. They were distracted by the pulleys that were now moving the casket over the grave site, about to lower it into the ground. This should be a private moment for Janet, Maxi knew. Giving her what she hoped was a reassuring hug, she headed off to find Wendy in the Channel Six news van.

After watching Maxi Poole's retreat for a few seconds, a tall woman in Harry Potter glasses, her hair pushed up under a floppy poor-boy cap, inserted herself squarely between the coffin and the widow. With pad and pencil poised, she asked, "How do you feel, Mrs. Nathanson?"

Janet felt a stab of discomfort. A reporter. Not television; there was no camera. Print. The *L.A. Times*? The *New York Times*, perhaps? Or *Variety*? The woman presented no credentials. Before Janet could respond, a burly man in jeans and a rumpled T-shirt jumped in front of them to the edge of the grave, hoisted a camera, and snapped off a series of flash-popping pictures as the coffin, with film legend Jack Nathanson in full-bodied view, descended into the ground.

Amid a cacophony of outraged protests, the man whipped around and said to no one in particular, "Sorry, I gotta bring in his box shot." With that, clutching his camera, he ran across the sodden grass toward a waiting van, funeral guests shaking their fists after him, Joan Collins among them, someone shrieking, ". . . fucking tabloid vermin!"

3

Pigs!" Debra Angelo had muttered in the backseat of the sheriff's radio car. "How *could* you do that in front of my child? I didn't kill the sonofabitch."

They took her to the sheriff's station in Malibu, venue of the crime, where she was booked, printed, strip-searched, and photographed. Next, they transported her to the Sybil Brand Jail for Women in East Los Angeles, where superlawyer Marvin Samuels was already waiting with bail money, having been alerted to her crisis by a friend at the funeral who happened to have a cell phone in his pocket and great affection for Jack Nathanson's first wife.

Everyone knows there's no bail on a murder rap in L.A. County, and nobody knows what Marvin Samuels did to get Debra Angelo out on bail—beg, plead, promise, bribe—but get her out he did, on a million dollars' bond. By the time the two walked out of Sybil Brand, a sizable contingent of media had gathered outside, flashbulbs popping, minicams cranking—this was hot stuff! Debra said nothing; you never heard her curse when there was press around.

Marvin, who loved the press, courted the press, shot some bon mots their way with his big teddy-bear smile. "No way they'll make this stick, lads and ladies. Tell me," he fired at them, squeezing Debra's shoulders, Debra in the too-tight designer suit, the too-high heels, the major hair, "does this look like a murderess to you?" Then he ushered her into his waiting limo and they screeched off.

Samuels had learned that they'd found Debra's fingerprints on the murder weapon.

"Of *course* my fingerprints are on the fucking gun," she told him. "It's *my* gun, for God's sake. I take target practice. Ask Tony Morano at the Lakeside Gun Club. My fingers are all over the damn thing all the time! If I'd killed the shithead, do you think I'd be dumb enough to leave the fucking gun on the fucking floor next to his fucking head?"

Still, Marvin thought, Marvin who had been there through the mutual carnage that was the Nathanson vs. Angelo divorce-and-custody trial—still, Debra's fingerprints were found on Debra's gun, which killed Debra's ex-husband in Debra's house.

4

"We should have brought a crew," Maxi said to Wendy. The two had ducked into Taglio's, a little bar near Forest Lawn, after the funeral.

"Yes, but with our budget cuts, I wouldn't put in for a crew for Madonna's funeral, let alone for some has-been's. Excuse me, Maxi, but Jack Nathanson was a has-been. Besides, we don't even *cover* celebrity funerals anymore. Well, maybe Madonna's—"

"But with Jack, there's always a story," Maxi broke in. "His funeral was more bizarre than the Ayatollah's. If you didn't think there'd be a story, what were we doing there?"

Wendy laughed out loud. "You know damn well what we were doing there, Maxi—you were there because you wanted that primal ex-wife satisfaction of seeing him dead, and I was there because you needed me to make it look like we were backgrounding a story so people wouldn't figure out that you just wanted to see him dead. And by the way, when did he get fatter than Ryan O'Neal?"

Maxi laughed. Wendy was a good friend, as well as the producer of everything that had Maxi's name on it—the six o'clock show she coanchored, the sweeps series, the spot news and specials. Maxi Poole and Wendy Harris were the tightest team in L.A. news.

Often, after the eleven o'clock broadcast, they would hang out in the empty newsroom, two news junkies, planning stories, watching tapes, dishing. Toward the end of Maxi's marriage to Jack Nathanson, these were the times when Maxi would confide to Wendy about how truly unhappy she was. No one else heard the tales; Maxi was very private. That's why everyone was astounded when she announced that she was divorcing Nathanson—everyone except Wendy.

Maxi was a sun-streaked, gold-toned, green-eyed beauty, whose classic features were kept from perfection by a deeply cleft chin and a left incisor that was decidedly crooked. She was trim and angular, despite her addiction to really thin pizza and really juicy burgers, which she paid for with daily workouts. Now she was raking a hand through her thick crop of straight blond hair, which telegraphed to Wendy that she was troubled.

"Debra didn't do it," Maxi said quietly.

"How can you be sure?"

"Because it's been years, it was over, they had worked everything out. More than that, Debra simply isn't capable of killing anyone."

"Well, the police seem to think she did. They must have *something* on her," Wendy countered. "And besides, it wasn't over. . . . For as long as they shared custody of Gia, Jack Nathanson was going to be in her life, making her crazy. I've seen how the man made *you* crazy."

"But Debra isn't crazy. You have to be crazy or desperate to kill, and Debra isn't either."

"Hah!" Wendy snorted. "That wasn't crazy I saw her doing at the funeral? Sure looked crazy to me."

"Theatrical, yes, that's her style. But not crazy," Maxi reflected. "Sure, I've heard her say more than once she wished the bastard were dead; she was probably ecstatic seeing him laid out in gardenias. But Debra never would have killed him."

"Then who did? Who would've wanted to?" Wendy asked.

"Oh, you could paper these walls with the glittering résumés of people in this town who've been heard to say they'd like to kill Jack Nathanson," Maxi answered, her eyes gazing up at the walls, which happened to be papered with bad Italian art.

"Including you." Wendy grinned.

"Including me. For that matter, why not Janet?"

"Janet Orson? That pillar of the community, sponsor of charities, distraught widow? They just got *married!* They just bought a *mansion*—"

"Which I'm sure *she* had to pay for," Maxi tossed out.

"Oh, come on, Max, he had tons of money."

"No, he was basically broke. That's why the IRS is hounding *me* for three years of his back taxes."

"But he starred in all those blockbuster films," Wendy persisted. "You think he didn't have loads of cash stashed in the Caymans or somewhere?"

"No," Maxi returned, shaking her head. "If he had piles of money, the IRS would have found it—they have ways." She said that with an air of finality, but to Wendy, who knew her every gradation of expression from years of scrutiny on the monitors in the control booth, Maxi didn't look completely convinced.

"Max, you told me he made seven million in points on *Black Sabbat* alone, back when seven mil was like twenty mil, not to mention all the big films that came later—so where did it all go?"

"He spent it." Maxi sighed. "He *had* to pick up the check, whether it was dinner for four or forty. He *had* to go first class, preferably on the Concorde. He *had* to buy lavish gifts for friends, expensive toy Ferraris that really drive for Gia, loads of pricey art, gigantic diamonds for his women—and given his track record with women, that's a lot of diamonds. And don't forget, half his money went to the government, ten percent to his agent, fifteen percent to his manager, another five to his business manager, hefty fees to his publicists, office payroll and overhead, huge living expenses—do the math, Wendy. He spent it all, it's that simple, and nobody was paying him the big bucks anymore."

Wendy looked thoughtful. "Listen, Maxi," she said. "Let's assume for a minute that he *did* have money left, and the Goon had it cleverly salted away." "The Goon" was Maxi's sobriquet for Sam Bloom, Jack's business manager. "Or let's say you're right," Wendy went on, "that it *is* all gone, but a lot of people don't think so. Like me. Like maybe Debra Angelo. Like folks who can't figure out how the guy could possibly be broke when he spent money like the early Elvis—"

"Oh, they just don't know—"

"Wait, wait, let me finish this," Wendy said, holding up a hand to stop her. "Take Debra Angelo. . . . Let's say Debra thought that he still had a few mil, but she could see that he was pissing it away big-time, and there wasn't any coming in. What if she decides she's going to off him before he spends the rest of her daughter's inheritance? She never made any really big money that she could hang on to, I'm sure. And you've said she's told you she put up with Jack's shit as much as she could because she didn't want to jeopardize Gia's trust fund. Suppose she wanted to stop the massive money drain. Suppose anyone with a vested interest in Jack's money, whether it's mythical or not, wanted to stop the leaking before he did spend it all. . . ."

"I've thought of that," Maxi said softly.

The way she said it struck a chord in Wendy, who was looking at Maxi now in that way she had, straight into her eyes with a little half smile, the look that if Wendy were a cartoon, a lightbulb would come on over her head. "You knew Debra was going to get arrested today, didn't you, Maxi?" she asked pointedly.

"Uhh . . . yes and no," Maxi said. "A contact downtown told me they were going after Debra, but it could have gone down anywhere. But yes, I thought it might happen at the funeral because it was so public, and the cops love their publicity too, as you know. Ever since the Rampart scandal, they've been going out of their way to make collars that get press attention."

Wendy was looking at Maxi with that intensity she burned when she was getting on to something, her pretty face crinkled in a frown. "So if you thought there was a chance in hell that it might go down at the funeral," she asked, "why didn't you insist on a crew? Dammit, Maxi, if you *really* wanted coverage out there you know I'd have begged for it, but you backed off! I said it wasn't worth tying up a crew, and you said okay. End of story. So how come?"

"I don't know. . . ."

"Come on, Maxi, you know," she prodded. "You *always* know what you're doing."

"Well," Maxi said, swirling the wine in her glass, "to tell you the truth, part of me wants to jump all over this story, and part of me wants to stay as far away from it as I can. Do you understand that?"

"Yeah," Wendy said. "I understand you're not as completely unemotional about this whole thing—or maybe as completely *uninvolved*—as you'd like people to think."

"What's that supposed to mean? Do you think *I* killed him?" Maxi laughed.

"Umm . . . Tell me again why you couldn't have killed him."

"No, Wendy, why I *wouldn't* have killed him. I wouldn't have killed him, first of all, because I don't kill people, and second, Your Honor, he's worth more to me alive than dead."

"Oh, fascinating! Tell me about that, Ms. Poole, and be mindful, please, that I'm the one who has listened ad infinitum to how this creep could wipe out every cent you've ever made if the tax man couldn't get it out of him, how they'd come after *you* with writs of attachment . . . and remember, you wouldn't listen to me when I begged you to do a prenup. But no, you were so in love!"

"I know, I know, I know. . . . Back to your question, may it please the court." Maxi laughed. "Look, if he's alive, he at least stands a chance of making another hit movie and paying his own debts. But if he's dead, that can't happen, and I get nailed for his hefty debts because our funds were commingled when he ran them up."

"Again, that's if he didn't have any money left," Wendy qualified, quieter now—she didn't like where this was going. "I bet he did, and maybe deep down, Max, in spite of everything his accountants tell your lawyers, maybe you think he had some, too. But you knew he was enough of a prick that he'd let you pay his debts if he could keep his assets hidden. He'd let you get wiped out financially and he'd still sleep like a baby at night; that's the kind of guy he was. Maybe *you* wanted to plug up the guy's money sieve before it was really all gone, and you knew if he was dead his estate would get turned inside out and the missing millions would turn up, and the IRS would seize what's theirs and you'd be off the hook, instead of having your salary attached for the next ten years and ending up at the Home for Impoverished Newswomen—"

"Whoa, hold it. Stop already . . . I didn't do it, okay?" Maxi laughed. "I don't even know where he lives. Lived, that is."

"Yeah, except with about two phone calls you and I can find out where anybody on the planet lives, as you well know," Wendy pointed out. "Besides, he wasn't murdered at his house—he was shot at Debra's house."

"Oh, right . . . Maybe Debra *did* do it."

"Do you really think so?"

"No. Come on, we've got to get back to work."

Maxi called for the check, and Wendy felt a little stab of fear. No, *couldn't* be, she chided inwardly. Still, she thought, if anyone in L.A. could get away with murder, popular Channel Six reporter Maxi Poole could.

5

". . . and thou shalt render obeisance upon the scaffold of the pillory whilst testifying to thine odious crimes, even as legions of disembodied souls wield firebrands from hell—"

"Shh!" Sally Shine put a comforting arm around her daughter. "Shhh, darling—I told you going to the funeral was a bad idea."

Sally helped Meg upstairs to her room, took off her clothes, eased her into bed, spoon-fed her a cup of hot tea laced with a strong tranquilizer, and said a silent prayer that she would sleep peacefully and wake up okay.

Sally Shine blamed herself for what had happened to her daughter. She had pushed Meggie into movies and television from the time the child was two months old and played Baby Number 4 in a Gerber commercial. There were eleven screaming, wailing infants on the set; Meggie was the only good baby, never uttering a sound.

From that time on, Sally ran her to every viable casting call. Meggie got more than her share of parts because she was so well known among casting directors, and, being such a good little girl, she was so well liked. Meg Davidson cooperated, Meg Davidson was smart, Meg Davidson knew how to behave, Meg Davidson was a natural, they'd say.

And heaven knows they'd needed the money. Sally was seventeen when Meg was born, the father having left town before she even knew she was pregnant, and her own mother having disowned the two; they'd had to make their own way, both of them children. So when Meggie read for the part of Hannah in *Black Sabbat*, a movie based on a best-selling novel that promised to be a huge hit because they'd signed America's hottest young actor, Jack Nathanson, Sally was thrilled that her daughter got a callback. The part of the little girl who was accused of being a witch could launch Meggie into a major motion-picture career.

They called her back three times to read with the star, Mr. Nathanson, who would play the minister, young Hannah's father in the film. Each time, Sally had washed and brushed Meggie's strawberry-blond hair, carefully chosen her wardrobe, and tirelessly coached her on her lines. At all of the readings, the child was perfect in every way. On the day they learned that Meg had the role, the room was filled with studio executives and press, and their pictures were all over the evening news. Heady stuff for mother and daughter.

What phantoms haunted her now? her mother anguished, as she watched Meggie in fitful sleep.

6

Settle down, Yukon," Maxi told her dog, a big, furry, friendly Alaskan malamute who was standing at attention next to the brown leather Eames chair in her study, where she squirmed into different positions, trying to get comfortable. "Just because *I* can't relax doesn't mean *you* can't."

Maxi had been jittery since the funeral that morning. She couldn't keep the horrific stream of events and their potential consequences from tumbling about in her head. Her well-ordered life had been unraveling on several edges since Jack Nathanson had come into it, and now it had turned downright precarious. She knew it would look dicey for her when Sheriff's Homicide began to sift through the flotsam of the late Jack Nathanson's affairs. Her lawyer had been working with her business manager to extricate her as close to whole as possible from Nathanson's financial twining. The lawyer had put her on alert, phoned her as soon as he'd heard the news of the murder that Saturday and told her to expect *a call*.

And Wendy was suspicious. Of course, newswoman Wendy Harris was more analytical than the average person. Still, Maxi thought, when the L.A. County Sheriff's Department and the various agencies working with them on this high-profile murder case unearthed the complex fiscal maneuvering ongoing between Jack Nathanson and Maxine Poole Nathanson, they would be dialing M for Motive, and Maxi's phone would ring.

Besides the IRS, several banks and lending institutions had filed for attachment of Maxi's salary, as well as all, *all* of her assets, to help cover unpaid taxes and millions of dollars in loans that Jack had taken out when they were husband and wife—loans that Jack had never told Maxi about. Not that she'd have objected. At that time, Maxi, and the *world,* thought that megastar Jack Nathanson had to be sitting on a fortune, from the way he lavished it on himself and others, from his track record as an extremely successful actor with his own production company, even from the way he talked—he *talked* rich.

Now that Maxi was privy to his books, she saw that Jack had *needed* those loans, needed those quick money fixes, because the top roles weren't coming his way anymore, and the money kept flying out the doors and windows.

Yes, he would pull down an occasional small-potatoes gig, which Sam would no longer allow him to turn down—a television *X-Files* or some such—but they didn't put a dent in the bills. And Janet had sold him to star in *Serial Killer* when Clint Eastwood turned it down, but that movie hadn't come out yet, and his points, *if* it was a hit, would pay off way down the road—too late to take care of his bills. The IRS had caught up with his tax debt, and the banks were calling their loans. Jack Nathanson showed zero assets on paper, but he'd had a wife when he'd piled up all that debt, a wife who was a well-paid television news reporter, and there was no legal contract separating their estates in those years. Which meant that Maxi had faced the possibility of being wiped out, and worse, the insane but very real prospect of working indefinitely to finish paying off his debts, while Janet Orson supported his continuing high lifestyle.

Maxi knew she was kidding herself, or at least kidding Wendy, when she'd said that Jack was worth more to her alive than dead. Not true, as the criminal investigators would plainly see. Money with the late Jack Nathanson's name on it, albeit in invisible ink, had already begun surfacing from hidden accounts, money that was pounced upon by his legion of creditors, which creditors in turn signed off on their claims to the assets of Maxine Poole. Since the murder, Maxi's business manager had been receiving notices letting her off her dead ex-husband's financial hook. Jack Nathanson was definitely worth more to Maxi Poole dead.

What to do? First of all, she determined to stop waffling on covering the story, and jump on it. True, under these circumstances it was inappropriate for her to cover this murder, but only *she* knew that. Unless her bosses found out and flashed her a red light, she'd get into it. She'd let everyone see that she was actively looking for the truth in the Jack Nathanson murder case.

The red light came sooner than she'd expected.

7

Take us through your day, this past Saturday, October twelfth, the day Jack Nathanson was shot and killed in your home," said Jonathan Johnson, the tall, quietly authoritative black detective who played "good cop" on the Cabello–Johnson L.A. County Sheriff's Homicide team. It was the day after the funeral, the day after Debra's high-profile arrest. Johnson, his partner Mike Cabello, Debra Angelo, and her attorney Marvin Samuels sat in a small office at the Malibu sheriff's station on Pacific Coast Highway.

"Well," began a subdued Debra, dressed in a loose-fitting light cotton dress, her bare feet in sandals, her hair tied back in a ponytail, "Gia got up early, as usual. Bessie supervised her wash-up; then she made breakfast—bacon and eggs for Gia, she loves eggs, and I don't think they're harmful for a growing—"

"When did *you* get up?" interrupted Mike Cabello.

"Before eight. Gia shook me because breakfast was ready. There's no sleeping in when my daughter is with me—"

"Then what?" Cabello, again.

"Then we had breakfast, of course. I had toast and fruit. I don't eat eggs—oh, before that I brushed my teeth and went potty, do you need to know that, too?"

Samuels shot her a look. He had specifically instructed her not to be flip, but even though apprehensive, she couldn't resist getting in an occasional little needle, disguised as "just a bit the dumb broad."

Cabello ignored the question. "What's the nanny's name?" he asked.

"Mrs. Burke. Bessie Burke. Elizabeth, actually."

"What did you do after breakfast?" asked Jon Johnson.

"I took Gia to her psychologist. Her appointment is at ten o'clock on Saturdays. With Dr. Robert Jamieson at UCLA. Gia has been lagging terribly behind in school, she's even been kept back a grade, second grade—"

"Where did you go from there?" asked Cabello.

"Well, let me see. . . . We got gasoline. In Westwood. Then we drove back to the beach, and we stopped at the grocery store, the one right near Big Rock. Anderson's Market. I bought bananas, lettuce, tomatoes, bottled water—"

"Then you went home?" Cabello cut in.

"Yes."

"What time did you get there?"

"I guess about noon."

"Then what did you do, Ms. Angelo?" asked Johnson.

"I looked at some snapshots of Gia—oh, I forgot to tell you, we stopped at Malibu Photo to pick up some pictures I'd had developed—"

"So you looked at the photos—what else?" demanded Cabello.

"I asked Mrs. Burke to pack Gia's bag; her father was coming at two. We talked about lunch—Gia wanted a chicken sandwich, with avocado. I checked my answering machine, hung out in the den awhile and watched Gia play her Team Arena game, then I kissed her and told her to have a great time at Daddy's and I'd call her tonight. Then I went into my room to wait until she left."

"You didn't want to see your daughter off?" Cabello asked.

"No. Unless we had something specific to discuss, I didn't like being around when Jack arrived. To avoid any possible unpleasantness, for Gia's sake. And Gia understood that."

"Okay"—from Cabello again—"so you were in your bedroom when your ex-husband arrived. Then what happened?"

"I heard what sounded like a gunshot in the house. Then I heard another. I was frantic. I called nine-one-one. The person who answered told me to stay on the line, the sheriffs would be there in minutes, and I said, 'But my little girl—I have no idea what's going on!' "

"Then what?"

"Then I heard the deputies arrive, so I went out of my room and down the hall to open the front door—we always keep it locked—and I followed them into the living room, and through the dining room, then to Gia's room, and there he was . . . on the floor."

"And where was your daughter?"

"In the kitchen with Bessie. She'd been eating her lunch. And Bessie was hanging on to her. They were hanging on to each other. They didn't know what happened."

"We'll be talking to Gia—" Cabello started.

Debra instantly reared up. "Marvin, can they do that? Gia is having dreadful nightmares with this. I have her shrink practically *living* at my house."

Samuels put a hand on her shoulder. "Perhaps you can hold off on that," he said to the officers, "see what falls together without questioning the ten-year-old, at least for now."

"What else can you tell us?" Cabello asked Debra. He saw her hesitation—clearly something was on her mind—and he added, "So we hear it from you, and not from somebody else."

"Maxi was there," Debra said quietly.

"Who?" Johnson and Cabello echoed in chorus.

"Maxi. Maxi Poole, his last wife. She was there, I think."

Cabello jumped all over that. “She was where? When? What do you mean, you *think?*”

“When I opened the front door for the deputies . . . I think I saw Maxi’s car driving away. I’m not sure, but I *think* I did.”

8

What evidence led to the arrest of Debra Angelo?" Maxi asked into the phone.

"Sorry, we can't divulge that."

"Are there any other suspects?"

"Can't divulge that."

Working the story, Maxi was talking to L.A. County Sheriff's Homicide detective Mike Cabello, head of the unit assigned to the Jack Nathanson murder case, and leader of the team who arrested Debra Angelo at the cemetery the day before. Maxi was getting no information out of him.

Not that she'd expected much—law officers rarely gave anything up to the press unless it was something they wanted leaked. Still, she expected to learn *something* from the conversation—a tone, an attitude, a feeling that they were really on to something, or not. This guy wasn't even friendly.

"Can you tell me anything at all that will help with the story, anything besides the who, what, where, and when that we already know?" she asked him.

"You were once married to the victim, weren't you, Ms. Poole?" Cabello shot back.

There it was. "Yes," she replied.

"Well, isn't it unusual that you would be covering this murder? Too close to home, conflict of interest, something like that?"

"I don't see a conflict," Maxi offered, feeling her way. "We've been divorced for more than a year. He had remarried. *Should* I see a conflict?"

"That's not for me to answer. What does Capra say?" Peter Capra was her managing editor, a hard-nosed newsman who had been around the L.A. crime beat for twenty-five years. Every law enforcement officer in Southern California knew Pete Capra.

"Pete hasn't said anything," Maxi returned carefully. Actually, Pete didn't know she was digging into the story. When he found out, she knew, he'd probably barge into her office, all six feet and two hundred–plus pounds of him, and bark something like "What the fuck issamatta with you?" Then again, Pete had no knowledge of the financial swamp she was navigating in the affairs of her late ex-husband. Pete just might read this case as no conflict. He could interpret it either way. And in fact, she had no intention of going to air with any part of it. Given her history with Nathanson, that would be irresponsible. For now, though, she was on a fishing expedition to assess her own exposure, and what she was finding out was that Mike Cabello knew something, or smelled something, something that involved her.

"Be sure to alert us if *you* learn anything, Ms. Poole," the detective was saying.

"Sure thing," Maxi said. *Fat chance*, she thought.

9

This is some knocked-out tootsie!" Pete Capra whispered in Maxi's ear as he took a seat next to her in the conference room at Channel Six News. The woman seated opposite them was digging in her purse. Taryn Zimmerman had called Maxi at the office, saying she had important information concerning the Jack Nathanson murder case. It was late afternoon on Friday, two days after the funeral. Maxi had asked her to come in, and when she sauntered provocatively across the bustling newsroom ten minutes ago, work stopped, and every male eye in the place locked on to her lank, luscious frame.

Six feet tall in heels, with loads of curly, fiery red hair, she was sheathed in a scarlet miniskirt, with a matching shirt tied under her astonishing breasts, exposing about a foot and a half of well-toned, well-tanned midriff.

Before they'd had a chance to get started, Pete Capra had popped his head inside the door. "I'd like to sit in on this, if it's about the Nathanson case," Pete had announced in his most officious boss tone. *Why am I not surprised?* Maxi thought.

"It was because of the fire hydrant," Taryn Zimmerman was saying now, as she applied crimson gloss to her pouty lips with what happened to be a fire-engine-red–tipped index finger, "and it was after that whole thing went down that I started sleeping with Jack. I mean, *that* wasn't because of the hydrant, but—"

"Wait, wait, wait, wait," Capra said, stopping her. "Slow down, and start from the beginning."

She pushed her chair back from the table and crossed her unbelievably long, golden legs in a gesture of impatience—she wasn't used to being slowed down.

"My husband, Irving Zimmerman, uh, my *ex*-husband Irving Zimmerman, well, he was my husband at the time—"

"Yuh, got that," Capra prompted, trying not to look at her legs, or her anything, trying to look her straight in the mauve-tinted glasses.

"Irving . . . *we* . . . needed a fire hydrant. We'd just bought the Benedict Canyon house, the big one, but it wasn't big enough for Irving, so he wanted to add on. When he applied for the permits they told him he had to put in a fire hydrant, because of a new city ordinance that covered hillside building. Or, since the property next door already *had* a fire hydrant, if we could get an easement from the owners, whom we hadn't met yet, an easement to use *their* fire hydrant if there was a fire, then we wouldn't have to put one in."

"Uh-huh," Maxi deadpanned. Ordinarily, either she or Capra would make the teller cut to the chase, but eyeing her boss's rapt expression, she guessed that this particular teller could take all afternoon and it'd be fine with Pete.

"Well, the fire hydrant turned out to be a whole lot more than just a fire hydrant, because they said we'd have to widen the driveway so a fire truck could get up it and another fire truck could come down at the same time, and that meant we'd have to tear out the walls, and a bunch of trees, and all the lights, and resurface the driveway, and put in a wider electric gate—anyhow, the whole thing was going to cost about two hundred and fifty thousand dollars."

Capra whistled. A quarter-million bucks for a fire hydrant!

That was twice what his *house* was worth. Pete Capra was still concentrating on not looking at this woman below the neck.

"Now, it's not as if Irving couldn't afford his own fire hydrant," she was saying, "but he saw no reason to pay for one if he could get one for free. That makes sense, right?"

That made sense to Capra.

"So," Taryn Zimmerman went on, "Irving invited our new neighbors, Jack Nathanson and Janet Orson, to come over for a barbecue, and Irving put some steaks on the grill, and popped some champagne, and we ate, and we drank, and we talked about Jack's movies and the shopping centers Irving built, and we got a little drunk and we were having a great time, and Irving put his arm around Jack and told him we needed an easement to hook onto his fire hydrant."

"And then what?" asked Capra, who was trying to stay focused on the narrative.

"And Jack said sure, just get a letter over to his business manager, and he gave Irving Mr. Bloom's number, and he said Sam would take care of it."

"But he didn't?" Maxi was trying to move this along.

"Well, what really happened, I mean much later, when, like I said, I was sleeping with Jack, and that's a whole other story, though it does have a lot to do with—"

Does this totally red woman know that she's talking about my ex-husband? Maxi wondered. She thought about getting up and leaving Capra alone with her; she had things to do.

"Anyway," Taryn Zimmerman was saying, "what Jack told me much later, like in bed, was that the next morning he called Sam Bloom and told him some asshole next door wanted something to do with a fire hydrant, so write him a letter and say that you've reviewed the situation and you're sorry but you have to turn him down."

"And your husband knew that?" Capra asked.

"Well, no, but when he got that letter from Sam Bloom, he

couldn't believe it. He ran over to Jack's house waving the letter and saying he didn't get it, it was no skin off Jack's ass if someone signed on to his damn fire hydrant, it wouldn't cost *him* anything—Irving couldn't believe that his new best friend next door was not falling all over himself to do him this favor, like people usually did. Jack just laughed at him, which *really* pissed Irving off! Jack said, 'Sorry, buddy, I gotta do what my business manager tells me; that's what I pay him for,' and Irving knew that was a crock of shit."

Irving Zimmerman was a name well known in the high-end commercial construction business, and also in police business. Years back, Maxi had investigated a tip from a source in the Department of Building and Safety, of all unlikely places, that a certain building inspector, who had turned up missing and was never found, was planted upright in the southwest abutment of the shopping center at Westwood and Pico that was built by Zimmerman Construction, a building inspector who had held up the project and pissed Zimmerman off. Irving Zimmerman had a reputation as a man you didn't want to piss off.

"So you think your ex-husband killed Jack Nathanson because he wouldn't give him an easement to his fire hydrant," Capra said, acting as though he thought this was totally plausible.

"No, no, it goes on. . . ." That's what Maxi was afraid of.

"Irving shelled out the money, had the engineering done, and put in the hydrant, built our new wing, two bedrooms with baths, an office and a gym, and he was mad as hell the whole time, and he never talked to Jack Nathanson again—"

"But obviously *you* did," Capra observed with a smile.

"Like I said, that's a whole other story, but I'm getting to that. . . ." Maxi wasn't interested in a story about yet another woman her ex-husband had slept with; Capra was rubbing his hands together—he couldn't wait to hear this woman tell it.

"Well, it just sort of happened," she said. "You know how those things happen. . . ."

"Yeah," Capra encouraged her. Maxi was ashamed for both of them.

"Anyway, long story short, one day Irving was at work, and I'm out by the pool getting some sun with no top on—I do that so there's no tan line—" Capra ran a finger under his collar.

"And I hear a noise, and I look up, and there's Jack Nathanson standing there, and I ask him how did *you* get in here, and he grinned like he does, uh, did, and said the gardener must have left the gate in the chain-link open, and I was so surprised to see him I forgot to cover up my tits, and, well, it was kinda too late by then anyway, and he said hey, *you and I* shouldn't be enemies, and he told me Janet was at work, and you know, we talked, and he said he knew a director who had a little part for someone exactly like me in his next picture, was I interested, and one thing led to another. . . ."

"So what happened?" asked Capra.

"Well, we had a thing going, usually in the afternoons. Janet was always working. He said he didn't have sex much with her anyway—"

Yup, that sounded like something Jack would tell a woman, Maxi thought.

"So how long did this go on with you and Nathanson?" Capra asked.

"Until he died," she said. "Well, till the week before he died, actually. Anyway, the point I'm getting at—"

Oh good, the point, thought Maxi.

"Irving came home early one afternoon. I mean, he *never* came home early. He was always late, if anything. But one day, he just walks into the guest room; that's where we used to do it. We couldn't do it at Jack's house because Carlotta, his housekeeper, was always there, and sometimes Gia and Ginny. Ginny was Gia's nanny at Jack's house—are you following this? So anyway,

Irving comes home early and asks Mrs. Hicks where I am, and the bitch tells him I'm in the guest room, so he walks in, and there we are. . . ."

"And?" Capra prompted. Maxi noticed beads of perspiration on his forehead.

"And he doesn't say word one to Jack, who gets up and puts on his clothes and leaves. He says to me, 'Get dressed and pack a suitcase.' I say, 'Why, where are we going?' And he says, '*We* are going to a hotel, and *I* am gonna drop *you* off, and I'll send the rest of your stuff wherever, and my lawyer will be in touch with you.'

"And he practically drags me into our bedroom, and he says, 'Get dressed,' and *he* threw a bunch of my things in a suitcase, all the wrong clothes of course, nothing went with anything, and he shoved me and the bag in the Range Rover, and I said, 'Aren't we gonna *talk* about this?' Like didn't it ever occur to him that he was forty years older than me and the three-minute sex didn't exactly get it done for me?"

"So now you're divorced," Maxi put in, "and you two are not friends." It was nearly four, and Maxi had to prepare for the six o'clock broadcast.

"Friends!" She spat it out. "Oh, I'm so *sure!* He made me sign a prenuptial agreement. It said if the marriage broke up before five years I'd get a hundred grand as a rehabilitative settlement, plus everything I had when we got married, and I had a green 1982 Toyota Corolla when we got married, so he had his people go out and buy me a frigging green '82 Corolla! It's parked right out there in your lot, that prick."

"So you think he killed Jack Nathanson," Maxi interrupted, wearying of this. She closed her notebook and stood, indicating an end to the meeting, at least for her.

"No, I don't think he killed Jack. He wouldn't actually *kill* a guy. But he sure as hell could *have* it done, and he was *majorly* pissed at Jack Nathanson, and if I understand my ex at all, it would take a lot less than—"

"So you and Nathanson had a thing going," Capra cut in. "You must miss him, huh?"

"Sure, I miss him," the ex–Mrs. Zimmerman said. "He was gonna get me in the movies."

10

Cabello and Johnson watched the dazzling Taryn Zimmerman sashay out the door. Having elicited no interest in her theory as to who killed Jack Nathanson from reporter Maxi Poole, she'd driven from Channel Six in Burbank to the Hall of Justice in downtown L.A. to tell it to the detectives on the case.

"So what do you think?" asked Johnson.

"I think I need oxygen!" Cabello grinned.

"Yah, yah," Johnson said dismissively. He usually got a kick out of Cabello's raging Italian hormones, but he had no time for them now. "So did Irving Zimmerman have Jack Nathanson done?"

"If you're seriously asking that, I'd like to sell ya the Hollywood Sign," Mike shot back. "But yikes! What a major babe!"

"Nathanson had a *lot* of major babes in his tent," Johnson said.

"Yeah, Debra Angelo, jeez!" Cabello offered, fanning himself. "And I wouldn't mind having Maxi Poole between the sheets. . . ."

"What *about* Maxi Poole?" Jon threw out. "We know she was at the murder scene. During the murder."

"No," Mike countered, "we know that dipstick actress *thinks* she saw her at the murder scene. She might just be covering her own ass. Besides, there are a lot of black Corvettes around town."

"You know," Jon said thoughtfully, "I don't think Debra Angelo is a dipstick at all. I get the feeling all of that's an act, that she knows exactly what she's doing, and exactly what she's saying. And if she says she saw Maxi Poole driving away from her house that day, I get the feeling she saw Maxi Poole driving away. She wasn't exactly bursting to tell us that, remember? Do those two know each other?"

"They'd have to. While Maxi Poole was married to Nathanson, Debra Angelo would have picked up and dropped off the kid."

"Oh, right, and they probably swapped notes on the kid, did their mother thing. Do they like each other?"

"Who knows?" Mike said.

"Still, I'd like to hear Maxi Poole tell us where she was last Saturday afternoon. Should we haul her in?"

"Uhh . . . What do *you* think, partner?"

"I think . . . I think . . . Lemme bounce this off you," Johnson tossed out. "I think no, not now, not yet. We know she's not going anywhere, and we know she's digging, for real or pretend, and we know she's good. And she's real close to the people in Nathanson's world. And the second we bring her in, the station's gonna take her off the story. I can't believe Capra hasn't done it already. I say let's sit on it for now and see if she turns anything up."

"Oh, right," Mike sneered. "Like she's gonna call us and tell us what she digs up."

"You've got a TV." Jon grinned. "We'll see it on the Six O'clock News!"

11

Maxi sat in a back booth at Land's End, a small café on Pacific Coast Highway, drinking coffee, scanning the *L.A. Times*, watching the door, trying to stay awake. It was 6:38 on Saturday morning, she was exhausted, and Debra was late. She'd managed about four hours' sleep between falling into bed the night before and falling into her car this morning for the hour-long drive to the beach. Debra had called—they *had* to meet, she'd said, but wouldn't say what was so urgent.

Maxi and Debra belonged to an exclusive club, whose membership roster was now permanently closed: former wives of Jack Nathanson. They'd shared some laughs at his expense, of course, but they also culled surprising insights from each other. It helped, because both women, different though they were, had the same misgivings about themselves when it came to Jack. Jack Nathanson wasn't a man you could dismiss from your consciousness when you signed the divorce decree.

Debra had just arrived and was climbing down from her jaunty vermilion-red Jeep, in exercise sweats and dark glasses, trying to keep a low profile. Still, she turned heads when she walked into the half-empty coffee shop. That was Debra. She slid into the booth opposite Maxi and took out a cigarette.

"I thought you quit," Maxi said. "This time was for good."

"Yes, darling, but it's better than doing drugs, don't you agree?" She lit up.

"They'll make you put it out," Maxi protested. Debra shrugged and took a deep drag.

"So how goes it?"

"Oh, splendid," Debra returned, exhaling smoke toward the ceiling. A few other diners shot her a look, but when she met each of them squarely in the eye and gave them a little nod and a smile, they all smiled back sheepishly and returned to their breakfasts, content with a personal acknowledgment from the extraordinary Debra Angelo.

"Oh, splendid. Everybody in this town thinks I gunned down my ex. I guess it's a short leap from I *should* have to I *must* have. Meantime, my phone isn't exactly ringing off the hook—the industry doesn't relish stopping production because one of its stars is sent up the river."

Maxi smiled. Debra went for the comic take even in the worst of circumstances. "So why are we here?" she asked her.

"Because I didn't want to talk about this on the phone, Maxi. I was brought in for questioning again, Marvin was with me, and they grilled me again, *intensely*, on everything I saw, heard, and did last Saturday. I told them I saw *you* driving away from my house right after Jack got shot."

Maxi blanched.

"What the hell were you doing there, Maxi?"

"I didn't know you saw me—"

"Well, I did. I didn't tell them at first, but goddammit, Max, I'm out on bail on a murder rap! I could go to prison for ten years! These guys aren't fooling around. I'm terrified," she breathed, grabbing Maxi's arm. "So talk to me. What were you doing at my house last Saturday?"

"I was running errands, and I was going to drop off that computer spelling program I ordered for Gia."

"So how come you didn't call? You always call."

"I just happened by the store and stopped in on a chance, and they'd just received it. I thought if I ran it out to you before Jack came for Gia they could work on it over the weekend. Jack was always great with helping Gia learn—"

"So why didn't you just drop it off at Jack and Janet's place? That would have been a hell of a lot closer."

"It didn't occur to me."

Debra looked dubious. "So you decided to drive all the way out to Malibu with it without even calling on the way? Let me know you were coming? You have a cell phone, Maxi."

"I was going to call, but you know you can't get a signal down through Malibu canyon, and when I broke out at the coast I was just about there, so I didn't bother."

"You knew Jack was coming at two. You knew he was never late. And neither of us liked running into him if we could help it. So you got to my house precisely when you knew he'd be there? Come on, Maxi."

"Hey, if I saw him it would've been, 'Hi, Jack,' a smooch for Gia, 'here's the speller that works with her Mac, the instructions are inside, happy spelling,' and out of there—I had nails at three back in town."

Debra's eyes narrowed behind her shades. "What was the big deal about rushing it out right away?" she asked. "We've been waiting for that spelling program for three weeks."

"Debra, you told me she flunked two spelling quizzes that week, remember? If I didn't get it to her that weekend, she'd have had to wait another week. You know I can only do errands on weekends, and you can't depend on the mail." Debra was interrogating her, and Maxi didn't like it.

"Okay, so out you came with the speller, all the way to the house. So why didn't you come in?"

"Because when I was driving down your street I heard sirens behind me, so I pulled over to let whatever it was pass. Turns out it was the Malibu sheriffs, as you well know, and I watched them screech to a halt in front of your house! So I just got out of there."

"That's not you, Maxi. You're a reporter—you don't take off when you see police action. You go find out what's going on. More important, you don't run when a friend might be in trouble. We *are* still friends, aren't we?"

"Well, I saw you at the door letting the deputies in, so I knew you were okay, and I knew Jack would never hurt Gia, so I thought maybe something was going on between you and Jack, and I didn't want to be a part of it. So I took off."

Debra digested this. "Okay," she said slowly, "all very innocent. So why didn't you tell the police?"

"Oh God, Debra, I know that was stupid, but I didn't know you saw me. I didn't think anybody saw me. And when I heard the news, heard what happened, I freaked. I knew it would *not look good* if they found out I was there when he was shot. It looks bad enough as it is."

"What does *that* mean?"

"Debra, I have not told you *half* the financial horror stories that have been landing on my head."

"You mean the back taxes?"

"I mean the income taxes, I mean the capital gains tax on the house he sold before he moved in with me, I mean another million-dollar signature loan that turned up, and on, and on, and on—it was looking like I might be working for his creditors for the rest of my life."

"So you figured they'd think *you* killed him?" Debra asked incredulously.

"Well, *somebody* killed him." It was Maxi's turn to look closely at Debra.

"It wasn't me, Maxi."

"And it wasn't me." The two women sat in silence now, and

Maxi could see that behind the dark glasses Debra was weeping. "I am so scared," she whispered, tamping out her cigarette.

Maxi took her hand. She had marveled that Debra had the mettle to talk to the press, video and print, tell how outraged she was, how she and Jack had made peace, how Gia needed her daddy, it was shock enough that her father was dead, and now they were actually blaming her mother, *think* of it, she'd tell them, choking up. It was a vigorous front, and an exhausting acting job, she'd confided to Maxi. That's why she'd wanted to meet at this early hour, and at this out-of-the-way place—to avoid them.

"Max," she said, "if something happens to me . . . I mean, if I have to go away, you know, even for a little while, I want you to take Gia. Will you? I don't want her in Italy with my mom and dad. I want her to continue with her school, and her friends, with no more disruptions—"

"Of course I will, you *know* I will, Deb," Maxi cut in.

But there was no stopping her. "There's only you, Maxi, and Gia adores you, and you'd be good for her. . . ." Debra was sobbing now.

"Shh, shh, shh," Maxi cautioned, squeezing her hand, looking around to see if people were noticing, and of course they were. Everyone, especially in the tight little community of Malibu, knew who they both were, and knew that movie star Jack Nathanson, their mutual ex-husband, had been murdered.

12

"Awful!" Maxi exclaimed aloud to no one. Driving across town on Monday night, a gigantic billboard perched across from Tower Records on the Sunset Strip had caught her eye, a huge ad showing a pair of female larger-than-life legs in fishnet stockings, spread apart, elongated in five-inch heels. Atop these legs, a black leather miniskirt cupped just under the butt of the woman we couldn't see. And between the legs crouched the Jack Nathanson character, the detective, looking up at her. It was an ad for Jack's movie, his last, *Serial Killer*.

She'd read on the wires that the studio, in the wake of the star's murder, was going to bring the picture out earlier than planned. Maxi knew the movie; she was married to Jack when they started shooting it. There was no female character like that in the film, no leggy sexpot in a leather micro-mini. The woman on the billboard did not exist in *Serial Killer*. Maxi looked up at it again. Large text beside the sleek pair of legs read: THE LAST TIME YOU WILL EXPERIENCE A NEW JACK NATHANSON THRILLER!

Maxi winced. Beyond tasteless. This exploitive publicity so soon after Jack's murder had to be the work of the notorious Alan Bronstein, Monogram's head of production. Bronstein—brilliant, charming, and a touch sinister by reputation—was coiner of the credo "It's not how you play the game, but whether you open at number one." He had met the young Janet Orson when she was the new "girl" in the steno pool back when they were both at Fox. He'd been her protector and big brother, and the one who'd encouraged her to become an agent. And she turned around and brought a lot of hot stars and great scripts his way. A symbiotic relationship. Diller and Von Furstenburg. And it was common knowledge in this company town that Bronstein was, and had been for years, in love with Janet Orson.

If it weren't for Janet, industry gossip had it, Bronstein wouldn't have *looked* at a Jack Nathanson movie. The two men had clashed famously several times through the years. Bronstein hated Nathanson, and he especially hated that the brash, charismatic actor had married the woman he loved. Also, Bronstein was a businessman, and Jack Nathanson hadn't made a hit movie in ten years. That Monogram was distributing *Serial Killer,* Maxi knew, was strictly a gift for Janet.

Alan Bronstein was thinking about Janet Orson on the drive over Coldwater canyon to his lunch meeting at Mortons, the restaurant where he and Janet had had a long-standing habit of having dinner together on Thursday nights. When Janet met Jack Nathanson, Alan had warned her not to get involved with him. This was a bad guy, Alan had told her repeatedly, citing atrocities, stories about how badly Nathanson had treated people in the course of business or pleasure. But Janet was not to be dissuaded. Then came her call saying that Jack didn't want her to have those Thursday night dinners with him anymore, because he wanted that time with her himself.

Soon after, Janet Orson became the third Mrs. Jack Nathanson. For a long time Bronstein had no contact with her, and that hurt. Until the day she turned up at his office unannounced. He'd surprised himself at how choked up he became. And then she laid it on him. Jack's production company needed a distributor for *Serial Killer,* and she wanted Alan to take the project on.

"Really!" Alan had said, raising his eyebrows. "But Jack doesn't even *talk* to me. Why would he want me bringing out his picture?"

He would, she'd told him, and she didn't have to explain why. Word was out that the picture was a dog, and nobody wanted to touch it. But Alan Bronstein could never say no to Janet Orson.

She'd looked so small in his office, sitting opposite him in one of the big leather club chairs, Janet gamely standing by her man. Bronstein, who had always been in the industry gossip pipeline, knew exactly what was going on in that marriage, what he'd known was bound to go on, because Jack Nathanson was an animal who wouldn't change. He was cheating on her in Vegas, partying with Sammy Minnetti and the good old boys when he'd go there to gamble or see a fight; he'd cheat on her on movie locations; he was even doing it right under her nose with some tough hooker disc jockey, Bronstein had heard.

He worried about Janet. He worried about Jack bringing home diseases. He worried that Janet would be publicly humiliated. And he worried about her assets, worried that being married to Jack, who was rumored to be pretty much tapped out, her money would go out a lot quicker than it came in. Somebody, he'd vowed to himself that day, had to stop Jack Nathanson.

He pulled into the parking lot at Mortons now, and a young parking attendant rushed over. "Hi, Billy," Bronstein said, getting out of his car. "Watch the doors, will you?"

"Sure thing, Mr. Bronstein." The young man beamed, jumping into the black Porsche Turbo. Bronstein was a regular at Mortons, one of that industry in-spot's more colorful customers.

Bronstein was *connected,* the stories went. He had no trouble finding Mafia money to fund his projects if he needed it, people said. Word was that Bronstein had even killed a man, that he was taking a meeting with a certain mob figure who was investing in a certain movie, and in some way there were drugs involved, and the gangster turned up dead that night, shot in his own den on his own green plaid sofa, which they showed on the television news. But there was no record anywhere that he had been meeting with Alan Bronstein that night, and Bronstein had flown to Vegas and gotten a room at Bally's, where the night manager was an old friend and predated his registration by a day. In a bit of revisionist history, the story went, Alan Bronstein had checked into Bally's in Las Vegas at ten o'clock at night, and Tony "Ears" Ergatti was killed in Los Angeles sometime after midnight.

If Billy was going to be denting doors that afternoon, he was not going to dent the doors of Alan Bronstein's Porsche!

13

Maxi had never seen this enormous villa on Benedict Canyon Drive, where, for the past year, her ex-husband had lived with his new wife. Janet Orson had called and asked if she'd like to have the two lovely pieces of furniture back that she'd given to Jack in their divorce. She wanted to give Maxi a chance to reclaim them, Janet had said, and she suggested that Maxi come by and see if there was anything else of hers in the jumble that Jack had amassed, before all of it went to the auction house tomorrow. Curious, Maxi had ducked out of the newsroom at lunchtime and driven over the canyon.

Maxi didn't know Janet well, though she had done several interviews with her through the years. She'd called Janet a few times since her marriage to Jack to say she'd just found some marvelous pictures of Jack in a drawer, or some books of his that he might want, and she was sending them over, that kind of thing. She'd always found Janet amiable and courteous.

And Maxi was fond of those two pieces of hers, a Winchester walnut chest of drawers with a serpentine front and carved feet, and a George Bullock mahogany collectors' cabinet with beautiful inlays that had fifty narrow file drawers. Jack had used them at their house—the chest had been filled with his underwear and the cabinet with his working files—so she'd told him to keep them. Now, she thought, she might as well have them back.

Carlotta let her in, and Maxi embraced the sweet-natured woman. She had always loved Carlotta Ricco, who'd taken such good care of Jack and his family, all his families. Jack used to joke that Maxi married him to get Carlotta. Standing in the foyer now, Maxi peered into the massive living room at furniture and artwork she had lived with in *her* home in what seemed like another life.

Janet appeared from around the corner, and Maxi pulled herself back to the present. The two women exchanged what seemed to both of them a self-conscious hug.

"Come in, Maxi," Janet said. "Take a look around; see if anything else is yours. Or if there's anything else of his that you want, for that matter."

"How did you know those two pieces were mine?"

"Jack told me. I'd wondered about them, because they're so different from everything else he owned."

Maxi scanned her ex-husband's cumbersome furniture crowded end to end, the antique mirrors leaning against the walls, the boxes stacked everywhere filled with books, tapes, clothing, and odds and ends, all of it the personal effects of superstar Jack Nathanson collected over thirty years.

And his artwork! Bulky, bizarre sculptures on pedestals, cryptic drawings and gigantic paintings on the walls, dark, frightening pieces of Expressionism, bloody, gory scenes portraying people cut in half, phantoms, ghouls, the devil in many forms, human and animal freaks of nature. Most of the work was by noted artists, Beckmann, Kandinsky, all superbly done, and all of it expensive. He even had a Corot, but the darkest, most dour example of that brilliant French Impressionist, a bleak forest of gnarled and decaying trees. Glancing at it on her *own* living room wall back then, Maxi would chuckle—she'd always figured that Corot must've been having a really bad day when he knocked that one out.

And it was voluminous, his art collection—Jack had been accumulating it with fervor since he'd scored with his first big movie and Sam Bloom had turned him on to the joy and prudence of investing in art. Jack never did anything halfway. Maxi could guess how Janet must have felt as she'd attempted to incorporate these grotesqueries into a tasteful, inviting home—a daunting task, Maxi knew, because she'd tried to do the same.

Two men in dark suits were wending their way through the clutter. "Anything with a red sticker is going," Janet said to them. And by way of explanation to Maxi, "They're the appraisers from Sotheby's. It's all going to auction."

Janet didn't seem at all bereaved, but Maxi knew that the shock of violent loss often left loved ones in denial for a time. Still, it was just a week to the day after Jack's funeral. Soon, it seemed, for his wife to be efficiently and matter-of-factly clearing out his things.

"You'll find those stickers on most of what's in the house," Janet went on to the appraisers. "There's more in my late husband's office, and the dining room, the den, bedrooms—"

"We'll go around and make notes, Ms. Orson," said one of the men, with the deference due a recent widow.

Maxi felt an odd sensation, being in the midst of Jack's belongings again. Big, heavy, dark, dreary furniture, Chippendale and Louis-the-Something, oversized, overstuffed, overwrought, cracked here, broken there, shabby in her view, and loads of it, most of the pieces undeniably ugly. Undeniable by everyone except Jack. He'd loved these things. Maxi remembered the day Wendy Harris had looked around their house in horror when they were moving Jack's belongings in. "What the hell are you going to *do* with all this shit?" Wendy had asked her. "What *can* I do?" Maxi had countered. "He loves it, and I love him. And in the scheme of things that really count, a few sticks and bones are unimportant, don't you think?" Wendy, a confirmed minimalist when it came to furnishings, had just rolled her eyes.

"Are you okay?" Janet asked now, sensing Maxi's discomfort.

"I . . . Yes, it's just . . . It's been a while since I've seen all this. . . ."

The two women were quiet for several moments. Memories. They both had them. Janet broke the silence. "Come with me," she said.

She led Maxi across the broad expanse of the crammed living room to four sets of French doors that looked out on a beautifully landscaped pool area. "Let's sit for a minute," she said to Maxi, indicating a pair of small, tasteful loveseats that seemed overpowered by the rest of the furnishings in the room.

"I don't remember these—" Maxi started, as they sat down opposite each other.

"No, these were mine," Janet said, running a hand gently over the ivory silk upholstery. The two women looked at each other then, and in that moment both realized that they had a lot in common.

"You know, Maxi," Janet said softly, "I was tempted to call you several times, when Jack seemed his most perplexing. To see what light you could shed on his behavior. But I never did."

Déjà vu, Maxi thought, remembering the day when she herself had first called Debra Angelo, sorely needing the same kind of enlightenment. There'd been nobody else to look to. Certainly not Sam Bloom, who thought all of Jack's wives were predators. Not wonderful Julian Polo, who knew the dark side of his client's movie plots, but not of his home life. Nor had she known anyone in Jack's family who could help. He'd told her he *had* no family.

Maxi's gaze drifted once again to the glut of furnishings in the room. "There's . . . just so much of it, isn't there?" she breathed, to break the mood.

"So much, and so *awful*," Janet returned, surprising Maxi with her candor. She relaxed into her comfortable love seat, dwarfed now by Jack's possessions engorging the enormous room. "I'm selling Jack's things at auction, according to the terms of his will," she said. "The proceeds will go to his estate for Gia." Maxi looked around her at this mini Hearst Castle, chock-full of Citizen Nathanson's stuff.

"I'm selling this house, too," Janet said. "I never really liked it."

"The upkeep alone must be exorbitant," Maxi said, for lack of anything more cogent to say. Again, this scene, with Janet confiding to her about her life with Jack, seemed hauntingly like when Maxi had first talked to Debra, *really* talked to her. *Jack Nathanson's wives*, Maxi thought. *The Club*.

"Let's not even *talk* about money." Janet sighed.

"I'm guessing you paid for everything," Maxi ventured, emboldened by Janet's willingness, her seeming need, to open up. Maxi was one of the few people who knew that Jack Nathanson was broke when he married Janet Orson.

"Everything," Janet affirmed.

"You were in love," Maxi put in kindly. "I certainly knew that feeling—"

"Yes, he was the romantic one, the artistic one, the outrageous one, and heaven knows, I needed that in my very conservative, cautious life," she said. "Jack was exciting—"

"*Were* you in love with him?" Maxi heard herself asking.

"Of course," Janet said. "Weren't you?"

"Yes. For a while."

"Me too."

"How do you feel now?" Maxi asked quietly.

Janet looked out the French doors into the middle distance. "Like I've been let out of prison," she murmured.

14

"This is Zahna, your late night rock 'n' roll dreamin' queen on Radio-KBIS, playin' 'em just for you on a Wednesday night. Call me and tell me what you wanna do . . . I mean what you wanna *hear* . . . I *know* what you wanna *do*, you maniacs. . . ."

Zahna was flying. She'd coked up before her eight-to-midnight shift, had to, just to get herself out of the house. Now, to bring herself down to that hazy, lazy, low-down soft-rock mode the station format called for, she was drinking straight tequila out of a paper cup, leveling out.

"This one's for Frank in Fontana. He's nuts about Lacy, but Lacy sez she needs her space. Hey, Frankie, lots of chicks would like to share *your* space, babe—bet we'll hear from a few tonight," she murmured, breathing heavily into the microphone.

What crap, she was thinking. Two hours into her show and she was getting very drunk. What else was new?

"Okay, boys and girls, this one's for Jack Nathanson. You know, Jack Nathanson, the big-deal movie star shot dead at his ex-wife's house . . . weekend before last . . . you saw the news. Hadda be an old wife or an old girlfriend dunnit, don'tcha think? Shouldn't mess with your women, guys, or look what happens."

The sound came up on Sting's "Every Breath You Take."

Zahna put her lips an inch away from the microphone and purred, "Oh, yeah, here's the *stalker* song—ever watch your lover's every move, every step, every breath?"

She punched her MUTE button. "I was watching *you*, you motherfucking, two-timing, three-timing . . ." she was muttering, knocking back the liquor, no ice, no lime, no frills, just anesthesia.

Her engineer shook his head. Blastoff time already, only 10:06. At her current rate of escalation, he was thinking, one of these nights she was either going to pass out cold, or confess on the air that she *killed* the guy. Good thing the bosses didn't listen at this time of night.

Everyone at the station knew that Zahna Cole had been having an affair with Jack Nathanson, an on-again, off-again, one-way kind of thing—it was on when he wanted it on, it was off when he didn't call her, and it was all one way, *his* way. Zahna was transparent, and her coworkers couldn't miss the signs—when he was around, Zahna was euphoric, and when he wasn't, Zahna was obsessed. Now he was dead, and she seemed dangerously close to the edge.

She'd met Jack Nathanson when she was cast for a small part in one of his movies, a voice-over disc jockey bit. The location was a brokerage company in a high-rise building on the Wilshire corridor. She'd never expected to see the star, but while she was recording her sequences, Nathanson actually came over to the microphone, bent down, and whispered in her ear that he'd heard her on the radio and had wondered if she was as sexy as she sounded. "When you're done here, come watch us shoot," he'd tossed back at her as he left the booth.

His hot breath in her ear melted her, and she was not an easy melt. This was Jack Nathanson—famous, glamorous, rich, dynamic, handsome movie star Jack Nathanson—wondering how sexy she was. She'd love to show him, she thought, and in fact he didn't make her wait.

Watching the shoot, it felt as if Jack was playing right to her. He made eye contact, he smiled, he winked, once he gave her a little finger wave. On the dinner break he came off the set, took her arm, and walked her to the chow wagon outside, where cast and crew were lining up. "We definitely don't want to eat this shit," he'd whispered with that impish grin, as they perused the assortment of hot casseroles, cold salads, baskets of rolls, and slices of fruit pie on paper plates. "When we're finished shooting, I'll take you to dinner."

"I have to do my radio show," she said.

"How about after your show?"

"At midnight?"

"Something wrong with midnight?" He laughed, and he asked for her address.

After work that night, when she pulled up at her small rented house in Sherman Oaks, his Ferrari was parked by the gate and he was sitting on her front steps, holding a bottle of champagne.

"Hi . . . How did you get in the gate?" she asked.

"An old army trick," he said with a wink.

Inside, he opened the champagne. He took her to bed. "Oh God," he'd groaned, "I've wanted to eat you since the second I saw you. Give it to me, give it to me, put it in my face, yes, *yesssss . . .*" Zahna couldn't believe she was rolling around on her king-size bed with this ravenous, insatiable man, this glutton for her body whom she'd just met that afternoon.

"Wait—what about condoms?" she'd breathed.

"What about them?" he'd slurred, burying his head deeper between her legs. She was too stoned to make an issue of it. She'd brought out cocaine. "Great combination," he'd moaned. "Champagne and toot—and sex."

She'd found herself drifting into one of her fantasies. He was a Roman soldier who had stumbled upon this beauty huddled in fear in the back room of a greathouse that his soldiers were pillaging. He pulled back his toga, revealing his bronzed, muscled body. His troops would have the jewels, he would have the woman. She was just settling into the scenario in her mind and the rhythm in her loins when he climaxed, big, fast, and he was up, and dressing. She rolled over on her stomach and reached for her robe.

"You're fabulous, Jack. . . . I'll make some coffee."

"No coffee, babe—gotta go." He was scrambling for his Nikes. "Early shoot tomorrow. I'll call you." And he was gone. She heard his car turn over and peel off before she got her robe around her. Home to the wife, she supposed—he was married to that newscaster Maxi Poole. Oh well, it had been a fun day.

But he did call, and he kept calling, and she lived for his calls. Every time they got together she fell harder. His wife was busy all the time, he told her. Maxi worked late, Jack got up early—their sex life was not exactly an Olympic event, he'd confided. "Frankly, Scarlett, she just doesn't turn me on the way my Zahna does, know what I mean? Spit in my face," he'd beg. "C'mon, Zahna, I'm your Roman soldier, I'm going to rape you, spit in my face. . . ."

She knew what she had with him; she was nobody's fool. Still, he kept showing up, and she couldn't resist him. The day would come, she'd tell herself, when he would realize that he was getting a lot better in the little house on Sumac Drive than he was getting at home, and he would leave Ms. Newsbitch and come to Zahna—and unlike his other two wives, she would know how to keep him happy.

Zahna Cole's time was due, she was sure of that. She'd had too many lousy relationships, and now she was alone, not getting any younger, and doing this dopey job. She had come to Los Angeles with moondust in her eyes. She was going to be a singer, make it big. Everybody said she was good, she was beautiful, she was gonna be a rock 'n' roll diva. Now, sixteen years later, she had dead-ended on all fronts, doing yeoman's service on a local FM station for thirty-six-five a year and spending half of it on drugs. Her ship was due to come in, and she was sure that sexy Jack Nathanson was at the helm.

"Here's Usher, with 'You Remind Me,' she breathed into the mike. "This one's for Linda, comin' atcha from Steve. He says he's your man, Linda; he loves ya, baby. . . ."

Where was *her* man? No more man. Going on midnight and her lights were nearly out. Just fifteen more minutes, then collapse city. Well, drive the clunker home and then collapse. Good thing there wasn't much traffic this late, couldn't handle it tonight. . . .

Came the day his second marriage broke up, hallelujah, it was Zahna's turn. He moved into a rental house in Bel Air, and she had a clear shot now. For the first time in the two years they'd had together, *she* could go to *his* house. When his kid was at her mother's, they'd get stoned, romp around naked, ball each other's brains out, and sleep till noon the next day in *his* bed. Those days were nirvana.

But they weren't for long. Jack would go for weeks without seeing her. When he'd finally take her call, he'd complain that he'd been really busy. One midnight, after she got off the air and was hurting bad, she drove over to his house, like he used to show up at her house in his married days. "Just took a chance, babe," he'd say. His big Spanish manse was all lit up—it looked like a party was going on. She pressed the bell.

"Who is it?" came his annoyed voice over the intercom.

"Surprise—it's your Zahna. I just took a chance, cuz I've got some very good blow—"

"I'm asleep, hon; got an early call."

"Oh, come on, half an hour. *I'll* put you to sleep, stud. I came allaway over the friggin' canyon—"

"Can't do it, too beat; call you tomorrow, babe." Click. Over and out.

A couple of weeks later, a friend told her she'd seen him at a Beverly Hills restaurant—he was with that agent Janet Orson and another couple. He was still having sex with Zahna every now and then. No restaurants, no dinners with friends, no plays, no concerts, no gala parties with the movie crowd—just sex. He just wanted to be alone with her, he'd say, not out at some boring hoo-ha making small talk with people he didn't care about; c'mon, baby, suck my dick, pretty please. . . .

She asked him about Janet Orson. Janet Orson was his new agent, he'd said. It was business.

Then she read in the *L.A. Times* that Janet Orson and Jack Nathanson got married in the Caribbean. But two weeks after that he was calling her again, with his "Let's get together, babe, I really miss you, I want to get it on with you." What *she* wanted was his balls cut off and served up on a plate.

Still, she had sex with him every time he came calling, even when he started bringing Clio around. He'd phoned her one night at the station and said he was coming over to her house when she got off, and he had a fabulous surprise for her. She soared through her show, fantasizing that the surprise meant the end of Janet Orson and the real beginning of Jack and Zahna, or even that Janet was going out of town for a month. But the surprise was Clio.

Zahna was waiting when he rang the bell, and she rushed to the door and pulled it open to see . . . Jack on her doorstep holding Clio by the elbow, both of them grinning. Clio was a lanky, leggy, exotic-looking black woman who worked at a dubbing house in Studio City. She headed right for Zahna, put both hands on her cheeks, and said, "We're gonna have some *fun*, girlfriend!"

"Wait, wait, wait . . ." Jack laughed, and ushered them both into the bedroom, where he popped the champagne he was carrying.

"I'm going to get some glasses, ladies." He beamed. "Now don't start without me." Zahna sat on the bed, trying to absorb what was going on, while Clio stood three feet in front of her and began to strip, slowly, down to black-lace bra and garter belt. She was touching herself, sensuously lingering on her nipples, when Jack came back into the room with three of the champagne flutes he'd bought for Zahna. He flipped on the stereo system, and Tina Turner's lusty voice filled the room while he poured the wine. Zahna was already intensely coked out. *What the hell*, she thought; *this could be fun.*

But he *did* love his Zahna best, loved her only, she knew. Clio was just another kinky diversion, and that was one of the things that made him the most exciting man she'd ever known.

She also knew that he'd just married Janet for business reasons, that he needed Janet Orson and her connections right now to help get his career out of stall, and when that happened he would divorce her like he had the other two and he would marry his Zahna. Otherwise, why was he still seeing her? Why had he never *stopped* seeing her, never stopped *needing* her?

Zahna shook out of her reverie as the station clock came up on midnight. *Oh yeah*, she thought. *Turned out* that *was a crock.*

15

Meg Davis turned her small sports car west onto Santa Monica Boulevard toward the ocean, headed for Malibu. It was a week and a day since Jack Nathanson's funeral, and she still couldn't stop the flashbacks. Driving stiff-backed, teeth clenched, a vise grip on the wheel, she tried to keep the thoughts from coming. She turned on the radio, punched in a heavy-metal station, turned the volume up high. But still, she couldn't push the waking nightmares out of her head.

She was ten years old again, on the set of *Black Sabbat*. It was late summer, and often above 100 degrees in the Massachusetts countryside that was meant to look like the Salem of 1692. She would spend hours clamped in the wooden pillory while extras heaved huge Styrofoam stones, dipped in slimy mud and ooze, that bounced off her head and face. The crew worked in shorts and sandals, T-shirts and halter tops, while Meg endured the stifling heat for hours on end in Puritan garb—a floor-length gown of coarse black wool, her head covered with a heavy wimple drawn and tied in folds under her chin—sweating for real, a good little girl, cooperating, getting it right.

Jack Nathanson was the star, playing her character's father, a minister, a once lofty clergyman of New England's Colonial days who now stood accused of being a warlock and harboring a coven of witches, including his beautiful wife and his sweet daughter.

Mr. Nathanson had told her mother that he could get a performance out of Meg that the world would remember if she'd let him work with her every day, just the two of them. After lunch was the best time, he'd said, because union rules dictated that the crew had to break for an hour. A golden opportunity, her mother had told her—this brilliant actor had taken a personal interest in Meggie's career. "Let's change Davidson to Davis," he'd said to her mother. "Davis is better. Meg Davis," he'd pronounced. And Sally agreed. Jack Nathanson knew best.

Meg's almost daily private sessions in the star's trailer were exciting at first. Mr. Nathanson would crouch in front of her and act out the scenes they had coming up. "Now *you* do it. *Scream* at me," he'd shout. "Spit in my face. Do it. Meg—spit in my face!"

"I *can't,* Mr. Nathanson," the good little girl would say. "I just couldn't do that. . . ."

Once he'd swooped her up, carried her to a chair, sat down, set her on his lap, glowered into her eyes, and said, *"Do it, Meg—spit in my face!"*

"I *can't,* Mr. Nathanson—" She was crying now.

He softened. "Trust me, Meg. Call me 'Father.' Do what I tell you—it'll help us play our scenes." He shifted her on his lap, took hold of her squarely by the shoulders, put his face inches from hers, and said, *"Now . . . spit . . . in . . . my . . . face."*

She spit, and she cried; he shouted "More!" and she tried. He demanded "Call me 'Father'!" and she sobbed, "Fa-a-a-ther," and spit, and dribbled, until finally he said, "That's enough for today," lifting her off his lap, wiping her face with his hand. "Very good, Meg," he'd praised with that wonderful grin of his, and scooted her off with a pat on the fanny to get into makeup and get ready for their next scene.

He'd repeatedly told her that she must never discuss their exercises—not with her mother, not with anyone. She didn't. Certainly none of the grown-ups objected to the closed-door sessions. "This costume looks perfect, Meg," the wardrobe mistress would say. "Now run along—Mr. Nathanson is waiting to run lines with you." And her performance reflected Jack Nathanson's personal coaching—the dailies were powerful, everyone said; young Meg Davis was brilliant in the part.

Sometimes she even liked it when Mr. Nathanson touched her, or urged her to touch him. But she was confused. Was what they were doing dirty? Or was this just what movie people did? A ten-year-old couldn't know for sure, but she couldn't help feeling that she harbored an awful secret.

Meg pressed down on the accelerator. She had to get to the child. She knew that ten-year-old Gia was the embodiment of herself at that age before the maligning spirits had ensnared her own soul. Gia was still an innocent, but her father lurked with the baneful specters now, the living dead, and would corrupt the daughter as he did herself if she wasn't shielded. Meg had to watch over Gia and pray; it was clearly her responsibility.

She made the turn onto Seashore Drive, where Gia lived with her mother in Malibu. She was always at her mother's now, since her father was taken to hell. Meg pulled up and parked a block away from their house. Tote bag slung over her shoulder, she hurried down the public accessway onto the sand, and carefully spread out a lightweight blanket at the foot of a jagged, blackened rock formation. There she settled, her back to the ocean, to watch the house. Gia would be getting home from school soon.

A relentless, white-hot sun moved lower in the sky on its afternoon passage over the ocean. Meg was calm, still, her eyes steady on the rambling, three-story weathered gray beach house with the white trim.

Finally, the back door opened and Gia burst out onto the sundeck, the housekeeper right behind her carrying a tray with drinks. Setting her bookbag on the table, Gia sat down and sipped her drink. Her mother came out and joined her. Peering from under a wide-brimmed hat, Meg kept her gaze fixed squarely on the girl, focusing on her, concentrating on her soul. If she could stay centered, she could keep the unearthly spirits from permeating Gia's being, but she could feel the antithetic tugging of the child's father, a menacing, potent pull from hell.

After a few minutes, the girl bounded into the house, then reappeared with her dog on a leash. Then mother and daughter came down the steps and onto the sand. Meg followed their progress, her eyes hidden behind dark glasses, her attention riveted on the child's blazing aura, which she could see emanating from her in an increasingly vivid flare as she came closer.

Do not inhabit this young soul; do not consume this child's essence, Meg chanted silently as they passed by, the youngster looking over at her curiously now, her spirited Irish setter tugging her forward.

"Come on, darling," she could hear the mother urging. "You mustn't stare at people; it isn't nice," and she nudged her lovingly along on their walk toward the surf.

Meg felt the familiar pain swelling in her chest and the fever rising in her head, her blood pounding as she repeated her invocation, half aloud now. "Gia must not die for my sins."

16

"You're covering the auction tomorrow, Maxi," Pete Capra said again.

"Come on, Pete," Maxi appealed. "You know this one's too close to home for me."

"That's exactly why I want you on it—you know what every piece is, where he got it, and why; you can bring behind-the-scenes stories to an otherwise boring furniture sale."

Maxi looked at him as if she didn't believe what she'd just heard him say. "You really have no heart, do you, Pete?" she said softly.

"Oh, stop it, Maxi—you were over the guy long before you divorced him. What's the big deal?"

Maxi could only shake her head. "Pete," she said, "there'll be movie stars there, there'll be celebrities, people from Jack's world. Put Jensen on it. He's the entertainment reporter."

"This isn't *entertainment*, Maxi. This is *crime*."

It was Friday afternoon. The newsroom was buzzing with preparation for the early news block, and Maxi sat at her computer in her glass-walled office, writing a story for the Six O'clock News. Pete Capra had barged in and was looming over her desk, waving some wire copy, bent on assigning her to cover the auction of the late actor Jack Nathanson's effects at Sotheby's in Beverly Hills the next day. Her ex-husband's effects.

"The only crime at the auction tomorrow will be Sotheby's charging big money for Jack's bad-taste stuff," she told her boss now, trying to lighten the mood, trying to get herself off the assignment. "People love to see big-time celebrities wasting their money—it's an Eric Jensen story."

"You know Jensen's a fucking prima donna—he won't work on weekends. It's in his contract."

"Well, it's in *my* contract too, boss. Check it out!"

"I know, I know, but you never give me any of that shit. Whatever has to be done, you do it."

"Not this time. Put one of the general-assignment reporters on it."

"Maxi, I want *you* on it."

"*Why*, Pete?"

Capra threw his head back in exasperation. "Because of the big picture. This is a *murder* story. A big, fat, high-profile, star-studded, scandal-ridden, loud, screeching, L.A. murder case. The *world* is interested in it. And a lot of the players will show up at that auction. Who knows what you'll see, what you'll hear, what you'll learn? Nobody on staff would be able to look at that scene tomorrow and see it with your insights. Just forget he was your fucking husband for a day, okay?"

"Pete?"

"*What!*"

"Why are you so cranky?"

Pete looked down, but not before Maxi saw his rumpled Italian face redden. "Because . . . I gave up smoking," he said in a small voice.

"Oh, *no!* Again?"

"Kris is on my back. And my doctor's on my back."

"The last time you quit smoking you punched O'Brian and

knocked him through an edit console." Dan O'Brian was a talented but cantankerous reporter who didn't edit a high-rise-fire story exactly the way Pete Capra had hoped. It would have been a much calmer situation if Pete had had a cigarette.

"So?"

"So you broke his collarbone!"

"He buried the lead—I shoulda *killed* him."

"He could have sued. I don't know why he didn't."

"He didn't sue because his drug bust would have come out. You know, when this station, thank you very much, bailed his sorry ass out of the tank and put him through rehab to the tune of forty grand."

"I don't want to cover the auction, Pete."

"Are you telling me you're refusing an assignment?"

Contractually, he had no case, of course, but Pete Capra never believed in fighting fair. Maxi's thoughts reeled back to her odyssey through Jack's things at Janet's house two days ago. It was dizzying. It was poignant. It was painful. She didn't want to relive it.

Acknowledging her reluctance, Pete softened. "Look," he said, "blow off the auction in a couple of minutes. Have your shooter isolate five or six things, voice over them, get me a couple of sound bites, with a star, with a family friend, whatever. I don't give a damn about the crap they're hawking. But you know the people in Nathanson's world. Talk to them. Listen to them. I want your eyes and ears there. Leave your heart at home."

Her heart had been all over the terrain on this story since it broke almost two weeks ago. Jack's murder had stirred up memories that she wanted to forget, and emotions that she didn't want to deal with, besides putting her in a potential vise that Pete, that nobody, could know about. All she could do was put one foot in front of the other, business as usual.

"Okay, Pete. You win. I'll cover the auction."

Pete gave her five. “What the hell,” he said with his mis-chief-making grin. “Maybe you’ll see something you wanna buy.”

Maxi looked at him incredulously. “Yeah, *right*,” she said.

17

The child was in the kitchen with me," Gia's nanny Bessie Burke was telling Mike Cabello and Jon Johnson, "and we heard sharp noises . . . shots, it was."

It was Friday afternoon, almost two weeks after the murder. The three were sitting in a small room at the Hall of Justice, L.A.'s central Sheriff's Headquarters. A paralegal who worked for Marvin Samuels had driven Bessie downtown.

"Did you notice anything unusual, Mrs. Burke?" Jon asked. "A car pulling up, a door opening?"

"No," Bessie returned, "there were always cars pulling up and doors opening. We're at the beach, you know. Neighbors and children come by to see Gia and Miss Debra. I don't pay much attention—"

"Mrs. Burke," Cabello asked her, "what time did you get up on that Saturday?"

"Seven o'clock. I always get up at seven."

"Was Gia up?"

"Oh, yes, she's up very early. She was already dressed and watching cartoons when I went into her room. I gave her a morning hug and left her be, and I busied myself in the kitchen with breakfast."

Bessie Burke was an ample woman, fifty-seven, from Cornwall, in England, and Debra had loved her on sight. She wasn't the most fastidious housekeeper in the world, but she adored Gia, played the proper British nanny to her, and to Debra, that was invaluable.

"So Gia and Ms. Angelo had breakfast, then went off to the kid's shrink appointment. What time did they get home?" asked Cabello.

"Umm, I never much mind the time, you know, but it was lunchtime, though Gia wasn't hungry—"

"So what did you all do, you, Gia, and her mother, before Mr. Nathanson arrived?" queried Jon Johnson.

"Well, we looked at some photographs of Gia and Skip playing volleyball on the beach last week. Miss Debra took them," she said. "And Gia wanted to play those video games that are all the rage with the youngsters these days," she went on. "She plays in the den, on the big TV, and Miss Debra was in there with her—she had her new magazines—and I went in the kitchen to fix Gia's lunch. I always made her eat before she went with her father, because the good Lord only knows what they feed her over there—" She stopped herself and looked down at her lap. She was twisting a lace handkerchief with both hands.

"And where was Ms. Angelo when Mr. Nathanson came?" Cabello quizzed.

"Why, in her room; I told you that," Bessie responded.

"Did you *see* her go into her room?"

"Uhh, no, not actually—"

"Then how do you *know* she was in her room?" Johnson pressed.

"Because she *always* went into her room before that man got to the house, unless she needed to have a discussion with him, and if she did, she made it short, *then* went to her room."

"She didn't like Mr. Nathanson, then?"

"I should think you'll have to ask *her* that."

"Yes, ma'am. But you do know how *Gia* felt about Mr. Nathanson. Did Gia like her father, Mrs. Burke? Or do you want us to ask *her?*" Bessie straightened in her chair, prim in her navy blue rayon suit with pleated skirt, white blouse, and sensible shoes, torturing the handkerchief now.

"I shouldn't think you'd force a little girl who's lost her daddy to come to this terrible place and make her talk about it," she reprimanded. "I should think you gentlemen would know better than to do that to a youngster."

"Well, then," returned Cabello, softening, "we know she loved her father; all kids love their dads. . . . But tell us, did she *like* her father? Was she happy to be going off with him?"

"She was pleased, yes. They were going to the lake. . . . Gia likes the lake—"

"What Mike wants to know, Mrs. Burke, is did Gia like her father?" Johnson interjected.

"Why, she *loved* her father. Gia loves everybody. She's a good girl," Bessie responded, appearing close to tears. Both detectives could see that this woman would do anything for Debra Angelo and her daughter, and she was terribly nervous about saying the right things.

"All right," Cabello said, shifting gears from the emotional to the practical. "Tell us about when Mr. Nathanson arrived. Ms. Angelo was in her room, you say; Gia was in the kitchen with you, and it was two o'clock when he came. . . . Oh, I forgot, you aren't mindful of time."

"Well, I was mindful just then, because we knew Mr. Nathanson was coming at two, and he's always directly on time, so we were watching for him, and it was exactly two, yes—"

"Okay, so it was two o'clock, and Gia's father rang the bell. Then what?" urged Cabello.

"Then Gia ran to the door to let him in, and they both came into the kitchen, and I'd finished making Gia's sandwich, and I asked if the child could eat up before she left. She'd missed her lunch—"

"And?" Cabello prompted. "When did Mr. Nathanson go into Gia's room, and why?"

"I already told you that, at our house the day it happened—" Bessie began.

"Yes, we know you did, Mrs. Burke," Jon Johnson put in, "but we want to hear it again. For the record, okay?"

"Very well," Bessie said stiffly. "Mr. Nathanson said they would need Gia's warm jacket because they were going up to Lake Arrowhead, and I said I'd just fetch it, but he said no, he'd get it, since I was still serving up Gia's lunch, and he said he wanted to see if there was anything else the child should take besides what I'd already packed for her, perhaps a couple of sweaters—"

"Then what?" Cabello prodded.

"Then he went in there, and, and—" Bessie broke down in tears. "And we heard the . . . heard the noise," she sobbed.

"How long was he in there before—"

"Five minutes . . . ten minutes—"

"Didn't you think that was a long time for him to be picking up a jacket?" Cabello asked. "Didn't you go into the room to help him find it?"

"No, no—I've told you, no, I did *not* go in there. Mr. Nathanson was searching about for what Gia might need at the lake, and I was feeding the child—" She was nearly hysterical now.

"It's all right, Mrs. Burke," Jon Johnson said softly, trying to calm her. "This is very important, ma'am. While Mr. Nathanson was in Gia's room, before you heard the shots, do you remember hearing, or seeing, anybody else?"

"No . . ."

"Did you notice *anything* that would have been unusual, out of the ordinary? Please think, Mrs. Burke. Take your time."

There was a long pause. "Well," Bessie ventured, quieter now, "only that that woman was out there again—"

"What woman?" Cabello pounced on her words, thinking she meant Maxi Poole.

"That actress woman, the one in Mr. Nathanson's movie, the one about the witches."

The detectives looked at each other. "Do you mean *Black Sabbat*, Mrs. Burke?" Johnson asked.

"That's the one. She was the little girl who was a witch."

"What do you mean she was 'out there'?" Cabello pumped. "*Where*, out there?"

"Out on the beach, but quite near the house, closer than where folks usually come, but Miss Debra told me once to leave her be when I mentioned it, so I paid the woman no mind after that, but she was out there regular, and she was out there that day."

"What do you mean by 'regular,' Mrs. Burke?" Jon Johnson asked. "How often, would you say?"

"Several times a week. She'd sit on her blanket, fully dressed—she didn't wear swimming outfits, so she wasn't taking the sun, or the salt water—"

"Why didn't you tell us that, Mrs. Burke?" Cabello demanded. "We've asked you before about that day and you didn't mention any woman near the house. How do you know it was that actress? Is her name Meg Davis?"

Mrs. Burke dissolved in tears under Cabello's hammering. "Because I didn't know it was important. . . . I didn't even *think* about it. She was there often—"

"Was it Meg Davis, do you know, Mrs. Burke?" asked Johnson.

"Yes, I know it was her, because the day I pointed her out to Miss Debra through the window, she said, 'Oh for heaven's sake, that's Meg Davis; she played the little girl in *Black Sabbat*, Bessie. She's not hurting anyone. She's probably found herself a favorite spot by those rocks, so let her enjoy it.' Miss Debra knows all the famous people at the beach."

"Did you tell Ms. Angelo that Meg Davis was out by the house that Saturday?" asked Johnson.

"Why, no, I never thought about it, until just now when you told me to think, think of anything I could—"

"Thank you, Mrs. Burke." Mike Cabello stood, dismissing her. "You've been very helpful," he said. He and Johnson were eager to follow up this new lead.

18

The bulky blue and white Channel Six News van scudded to a stop on Wilshire, across the wide boulevard from Sotheby's in the heart of Beverly Hills. It was after noon on Saturday, and the auction was already in progress. Several other big vans bearing the logos of competing news outlets, local and national, were already parked along the curb, which was a red zone, but the police rarely ticketed newsies. They cultivated good relations with journalists and news operations, to come off in the best light possible in the day-to-day fracas that was news in L.A.

Maxi hopped down from the truck as her cameraman, Rodger Harbaugh, raised the big, unwieldy microwave mast to feed the signal back to the station. Rodger was a street-smart news wars veteran, a wiry man with short brown hair and a sun-weathered face, who always got his shots with the least possible fuss. Maxi was glad she drew Rodger today, and not one of the station's puffed-up auteurs who would try to make *Gone with the Wind* out of this shoot. She didn't want to be here, she fervently hoped none of her colleagues would make her part of *their* story because she was once married to Jack Nathanson, and she intended to get in, get her footage, do her stand-ups, and get out. Hoisting her bag onto her shoulder, she walked around to the back of the van where Rodger had begun unloading gear.

"Down and dirty on this one, Rodge—no frills, okay?"

"You got it, Max. How'd you draw this duty, anyway?" Everybody at the station, in fact everybody in the business, knew that Maxi Poole was one of the late Jack Nathanson's exes.

"Pete had a bug in his drawers about me doing it—"

"You couldn't reason with him?"

"He quit smoking again."

"Aah."

Rodger hoisted the heavy minicam up on his right shoulder, lugged a leather bag filled with tapes, lights, filters, lenses, battery packs, and other assorted photographic supplies, and hefted the big aluminum tripod with his left hand.

"Sorry I can't help you with any of that," Maxi said.

"I know. We'd get nailed." It was against union rules for reporters to touch any camera crew equipment. Maxi broke that rule routinely when there were no other news personnel around who might feel strongly enough to file a grievance. They crossed the eight lanes of Wilshire and climbed the stairs into Sotheby's lobby, showed their credentials, and went inside the auction hall.

There were the usual greetings and camaraderie between competing news crews. If any of them thought it odd that Maxi Poole was covering the auction of her deceased ex-husband's effects, none of them let on to her. There would be some wagging about it, Maxi knew, but she shrugged it off—they didn't pay her mortgage. Still, she couldn't help feeling uncomfortable, especially being confronted yet again with all the pieces that had furnished her own home for years. Seeing it all jammed together here, lined up row after row in Sotheby's showrooms, unrelieved by a plant, a lamp, a book, the pieces presented even more of a drab lot than they had at Janet's house three days ago.

Rodger scoped the place for a spot where the light was best, while Maxi scanned the hall to see if she recognized anyone she could grab for a sound bite. Feeling a touch on the shoulder, she jumped. *Tension*, she thought. When Jack Nathanson was in a room—and she could definitely feel him in this room—there was tension. Sexual tension, excitement, anxiety, hostility—conflicting emotions, but never indifference.

"Hi, Maxi . . . Forgive me for startling you." It was Janet Orson.

"Hello, Janet." She smiled. "How's it going?"

"Oh, it's *going*," Janet said. "It's *all* going! Sotheby's has agreed to take whatever's left for a lot price, so today will be the last of it."

"You got a good turnout," Maxi said, attempting to ease the awkwardness they both felt in this situation. The two looked around the room. A tall, stunning woman with titian hair, in leather shorts and suspenders over a halter top, was ambling about, inspecting the paintings.

"That's Taryn Zimmerman," Janet offered. "Lived next door to us for a while. She was married to Irving Zimmerman, the developer."

"I know," Maxi said. "She came to the station and tried to sell us on doing a story suggesting that her ex-husband had Jack killed."

"Did she tell you she was having an affair with Jack?"

"You knew?"

"Of course I knew. Wives know."

"The old Jack Nathanson mystique." Maxi sighed.

"Yup, they can't get enough of him, even after he's dead."

At that, Maxi scrutinized Janet's face—the widow looked surprisingly like she didn't give a damn.

"Oops, there's another one," Janet said, mischief in her eyes. Maxi followed her gaze to an emaciated young woman who might have been beautiful once, but now, her eyes hooded, her skin pasty, her auburn hair hanging in tired clumps, she looked like another casualty of hip L.A.'s love affair with drugs. "Meg Davis, the child actress in *Black Sabbat*."

"She was at the funeral," Maxi observed.

"And now she's here. Probably was also hooked on Jack."

They took another look at the woman, who was unsteadily holding a glass of champagne in one hand and a bidding card in the other. "She looks like she just got here on the mother ship and she's still on Venusian time," Janet commented with an impish smirk, again surprising Maxi with her lack of even a trace of bitterness.

"Guess Jack collected them," Maxi offered absently, then quickly added, "I'm sorry, Janet; that was probably offensive."

"Hardly," Janet said with a wry lift of her brow. "You've *been* there. By the way," she added, "I'm surprised to see you here."

"I had no choice," Maxi rejoined. "My boss has some goofy idea that by cozying up to the people who knew Jack, I might sniff out his killer."

"Not so far-fetched," Janet remarked, scanning the massive auction hall. "I can see at least half a dozen people right now who might have had the motivation to do it."

A couple in their fifties, conservatively dressed, were approaching them. The woman reached for Janet's hand. "Hello, dear," she said. "My husband was the director of photography on two of Jack's films. We had dinner with him several times. He was charming and witty, a wonderful man. . . ."

After some reminiscing the couple drifted off, and Janet surreptitiously rolled her eyes. Maxi was seeing a whole new side of Janet Orson, and she was enjoying her.

"I've got to get to work, Janet," she said now. "If you spot the killer, bring him over to my camera, would you? My boss would be so proud."

Janet's smile reached her eyes. "You've got it. Meantime, if you see anything here that you want, let me know. For you, it's free."

Maxi scanned the hall. "How about that black boxwood corner number adorned with the ormolu gargoyles with the ivory teeth?" she said, pointing to an oversize, dreary-looking Gothic cabinet propped against a far wall. "I used to keep Yukon's toys and dog food in that thing."

"I'll have it shipped to your house," Janet deadpanned, and she gave Maxi a gentle elbow to the ribs. Maxi couldn't wait to tell Debra—this woman was definitely a new member of the Club.

She moved off through the furniture and the crowd to where Rodger had set up lights and was shooting B-roll. As soon as she came close enough, his eye still in the camera lens, Rodger grabbed her arm with his free hand. "Here's your story, Max!" he whispered. He was rolling tape on Meg Davis, who was now bidding on some kind of movie prop that had been used in *Black Sabbat*.

The auctioneer's voice droned on, and each time the bid price escalated, Meg Davis raised her bidding card again. Rodger was getting it all on tape. Maxi checked out the item on the block, an ornamental crucifix of some kind.

"*Sold*," sang the auctioneer with a bang of his gavel, "to the woman with bid number three-eleven. Congratulations, ma'am. You can claim your purchase at the desk in about an hour, after it's processed. Next item, lot number fifty-six, a painting by . . ." And on it went.

"Let's go," Maxi said to Rodger, and as she ran ahead to where Meg Davis stood, she spotted other reporters rushing toward the woman. Maxi got there first, with Rodger on her heels, toting the camera.

"Ms. Davis," she said, "I'm Maxi Poole from Channel Six. Can you tell us about the purchase you just made?"

"N-no. Please . . ." the actress stammered, holding her hand up in front of her face, palm out, as if to ward off something evil. Maxi saw fear in the woman's eyes. As other reporters swarmed around, Maxi held her own hand out to keep them at bay. Meg

Davis dropped her bidding card, turned on her heel, and fled. The press contingent, Maxi included, stood and watched as she pushed her way through the crowd, stepping on shoes, causing one startled woman to spill a drink, until she made it to the front of the hall and disappeared inside the women's rest room.

Maxi looked at her colleagues. "Guess she isn't giving interviews," she said to no one in particular.

"What the hell did you say to her, Maxi?" a friend from Channel Four asked.

"Nothing, honestly—" Maxi started.

"Shit, I think she's still in the coven," a cynical reporter from *Access Hollywood* threw out, causing the rest of them to laugh as they began to disperse in pursuit of more willing interview subjects.

Maxi stood alone with Rodger. "You got the bid from the beginning?" she asked him.

"Almost the beginning. I got more than enough."

"And did you get a close-up on the item she bought?"

"Of course."

"Great. Let's go grab someone from Sotheby's to talk about exactly what the thing is. Then I'll voice over your setup shots of the merchandise, and do a stand-up close in front of the auctioneer's podium. Then we're done."

The reporters' mandate at Channel Six News was that no story was worth more than a minute-thirty, unless it was the Second Coming; then you could go a minute-forty-five. And Maxi wanted to get out of there. She had just learned that the movie prop Meg Davis had purchased was the cross that the child witch had masturbated with in *Black Sabbat*.

19

Zahna Cole had walked into the crowded auction hall just as a strange-looking woman was making a successful bid on a strange-looking artifact, a heavy, ornate metal cross about fifteen inches high, painted in a medley of faded colors and peculiarly cast into a sharp point at the bottom. Circling the massive showroom, she'd picked up the buzz in the crowd—it was the *Black Sabbat* cross, people said, fashioned expressly for that period movie twenty years ago, and frighteningly memorable in it. And it was whispered that the woman who bought it was the now grown-up actress who had played the child in the film, Meg Davis.

Zahna had watched as Maxi Poole and a man carrying an intimidating-looking video camera on his shoulder aggressively approached this Meg Davis, which seemed to frighten her into running from them. Jack had told Zahna plenty about his then-wife Maxi Poole. He'd said she cared only about herself and her trivial news stories. Watching her now, acting so important while other reporters crowded around her, Zahna could see that in her. Jack was dead, but that didn't seem to bother Ms. Maxi Poole at all, or upset her perfect life.

Zahna ran her hand along the curved contours of a cherrywood table that had once stood in the foyer of Jack's Stone Canyon house, with a Tiffany lamp on it, a small silver tray where Carlotta had always put Jack's mail, and usually a bowl of fresh flowers. She sat down on a glossy German leather couch that they had made love on in the days before he married Janet Orson.

She had never met Janet Orson, but she'd seen pictures of her in the press. And there she was, cool as you please, moving all businesslike among the furniture, speaking to people like some detached vendor. Janet Orson was certainly a woman who got the job done. She got Jack to marry her because she had the power to help his career. Looking over at her, so attractive and self-assured in her chic white suit and gold jewelry, Zahna was sure that Jack's widow didn't much care that he was dead, either.

Zahna cared, and she could tell that the woman who bought that curious-looking cross, Meg Davis, cared. Spotting her in the crowd again, she studied her. About her own age, taller than average, excessively thin and carelessly dressed, no makeup, long hair untamed. Zahna watched her as she made her way unsteadily to the front desk. This was no seasoned auction-goer, no Saturday afternoon bargain hunter, Zahna knew, nor a former colleague or fan of the late Jack Nathanson simply interested in owning a part of his legacy. This woman was damaged goods, like herself, and Zahna's instincts told her that the damage was somehow attributable to the ghost whose palpable presence stalked these rooms among his own worldly possessions.

Zahna stood a few feet away as Meg Davis presented a credit card that had to be verified—it was a joint card in her mother's name, she heard her explain. She paid $1,400 for the movie prop; Zahna had the feeling that, like herself, she had paid a whole lot more than that in emotional currency. The woman picked up the cross in both her hands and headed uncertainly toward the exit. Zahna followed her out the doors.

"Hi there," Zahna said, catching up. "What'd you buy?"

"Oh, it's just a prop from one of his movies," Meg Davis answered.

"No kidding—which movie?"

"Uh, *Black Sabbat*. It's the cross that the minister used to ward off evil," Meg Davis said. "It's sentimental to me."

"Yes, you played the child in *Black Sabbat*, didn't you?" The two walked together toward the parking lot. "You were great," Zahna said.

"It was a long time ago," Meg responded. "Excuse me; they're bringing my car."

"I'm Zahna Cole. I knew Jack, too. Would you like to have a drink?" she asked, extending her hand.

Meg accepted it uneasily. "No, I have to be somewhere," she said, "but thank you."

"I have some really good grass," Zahna whispered, smiling.

Meg hesitated. It had been a long time since she'd toked up, and it was tempting. "No, I don't have time," she finally said. "I have to get out to the beach."

"Oh, do you have a date?" Zahna asked. She had a compelling need to talk to *somebody* about Jack, but there wasn't anybody. In those rooms full of people at Sotheby's, there were many who knew Jack Nathanson, but none she could talk to. She sensed that Meg Davis was a kindred spirit, would have stories to share.

"No," Meg replied, "I just like to sit on the sand near the ocean—it calms me."

"That sounds like a great idea," Zahna returned. "I could use some calming myself. Would you mind if I tag along? I'm a disc jockey and I work nights, but not on weekends, so I'm loose tonight, and I don't feel like going home just yet."

Meg shrugged. "If you want to," she replied, feeling some kind of kinship with this offbeat woman, and thinking that it would actually be nice to smoke a joint again. "Just follow me," she said, and she climbed into her car.

Meg waited until she saw Zahna's car come up behind her, then headed out to the beach. She would listen to music and concentrate on this interesting new acquaintance, and try to keep the thoughts from taking over.

She focused on the headlights of the dented black Volkswagen Rabbit. She didn't want to lose it; she was looking forward to getting high now. Meg had made frequent forays into drug rehab over the years; now the twelve steps didn't seem to mean much in the ragged framework of her life. She'd dropped out of high school, moved into her own apartment, had a series of sexual encounters and love affairs, two abortions, a short-lived marriage to a guitar player in a rock band. She hadn't achieved any real success at acting. She had always been famous, of course, for her role in that one very famous movie, but she'd never again come close to that single, memorable, brilliant performance.

Six months ago, when she became unable to care for herself physically, emotionally, or financially, she'd moved back in with her mother, who was married to a good man, Dr. Alexander Shine, a dermatologist. But her presence in the home put a tremendous strain on her mother's marriage. Tension hung in the air, all generated by Meg and her formidable problems. Husband and wife decided to try a separation, and mother and daughter moved into the high-rise in Century City. Now Sally's first priority was Meggie.

And Meg's priority was the girl. She had to protect Gia from being permeated by evil like *she* was; she had to make that child's life worth living, as hers was not. It was her mission, she knew, and God had now sent her the cross, the talisman that would enable her to do it.

She'd read about the auction in the trade papers and she went to Sotheby's, and there it was. The multicolored cross that tied her youth together with Gia's, that drove the spirits out of the fictional child of Jack Nathanson in the movie, and would now keep them from invading the child born of Jack Nathanson in life.

Zahna tailed the little red Fiat out to Malibu until it came to a stop on Seashore Drive, and the Davis woman stepped out. To Zahna's amazement, they were just a few doors away from Debra Angelo's house, the house where Jack Nathanson was murdered.

She caught up with Meg, who motioned her to be quiet. The two walked down a path to the beach, and Meg led the way to a formation of jagged rocks almost directly in front of Debra's house. Meg reached into her tote bag and produced a blanket, which she spread out on the sand in front of the rocks. Zahna saw the newly purchased crucifix in the bag. The two women sat on the blanket, but Meg Davis did not face the roiling ocean, she faced the house.

"Who lives there?" Zahna asked.

"Gia."

"Gia, Jack Nathanson's daughter?" Zahna pressed.

Zahna, of course, knew the house well. She remembered the first time she'd come here. It was after Jack and Maxi Poole had split up, and she was seeing a lot of Jack. He had taken her along one Saturday to pick up his daughter. When they'd pulled up out front, he told her to wait in the car. She'd asked if she could come in, she would love to see this charming old home and the beach beyond, but he'd insisted that she stay put. He was gone nearly an hour. He'd sent her a message that day: Even though he was now a single man, Zahna was still a second-class broad, good for hot sex, but not important enough to shield from the blazing heat and boredom of an hour wait in a closed car. And not good enough to introduce to his ex-wife once removed. Yes, Zahna knew this house.

"Gia lives here," Meg Davis was saying, "and I have to protect her—"

"Excuse me?" Zahna said.

"God wants me to keep Gia from being hurt by evil spirits," Meg returned, her eyes riveted to the big, ramshackle house with the wraparound sundeck, lights coming on in its windows now.

"Uh . . . why?" Zahna asked, studying the other woman's hypnotic gaze.

"Because if I don't keep the demons from stealing her soul, Gia will be spirited to hell with her father."

"Uh-huh," Zahna said guardedly. She lit a marijuana cigarette, its tip glowing red in the gathering twilight, and took a deep drag. "How often do you come here?"

"As often as I can," Meg responded. Then she removed the *Black Sabbat* cross from her tote bag and held it out toward the house with both hands, like a priest holding the sacred chalice toward the altar as he's saying Mass.

Zahna watched Meg's bizarre behavior in fascinated silence. The woman seemed oblivious to her now, in a trance, and she began uttering some sort of singsong chant, softly at first, then louder: ". . . *May this cross compel redemption, may it frustrate Satan's evil ends. . . .*"

Whoa, Zahna thought, *this chick is loony-toons*. She passed her the joint. As darkness fell, the two women sat silently on the beach, pondering their own private torments, and getting stoned.

20

Good morning!" Alan Bronstein said, looking up from the Sunday *Times* as Janet came out onto the poolside patio. The Monogram Studios exec was wrapped in one of Jack's blue terry-cloth robes, drinking coffee, the remains of a toasted bagel on a plate in front of him, a bud vase spilling over with magenta bougainvillea by his place, Carlotta's signature.

"Why don't you make yourself at home?" Janet laughed. Then, "God, Carlotta's going to think I slept with you, only two weeks into widowhood."

"Hardly," Alan said. "When she bustled through the living room this morning she couldn't miss my six-foot-two body doubled up on one of your four-foot-two love seats, and she couldn't fail to note that your bedroom door was shut and presumably bolted against this big, bad wolf—big, bad, *aching* wolf," he grimaced, stretching and rubbing the small of his back.

"My last day in this *auditorium*," she said, looking back through the French doors at the massive living room littered with boxes, packing scraps, lamps on the floor, planters at the periphery, and her exquisite pair of Lawson love seats dwarfed in the expanse.

"Let's get thee to a hotel," Alan said, "before you start getting melancholy."

"I can't wait. I just have to sort out what to bring."

"You don't have to bring the world," he reasoned. "It's not as if you don't have the keys to this joint. You *can* come back and pick up a hair dryer, you know."

"I know. But I don't *want* to come back."

"Well, Carlotta will be here, and she can run anything you need over to the bungalow."

Janet had reserved a bungalow at the Beverly Hills Hotel for a month. Now that the auction was over, she would get out of this mammoth villa that she had shared with Jack. She had put it on the market, and she would stay at the hotel while she looked for an apartment for herself and Carlotta, something minimal, until she could get her bearings and figure out where she wanted to live next. Meanwhile, Carlotta would oversee the big house, clean it up, and get it ready for sale. *Thank God for Carlotta,* she thought.

And thank God for Alan. During the late hours of the auction yesterday she had felt a tremendous letdown, seeing Jack's things scrutinized and pawed over, each one eliciting memories, good, bad, and bittersweet. When it was finally, mercifully, over, she'd walked out of the hall without looking back, Alan at her elbow. He took her to a small restaurant on Beverly Drive, a low-profile bistro where it was unlikely they would run into friends. The waiter brought drinks, she took one sip, and that's when she dissolved into a deluge of tears.

"Go ahead; let it all out," Alan had urged. "There's nobody here but us, and you don't have to worry about your makeup; it's all gone anyway. What are you feeling?"

"Nothing," she'd sobbed. "I just feel . . . empty."

"Well, let's fill you up," he'd said. "When you're ready to talk, you'll talk. Or not. Meantime, let's order some dinner."

He'd summoned the waiter and made a show of choosing.

This salad or that? A little caviar to start? Why not? Go over the fish entrées, please, he had a woman here he had to feed. Look at her, he told the waiter; she was actually crying with hunger pains. Janet was blowing her nose and laughing at the same time.

"Oh, this is attractive," she'd sniffled. "Give me a minute; I'll pull my act together—"

"I'm enjoying your act," he'd said with a smile. "I like *all* your acts. . . . This one's good. Oh, splendid, here's the bread. A little bread for you, no butter, I know. . . ." He broke off half a roll and extended it to her. "Comfort food," he said, "good for you." *He* was good for her, good therapy.

After dinner, they drove back to Sotheby's to pick up her car. "I'm going to follow you home," he'd said, and when she protested that it wasn't necessary, he said he thought it was. And she did need his bolstering.

When he ushered her back into the big house, she was engulfed by an overwhelming loneliness. In the cavernous living room, mostly barren now except for a few skeletal pieces and the detritus from the auction preparations, the emptiness was underscored by the hollowness inside her.

"Stay for a while," she'd pleaded.

"Sure, but Janet, you're exhausted," he'd responded. "And I don't think you should have any more to drink."

"I guess I just don't want to be alone," she'd said.

"Tell you what," he'd rejoined, "I'll sleep on your couch. Oh, right. You don't *have* a couch anymore."

"There's a daybed in the sewing room," she offered. "I'll get some sheets and blankets—"

"I have an idea," he said. "You go get into your comfiest feet-in jammies with the buttoned-up dropseat, and we'll tuck you into bed, and I'll sit out here and read *Time*." He'd picked up the magazine from the bar. "You'll go sleepy-bye, and I'll be out here, and after you're long gone to dreamland I'll slip out, how's that?"

"You mean you'll baby-sit me?" she'd asked, laughing.

"Sure. Now hurry up; get ready for bed. I get eight dollars an hour."

Wonderful Alan. He had ended up falling asleep all cramped up on one of her small love seats in the living room, and she was surprised and pleased to see him here this morning. She sat down across from him at the patio table, and Carlotta appeared with her usual fresh grapefruit juice and cereal. Life was definitely looking sunnier. They lingered, reading the papers, enjoying Sunday morning.

"Okay," he said at last, "I'm going home before my dog sends you a nasty fax—Bruno's hungry."

"Thanks, Alan; you're the best," she said. He was going to help her move today.

"You dress and pack your stuff." He looked at his watch. "I'll be back with the Cherokee at two o'clock. And anything you forget, we'll get it tomorrow, or Carlotta will bring it, or we'll buy a new one, okay? Now, I've gotta go home and change. I feel like a hooker in last night's suit."

He made her laugh. She was grateful that he wasn't going to give her the time or opportunity to feel sorry for herself.

The bungalow was cozy. It had two bedroom suites—the second one would be her office. They stopped at a gourmet shop and stocked her little kitchenette with wine, bottled water, coffee, juice, cereal, fruit, and cheese. Alan had sent over a huge bowl of tulips; they graced the living room coffee table in a profusion of pinks and reds. The card read, "Don't forget to water us!" It was comfortable being contained in this limited space; Janet felt in control again.

"I'd say you're settled, darlin'," Alan observed, looking around in satisfaction. "Let's wander over to what is now your own personal dining room and see what's for dinner."

At the Beverly Hills Hotel dining room, they ordered Rex

Harrison salads, a longtime specialty of the house. Alan started laughing.

"What's funny?" she asked. The whole weekend, of course, had been theater of the absurd.

"The last time I was here and ordered a Rex Harrison salad, my date was so young, she said, 'Wasn't he one of the Beatles?' "

"Alan," she said with a grin, "you are a dirty old man."

They meandered back through the night-blooming jasmine to bungalow 16. Inside, he dropped the key on the kitchen counter and kissed her on the forehead.

"Umm . . ." she whispered, "I don't want to be alone . . . again."

"Fine," he said. "I have a huge, well-appointed house, as you know. But hey, where do you want me? On the miniature couch in the living room? Or how about the bathtub off the office? It's deep. I'll have housekeeping bring some blankets—"

"How about my bedroom?" She smiled.

"What?" he questioned, not sure he'd heard right.

"It can be a nice, friendly thing. Like old times. Oh, God, Alan, it's been so long—"

"Janet, it's been two weeks since you lost your sex partner," he reminded her.

"No," she said. "It's been a long time."

He put his arm around her and steered her into the bedroom.

21

Okay, computer says, spell *monkey*—type it in, Gia," Maxi said, staring at the screen. "Now spell-check, control, function key F-2, you are *correct*, missy. Next, computer says, spell *morning* . . ."

"This is fun, isn't it, darling?" Debra fairly sang, giving her daughter a squeeze. The two women sat on either side of Gia in front of her Mac terminal, working through the new spelling program that Maxi had brought to the beach.

"You are a computer wizard, Gee," Maxi pronounced. They'd been at it for two hours, and Gia's mother was delighted that she was actually enjoying the spelling exercise, making a game of it. It was Sunday, fifteen days after Gia's father had been shot to death in her bedroom, and Debra felt that, for a while at least, the terrible weight of that knowledge seemed to be off her daughter's mind.

"Lunch is ready," Bessie announced, peering into the den. "Pasta and salad. It's a lovely day," she said. "Will you have it out on the deck? Get some fresh air?"

"What a nice idea," Debra responded. "Let's do, shall we?" She started to get up.

"Just two more," Gia pleaded. "Then we'll be done with the M's. Please, Mom?"

"Who *are* you?" Debra laughed. "Are you *my* daughter, actually *begging* to spell? This program is brilliant, Max."

Debra was troubled by Gia's behavior since the murder. She never talked about it, nor spoke of her father, but she'd been listless and unmotivated, had no interest in playing with her friends, or even with her toys. Her teachers were telling Debra that Gia wasn't concentrating in class—she was lagging far behind in reading, doing poorly in math, flunking almost every test. And she wasn't getting on with her schoolmates. She was picking fights at every turn. Debra was told that Gia was being tolerated for the moment because the poor youngster had lost her father, but if she didn't improve markedly, and soon, they wouldn't be able to keep her there. Debra was also getting negative reports from Gia's therapist. Dr. Jamieson was coming out to the house now, to observe Gia in her home environment; he didn't feel he was making progress with the girl, he said. Now, as they sat down to lunch on the broad redwood deck overlooking the surf at beautiful Malibu beach, Debra felt it was the closest to a normal day that they'd had since the murder.

"Gia," Debra said to her daughter, "after lunch, Sunshine and Kip are coming over to play. I've invited them, okay?" Sunshine and Kipper were the daughter and son of a film producer and his wife who lived a few houses down the beach.

"Where are we going to play?" Gia asked. She wouldn't go into her bedroom, hadn't since the murder. She alternated between sleeping with Debra, or upstairs with Bessie when Debra was out.

"Well, darling, since all your toys are in your room, and Sunshine and Kip haven't seen your Sports Flyer game yet, you could play in there, and Bessie will bring you lemonade. . . ." Gia was vigorously shaking her head.

"Okay, sweetheart." Debra sighed. She'd hoped that by associating Gia's room with play, she might disassociate it from the murder. But she didn't blame her daughter; even she avoided that bedroom. She'd decided to convert the guest room upstairs for Gia. It was bigger, she was old enough now to be a floor away from her at night, and Janet had sent over all her things from Jack's house, so she needed more room.

"Oh, here they come, Gia," Debra said, as the two blond neighbor kids came tripping across the sand. She hoped her daughter would enjoy playing with them. She hoped she wouldn't fight with them and come in crying. The youngsters came up on the deck, had some lemonade and cookies, then all three cantered off onto the beach with giant squirt guns. As Bessie gathered up the lunch dishes, Debra and Maxi went over to the reclining chairs to talk and watch the kids.

Debra suddenly felt very tired. "So," she said, "the grand jury won't convene until they get more solid evidence, Marvin says. Meantime, I wait. I'm in limbo. I can't work. Even if anybody were crazy enough to hire me, I can't commit. This is hell, Max; I'm terrified."

"I know," Maxi said. "At least the press has backed off—my esteemed colleagues."

"They're not your colleagues, Maxi, they're the *crap* press! The *Enquirer*, the *Globe*, that whole scum bunch. Going to them and spilling my outraged and deeply offended guts pacified them somewhat—they love it when you cry. They've all slithered off for now, until . . . I mean *unless* something happens."

"But no preliminary hearing has been set—that's good."

"Yet! Not *yet!* Marvin's dragging it out, but charges have been filed, I've been arraigned, and they're digging hard," Debra said.

"What do they have?"

"Not much. They've had me in three times; we go over the same stuff—Marvin says the Italian detective wants to get in my pants. In his dreams! He *is* kinda cute, though—"

"Jeez, Debra, how can you joke?"

"What *should* I do? Slit my wrists? Christ, don't they get it that if I were going to kill him I would have done it years ago? Maxi, speaking of killing someone, would you believe that during the custody trial he told me 'friends' of his offered to *do* me for him? Offered to *kill* me! Friends in the mob—he loved to pal around with them. He thought he could scare me into giving up my child. You know," she went on, "he used to pass counterfeit twenty-dollar bills they'd give him, just for kicks. He'd give bogus bills to maître d's, parking attendants, store clerks—then he'd brag to me that it was funny money."

"Oh, God," Maxi gasped. "He did the same thing with me once. I was shocked. I told him he was putting me in the position of knowing about an illegal act. If I knew the bill was counterfeit, by law I had to report him. He said, 'Oh, *please*.' "

"He cultivated that bad-boy image, and the fact is, Maxi, he *was* bad. He had the soul of a criminal."

"You don't really think he'd have had you killed, do you?"

"Trust me," Debra said. "I was looking over my shoulder. Maybe he wouldn't have ordered the hit, because he wouldn't want some goon testifying in court that he'd asked him to do it, but he would definitely have popped a bottle of champagne if somebody whacked me because he thought it would please the boss. Can you believe, Maxi, they called him the *boss!*"

"I know," Maxi said. "They'd call the house and say, 'Is the boss there?' Once I asked one of them if he meant Bruce Springsteen. They'd come over with cartons of antipasto and baked ziti, and eat like the Sopranos. Jack would whisper to me that our guests were packing."

"Did he ever tell you that one day two of the 'consultants' on the *Hell-bent* set, two ex-cons, went across the street on the lunch break and robbed a factory of its payroll?"

"Oh sure, I heard that one ten times. That was one of his favorite dinner party stories."

"Yeah, well, now I've gotta get through this," Debra mused. "You know I'm strong, Max—whatever happens, I'll handle it. But can Gia? That's what has me sick with worry. . . ."

Maxi was watching a woman spread a blanket on the sand by the rocks near the house. Debra looked around to see what had caught her attention.

"Oh, Lord," Debra said, "now there's another whole story. Do you know who that woman is? Take a good look, Max."

"I can't make her out."

"Here." Debra picked up a pair of binoculars from a side table and handed them to Maxi. "We usually gaze at the stars with these—you are now about to gaze at a burned-out star."

Maxi looked through the glasses. "Whoa!" she exclaimed. "Meg Davis! She was at the funeral. And at the auction of Jack's things yesterday. I put her in my story. She bought a movie prop, the cross they used in *Black Sabbat*. . . ." Maxi was focusing the eyepiece.

"I know. I know. But listen to this," Debra said. "She's been camping out there all summer, two, three, four days a week, lately *every* day. I didn't think anything of it, until the detectives got very interested that she was out there on the day Jack was shot."

"What?" cried Maxi, putting down the glasses. "Did you see her?"

"No, but Bessie did, and Bessie told the investigators. They told her to think hard about anything out of the ordinary that went on that day—and she told them that the actress Meg Davis was on the beach in front of the house at the time of the murder. Bessie was a nervous wreck, being hauled in to the Hall of Justice. She told me all about it when she got home."

"Come on, Deb, how can you say you didn't think anything of it? This woman goes way back with Jack, and who knows what went on between them? Word is she's a drug addict, hasn't worked in a long time; maybe she blamed *him*—"

"Maxi"—Debra stopped her—"I keep my doors locked; the

police found no evidence of forced entry. There were no foot-prints around the doors or windows that they couldn't account for. There were no unfamiliar fingerprints anywhere inside—God knows, *mine* were on the goddamned gun. There weren't any hairs anywhere—evidently hairs are a big deal. They vacuumed meticulously for hairs and fibers; Bessie should only do such a good job. And they took some strands of *my* hair, and Gia's and Bessie's too, to compare with what they swept up. Marvin says they found nothing. Now, take a look at that woman out there. You had her on the news last night—she's a zombie! She looks like she couldn't *dress* herself. How the hell could she get in my house, kill somebody, and get out without a trace?"

But Maxi was setting up the audiocassette recorder that she always carried in her purse. Getting up out of her chair, she said, "I'm going to go have a chat with her."

Debra watched Maxi saunter across the sand toward the rocks where Meg Davis was sitting, intently watching the three children playing on the beach.

22

"See that lady over there?" Gia said to Kipper and Sunshine, pointing her squirt gun in the direction of the woman who was sitting by the rocks, watching them. "She's a witch," she told them. "Honest, she's a real live witch!"

"How do you know?" asked Kip, wide-eyed.

"Jason said so. His mom told him." Jason's family lived next door.

"Let's go ask her if she's a witch," Sunshine suggested.

"No, we can't; my mom says we're not allowed to bother her, I think because witches need their privacy," Gia said.

The three children were cavorting on the sand on this late October Sunday, still swimsuit weather on Southern California beaches. Meg Davis was sitting motionless with her back against the rocks, holding the *Black Sabbat* cross upright in her lap, staring fixedly at the younger girl, Gia Nathanson. Now that she'd been granted the cross, her grail, it was all very clear to her. She knew exactly what she had to do. God had made her mission known to her. She had to protect Gia; she was the only person on earth who could save her.

She'd needed to know her possessor, this man whom she hated, feared, was in awe of, and, on some level, loved. She came to understand that Satan was powerful, and able to inspire all of those feelings; that was his way. That's when she began diligently following Jack Nathanson's activities in the press, tracking the progress of his movies, his many awards, his romances, his marriages. Sometimes she would call his office, give his secretary the name of a prominent star or producer, and when he would come on the line, she'd hang up. When she knew his movements in advance, knew where he'd be, which studio, what location, she would be there waiting for him to arrive, watching from some hidden vantage as he drove his menacing-looking black Ferrari through the gates. And she would wait, watching, sometimes all day long, until she saw him leaving.

Sometimes she would tail him at a discreet distance, follow him home, to a restaurant, to a romantic rendezvous. She always knew who he was having affairs with, where he was living, when he was about to move, where he and Carlotta would next set up housekeeping, and with what new woman.

Until now she'd been guarded, careful to let no one know of her appointed task. She could never tell her mother. She could never tell the many different therapists who had tried to pry her thoughts and plans and reasons from her. They wouldn't understand. They would try to dissuade her. They would lock her up in hospitals. They would conspire to keep her from fulfilling her God-given assignment. But she realized that the woman she'd met last night at the auction, Zahna, was sent from God, because she'd felt compelled to talk to her, and like a soul mate, this Zahna had listened and understood. It was a tremendous relief to finally be able to tell everything. She no longer needed to keep it secret. Now she was meant to divulge her work to those whom God designated to rally round and help.

She was distracted suddenly by Gia calling out, "Maxi! Maxi! Do you want to play with us?" Looking up, she saw a woman walking toward her on the beach, a woman with swinging blond hair—*Maxi,* the girl called her. Of course. Maxi Poole.

"Not now, honey," the woman called to Gia. "I want to talk to Miss Davis."

Meg's initial instinct was to flee, just as she'd fled from her at the auction. But the woman was smiling at her as she approached. Maybe *she* was being sent to help, too. Maybe Maxi Poole was one of God's archangels, called upon to spread the word now that Meg had been given a sign that secrecy was no longer useful. After all, this woman was on the news. Meg made the decision that she would talk to her. Maxi Poole was being sent to help her save Gia.

23

Debra had a screeching headache. Bessie was full of questions about what Maxi was doing down there on the beach with that weird actress who was loitering around their house all the time. Maybe Maxi was right, maybe Meg Davis *was* some kind of threat. Debra had dismissed her as just another druggie, as industry gossip suggested—she had certainly looked stoned on the news last night. But lately she seemed to be a fixture out there by the rocks. And she'd showed up at the auction—maybe it *wasn't* just a coincidence that the woman's favorite spot on the beach was right outside the house where Jack was murdered. Debra was relieved that Maxi had decided to talk to her. Maxi knew how to get answers out of people.

Suddenly, Bessie called from the sundeck, urgently, "*Miss Debra, come quickly!*" Thinking something had happened to Gia, Debra lunged for the door.

"Look!" Bessie said to her, pointing down the beach. Maxi was walking toward the house with Meg Davis in tow. And the three kids, curious that the weird woman was going to Gia's house, were following. *Give me strength,* Debra thought, and she sank into a deck chair to await their approach.

"Debra, I want you to meet Meg Davis," Maxi said brightly,

as she and her entourage lumbered up the steps. "Meg, this is Debra Angelo, and Bessie, Gia's nanny . . . and this is Gia, and her friends Kipper and Sunshine."

What the hell is Maxi doing? Debra wondered, even as she extended her hand and offered Meg a seat at the redwood table in the shade of the umbrella. Maxi and Debra joined her, while Bessie settled resolutely into a deck chair, looking vaguely disapproving, and the kids huddled together on the hammock, enthralled by the eerie-looking stranger.

In the harsh light of the blazing midafternoon sun, Meg Davis looked sallow, haggard, old beyond her years, her eyes sunken, harsh lines around her mouth, her once lustrous auburn hair dull and matted. Debra said nothing, waiting for Maxi to make the first move, to let on what this odd visitation was about.

"Meg has the most fascinating story to tell," Maxi began, "and I want you to hear it from her yourself, Debra."

"Yes?" Debra responded, turning to Meg.

"Well," Meg said, glancing uncertainly at Maxi, who nodded encouragement. "God has directed me to protect your daughter Gia from evil. That's why I come here. I can't let her down, because if I do, the spirits will possess her soul, and she'll be taken to hell with her father. I promise I won't let that happen. I have the cross, now—" Suddenly she became flustered. "The—the *cross!*" she stammered. "I left it on the blanket. . . ."

"I'm sure it'll be safe," Maxi said. "Go on, Meg, please."

Scrutinizing this frail, spacey-looking woman sitting here on her deck, listening to her spin a yarn that sounded like *The Twilight Zone*, Debra was nonplussed, astounded at the gibberish she was spouting, and frightened at the way she was staring at Gia, intensely, proprietarily. Debra got up. She went over to the hammock and took Gia firmly by the hand.

"Excuse me, Meg," she said, "but I see that Gia is sunburned and I need to get some lotion on her. Maxi, Bessie, would you help me?" She nodded deferentially at Meg, then led Gia inside. Maxi and Bessie followed.

"My God, Maxi," she whispered, as soon as she had shooed Gia into the kitchen with Bessie, and they were out of earshot of the deck. "She's *crazy!* And she's obsessed with my child!"

"I know; I know that," Maxi said, "and I wanted you to hear it for yourself, or you wouldn't believe me. I have it all on tape," she said, patting her bag. "I'm taking it to sheriff's headquarters in the morning."

"Fine," Debra said tersely. "Now please get her the fuck out of here, Maxi—she's giving me the creeps!"

24

Carlotta Ricco was nervous, alone in the big house. She kept imagining that she heard sounds, whistling noises, creaks on the stairs. Mr. Bronstein had taken Miss Orson to the hotel a few hours ago, and this was her first night here by herself. She'd get used to it, she told herself. And it was only for a few weeks, until Miss Orson could find the right apartment, spacious enough for her office and a gym, and a guest room, she'd said, plus a comfortable room for Carlotta with space for her ironing and sewing. That would be perfect, Carlotta thought—then she would be moving out of this cavernous house, too.

Meanwhile, she had a lot of work to do. Joe Babajian, the famous Beverly Hills Realtor, was coming by in the morning to videotape, and she intended to be up very early to get the place as presentable as possible.

Stopping short, she thought she heard a noise again. She was in her quarters upstairs, with the door locked and bolted; the entire house and the gates were completely secured, the alarm system was armed—she shouldn't be anxious, she knew. She would get to sleep early, and tomorrow she'd finish straightening up the mess the auction people had left; then she'd start packing up the kitchen things, the cooking utensils, the good china, the linens, and the rest, to get organized for the move to a new apartment.

Wait—there it was again. This time she was sure she heard a noise downstairs. She strained to listen in the stillness. No, she was being foolish. She would watch a little television to ease her anxiety and help her get to sleep. She got up from her wicker sofa and started over to the TV set to pick up the clicker. And she heard it again.

Someone was in this house! There were definite footsteps, muffled sounds coming from downstairs. Maybe Miss Orson had come back for something. She was sure she would overlook something or other, she'd said, a suit blouse, a pair of shoes. The Beverly Hills Hotel was less than ten minutes away. Maybe she'd realized she needed more clothes before the workweek began tomorrow.

In bathrobe and slippers, Carlotta opened her door and padded noiselessly down the hall, stopping to peer over the banister to the floor below, into the large, mostly barren living room that was dimly illuminated by an amber lamp on a table in the foyer. She stood still. Then she heard it again. A shuffling noise, coming from somewhere below.

"Miss Orson?" she called. No answer. She turned the corner and started down the stairs. "Miss Orson!" she called out again. She went on down the staircase and across the wide expanse of the living room, then through the hall toward the lower bedroom wing, following the direction that the intermittent noise was coming from.

Abruptly, she stopped. In the dark corridor she could see a sliver of light coming from under the door to the master suite. Had Miss Orson left the lights on? Or was she inside the room now, picking out some things she needed? Carlotta hadn't heard her come in. Maybe she had been especially quiet, thinking Carlotta might be asleep and not wanting to disturb her.

She knocked on the door. No answer. She tried the knob. It

opened. She stepped into the entry hall of the suite. At the archway to the bedroom, she froze. Someone, something, a figure in voluminous black robes with a black hood, facing away from Carlotta, was pawing through the top drawer of the dresser on the far side of the king-size bed.

"Who *are* you?" Carlotta cried out inadvertently, clamping her hand to her mouth as if to take back the sound, but before she could respond to her instincts to turn and run, the figure whirled around, robes flowing, only eyes visible through the slitted hood, and with black-gloved hands, held up a sinister-looking object, a knife of some kind, a cross!

"*God forgive you*," the person said in a low, guttural voice, raising the painted crucifix higher and toward Carlotta. In a gravelly, raspy cadence, muffled by the hood, which had no opening for the mouth, the figure began reciting a chant of some kind. "*May corruption be rebuffed from the deepest reaches of your soul, may black magic be quelled by a host of angels, and your spirit be lifted—*"

Carlotta screamed out and ran from the room, stumbled down the bedroom hall, and was bolting through the door she'd left open to the outer corridor and the living room beyond, when suddenly, violently, the dark figure pounced on her back and knocked her to the floor.

"Please," Carlotta sobbed hysterically, "take anything you want—" A hand pushed her head to the floor, and she felt a stab of ferocious pain, felt the jagged cross gouging the flesh between her shoulder blades, again, and again, and again, the hand shoving her face into the carpet, her own warm blood gushing across her back, until she felt nothing.

25

Tell us again—under what circumstances did you make this tape?" Jonathan Johnson asked Maxi Poole. She sat with the two detectives in a small cubicle at the Hall of Justice downtown.

"This woman sits on the beach outside Debra Angelo's house almost every day," she said. "She was there yesterday when I happened to be visiting, so I went out and introduced myself, and I had this extraordinary conversation with her," Maxi told the detectives, indicating the audiocassette on the table between them.

"And your tape recorder just happened to be in your purse?" Johnson quizzed.

"Uh-huh."

"And she didn't know it was there?" he continued.

"No."

"Well, it's not admissible—you know that," Cabello snapped.

"Of course I know that," Maxi said, "and I can't use it in a story, either, but I think you gentlemen should hear it, in view of the fact that Meg Davis was there, outside Debra Angelo's house, at the time of the murder."

"You also know that running a hidden tape on someone, unknown to them, is illegal, don't you?" Cabello asked.

"I always carry a tape recorder, for my work. That's *carry*, as in thrown in my purse, not strapped to my body," she emphasized. "And the ON button must have got accidentally pushed when it was jostled in my bag."

"Yeah, right," Cabello sneered.

"Look, do you want to hear it or not? If not, no problem; I have things to do," Maxi said, getting up and reaching for the cassette.

Cabello looked at Johnson. "Tell ya what," he said. "Why don't you leave it for now, but we probably won't have any reason to listen to it, and you can have it back any time you want—does that work for you?"

"Sure," she said. She expected something like that. She knew they wouldn't listen to it in her presence. "By the way, is Meg Davis a suspect?" she asked.

"No more than you are," Mike Cabello said, watching her closely.

"I wondered when you were going to get around to that," Maxi rejoined.

"Do you want to tell us something?"

"Do you want to *ask* me something? Because if you do, you can notify me properly, and I'll notify my attorney," she said with a smile.

"Do we want to ask the second ex–Mrs. Nathanson anything, Jon?" Cabello asked his partner.

"Well, we know *where* she was that Saturday. We might want to ask her *why*," Johnson replied.

"Yeah, and how come she's going out of her way to illegally record *other* people who might have been in the same place she was on the afternoon of October twelfth, at exactly two-fifteen."

"Are you going to ask me to sign a Miranda waiver?" Maxi threw out.

"Not today," Mike Cabello said. "We've got other fish in the pan."

"Really! May I inquire about those fish?" she asked.

"Sure," Cabello said. "The Nathansons' housekeeper was murdered last night."

Maxi's hands flew to her face. "Oh my God . . . Carlotta? Please, not Carlotta . . ." She looked stunned.

"You knew her?" Johnson asked.

"Of course—she'd been with Jack for years. Oh God . . . what happened?"

"You'll have it on the wires by the time you get back to the station," he told her. "Beverly Hills P.D. got there about twenty minutes ago."

"Do you know anything at all—?" she started.

"No," Cabello said. "They're still securing the place."

Maxi got up and hastily left. She had truly loved Carlotta. During the last year of her marriage to Jack, when she'd felt like she was drowning, Carlotta sensed it. Though neither of them ever talked about it, Carlotta invariably made an effort to cheer her up. Yet the woman was always loyal to Jack, would never utter a derogatory word about him. Maxi had great admiration for Carlotta Ricco.

She raced to her car, turned on the ignition, then slumped back in the seat and cried. She thought about Carlotta's son, a sophomore at Arizona State. He was an honor student, and he was on the varsity baseball team. Carlotta had been so proud of him. He probably didn't even know about his mother yet.

"She was pretty broken up about the Ricco woman," Jon Johnson said.

"Maybe she was *acting* broken up," Cabello mused.

"Jesus, Mike, you give cynicism a bad name," Johnson told his partner.

"Hey, buddy," Mike shot back, "bring me a suspect that maybe *did* this murder and I promise I won't be cynical, okay? Right now we got nothing solid, except for another damn dead body. Maybe Ms. Poole *did* off her ex. Can you prove she didn't?"

"You think the housekeeper's murder is connected to Nathanson's?" Johnson asked. "Frank Rey says it looks like a burglary. They're getting the widow over there now. She'll establish whether anything was taken, but Frank says the place looks ransacked pretty good; most of the furniture's gone."

"Janet Orson—where was *she* when all this went down?"

"Frank says her office referred them to the Beverly Hills Hotel," Jon said. "She spent the night there."

"Really!" Mike was interested. "With who?"

"In a bungalow registered in her own name. She'll be at the house in about thirty minutes. We should let Beverly Hills Homicide have first crack, see if she tells us the same story."

"Yeah," Cabello said, picking up the cassette that Maxi had left on the table. "Meantime, let's see what's on this sucker for our listening and dancing pleasure."

The two men were astonished at the conversation on the tape between Maxi Poole and Meg Davis. It was evident that the actress was seriously disturbed, and was obsessing over Jack Nathanson's child. And according to both Maxi Poole and Mrs. Burke, the Davis woman was spending most of her time these days, in full view of the family, loitering outside the girl's house in Malibu. Cabello played the tape twice.

"You think it's authentic?" he asked his partner.

"Has to be," Jon said. "Nobody would dummy-up something like this, least of all Maxi Poole. But why would she bring it to *us?*"

"They can't use it on the air over there," Mike answered. "It's got 'lawsuit' written all over it. In my opinion, she brought it to us because she knows she's not off the hook on this rap herself, won't be till we get our man. Maybe she'd like this woman to be our man," he said, gesturing with the tape.

"By the way," Johnson said, "I guess she thinks we believe she's on the story, huh?"

Cabello shrugged. The department subscribed to a service

that provided tapes of all radio and TV coverage of their cases. Not once had Maxi Poole reported on the Nathanson murder—the story was always handled by Richard Winningham, the new Channel Six crime reporter. So Cabello had called Pete Capra, the station's managing editor, and asked what was the deal, was Poole on the Nathanson story, or was she just *talking* about working it? Capra had told him she wasn't assigned to the story, and when Mike asked him what did that mean, he'd growled, "What that means, Cabello, is she ain't on the fucking story!" Pete Capra blustered a lot, but he would protect his people even if they locked him up.

"So what about this Meg Davis?" Cabello asked Johnson now. "Besides the fact that she's a raving ding-dong who hangs out at Jack Nathanson's ex-wife's house so she can lay some voodoo on his kid? Do we have a murderer, d'ya think?"

"I think we have to bring her in, don't you?"

"Yah, I do," Mike said. "Let's talk to her tomorrow. We got a full slate today."

"Okay," Jon said. "I guess we can wait a day. It's not like we don't know where to find her."

"Yeah." Cabello laughed. "We'll just call Tim Randall out at the Malibu station—the guy works out every day. Tell him to pin his badge on his Speedo and oil up for the TV news, we need him to go out on the beach and pick us up a movie star."

26

When Johnson and Cabello ducked under the yellow crime-scene tape at the big house on Benedict Canyon Drive, they found Dave Billings examining the body. Billings had seen a lot of stabbing victims in his seventeen years in the coroner's office, he told them, but this one looked like she was carved up with a railroad spike. The lab boys would be able to shed some light on what the weapon might have been after they ran their tests, he said.

The detectives had swapped notes with Frank Rey and his partner Ed Mallory from Beverly Hills Homicide. The uniformed officers had secured the house. A photographer from the mobile crime lab was taking pictures; other personnel were gathering evidence. Cabello and Johnson walked around, observing, getting the feel, and waiting for the woman who owned the place to show up. She was late. Meantime, the two were mentally weighing everything they saw in relation to the big question: Was there a connection between this killing and Jack Nathanson's murder?

On the surface, at least, this one smelled like burglary. Specifically, a junkie burglary, which they'd seen a lot of. Messy raking through drawers and closets, random looting, yet leaving obvious targets behind—easy-to-carry, highly salable items like the

Olympus camera on top of the dresser, the portable TV in the master bath. Pros didn't do that. Druggies did.

It could've been someone who'd known Janet Orson would be away for the night, had broken in to steal, and was surprised by the housekeeper. There had been nothing at all stolen in the Jack Nathanson murder case, but this house was emptied out. And they had very different M.O.'s. Nathanson was shot; this woman was hacked to death. There had been no sign of forced entry at either house, but that didn't tell the story. Professionals know how to get into a place. *Master* pros know how to get in and out without leaving incriminating tracks.

The detectives were watching Billings now as he bent low over the body, looking up into the dead woman's eyes with a pen-light. Beverly Hills Homicide detective Ed Mallory came into the hallway. "Mike," he said, "the Orson woman is just pulling up. Since she's late, why don't you guys go first with her?"

Cabello went to the front door to meet the lady of the house, who had just arrived in a black Porsche. Film studio executive Alan Bronstein was in the driver's seat—Mike recognized him from pictures he'd seen. Johnson had made a run over to the nearby Beverly Hills Hotel and found out from a couple of employees that Mr. Bronstein had apparently spent the night in her bungalow. Rule him out of *this* one, at least, Cabello thought—if he was with the widow all night, he's got a tight alibi. Still, if this guy was connected, as word on the street had it, he'd have had a mechanic do it.

Bronstein opened the passenger door and helped Janet Orson out into the blazing sunlight. She looked disoriented and badly shaken. As he guided her toward the house, Cabello stood at the front door observing them. Two weeks after Jack Nathanson was lowered into the ground, his widow and this guy sure looked like a couple to him.

Cabello ushered them inside to where Billings was examining the remains and Johnson was taking notes. The dead woman was facedown on the floor; on her upper back, encrusted with dried blood that had spilled in thick, gooey puddles onto the ivory carpeting, were some of the meanest-looking wounds he had ever seen. They appeared to be a series of gashes delivered with frenzied violence. It didn't look to Cabello like the work of a professional burglar, or even a drugged-out snatch-'n'-grabber. It looked like overkill.

"I'm sorry we have to put you through this," he said to Janet Orson, "but it's important that you tell us anything you notice that might help us. Anything that doesn't look quite right to you." His sense of irony caught up with him. *Nothing* in this bedlam, he realized, looked quite right.

"Was Mrs. Ricco alone in the house last night?" he asked. He looked from the body on the floor up to Janet Orson, who was leaning on Bronstein and looking like she was going to be sick. She nodded. He led the two of them into the master bedroom suite.

"I'd like you to look around," Cabello said to Janet, indicating the ransacked closets, the rifled drawers, "and tell me what, if anything, is missing." Bronstein stayed at her elbow as they moved to her built-in dresser drawers, she to examine, Bronstein to support her. Jon Johnson had come into the room.

"Now, don't touch *anything!*" Cabello cautioned them. He produced the collapsible metal pointer he always carried, and used it to gingerly stir some scarves around in a top drawer. "Indicate to me what you need moved to get a good look," he said, "and I'll do the moving."

"Some of my jewelry is missing; it was in this drawer," Janet said. "Bracelets, rings, a diamond pendant on a chain, several pairs of earrings. And the cash—there was about a thousand, maybe fifteen hundred dollars in a little leather box; the box seems to be gone. I can't remember everything that was in here. . . ."

She'd explained why most of the house was empty, that

Sotheby's had sold almost everything, and she had moved into the hotel yesterday. That ruled out a big one, Cabello thought, the possibility that pros had rolled up here with a huge truck last night and hauled everything off without being noticed. Pulling that off would have been a minor miracle, but it certainly had been known to happen.

The slow, painstaking inventory went on for a couple of hours, Janet seeming dazed the whole time. When finally it was finished, after answering more questions, she told the detectives that she'd be at the Beverly Hills Hotel if they needed her. Bungalow 16.

Several hours later, after Billings and his people had rolled out with the housekeeper's body, after everyone else had come and gone, and their own initial work at the crime scene was done, Cabello and Johnson sat down on Janet's love seats in the near-empty living room to compare notes.

There was no forced entry. The alarm system had not been activated when the police arrived in response to the gardener's call, and there was no record at the security company that it had gone off, but Janet Orson said she couldn't imagine Mrs. Ricco leaving the system unarmed. They didn't know yet if the prints they'd turned up were significant; that would take days. None of the neighbors they'd talked to had heard or seen anything out of the ordinary. Billings had put the time of death at somewhere between seven and ten last night, but lab tests would pinpoint it closer.

The murder weapon was some sharp, jagged, probably metallic object. Definitely not a knife. Billings said he saw what looked like paint fragments in the wounds. The lab tests would tell more. What was missing was some cash and jewelry belonging to Ms. Orson. She thought there might be other things stolen, but she couldn't be sure. The woman had seemed to be just going through the motions; she would probably realize that other items were gone when she was up to a more thorough inspection.

Nothing in the victim's quarters had been touched—Mrs. Ricco had $460 in cash in a ginger jar on her dresser, plus some money and credit cards in her purse. And though the huge place *looked* like it had been plowed through with a bulldozer, the widow had confirmed, as they moved from room to room, that it was the auction people who had cleaned the place out. It looked to her that only the master suite had been scoured and looted.

The two outside gates were closed and locked when the gardener had arrived in the morning, but a person could climb over them because they were not wired for alarms. Johnson had made an appeal to the public with the reporters at the scene earlier for any information that could help. It was possible that someone might have seen a person or persons climbing over the gates or the iron grating that surrounded the property, and would come forward.

Neither of the detectives had a definite take on Alan Bronstein, or how he might figure in the picture, beyond the obvious—he was very much involved with Jack Nathanson's widow.

"So you wanna be a millionaire?" Cabello asked his partner. "Here's the million-dollar question: Do we have a connection to the Nathanson case here?"

"I think so," Johnson replied. "Do you?"

"Absolutely," Cabello told him. "But let's agree that it's not for publication right now. Here's what I think," he said. "I may be way off base, but I think somebody came here last night *looking* for something."

27

Maxi roared out of the parking lot at the Hall of Justice and maneuvered her black Corvette up the Hollywood Freeway, across Barham Boulevard, and down into Burbank, ignoring the tears streaking over her cheeks. She pulled into her parking spot on the station's midway and slumped over the wheel. *Why Carlotta?* she raged inwardly. She was the last person on earth who deserved this.

There I go, she thought, *looking for justice again.* Jack used to call her an injustice collector. Twelve years in the news business, reporting the most brutal, inhumane, gut-wrenching acts of violence known to humankind, and she was no more reconciled to it now than on the day she started. Looking into the rearview mirror, she wiped her eyes and put on her sunglasses. Never let them see you sweat; *definitely* never let them see you cry.

Upstairs in her office, she logged on to her computer to check the wires—she wanted to see what they had on Carlotta's murder. Interrupted by a rap on the door, she looked up as producer Wendy Harris opened it and thrust her head inside. "Heads up, Max—Pete alert!" she whispered, and she was gone.

"Just what I need," Maxi groaned, as Pete Capra loomed large outside the glass and barged through her door.

"*What kinda game are you playing, Maxi?*" he roared, stomping inside. "Cabello says you're pumping his partner and him for information, saying you're working on the Nathanson murder."

" 'Pumping' is a little strong, Pete," Maxi said. "Look, I just found out about Carlotta Ricco, Jack's housekeeper, and she was very close to me. Can this wait?"

"No, this can't wait." Shoving stacks of files aside on Maxi's small couch, he sat down. "Cabello told me," Pete said, leveling his gaze at her, "that *you* have not been ruled out as a suspect in the case. A *murder* suspect, Maxi! What the hell is going on?"

"I didn't do it, boss," she said.

Ignoring that, he growled, "Why do they consider you a suspect, Maxi? This station has a right to know."

"You'll have to ask *them*," she answered quietly.

"Listen, Maxine," he said, getting up and putting his two hands on her desk and looking down at her. "There's a clause in your contract that says offending public decency is grounds for termination. I think *murder* just might *offend* some people, don't you? Look," he added, softening, "has it occurred to you that I might be able to help?"

Maxi regarded him wearily. "Okay, Pete," she said. "Help me with Carlotta. Find out what really happened over there, or what they think happened—they won't give *me* any information." Pete could see now that she'd been crying.

"Okay, I'll call Cabello and see what I can get," he said. "But after that, you're going to talk to me."

Maxi sighed audibly as she watched Pete's large frame rumble out of her office. She picked up the phone and asked Information for Arizona State University in Tempe. The switchboard put her through to the dean of students, who assured her that he would track down Ronald Ricco and have him return her call.

Maxi scanned the Associated Press wires. The story was slugged NATHANSON DOMESTIC:

Mrs. Carlotta Ricco, who had been employed as a housekeeper for the late Academy Award–winning actor Jack Nathanson for 21 years, was found stabbed to death this morning in the Nathanson home in what appears to be a burglary. The mansion in Beverly Hills was ransacked, and cash, jewelry and personal belongings of Nathanson's widow, talent agent Janet Orson, were stolen . . .

The report went on to detail the crime scene, recap the recent Nathanson murder, profile the actor's life and career, list his films, delineate Janet Orson's career and personal life, characterize Nathanson's previous wives with thumbnail sketches, and identify and describe his known survivors, beginning with his only child, Gia Nathanson. *Poor Carlotta,* Maxi thought. *She's the lead, but she only gets an inch in a three-page story.*

She picked up the phone and called Debra. "You heard about Carlotta?" she asked her.

"Yes, it's all over the news—it's dreadful. That woman was a saint."

"They're calling it burglary. Pete Capra is trying to find out if they think there's more to it," Maxi told her.

"Burglary—oh, *sure!*" Debra spat out. "Maxi, has it occurred to you that maybe somebody wanted to get to Janet? I've been thinking about it all morning, and I'm terrified that there's some nutcase out there. Maybe Meg Davis *isn't* so harmless. From now on, I'm going to drive Gia to school and pick her up myself every day, and check behind my back. And you'd better do the same. I don't have to tell *you* that Jack knew a lot of weird and unsavory people, and as you well know, Maxi, he had a way of pissing off the world."

"Listen, Debra," Maxi responded, "I'll call you back as soon as I find out more about what happened to Carlotta, but meantime, try not to overreact, okay?"

"*Overreact!*" Debra fairly screamed. "Maxi, for God's sake—

look at what's happened to my life in the last two weeks! I'm living in hell! Don't overreact? How *should* I react? Would you like to write me some guidelines?"

"I'm sorry, Debra," Maxi countered, trying to calm her down. "You're right. Keep your doors locked, and be cautious. Give Gia a hug for me. I'll call you back." She hung up. Debra was in frantic mode, and Maxi didn't blame her.

Both her other lines were ringing. The dean at Arizona State was calling to tell her that Ronald Ricco had gotten the news about his mother's death, and he was on his way to his dorm now to pack and leave for California. And Pete was calling to tell her he wanted to see her. And Richard Winningham was tapping on the glass door to her office. She beckoned him inside. Winningham was a new hire; he had been a crime reporter for the ABC station in New York for fifteen years. Maxi had just a nodding acquaintance with him. She'd spoken to him only once, on his first day at the station earlier in the month when Pete brought him around to meet everyone.

"Hi, Richard," she said, as he came into the office.

"Bad day, huh?" he remarked, lowering his lanky frame onto her rumpled couch. Well over six feet tall, and spare, Richard Winningham looked like a runner. He had tousled sandy hair that seemed to have a will of its own, 180 degrees from the usual television newsman hair-sprayed look. Handsome in a rugged way, it looked to Maxi as if he'd had his nose broken a time or two. And he had a small craggy scar over his left eyebrow.

Having observed him in the newsroom and on the air over the past couple of weeks, she had detected a definite New York–style "Don't mess with me" attitude, but today, this close, she could see that his eyes were kind. Word on the company grapevine was that he had moved here alone, no family.

"Except for his movies, I don't know anything about your ex-husband, or his housekeeper," he said now, "but you must be on edge with all that's going on, and I thought maybe I could help."

In less distressing circumstances, Maxi might have taken this as a bit of personal interest, and were she not so devastated right now, she might even have welcomed it—which was heartening, since from the time she had started divorce proceedings against Jack Nathanson, she hadn't felt a flicker of interest in any man; she was beginning to wonder if she ever would.

"Help how?" she asked.

"I was at the Benedict Canyon house this morning, and I'm going back to do live shots for the early shows," he told her. "The Beverly Hills cops and the L.A. sheriffs are calling it a routine burglary, but I have a hunch they don't really believe that, and for what it's worth, it doesn't smell like anything routine to me." He paused.

"Meaning . . . ?"

"Well, I've been around a lot of crime scenes, and this one has an element of, I don't know, *lunacy* about it. I'm not sure what I'm talking about—all these kinds of things are insane, of course—but from our vantage they usually have their own crazy order to them, if you know what I mean. This one doesn't. I'll know more later, but meantime, I wondered if you have good security."

"Um, I have the usual—"

"*What* usual?"

She didn't know this man at all, and she wasn't sure if she should be offended at his brusqueness or flattered by his concern. *God,* she thought, *I'm really losing it. He's an experienced crime reporter who's just trying to be helpful to a colleague.*

"Like a good alarm system, dead bolts on the doors—you know, the usual," she said.

"Do you drive home the same route every night?" he pressed, and continued with a barrage of questions that made her wonder if she actually *was* cautious enough, not only for now, but even in ordinary circumstances, given her high-profile job. After making her promise to be more mindful of her safety, he offered to look around her house to see that it was as secure as it could be. As he got up to leave, Maxi thanked him. He had actually made her feel better.

She picked up her notebook and was about to go over to Pete's office when her phone rang again. It was Ronald Ricco calling from Tempe.

"I'm so sorry, Ron," she said. "I loved Carlotta—"

"I know," he said. "I'm coming in this afternoon. Do you know anything?"

"Not really, Ron, beyond what you've probably heard on the news, but we're looking into it. Where are you staying?"

"I'll make some calls when I get there, see if I can bunk with a friend," he said.

Maxi knew he must be on a tight budget. "Stay with me," she offered.

"Oh, I don't want to bother you," he said. Carlotta had taught him to be proud, but Maxi could hear the anguish in his voice. He had been the man of Carlotta's little family ever since his father was killed in a construction accident when the boy was six years old. It wasn't until he left for college that Carlotta gave up her apartment in West L.A. and became Jack's live-in housekeeper. Maxi remembered that Ronald had been pleased with that move; ironically, he'd thought it would be safer for his mother than living alone.

"It's no bother," Maxi insisted. "I have a comfortable guest room, and I'd like to have you with me." When he still hesitated, she said, "Ron, I want to do it for Carlotta, okay?"

"Okay, Maxi. I really appreciate—"

"You can get a cab to my house," she said, cutting him off. She spelled out her address. "Or will you be renting a car?"

"Uh . . . yeah, I guess," he replied uncertainly. *Poor kid,* Maxi thought; *it hasn't sunk in yet*. She told him her extra key was hidden in a magnetic holder stuck underneath a drainpipe behind the house, and she gave him the alarm code. "Make yourself comfortable, use the phone, fix yourself some food—Ron, I want to help, okay? I'll be home later tonight."

She hung up and walked over to Pete's office.

"Everything, Maxi," Pete repeated. "You gotta tell me *everything*."

"I *told* you everything," Maxi insisted. "Jack was holding me up to pay off exorbitant bills that he'd run up while we were married, debts in the millions, and legally, he might have gotten away with it. So it looks like I had quite a bit to gain by his death, and of course the detectives know that."

"Aren't you forgetting to tell me something?" His bushy eyebrows shot up.

"Like what?"

"Like they know you were at the scene the exact minute your ex–old man was croaked," Pete said.

Maxi felt her throat constrict. "I'll tell you about that, Pete, if you promise you won't tell Baker." Lon Baker was the young news director who had recently been brought in to head up the news department, along with his even younger assistant, Chaz Crawford. Pete and Maxi had been at the station through several management teams, and this one seemed far more interested in cosmetics than in solid news coverage. Pete called them "the idiot" and "the underjerk."

"No," he said, "I won't tell the idiot unless this gets dicey, but if it does, all bets are off."

"Yes, I know that, but for now, if the rank and file hear about this"—she gestured outside his office toward the enormous newsroom teeming with writers, producers, camera crews, editorial assistants, graphic artists, researchers, and the rest—"you know *somebody* will drop a dime on the print press and it'll be all over the papers. Then—"

"Right, then you'll be off the air and maybe out of a job," he finished. "Sorry, Max, but that's out of my hands. Now spill it."

Maxi told him about that Saturday, and Pete's eyes widened. "Worse than I thought," he muttered. "Why didn't you come forward?"

"Because I didn't think anyone saw me."

"Jesus, Maxi, of all people, you know better than that."

"You don't know how you're going to react until you're in that kind of situation," she offered, realizing the weakness of her position even as she uttered the words.

Pete let it go for now. "Mike Cabello told me he's not convinced the Ricco woman's murder was just a burglary."

His words triggered icy fear in her. "Tell me everything," she demanded.

"There's not a lot to tell, but he swore me to secrecy—he specifically told me not to tell *you.* Winningham doesn't even know, and he's on the story."

"I give you my word, Pete." She was well aware that when confidentiality was breached, sources dried up, and sources were the lifeblood of the news business.

"Okay. All he's saying is it feels wrong. He says he knows they're missing something, and that something feels eerily . . . *inhuman.*"

28

"Gia, I have a message from Mrs. Daugherty," Debra said sternly to her daughter. It was Monday, late afternoon—she'd just got Gia home from school and checked her phone machine.

"Is there something you would like to tell me before I return her call?" she asked her.

"I didn't do anything," Gia said with an anxious half smile. She spoke with no trace at all of Debra's own Italian accent.

"Gia, she is the principal of your school. If she tells me that you have done something nasty, I'll be very angry with you for lying to me."

Gia started crying. Debra felt like crying too. She went to the phone.

Mrs. Daugherty had left for the day. *Just as well,* Debra considered, sighing. She didn't think she could handle one whit more of bad news today. Carlotta dead, stabbed in the back in a very brutal killing. She was waiting to hear from Maxi, hoping for a report that it was, indeed, nothing more than burglary. But all of her instincts told her that wasn't the case.

She went back into the kitchen where her daughter was sitting over her math homework. Gia looked up at her nervously.

She's going to try to tough this out, Debra thought. *Why does she actually believe she can fool her mother?*

"Gia, I would like to hear it from you," she said crisply, sitting down across from her at the table. "What exactly happened at school today?"

"One of the kids got bit," Gia said, continuing to stare at the numbers in her looseleaf notebook.

"Who got bit?"

"Umm, I don't remember," Gia muttered, her head dropping lower.

"Look at me, young lady," Debra fired at her. "Just how did this mystery child get bit?"

"Well," Gia replied, "one kid wouldn't let anybody have some of his fruit bar, and, uh, so he got bit."

"Really," Debra remarked dryly, making an effort to maintain her calm. "And who bit him?"

"I don't know."

"Bessie?" Debra called to Mrs. Burke, who was working at the sink, chopping vegetables, trying tactfully to ignore the unpleasantness. "Would you please get Gia's class picture, the one of all the youngsters in fourth grade, and perhaps Gia will be able to remember who exactly got bit, and who exactly did the biting. It's hanging above her dresser; you know the one—just take it down off the wall, Bessie, and bring it here, would you?"

Bessie returned and wordlessly handed Debra the class picture. "Thank you, Bessie," she said. "Now, Gia, have a look at this, will you? Please pick out for me which child got bit." Sullenly, Gia pointed to a child in the second row of the group portrait.

"Aah," Debra intoned, "and what is that boy's name, Gia?"

"Jimmy Bracken."

"Uh-huh. And on what exact part of his body did Jimmy Bracken sustain this bite?"

"His arm."

"I see. Now a very important question. *Who bit Jimmy Bracken?* I'm sure this picture will jog your memory. Please point to the child who bit Jimmy Bracken. *Now*, Gia."

Gia turned away and started to cry again. Debra took her arm and yanked her up to face her. "Stop it," she ordered. "Tell me the truth immediately, Gia. Did you bite Jimmy Bracken?"

Gia nodded.

"Tell me *why* you bit him, Gia, and I don't want to hear about fruit bars. You *do* know better."

"I don't know—"

"Fine," she snapped. "Finish your homework, and then you're going right to bed. Tomorrow, you will apologize to Jimmy Bracken. Then we'll call his mother, and your teacher, and Mrs. Daugherty, and you will tell them all that you are very sorry, and that you will never, ever do a horrid thing like that again."

"Okay, Mom."

Gia was sobbing. Debra wanted to take her in her arms and comfort her; none of this was the child's fault. But the lesson had to sink in. *God help her, and help me*, she thought. *I hope it's not too late*.

She escaped into the small sitting room adjoining her bedroom and sank into the sofa. Her nerves were raw. That crazy Meg Davis had been squatting out on the beach for hours again today. Debra's first impulse was to march out there and let her have it, demand that she go away and stay away, leave her family alone. But she was frighteningly aware of stalkers in the news, obsessed psychopaths like the deranged drifter who killed the beautiful young actress Rebecca Schaeffer, or the monster who'd stalked and slashed her friend Theresa Saldana. Debra knew there was no appealing to logic with these people, that confronting Meg Davis could possibly trigger catastrophe.

Her second instinct was to call the police. But what could she tell them? The woman wasn't breaking any laws. That area by the rocks was public beach. And Maxi had taken the tape recording of the woman's bizarre rantings to the detectives investigating Jack's murder, and they'd evidently seen no reason to detain her, nor to deter her from keeping her eerie, twisted vigil outside this house every damn day. *Guess there's no law against being nuts*, Debra thought.

Shoulders sagging, she contemplated her life. A prisoner in tony Malibu, with a wacko camped outside her door, murder charges hanging over her head, a hard-earned career in tatters, terrible apprehension that she was losing Gia's soul, and an overwhelming dread of some killer out there who had viciously stabbed Carlotta Ricco to death last night.

She shivered. It was getting cold at the beach. Halloween was three days off. And Thanksgiving would soon be here. Would she have anything to be thankful for? she wondered.

Have to shake off this mood, she told herself. She would do her nails, save herself sixty bucks on a manicure and pedicure. Her expenses were high, and now she had to find the means to manage all of Gia's support and schooling alone. She was laying out the polish and emery boards when her phone rang. Maxi, she hoped. But it was Marvin Samuels, her attorney.

"Debra, where were you last night?" he asked.

"I was here," she said.

"Between seven and ten, you were home?"

"Well, I did go out for a little while, for a run on the beach. I've really been feeling cooped up. Why?" she asked.

"Were you with anyone? Did anyone see you?"

"Marvin, for God's sake, what's this about?"

"We have to go downtown tomorrow, Debra. You're wanted for questioning in connection with Carlotta Ricco's murder."

29

That night, Maxi bustled about getting Ron Ricco settled in with linens and soaps, keys to the house, instructions on the burglar alarm, phone system, TV, VCR, and clock-radio in his room. Next, she conducted a full tour of the kitchen, showing him where everything was and how it worked. Then she put the kettle on for tea.

Ron protested that she was making too big a fuss over him, and in fact she knew she was. A bright young college athlete didn't have many needs beyond a bunk and running water, and he could certainly figure out how to make himself some toast or pour a glass of juice, but the ritual forced both of them to focus on something other than his mother's murder, at least for a while. By the time Maxi had exhausted every bit of business making her guest comfortable, she actually had Ron laughing. "I feel like I'm buying the house," he said.

The two sat down over tea, and talked. Ron was in his teens when Maxi was married to Jack, and he would drop in on his mom now and then—Carlotta would chuckle that usually the reason he graced her with an after-school visit was to borrow money against his allowance. When Ronald was around, you couldn't miss the enormous pride she had in her only child. "Mrs.

Nathanson," she'd call, "come see how much Ronnie's grown in the last couple of months," and Ron would turn shades of crimson and be uncomfortably polite until he could manage to escape out the door, leaving Carlotta and Maxi laughing. Now he was red-eyed, and Maxi ached for him. She walked him to his room, turned down his bed, plumped up the pillows, and gave him a hug, feeling a need to mother him, for Carlotta.

With a heavy heart she went into her study, booted up the computer, and logged in to the Basys system in the Channel Six newsroom. She had research to do for an interview she had scheduled in the morning. Minutes into it, she was distracted by a noise outside. She turned and cocked her head. Probably Yukon, who had bolted out of the room a few minutes before. Yukon had the run of the house, and no conception of grace when he lumbered across floors and down hallways. She figured he'd heard something that she couldn't hear, one of the night sounds that so intrigued her about L.A. canyon living.

"Yukon!" she called, trying to smoke him out. "Come here, Yuke!" He came bounding into the study. She gave him a rub behind both ears and turned back to her work, the dog settling down on the rug beside her.

Again she heard a noise. Beverly Glen canyon was populated with raccoon, deer, coyotes, and other animals that would wander down from the high ground at night looking for scraps to eat. Or maybe Ronald was rustling about in his room and needed something.

"Is that you, Ron?" she called. No answer. "Ronald Ricco!" she shouted louder. Silence. He was probably asleep.

She returned to tapping out questions for her interview, when Yukon let out a growl and leaped to his feet, pointing four-square toward the door.

Maxi whirled, and gasped in horror. In the doorway was a spectral figure dressed entirely in black, in some kind of macabre getup of flowing robes and capes, with a black hood that covered the entire face except for the eyes, which Maxi could see were staring fixedly at her.

"Who are you?" she demanded, her heart pounding wildly. "How did you get in here?"

The figure didn't answer, didn't move. Maxi felt tentacles of fear churning her stomach and raising bile in her throat. The doors and windows were closed and locked, the alarm was set, and all accessible means of entry were wired into the system. She flashed on Richard Winningham's warning: "Are you sure you have adequate security?" The eerie, terrifying figure didn't stir.

She turned back to her computer keyboard and pressed four characters that connected her to the newsroom assignment desk. Martin Reese, an alert, aggressive newsman, was heading up the desk tonight, she knew. She tapped out a message that would trigger a beep and scroll across the top of his computer screen, along with her personal ID code to indicate where the message originated from:

MAX*P: SEND POLICE MY HOUSE ASAP—INTRUDER INSIDE

She turned again to the figure, who now had two black-gloved hands extended toward her, holding a cross—*the* cross, Maxi realized, stunned—the *Black Sabbat* cross from the auction of Jack's effects, the one she had shown on the news, the one Meg Davis had purchased and had with her yesterday afternoon when they talked at the beach. Held this way, it looked lethal. *My God,* Maxi thought, *is this what killed Carlotta?*

"Meg?" she said to the figure. "Meg Davis, is that you? Meg, will you talk to me?" she attempted again, knowing in her heart that whoever was under those ghoulish robes was most likely beyond reasoning with. Looming in the only doorway to the room, the phantomlike figure blocked all escape.

A beep sounded from her computer. She glanced at the terminal. Martin Reese's ID code flashed at the top of her screen, followed by a one-word message:

MAR*R: DONE

Thank God. Reese had been canny enough not to call her on the phone, lest it trigger a response from the intruder.

The figure had begun some sort of unearthly chant now, its voice raspy and guttural and muffled by the hooded mask, indistinguishable as male or female. At the outlandish sounds, Yukon let out a growl. Maxi reached down and grabbed his collar.

Slowly, the figure, still intoning the dirge, raised the cross on high. The gesture caused its robes to lift somewhat, and Maxi saw black running shoes; they looked like Reeboks. She remained rooted to her chair, nearly frozen with fear, thinking about Carlotta, praying for the strength to bolt and run if she saw a chance, still hoping to talk this maniac into backing off.

"Meg," she said as calmly as she could, "I can help you with Gia—" The chanting grew louder, as if to drown out her pleadings, and though the voice was muffled, Maxi recognized the same drivel that Meg Davis had raved into her tape recorder yesterday, phrases about the black art . . . spells and divination. . . .

Suddenly the figure took a deliberate step toward her, and with that, Yukon broke from Maxi's hold and charged at it, lunging fiercely with the force of his hundred-plus pounds. The hooded creature emitted a howl and stabbed at the dog with the cross, landing several gashes to his throat that sent the animal staggering to the floor, yowling in pain.

Maxi let out a scream and rushed for her dog, just as Ron Ricco came bounding down the stairs waving a baseball bat. The specter spun and flew out of the room, down the hall, and out the front door. Ron rushed to Maxi, who was kneeling in a pool of blood beside her dog, using her sweatshirt to stanch the flow pouring from the animal's neck and head.

A car screeched to a stop out front and two uniformed police officers sprinted in through the open front door. "Maxi Poole?" one of them shouted, as they skidded around the corner into the study where Maxi was ministering to her mutilated dog. Ron was standing over them, still gripping the baseball bat.

"What the hell's going on here?" one of the cops barked, while the other one wrenched the bat away from Ricco and pinned his arms behind his back. Maxi protested that Ron was innocent, and blurted the gist of the story, pointing out the door where the intruder had fled. As the two officers ran out in pursuit, one of them flung back, "Don't go anywhere; we'll be back."

"Ron," she cried, "you have to take Yukon to the emergency vet for me, please, right away."

"Of course." He gently hefted the dog's bulk away from Maxi. "He's alive," he said. "Quick, Maxi, where do I go?"

She got up and pounced on her computer, dripping blood across the carpet. She called up her Rolodex program and typed in VETERINARIANS, then cursored to a name with the notation *twenty-four hour emergency service* beside it. Quickly, she pressed the PRINT key, the printer clacked out the file, and she ripped it off and handed it to Ron. He'd grown up in L.A.; he knew the streets.

"It's on Robertson," she said, "just south of Beverly. I'll call and tell them you're coming." Maxi ran to get some sheets, and they wrapped Yukon, who was shivering and letting out low whines, obviously in shock. Ron carried Yukon to his rental car and settled him on the front passenger seat so he could hold on to him with one hand, to brace the dog and to comfort him.

"Go inside and lock the door, Maxi, and don't open it unless you're sure it's the cops," he called, as he backed out and headed south to the animal hospital.

Lock the door, Maxi echoed to herself as she sprinted back inside the house. It was locked, bolted, and alarmed before, and that hadn't done a damn bit of good! She was shaking uncontrollably as she secured the door behind her and rearmed the alarm system. She sat in her living room and wept aloud. *What kind of monster is this who can walk through locked doors?* she asked herself, oblivious that she was smearing the white upholstery with blood.

In minutes the police returned; they'd found no sign of the bizarre creature Maxi had described. Still whimpering, she led them into her study to recount the macabre events that had taken place there. When they were satisfied, Maxi told them she was going to the vet's to be with her dog, and she gave them the address. Crime-lab technicians would be out here in the morning, they informed her, looking for evidence in daylight, most specifically for footprints from a pair of black Reeboks.

"I feel sure," Maxi reiterated to the officers, "that it was the actress Meg Davis."

30

This is glorious." Sally Shine beamed at her husband. It was Monday night, a bracing, early fall evening at Santa Monica beach, and they were enjoying soft-shelled crabs, the specialty of the house at the Ivy at the Shore.

She was surprised at how relaxed she felt, how she had laughed tonight for the first time in so long, and most of all, how good it was to be with her husband again. She and Alex had been living apart for five months, and having focused intently and exclusively on Meggie all that while, Sally had numbed herself to such feelings, forgotten how much she'd missed him.

When Alex had called and suggested dinner she'd demurred, concerned that the evening would be another emotional minefield, but he'd persisted—he needed to see her, he said, for no other reason than he missed her. "No questions, no plans, no talking about what's going on or what we should do," he promised. "Let's just get together, go to a great restaurant, have a terrific dinner, and enjoy each other—what do you say?" She couldn't resist.

And he was being faithful to his word. They kept the chat impersonal. They discussed George W. and the economy. They talked about books, movies, theater, their Lakers—the incredible Shaq and Kobe show.

Sally smiled at her husband.

"What?" he asked, savoring her joy.

"I was just thinking . . . that I'd like you to make love to me tonight."

He laughed. "Are you asking for cheap sex?"

"With what we've been through, I'd say we've paid a high price for it."

"Uh-uh-uh-uh!" he said, raising his hands to stop her. "Nothing heavy—those are the rules, remember?"

Bless this man, she thought; *I really do love him.* "Let's have more nights like this, shall we?"

"Absolutely. And let's *do* make love tonight," he whispered, taking both her hands in his. "Please."

They left the restaurant and walked hand in hand along the shoreline in silence, high on the heady salt air, and on each other. This night was a revelation that there was life to be lived, Sally thought, and she wanted to live it. He was right to insist that they not discuss any future plans tonight. And it made her want to discuss future plans.

Driving back into town, listening to one of Alex's old Neil Young tapes, inhaling his familiar Aramis fragrance, looking up at his strong profile from the safe haven of his shoulder, she allowed herself to be wrapped in the delicious anticipation of lovemaking with this wonderful man, her husband.

They pulled into the parking garage beneath her apartment building, taking no special note of the police squad car parked out front. On the elevator ride up to the nineteenth floor, Alex turned her to face him, drew her into his arms, and kissed her tenderly, until the doors opened at their stop. They walked arm in arm down the hall, and rounded the corner to see two uniformed LAPD officers standing in front of the door to her apartment.

As they approached, one of the policemen presented credentials. "I'm Officer Bob Brown, and this is Officer Juan Salinas," he said. "Is this the residence of Margaret Davidson, also known as Meg Davis?"

"Why . . . yes," Sally said tremulously. "I'm her mother. Has something happened to her?" She gripped Alex's arm.

"Where is she, ma'am?" the officer questioned. His partner was talking on a cell phone.

"She's out for the evening, I'm not sure where. Why?"

"May we come in, Mrs. Davidson?"

"This is Mrs. *Shine*," Alex put in. "I'm her husband, Dr. Alexander Shine." He took Sally's key out of her trembling hand and opened the door. The four filed into the living room.

"Now," he said confronting the officers, "what is this about?"

"Your daughter is wanted for questioning in connection with an assault with a deadly weapon," Brown told them. "My partner is alerting Sheriff's Homicide that you're home now, and they'll be sending personnel here with a search warrant."

"*What* assault? What are you talking about?" Sally begged.

"I have to ask you both to stay in this room," Brown said, "in the presence of my partner or myself."

"Just a minute," Alex retorted. "It sounds like we need an attorney—"

"You won't need an attorney for yourselves, Dr. Shine," the officer answered. "This doesn't involve you."

"Then why the order not to leave the room?"

"To ensure that nothing is moved, Doctor."

"What would we move? For God's sake, what are you looking for?" Sally asked. "Just tell me, and I'll get it for you."

"Shhh, darling." Alex put a restraining arm on her, coaxing her onto one of the sofas and settling down beside her.

Salinas folded his cell phone and put it in his pocket. "It'll be about ten minutes," he notified his partner. And to Sally, "Do you know what time your daughter will be home, ma'am?"

"No," she whispered. The gravity of the situation had suddenly hit her.

In the silence that followed, the four of them heard a key turn in the lock, the front door open, and footsteps in the hall; then Meg appeared in the wide-arched doorway to the living room. She looked frail and ethereal in the half-light, dressed in a loose-fitting, pale yellow cotton dress that seemed scant protection against the chilly autumn night, and clutching a straw tote bag in both her arms. For a few seconds, her mother, her stepfather, and the two policemen stared at her as though they were seeing a ghost.

"Meg Davis?" Brown queried after a moment. Meg looked at her mother in bewilderment.

"It's all right, darling," Sally murmured, getting up and moving to her side. She put her arm around her daughter.

Officer Brown approached them. "Meg Davis," he said, "you are under arrest for assault with a deadly weapon tonight on the person of Maxine Poole. You have the right to remain silent. . . ."

31

Maxi stood motionless in her study where the horrifying scene had taken place earlier that night, staring at her trembling hands. The police had hustled out her front door, to try to find Meg Davis, she presumed. Ron was at the animal clinic with Yukon; no word from him yet. She stood alone, scared, listening intently to the silence. A beep from her computer breached the stillness. She turned to the screen to see a message flash across the top:

R*WIN: CALL ME—3402

Richard Winningham. She dialed the office, and his extension. "News, Winningham," he answered curtly.

"Richard, it's Maxi—"

"Are you okay?" he blurted. "What the hell's going on? Reese doesn't know anything except that somebody broke into your house. We picked up a report on the scanner that the police got there, but we couldn't get any information."

She gave him the highlights, then told him she had to rush to the vet to see her dog, and besides, she was too spooked to stay in the house for another minute. Meg Davis must have come in through the *walls*, she told him, because everything was locked up and alarmed.

"Give me the vet's address and wait there for me," he said. "I'll go over there right after the Eleven O'clock News. You shouldn't go back to your house alone."

"I won't be alone," she said. "Ron Ricco is staying—"

"What's the vet's address, Maxi?" he interrupted. "I'm on in twelve minutes, and I'm hammering my piece together."

"I'll dupe it to you."

"Great; see you there," he said, and hung up.

The animal clinic information was still up on her screen. She typed in Richard's code and tapped the DUP key, sending it electronically to his file. Sprinting into her bedroom then, she grabbed her purse and keys and went out through the back door to the garage. She took her old SUV, in case by some miracle Yukon had sustained only minor injuries and she could take him home. Urging the beat-up Chevy Blazer toward the Eagle Veterinary Clinic, well above the speed limit, much faster than the creaky old hulk was used to, she begged God to let Yukon live.

Though the clinic was open twenty-four hours, the doors were kept locked at night. She rang the bell and was ushered into the lobby, where Ron Ricco gave her a supportive hug.

"Yukon . . . is he—" she began.

"We made it, by seconds, Maxi—he's still alive. His trachea was severed and he wasn't breathing. The doctor set up a tracheostomy site through the wounds, and he's treating him for shock. Come on back; he'll explain it better than I can."

Ron steered her into a treatment room. Yukon was lying on his side on the table, an assistant holding him steady, dried blood matting his coat, an IV tube connected to the cephalic vein in his front leg. His body was quivering, and he seemed to be gasping for breath.

"Oh, God," Maxi cried.

"Doctor, this is Maxi Poole—Yukon's her dog. Maxi, Dr. Bill Sullivan."

"I watch your news," the doctor said, not looking up from the table where he was massaging Yukon's head. "He's responding. I'll be honest with you, it's touch and go, but this is a strong dog. He has a slashed jugular vein, lost a lot of blood—"

"Slashed jugular! Good Lord, can you repair it?" Maxi pleaded.

"No," the doctor said. "We'll have to sacrifice that vein, but other vessels will take up the slack. I've given him a transfusion. When the shock subsides, we'll do surgery to repair his trachea."

Maxi was sobbing now, seeing her big, lovable pet so critically hurt. "He's five years old, Doctor. . . . Is he going to make it?"

"I can't promise that," the vet answered. "In severe trauma there's always the danger of complications, the most common being infection, which usually doesn't show up for several days. He's on heavy antibiotics—we'll watch him carefully."

Yukon was visibly shivering. "Can I stay with him during the surgery?" Maxi asked.

The doctor looked up at her. "You don't want to do that," he said. "It'll be about three hours before we get him stabilized, then I'm going to operate. The surgery will take another couple of hours. It won't help you, it won't help me, and it wouldn't be good for old Yukon if you hang around here and cry," he said kindly. "Go home and get some sleep, Maxi, and come back in the morning." He rubbed Yukon's head gently, saying to him, "And you'll be more presentable then, won't you, buddy?"

"Can I hold him for a while?" She was still weeping.

"Now, *that* would be good for him," the doctor said. "He knows you're here, he can hear your voice, but you're going to have to calm down. If he senses that you're upset, *he'll* be upset, and we need him to feel secure."

The outside doorbell rang, and the vet's young assistant went to answer it. She brought Richard Winningham into the treatment room; he gasped when he saw Maxi covered with blood. It took him a few seconds to realize that it wasn't her blood, it was Yukon's. Dr. Sullivan had moved Maxi close to the examining table and was showing her how to apply light, soothing pressure to the dog's head and body, and talk to him in tranquilizing tones.

Maxi smiled wanly at Richard. "I'm going to comfort Yuke for a while," she told him. "Then the doctor's throwing me out of here. He's going to operate."

"I'll stay with you," Richard said, "and I'll follow you home. I know the evidence guys will be out in the morning, and they don't want my fingerprints all over the place, but I'd like to take a quick look at your locks, okay?"

"You don't have to do that—" Maxi started.

He raised a hand to stop her. "I want to," he said.

"Then I'm grateful." She sighed.

The doorbell rang again. "We're an all-night clinic," the doctor reminded them, and leaving Maxi to stroke Yukon, he went to the door himself. Through the glass partition he saw a man and a woman standing at the top of the stairs. The man held up an ID card that read *Los Angeles County Sheriff's Department, Serology Technician*. Dr. Sullivan let them in.

"I'm Officer Jim Peterson, and this is Officer Valerie Craner. We understand you have an injured dog here belonging to Maxine Poole—we need to see the dog."

The vet brought the pair back to where Yukon was being treated. The two looked at the dog; then Peterson informed the doctor that they were there to examine his wounds.

"What kind of examination?" Sullivan asked.

"We need to measure the lacerations and cut away some of the surrounding tissue to bring to the lab for tests. We're attempting to identify the weapon that did this."

"No," Sullivan said, "I can't let you do that. This animal is severely compromised, and may not pull through surgery in the best of circumstances. If you touch him now, it will kill him."

Maxi let out a cry. "Please, no—" she begged.

Reaching into his inside coat pocket, Peterson produced a piece of paper and handed it to Dr. Sullivan. It was a court order mandating the examination. "Can't help it," the officer countered. "We've got a murderer out there."

"I'm going to ask you to wait until the dog eases out of shock and gains strength from the transfusion, and can be prepared for surgery," he told the technicians. "This animal absolutely cannot sustain the kind of assault you intend right now. You can't cut without anesthetizing him, and if you put him under now, before he's stable, the dog will die. There's no question about it."

Richard came around and put an arm around Maxi, who continued to massage Yukon. She tried, but she couldn't control the deluge of tears.

"How long is it going to take?" Peterson asked.

"Two to three hours," Dr. Sullivan answered.

Peterson was silent, weighing the life of this dog against the urgency of a murder case in which one woman had been killed and the owner of this dog *might* have been killed. It struck him that Maxi Poole almost certainly would be dead had it not been for this big, shuddering husky who was now fighting for his life.

His partner looked at him. "Let's give them the time," Valerie Craner said quietly. "I have a golden retriever who's my only family. I know how Ms. Poole feels."

"Okay, you've got it," Peterson said, shrugging. "We'll be back in a couple of hours." He justified that decision by telling himself the most likely suspect was probably already in custody.

"One more thing," the vet said to Peterson and Craner. "I'd like to assist. I can give you what you need with the least intrusive technique. I want to save this dog."

"We'll welcome your help, Doc," Peterson returned, and he and his partner left the clinic.

Dr. Sullivan approached Maxi. "I don't want you here when they get back," he said, "but believe me, I'm going to do my damnedest to save Yukon." She thanked him, and wiped away her tears. She felt her world slipping further out of control.

Ron told them he was going to start back to the house. "Maybe you shouldn't be there alone," Maxi whimpered. "That woman had no trouble getting through all the barricades—"

"I hope the hell she *does* come back," Ron said. "Believe me, I'll be ready for her." Steely hatred blazed in his eyes.

"Ron," Maxi said, "she's *insane*. . . ."

"She killed my mother," he uttered through clenched teeth.

It was nearly two in the morning by the time Maxi drove the Blazer up through Beverly Glen canyon, with Richard Winningham following behind in his Audi TT convertible. She kept turning everything over in her mind. Could it have been Meg Davis who killed Carlotta? But why? Was Debra right—had she been trying to get to Janet? And then to herself? For some twisted reason, was Meg Davis trying to kill all of Jack Nathanson's wives? But it was useless, she knew, to try to bring logic to the scenario, when Meg Davis's mind was in chaos.

She was exhausted, but the closer she got to her house, the more intensely her fear grew, until with a sudden lurch she pulled over to the side of the road. Richard drove up beside her in his open car. "What's wrong?" he asked.

"I'm scared to go home," she said.

Richard studied her in the dark, pale and drained behind the wheel of her battered Blazer. He could see that she was weeping.

"I'll stay with you. Maxi," he said quietly, "I have a gun."

"I can't," she whispered. "I can't go back there. I don't know what to do."

"Okay, I'll take you to my place. I'll put you in my bedroom and I'll sleep on the couch. Tomorrow, we'll bring candy and flowers to Yukon, and we'll find out what's going on. I'm sure the police will have Meg Davis in custody by then, if they don't already, and you'll be safe."

Tears were streaming down Maxi's cheeks. Richard pulled ahead and parked in front of her. He walked back to the Blazer and put his two hands on the door. "You've been through hell tonight," he said. "I'm taking you home with me—you've got to let someone take care of you, and I've just appointed myself the guy. Dry your eyes and follow me, okay?"

"Okay," she sniffed. He got back in his car and made a U-turn, and she followed.

Richard's high-rise apartment in the Marina was spacious, efficient, minimal, and male. He presented her with a new still-packaged toothbrush and a pair of his pajamas, and showed her to the bathroom, a definitely masculine space carved in black granite, chrome, and glass.

"Is there toothpaste?" she asked. He laughed, following her gaze over the gleaming black countertops, empty except for a stainless-steel soap dispenser. "I have few needs," he told her, pressing a panel of glass, which opened to reveal a medicine cabinet with very little in it. He produced a tube of Crest.

"If *I* lived here, I'd have the whole place completely cluttered in fifteen minutes." She chuckled. *Good,* he thought. *She's cheering up a little.*

"Okay, now let me show you how the shower works," he said, opening a glass door. Black granite steps led down into a steam Jacuzzi shower with a panel of high-tech controls.

Maxi put her head inside. "Whoa, you have to start it for me," she said. "I'm not checked out to pilot a nuclear sub."

"Okay, are you ready?"

"Yah, uh, start it, then leave. But don't make it too hot, okay?"

She stayed in the shower for so long she was afraid Richard would begin to worry, but she hadn't realized how good it would feel. There was a selection of soaps and shampoos tucked into a niche in the wall, and she helped herself. Idling in the steam, and surrendering to the cleansing rivulets of warm water surging over her body, she felt the blood and filth of this day and night being purged from her being.

Finally, she stepped out of the steamy bathroom into the bedroom, damp and rosy and very small in Richard's black silk pajamas, carrying her own clothes wadded up in a crumpled, bloodied, forlorn pile. Richard was sitting in a leather chair with his feet up on an ottoman, his hands behind his head, getting an enormous kick out of the picture she presented.

"Gosh, what'll I wear tomorrow?" she asked, as she set her ruined things down on the stone surface of a built-in bank of drawers.

"Well, let's have a look," he said, getting up and opening one of the drawers. "Here's a possibility—" He pulled out a pair of black stretch bicycle pants that he wore for running. Then he went over to a mirrored wall, touched something, and the glass doors parted, revealing a massive closet with very little wardrobe and several rows of empty poles.

"Wow," Maxi gasped. "You actually have unused closet space. I've never *known* anybody who had unused closet space."

He shrugged. "What can I tell you? Few needs. How's this?" He held up a large blue denim shirt.

"Perfect," she said. "Now what about underwear? Do you have underwear?"

His turn to be shy. "Well, yeah, I have underwear. You wanna look?" He opened one of the drawers and gestured to it.

"Oh, Calvin Klein! I have some just like this," she whooped, holding up a pair of black cotton briefs with a white waistband. "They're a little big, but they'll work."

Richard dropped his head into his hands. "Okay, but do me a favor. If you're going to return them, please don't toss them on my desk at the office, okay?" She giggled.

"I'll need some socks," she said. "One of these drawers?"

"Yeah, yeah, yeah, third drawer down, right side. But I definitely don't have a bra."

She laughed. "That's okay. I don't need a bra."

The phone by the bed jangled, and they both jumped. Richard grabbed it. "Yeah?" he barked.

"Winn, you up?" It was Pete Capra. Richard glanced at the clock-radio on the nightstand—2:40 A.M.

"I'm up *now!*" he said, pretending to yawn, winking at Maxi.

"Listen," Pete growled, so loud that Maxi could hear him from across the room. "I just got a call from one of my tipsters downtown. They're about to haul that actress, Meg Davis, in to Sybil Brand. *She broke into Maxi Poole's house tonight and tried to kill her!* The detectives on the case won't take my calls, and Maxi's not answering her phone. Poor kid—the guy told me that bitch killed old Yukon. Maxi loved that hound. Anyway, get down there; it's a helluva story. We'll break in live tonight, then go with a lead on the morning show—"

"Did she confess—?" Richard began.

"How the hell do I know?" Pete roared. "Get your ass in the car and call me on my cell; I'm going over to Maxi's house, make sure she's okay. Then I'm going in to the station. I'll fill you in while you're driving to East L.A. This is looking like a weird pattern to me—the Ricco woman, Maxi Poole . . . This nutso broad just might be Jack Nathanson's killer."

32

I'm sorry, Mrs. Shine, you can't ride with your daughter," Mike Cabello told Sally. "You can follow us in your own car." Cabello and Johnson had arrived with the search warrant and had taken charge.

"Wait; let me at least get her a jacket," Sally pleaded. Alex was on his cell phone talking to Neil Papiano, his lawyer. Neil would meet them at the Sybil Brand Jail for Women.

Officer Salinas came into the living room. "We got the shoes, Detective," he said, holding up a pair of women's black Reeboks in a plastic bag.

"Good. You guys done?" Cabello questioned Salinas.

"Nowhere near."

"We can't leave them alone here," Sally protested.

"Stay here with them, or come in with us—suit yourself," Cabello said. "The officers will leave a copy of the search warrant and a list of everything they take on this table. Do whatever you like, but we're leaving now." He held the front door open and gestured for Meg to precede him. Jon Johnson had already gone down to the car.

Meggie was in a daze, and Sally was in a panic. "Meg needs you with her," Alex said, "and I want to be there to meet Neil.

Jesus, if we can't trust *these* guys"—he tossed his head toward Salinas, who was standing there holding the bagged-up shoes—"who the hell *can* we trust? Would you please pull the door shut behind you when you leave?" he asked the officer. "It'll lock automatically." He followed the disparate group out the door.

Thank heaven Alex happened to be here tonight, or I'd fall apart, Sally thought, as they drove wordlessly behind the deputies, inbound on the Santa Monica Freeway toward the east side of downtown Los Angeles.

Neil Papiano was waiting for them just inside the prisoners admittance doors. He updated them on what he'd been able to find out. Earlier tonight, someone had broken into the home of Maxi Poole, the television news reporter, and threatened her life. Evidently Ms. Poole's dog, or a house guest who was staying with her, or both, had scared the intruder off, but not before he, or she, had brandished a large metal cross.

Sally watched helplessly as her daughter was being put through the police booking process, while Neil continued quietly telling them what he knew. Maxi Poole had told the investigators that she was sure the cross was the one Meg had purchased at the Jack Nathanson auction—she'd shown that cross on the news—and Ms. Poole said she happened to see Meg Davis with it just yesterday on the beach at Malibu.

The attorney went on to tell them that the investigators were looking for a possible connection to the murder of the housekeeper at the Nathanson estate, who had been stabbed to death the night before with some kind of sharp, jagged instrument. Sally and Alex had heard about it on the news.

"And of course," Neil continued in subdued tones, "they're looking for an ultimate link to the murder of Jack Nathanson."

"Not Meggie!" Sally pronounced. "Meggie is not capable of killing anyone," she reiterated to her husband and the lawyer. "I know my daughter!"

But do I? she wondered, as she looked up to see Meggie, who was being fingerprinted now. She was pallid and deathly frail, and she was chanting. Sheriff's personnel were asking her questions but she stared straight ahead, seeming to look right through them, ignoring them, chanting.

Sally had been hearing this same dismal chant lately, filtered in the early mornings through the closed door of Meggie's room. Since Meggie was gone most of the time, Sally routinely scoured the room for clues to her increasingly disturbing behavior. The notion that she was invading her grown daughter's privacy gave way to the urgent priority that she find a way to help her.

On Sunday morning, before her daughter left the house, Sally had spotted a makeshift shrine in Meggie's room, dried flowers and candles that had burned halfway down arranged around that cross Meggie had bought at the auction and that Sally would get the bill for. The thing was perched upright atop a copy of the Bible that Sally had given her daughter years ago, its lethal point cutting into the book's fragile leather, the top leaning against the mirror above the dresser. Underneath the Bible, she saw with horror, there were three pictures of Meggie, old photos of her as Hannah, the character she played in *Black Sabbat*. Sally didn't disturb anything, but she called Dr. Cohen. "Don't you see," Angela had entreated, "she needs help, *real* help. You have to commit her, Sally, for her safety, and for your own."

"What do you mean, for my *own* safety?" Sally had demanded.

"Just that in her possibly psychotic state—and yes, it could very well be psychotic, because she's not in control—there's no guessing what Margaret might do. Listen to me, Sally. Give me your permission to start the legal process."

She didn't. She couldn't. And now the worst had happened. Sally was gripped with terror for Meggie.

But Meggie displayed no outward fear, no emotion of any kind. "*Malign spirits will claim the revenants*," she chanted, louder now. "*God forsakes those who are in league with witchcraft, and evil in many forms possesses His own kindred. . . .*"

One of the uniformed deputies was taking 35-millimeter booking photos of Meggie, and a female clerk was snapping Polaroids. She took three shots, and spread them out on the counter to let them develop. Meggie's chants resonated through the room, and although everyone appeared to ignore her and go about their business, an eerie hush infused the usually down-to-earth atmosphere in Inmate Reception.

After a few minutes it became apparent that no images were going to manifest on the Polaroid prints. One of the deputies whispered to the photographer, "She was the child in that movie, you know. Maybe she *is* a witch."

"It's more likely that this film is defective," the woman muttered, but still, the mood was somber.

At 5:47 Tuesday morning, Channel Six reporter Richard Winningham and his crew were jockeying for position among the local and national television, radio, and print journalists and photographers outside the gate from the release area at the Sybil Brand Jail for Women, all of them vying for the best vantage to catch Meg Davis being hustled out of there.

"Here she comes!" somebody yelled, and all eyes, and cameras, turned to the release gate. Winningham was stunned at the forlorn figure of Meg Davis, looking like a latter-day Joan of Arc, her tall, lank frame draped in a drab cotton dress, her back straight and her head held high; she was chanting some kind of dirge as she was guided to a waiting car by her attorney, her mother, and her stepfather.

Chanting *what?* Richard asked himself, while his cameraman shot the curious scene. Something about the occult, wickedness, sin. *Black Sabbat* was the movie she was internationally famous for, and here, outside the cold, dun-colored walls of a county jail just before dawn, the woman who had starred in it as the mystical child marked with the sign of the witches was giving an encore performance. Winningham made a mental note to look into the making of the film, to find out if something could have turned that child star into this seemingly demented woman.

33

Maxi had set Richard's clock-radio for 7:00 A.M. She was awakened by the news at the top of the hour, blaring the sensational events during the night surrounding the arrest of actress Meg Davis. When Richard had left for Sybil Brand it was almost three in the morning—she felt as if she'd just dropped off to sleep. Reaching over to the nightstand, she turned off the radio, picked up the TV remote control, and clicked on the Channel Six morning news. Richard Winningham was on in close-up, leading in to the footage that his crew had shot at the jail. The tape ended, revealing Richard in a wide shot standing in front of . . . good God, standing in front of *her* house!

"How *could* he!" she sputtered out loud, watching as he traversed her lawn and went up her front steps, explaining, as he walked, how the spectral figure had entered and confronted the owner of this house, Channel Six reporter Maxi Poole, along with a houseguest who was the son of the murdered Carlotta Ricco . . .

Maxi was barely able to stifle the urge to throw his high-tech clock-radio at him right through his high-tech giant TV monitor in his high-tech bedroom. As he described in detail the attack by the black-robed intruder, an EXCLUSIVE graphic flashed across the lower screen. *I'm going to kill him,* she thought. *I will kill him!* Of course he had an "exclusive"—she had spilled her guts to him in the innocent pillow talk they'd had last night.

She picked up the phone and called Pete Capra at the station. "I'm not coming in this morning, boss," she told him. "Got hardly any sleep last night, my dog may not recover, the bulls from the police crime lab are going to be swarming all over my house in an hour—"

"Where the hell have you been all night?" Pete interrupted. Good—at least Richard hadn't blabbed at the office that she'd slept at his apartment. In his bed.

"I stayed at a friend's—"

"When you didn't answer your phone I went over to your place, and the Ricco woman's son said he didn't know *where* you were. Jesus, Maxi, why didn't you call in?"

"To let you know I was okay, or to give you the story, Pete?" she asked, an edge in her voice. She wondered how much Richard had told him.

"*Not fair!*" he barked. "You *know* I was worried about you! Okay, okay, so I wanted the story, too—my new best friend, Mike Cabello, wouldn't take my calls." Maxi had to laugh. Pete was Pete, and Pete was a newsman, arguably the best in the city.

"So where *did* you get the 'exclusive' I just saw on the morning show, in front of *my* house?" she asked. He told her the sheriff's department had held a press conference at Sybil Brand after Meg Davis was released, and the station had Winningham there, so they shifted him to her house with his crew.

"How the hell could you send him to my house?" she demanded.

"*Everybody* went to your house," Pete told her. "Finding your house wasn't exactly rocket science. This is gonna be the lead story all day on every newscast in the country. The whole industry is doing live shots from your front door. Your grass is gonna be fucked!" he added.

Maxi groaned. But she was grateful that she wasn't there. And grateful that Richard had not breached her trust after all. That information had just saved his clock-radio and his TV tube. And he hadn't led the caravan of news troops to her home, either. In fact, at this very moment he was probably doing his best to keep the news gang-bang out of her geraniums, she supposed. Not only were his TV and his clock-radio safe, she'd have to buy him lunch one day when this was all over.

"So how come you chyroned the story 'exclusive' if *everybody* was there, and *everybody* had it?" she asked Pete.

"You, of all people, have to ask?" he returned, with more than a hint of exasperation. "You know the idiot slaps 'exclusive' on every piece of shit we run! He put an 'exclusive' on the mayor's press conference announcing the new metro-rail lines yesterday—the *world* was there! Sanders came up with a sidebar that they were planning a program to let neighborhood kids do some artwork for each train station, so the idiot and the underjerk decided that we therefore had an 'exclusive.' Are you looking for integrity this early in the morning? It's a Tappenoid thing!"

Maxi sighed. Tappen was the station's consultant company, whose job was to "consult" on its news coverage with an eye to making the stories more glitzy, more razzle-dazzle, more compelling to the viewer. Pete and all the hard-news pros in the business called the consultants "Tappenoids." One night at Haley's, the bar across from the station where newsies hung out, she had heard Pete characterizing the "Tappenoids," in his loud, blustery voice, as "a bunch of snot-nosed college kids and yuppie clowns in striped shirts and suspenders who charged money for suggesting that news reporters take their pants down and tap-dance to make a story 'more compelling to the viewer.' "

"So why were we 'exclusive' on this one?" she asked.

"Who the hell knows?" Pete growled. "I guess they figured because you're ours, that made the story our 'exclusive'—did you see the chyron 'Home of Channel 6 news reporter Maxi Poole'?"

"Great!" she groused. "I'll have to move." She meant it. "Look, Pete, I'm going to the vet's to see my dog; then I'll be at my house to fend off the vultures and protect what's left of my property. I'll try to stay out of all the other stations' live shots, since they don't sign my checks." With the telephone receiver tucked under her chin, she was pulling on the assortment of Richard's clothes that he had set out for her.

"Maxi, *are* you okay?" Pete asked, knowing the bravado was her way of getting through this.

She took a deep breath. "Not really, Pete. I'm devastated over Carlotta, I'm aching for her son, I'm worried about Debra Angelo and Gia, I'm terrified that my dog will die, I'm exhausted, and . . . and I'm scared."

Maxi found Yukon curled up on the floor of a small cage lined up with several others in a foul-smelling hallway behind the treatment rooms, cages that held yelping, whining, ailing animals. She was told by a woman at the front desk that Dr. Sullivan had gone home—Dr. Brice would be in to update her on her dog's condition when he was finished examining an arthritic Great Dane.

Maxi knelt on the floor and lowered her head to Yukon's level. He was lying on his side, bandages wrapped around his throat and upper body, his only movement the heaving of his chest with his labored breathing. His big, mournful brown eyes gazed out through the slats of the cage at Maxi.

The day-shift vet walked into the hallway. He was very young, very tall, very skinny, had very short dark hair, and wore huge black-framed glasses that were much too big for his face.

"How's he doing?" Maxi asked him, without getting up from the floor.

"I'm Dr. Ray Brice," the doctor said, kneeling down beside her, putting his hand through the bars and stroking Yukon's head. "He's doing okay, but he's had a rough time. His surgery was more complicated than we'd anticipated, and those crime-lab techs demanding specimens didn't help. He's getting antibiotics for infection, and we've got him on heavy sedatives so he won't move around and rip his stitches."

"Is he out of the woods?" Maxi asked.

"Can't promise that, Ms. Poole," the doctor said. "We'll be watching him carefully for a few days."

"He looks so . . . so lonesome, cooped up in this little cage," she mused. "I didn't expect—"

"What *did* you expect?" Dr. Brice asked.

"I don't know. . . . I thought—"

"I'll bet I know," the vet put in with a smile. "You expected old Yukon to be sitting up in bed in a private room, munching doggie treats and watching game shows."

"Yes," she said, realizing that she was being silly. "And I expected that his doctor would stay by his side night and day, and never go home to his wife and children."

"Yeah," Brice said wistfully, "they all do. Dr. Sullivan is the Marcus Welby of veterinarians, and instead you got me, the Ichabod Crane."

Maxi stood up and extended her hand. "Thanks," she said. "You've cheered me up—you don't know how much I needed that."

"Yes, I do," he said. "I saw the news this morning." She'd completely forgotten that the private life of Maxine Poole had probably been the subject of half the breakfast table conversations in Southern California.

"What can I do for my baby here?" she asked, looking solicitously at Yukon.

"You can go about your day, think good thoughts for him, and call us later this afternoon. Meantime, we have your number—if anything changes, we'll call you."

"Thanks, Doc." She smiled, feeling reassured that Yuke was in good hands.

* * *

Maxi drove slowly by her house to assess the situation there. News trucks were parked all over narrow Beverly Glen Boulevard on both sides of the road. Her gate was open, and one of its hinges had been ripped off, causing it to list drunkenly against the wood slat fence. Peering inside, she saw a strip of yellow crime-scene tape blocking off the walkway, and a police officer snapping photos of the ground behind it. Outside the tape, news crews camped on her front lawn, talking, smoking, drinking coffee. Cable was strewn everywhere, tripods dug into her flower beds, Styrofoam cups littered her grass.

She had borrowed a New York Yankees cap that she'd found in Richard's apartment. Pulling the visor low on her forehead, she wondered if she could somehow get inside her own house without being noticed. Not a chance. These were news people. She kept moving.

One of the live trucks was coming toward her. It was her own station's; she could make out the Channel Six logo painted on the sides. As the cumbersome van approached, she could see Richard Winningham in the passenger seat, with his cameraman driving.

When they'd pulled alongside, Greg Ross rolled the window down and Richard mouthed, "Go up past Briarwood and take a left on Nicada. We'll meet you right around the corner—we've got a plan to get you in." Then they rolled on past.

At work, they called Richard Winningham the "crime dog," and they called Greg Ross, his cameraman, the "crime pup." Greg was twenty-six, with boyish good looks and wavy blond hair that fell to his shoulders. His usual dress was surfer clothes—Richard kidded him that he looked like he had time-traveled from the sixties. But he was tough, bright, expert with a camera, and fearless in the trenches. The two were a good team. Maxi was waiting for them when they pulled around the corner.

"Hi," Richard said as he approached her Blazer. "These

goons—excuse me, our esteemed colleagues—are staked out, expecting to get you on camera. Even if you refuse to stop and talk, they'll yell questions at your back as you drive in, and you'll be at the top of every newscast on the air tonight. Do you want that?"

"God, no," she said. "That'd be awful!"

"Yeah, especially in those clothes," he said, grinning. She looked down at herself in Richard's bicycle pants and huge denim shirt, his argyles jammed into her Nikes, and his baseball cap pulled down over her eyebrows. "Not exactly proper business attire," she agreed. "So what's the plan?"

He told her he would walk into her front yard and tell everybody that he'd just talked to Pete Capra on his cell phone, and Maxi was already at work, so she wouldn't be back here until after the Six O'clock News tonight. A few of them would figure out that it was probably a ruse, but even if they hung around, she'd be able to use her zapper to get into the garage while he distracted them. They would definitely not be expecting Maxi Poole in a beat-up old truck dressed in Salvation Army gear, he told her. And the Blazer had tinted windows, so she wouldn't be seen clearly. By the time they realized it was her, *if* they did, she'd be inside.

"They'll hate you for this," Maxi said, "and you've got to live with them on the street."

"Nah." He laughed. "They'll give me points for it."

She looked at her watch: 8:40. The police crime lab crew was already inside—she had given one of the officers a key last night in case she had to stay overnight with Yukon. She waited for about a minute before following the news van back to the house. When she tooled past her own gate, she saw the newsies gathered around Richard, listening to him. She opened her garage door with the remote control in her Blazer, scooted inside, and zapped the door shut behind her. Made it.

She slipped through the kitchen and into her living room.

An officer was dusting surfaces for fingerprints, another was photographing the front door locks and the alarm system.

"Find anything significant?" she asked.

"Maybe," said one who'd introduced himself as Delaney. "We photographed some footprints we're pretty sure were made by the intruder. And we've got shots of footprints at the Nathanson house where the Ricco woman was murdered. We'll see if they match."

"What do you think?" Maxi asked.

"Can't tell, and even if we could, we wouldn't. It's not up to us to release any information, especially to you folks."

"Off the record, I swear," Maxi entreated.

"Off the record—and I'll hold you to that, Ms. Poole—I'm betting we have a match. And I think you're lucky to be alive."

34

Debra Angelo watched the morning news with a mixture of fascination, horror, and relief—fascination that frail, unbalanced Meg Davis might actually be a vicious killer, horror at the realization that all the time the woman had spent lurking near her house, Debra's own family could have been targets, and relief that this high-profile arrest should take the heat off *her*.

And Maxi could have been *killed!* She'd been trying to get Maxi on the phone since she heard the news, but had only reached her answering machine.

Her lawyer, Marvin Samuels, had phoned earlier this morning. He and Debra were due at sheriff's headquarters in downtown Los Angeles at ten, but as soon as he'd learned about Meg Davis's arrest, Samuels called Mike Cabello to challenge the detective's reasons for questioning his client. He was told they would table the session, for now. When he was notified yesterday that they wanted Debra for questioning, he'd asked why they were calling his client in on the Carlotta Ricco murder. He reminded Cabello that Sheriff's Homicide had managed to come up with nothing on Debra Angelo in the Jack Nathanson case, and that the county was courting a wrongful-arrest suit as it was, not to mention civil charges for destroying her livelihood. Cabello told him that whoever killed Carlotta Ricco had sailed right through the locked front door, so they would be talking to everyone who had keys to the Nathanson house, including cleaning help, gardeners, and other service people. Debra had a key, and she knew the Nathansons' alarm code. She said it was in case she ever arrived there to drop Gia off before anyone in the household got home—rather than keep her daughter waiting outside on the doorstep, she could take her inside and sit with her.

Debra had told Samuels that the Nathansons' key usually hung on a hook in her kitchen, near the garage door. When Bessie would drive Gia to her father's house, she, too, always took that key with her. And, in fact, Jack had had a key and knew the alarm code to her house, too, for the same reason.

She jumped when the phone rang. It was Mrs. Daugherty, the principal at Gia's school, sounding even more rigid than usual. It was necessary that she come to the school immediately and take Gia home, the woman told Debra in icy tones. Westview could no longer accommodate her daughter.

"Please, Mrs. Daugherty," Debra tried, "this is the worst possible time for Gia to have more changes in her life. Tell me what happened, and I promise I'll see that she does better."

"It's too late," the woman responded. "Please come in immediately and pick up your child. She's sitting outside my office, she's crying, and she is not welcome back in class."

Sensing she'd get nowhere on the phone, Debra told the woman that it was a forty-minute drive from her house to the school, and she would leave right away.

Now what? Debra thought, as she drove through Malibu canyon toward Westview Elementary. She could tell from Mrs. Daugherty's tone that she would have to muster all of her powers of persuasion to turn this one around, but she was pretty sure she could pull it off. Again. Ridiculous as it seemed to her Italian mentality, movie stars were this country's royalty, and she might as well take advantage of it.

Debra pulled into the parking lot. The school looked more like a country club, she considered, as her gaze traveled to the tennis courts, the Olympic-size swimming pool, the high-tech playground, the performing arts theater. She walked up the stairs and down the long corridor to a door marked PRINCIPAL, and went inside.

Gia was sitting on a bench against the wall of the outer office, head down, one pink sneaker on top of the other, tears streaming down her cheeks. She looked very small in her regulation pleated plaid skirt and navy blazer, white shirt, and white socks. Debra sat down on the bench beside her.

"What happened, Gia?" she asked.

"Nothing."

"Don't tell me *nothing,* young lady," Debra fumed. "Tell me exactly why I've been called here." Gia started to cry again.

Mrs. Daugherty's assistant appeared at the doorway and beckoned the two inside. The principal sat behind her desk, imperious in a severely tailored gray suit with a white ruffled blouse, her dyed black hair pulled up in a knot. She peered down at them through wire-rimmed glasses, and Debra had a palpable sense of how intimidated Gia must feel. "Please be seated," Mrs. Daugherty said crisply, indicating the two chairs in front of her desk.

"Tell your mother," she addressed Gia, "what you did to Susan Kostner in class this morning."

Gia lowered her head. Debra looked from one to the other, waiting. *I can't make her talk*, she thought dismally. *Let's see if this poker-faced harridan can*.

"I hit her," Gia said in a small voice.

"And would you tell your mother *why* you hit her, Miss Nathanson?" Mrs. Daugherty pressed.

"Because she said dirty things to me," Gia whimpered.

"What dirty things?" Debra asked her daughter.

"I said I wanted to play with her at recess, and she said she wouldn't play with me," the girl responded weakly. Debra's heart was breaking. Of course Susan Kostner didn't want to play with her. Given Gia's misanthropic behavior, she didn't wonder that other children shunned her.

"And so you slapped her across the face!" Mrs. Daugherty snapped. She turned to Debra. "Parents entrust their children to us, to teach and to safeguard while they're in our care. We can no longer expose them to unprovoked attacks by your daughter. At the very least, she puts us in danger of lawsuits," the woman intoned. "Furthermore, she thrusts her classes into disarray, destroying the kind of climate in which teachers are able to teach and students are able to learn. We can no longer tolerate her behavior."

Debra's heart sank at the finality in her tone. She could not disagree. Everything the principal said made dreadful sense. "Please, Mrs. Daugherty," she implored. "It's so soon after Gia lost her father—all I ask is one more chance."

"I'm sorry," the woman said. "We've had complaints from other parents." With that, she turned her attention to some papers on her desk. Debra was dismissed. The doyenne kept her stolid gaze riveted on her paperwork. Debra straightened, scooped up Gia's hand, turned, and slammed out the door with her daughter.

In anger and frustration, she propelled Gia toward the parking lot and ushered her into the Jeep. Mother and child drove through the long canyon to the beach without speaking. When they emerged at the coast, the sight of the rolling ocean waves and the briny smell of the salt air restored Debra's spirits, as they always did. Looking over at Gia sitting silently, studying her own hands twisting in her lap, thoroughly ashamed, she knew it wasn't her baby's fault. Children are given to us as so much clay, she reflected, and this, sadly, is what she and Jack had molded. When Jack died, she'd committed herself to do whatever it took to repair the damage.

* * *

At home, Debra found a message from Maxi on her answering machine. She reached her at her house, and Maxi filled her in on the bloodcurdling events of the night before. And she told her about the tests that the police technicians had done on Yukon's grisly gashes.

"Meg Davis has been released; they couldn't hold her," Maxi went on. "The investigators have put a gag order on the crime-lab information, but Detective Cabello told my boss the results off the record, and Pete told me off the record, to warn me—and now I'm warning you, Debra. The stab wounds that nearly killed my dog were made with the same weapon that killed Carlotta—Meg Davis's *Black Sabbat* cross!"

35

Meg, Sally, and Alex were silent on the drive home from Sybil Brand. As the sun lightened the early-morning sky, Sally felt that it heralded a new dawn for her small family. She and Alex would not remain separated; they loved and needed each other. And Meggie would get the help she needed—Sally was prepared now to have her legally committed.

Alex had guided the two women through the clamoring crowd of media at the jail to his waiting car. All the while the cameras followed them, Meggie was chanting the doggerel that Sally had heard her droning since the morning of Jack Nathanson's funeral. When they were at last alone in the safe haven of Alex's BMW, she'd gently told Meggie to stop it, stop the chanting, and she did. Her daughter sat quietly now, staring out through the windshield at the blurred lights of moving traffic on the Santa Monica Freeway, clearly in another world.

Sally prayed for strength to wade through the medical and legal morass she knew was requisite to getting Meggie into treatment. Once they were through it, the chaos that ruled their lives would subside. Meggie would thrive in an atmosphere of healing—they would be able to look forward to a happy, healthy future for her.

She refused to allow herself to think about the criminal charges—*murder* charges, Neil Papiano had said. Her fragile child was not capable of violent behavior; they would find that out. They had made a terrible mistake.

It was nearly seven in the morning when they once again walked through the doors of their apartment tower in Century City. Sally's mind flashed back to the night before, when she and Alex had approached the same doors arm in arm, enveloped in love and hope, only to be met by two policemen waiting for them in the hall. And so the nightmare had begun.

They had been gone from the apartment for about eight hours, but it seemed like days. On the table in the entry hall there was a copy of the search warrant, along with a handwritten list of the items that had been removed from the premises.

Meg disappeared into her room and closed the door, as Alex scanned the list. He read aloud:

1. Straw tote bag
2. Contents of above:
   Billfold, ID Meg Davis
   Key ring w/ five keys
   Journal notebook w/ attached metal pen
   Case containing makeup products
   Multicolored fabric scarf
   Paperback book, *Black Sabbat*
3. Pair women's black Reebok leather shoes, size 8
4. Pair black fabric gloves
5. Pair black leather gloves

"What does it mean?" Sally asked.

"It's pretty obvious," Alex responded, concerned. "They're looking to match Meggie's shoes and gloves with garments that the intruder wore."

"I saw the cross in her room," Sally said, glancing up at the closed door to Meggie's bedroom, from which drifted the incessant sound of the incantation. "I don't know if it's still there."

"Darling, of *course* it isn't still there," he said. "The cross would have been the key piece of evidence they were searching for. Obviously they didn't find it, or it would be on this list. They searched her car, too, it says on the warrant, and they didn't find anything they wanted. Be thankful she didn't have drugs," he added, "or they'd have had reason to hold her."

Neil Papiano had warned Alex that if they held Meggie they'd probably put her in the "ding tank," which, he explained, was cop talk for the Constant Care Section, the holding cell for inmates who are mentally unstable. Throwing her in with the criminally deranged until her arraignment might well have pushed her over the edge. If she had to be in custody, Alex thought, let it be later, after a trial, after sentencing, and after psychiatric evaluation dictated that she serve her time in a clinic.

"You don't believe that she could have hurt anyone, or *killed* anyone, do you?" Sally asked.

Alex put his arms around her. "I've been away from the two of you," he answered. "I don't have a feel for how she's been. I don't know what to think."

In truth, Dr. Alexander Shine did indeed believe that all signs pointed to Meggie, but he would indulge his wife's fantasy that no charges would be filed against her daughter, and that Meg would soon be safely settled, not in state custody, but in a private facility.

Deriving strength from her husband's presence, Sally steeled herself for the onerous task she faced. She would call Dr. Cohen now, she told him, and they would do what had to be done to get Meggie into a hospital.

"Wait awhile," Alex protested. "We've been under terrible strain, we're exhausted, we haven't slept all night. I've canceled my morning appointments. Please, darling, let's get some sleep. Then later, with clear heads, we'll decide what to do."

"No, I've already decided what to do. I couldn't sleep now, Alex. I have to call Angela before she leaves for the office."

She wouldn't be dissuaded. She reached Dr. Cohen, who, of course, had seen the news. Angela would drop everything and be at the apartment within a half hour, she said. Sally sighed with relief.

She had to talk to Meggie now. She knocked on her daughter's bedroom door. No response, but she could hear the faint undertones of the rhythmic chanting from within. Slowly, she turned the knob; the door was unlocked. The curtains were drawn against the morning light. Sally peered into the semidarkness illumined by candles.

As her eyes narrowed to adjust to the gloom, she saw Meggie sitting cross-legged on the floor, her arms raised in supplication toward the improvised shrine atop her dresser. The cross was gone, but the Bible, the candles, the flowers were there. Meggie was chanting in low tones, the glint of candlelight revealing her eyes glazed in an unearthly stare, transfixed, unseeing.

Something in Sally snapped. "Stop it, dammit! Stop that, Meggie!" she cried.

Meg continued chanting, without hearing, without seeing. Sally barged across the room, tore apart the heavy drapes, threw open the windows, then strode over to the makeshift shrine and blew out the candles. She dropped to her knees in front of her daughter, took hold of her by the shoulders, and shook her. She had to quell the urge to slap her, to wake her up from her stupor.

"What is it, Mother?" Meg spoke as if from a far-off place.

"Come with me," Sally said. "I'll make coffee. We have to talk." Taking Meg by the hand, she led her, like a submissive child, into the sunny kitchen, and seated her at the glass-topped table.

"How do you feel after that frightening ordeal?" Sally attempted gingerly, as she measured coffee into the basket.

"I'm tired," Meg whispered.

"Why do you suppose you were arrested, Meggie?"

"I don't know," came the meek response.

Sally set two steaming mugs on the table and sat down opposite her. "Meggie," she questioned gently, "where is that cross?"

"I don't know," Meg said. That's what she'd told the detectives at Sybil Brand this morning. Just "I don't know."

Sally reached over and took both her daughter's hands. "Listen to me, Meggie," she said. "Angela is coming. She's going to arrange for you to go to a care facility where you'll get well."

Meg's eyes came alive with sudden fury. "*No!*" she shouted. "I've told you, Mother, I will *not* go away! I must complete my mission!"

Dear God, what mission? Sally wondered, but didn't dare ask. "You no longer have a choice," she told her. "You've *got* to go. You'll be helped, Meggie. Angela is going to make the arrangements. It has to be done today, darling."

"No," Meg bellowed, in control now. "If you do this to me, Mother," she said in menacing tones, "you'll be very, very sorry."

Sally was horrified to see naked hatred in her daughter's steely gray eyes. Her mind flashed on yesterday's news coverage of the brutal slaying of Carlotta Ricco. This time she had to stand up to her. She leaned in, hardening her expression. "Don't threaten me, Meggie," she said. "Don't ask, don't beg, don't demand, and don't threaten me. You're no longer able to make decisions for yourself. You're going to a hospital, today, and you're going to get help."

"*No!*" Meg shrieked, and she leaped out of her chair, knocking it backward to the floor. She picked up the cup of coffee in front of her and hurled the scalding liquid at her mother.

As Sally screamed and clutched at her face, Meg burst out of the room, colliding with Alex, who had come bounding through the kitchen door at the sound of his wife's screams. Seeing what had happened, he pushed Meg out of the way, rushed over to the sink, grabbed a towel and doused it with cold water, then quickly applied it to Sally's skin. Sally was sobbing, as much in shock, hurt, and fear as in pain.

"I'm going down to my car to get my case," he told her. "Don't move!"

"Don't let her leave!" Sally pleaded, holding the wet towel to her face. Alex turned and ran out of the kitchen into the living room, but he was too late. The entry door was open, and Meg was gone.

He raced down the hall to the elevator. The light indicated it was on the sixteenth floor and descending. He knew Meg didn't have her car keys with her because they were listed on the search warrant form. She couldn't get far, and he had to treat Sally. He leaped across the hall to the stairway entrance and vaulted down the steps three at a time.

Dr. Angela Cohen maneuvered her car through the streets of Beverly Hills toward Century City. She had been gripped with dread since she saw the story about Margaret's arrest on the morning news, and she was shocked at the videotape of the emaciated figure walking in a trance and chanting something about witchcraft. Sally's frantic call had come shortly after, and Angela canceled her appointments. She'd long been fearful that Margaret's fragile center wouldn't hold, that something horrible would happen. And now it had.

Margaret. Angela had gained her confidence immediately, it had seemed—from the moment they'd met, doctor and patient had struck an instant rapport. What did she want to be called? Angela had asked her—*Meg,* as she was known professionally, or *Meggie,* the name her mother always called her. She was surprised when the young woman asked to be called Margaret, her given name.

Angela had thought a lot about that. Margaret had perceived, on some level, that for the doctor to rehabilitate her, she had to bring her back to the person she was before she had been in *Black Sabbat*. And as her therapy progressed, Dr. Cohen came to understand why.

As she pushed through the double doors that led into the apartment building, she was stunned to see Margaret running through the lobby, still dressed in the wrinkled, faded yellow dress she'd had on in the news reports from Sybil Brand earlier this morning. She had no shoes, no purse, no sweater or wrap. She was clearly agitated—people had to move out of her way as she bolted toward the front doors.

"Margaret! Margaret, it's Angela," the therapist called out, hurrying to catch up to her. Meg stopped and turned around. She hesitated for just a moment, then ran into the doctor's arms.

"Come on, dear," Angela murmured, as her patient broke down and wept against her shoulder. "I'm going to take care of you, I promise. Everything's going to be all right."

At that moment, the door to the stairwell was thrown open and Alex burst through, red-faced and out of breath. Angela looked up. "Dr. Shine!" she cried.

"Sally's been hurt," he gasped, relieved to see that Dr. Cohen had stopped Meg. He loped past them toward the door to the parking garage. "I'm getting medical supplies," he called over his shoulder. "Take Meggie upstairs."

As people turned to stare, Angela propelled Meg into the elevator and up to the nineteenth floor. The front door to the apartment was still ajar. With her arm around Meg's shoulders, she found Sally in the kitchen pressing a cold compress to her red-blotched face, her clothing drenched and stained with coffee.

"Good Lord, what happened?" she cried. Sally held a hand up to stop her. Angela deduced immediately that she'd been burned, and that Meggie was responsible.

Minutes later, Alex rushed back into the kitchen, carrying his medical bag. He slammed the case on the table, snapped it open, spread out supplies, and took Sally's face in his hands.

"Luckily, the burns are superficial," he muttered. "No serious damage, darling. You won't have any scars."

He began treating her with ointment. Sally was still wearing the sleeveless, low-cut black Alaia dress she'd had on the night before when they'd gone to dinner at the beach. Her face, neck, and shoulders were splattered with angry, stinging red welts.

It was 8:15. The County Health Department opened at 8:00. Angela lowered Margaret into a kitchen chair and kept a comforting arm around her; with her other hand, she picked up the wall phone, tucked it under her chin, punched in a number, and asked for Gail Rosenberg, a social worker whom she worked with often. Angela explained the situation.

Mrs. Rosenberg had seen the news reports, she said. She agreed that what Dr. Cohen described constituted an emergency, and on that basis, the patient could be brought in and held under observation for seventy-two hours. That would give them time to arrange for continuing care. She would dispatch an ambulance to the Century City apartment right away, she told Dr. Cohen.

Hearing Angela's side of the conversation, realizing what was happening, Meg wrenched herself out of the doctor's grip and struck at her ferociously. Alex leaped around the table and restrained her, and at the same time, he reached into his bag for a hypodermic needle and deftly prepared a shot.

"This won't hurt much, Meggie," he said, "and you're going to feel a lot better." He picked up her arm and quickly administered a strong tranquilizer. Almost instantly, Meg began to calm down.

Alex turned his attention back to Sally and continued dressing her burns. She was in pain, and terribly distraught. "Angela," she said, "I don't want her at the County, I want her in a private facility . . . Westwood Psychiatric . . . somewhere clean, and close by—"

"There's no time," Angela said resolutely. "As long as Margaret won't consent, to commit her to private care would take days, maybe weeks, of legal red tape. Yes, I know that's what I told you we'd do, but that was months ago. Now . . ." she said, looking down at Meg, who'd been anesthetized into docility, "now it's too late for that."

"No, I won't have it!" Sally was sobbing now. "I've worked in hospitals all my life. County facilities are like bus terminals. Cigarette butts on the floors, inmates walking into walls, ranting, urinating in the day rooms . . . Meggie would have to sleep in a dorm with them—"

Angela didn't have the heart to tell her that in the extreme stages of schizophrenia that she now observed in Margaret, she simply could not be trusted in a private facility. Those hospitals were open, they often had spacious grounds, there were very few restraints. Margaret would be up and out of there in a heartbeat. In her present condition, she was a danger to herself and others, and at the rate her psychosis was escalating, they couldn't afford a week, even a day. She had to be taken in immediately.

"Please trust me, Sally," Angela implored. "This is what's best for her right now."

"She's right, darling," Alex concurred.

The doorbell rang; the ambulance had arrived. Alex told the doorman to send the attendants up to the apartment. Meg sat in a stupor, the result of the sedative combined with lack of sleep. Angela helped her up and steered her into the living room, and Alex and Sally followed.

Alex opened the door to two white-coated paramedics, a man and a woman, who offered identification. "This is Margaret Davidson?" asked the man, indicating Meg. As he removed a pair of soft plastic cuffs from his kit and started to approach her, Meg's vacant face was suddenly stricken with fear.

"What are you doing?" Sally asked. "You can't put *handcuffs* on her!"

"It's regulation, ma'am," the attendant said.

"No!" Sally appealed to him. "It's not necessary. We'll be with her."

"I'm afraid that's not possible," he countered. "We're responsible if anything happens, and regulations are that the patient must be restrained for transport."

"Sally," Alex said gently, "don't fight this. It'll only make it harder. Tell her, Angela."

No one had noticed that Meg had gotten up and moved across the room to the French doors that led out onto the terrace. At the sound of the doors opening, they all turned. Before anyone could get to her, Meg walked out onto the balcony, climbed up on the stone parapet, and jumped nineteen floors to the pavement below.

36

Richard Winningham sat at his desk in the newsroom, studying the twenty-year-old yellowing crew sheet from the production of *Black Sabbat*. Channel Six's entertainment editor, Eric Jensen, had dug through his files and come up with it. Everyone who worked on the film was listed, along with their titles and phone numbers, both at home and at the New England location. Winningham had tried the home numbers of those on the first page of the list—the producer, the line producer, the associate producers, production coordinator, casting director, location manager, first assistant director, second assistant director, and on down the line. So far, not one of the phone numbers was current.

He went on to page two, starting with one of the three costumers—it was a Los Angeles number. A woman answered. He identified himself and asked for Shirley Horowitz. Yes, she told him, she was Shirley Horowitz. *A small miracle*, Winningham thought, and he asked her about her work on the old movie, *Black Sabbat*, and particularly what she remembered about the young actress, Meg Davis. Mrs. Horowitz said she had seen the news coverage that morning of Meg's arrest.

"Such a shame," she said. "I haven't seen her since the picture, but she was a lovely youngster. Do they really think she killed those people?"

"I don't know," he responded. "They couldn't make the charges stick this morning, and as you saw, she was released."

"Well, that Mr. Nathanson, he was a hard one, but I can't believe Meg could do a thing like that," she went on.

The newsman asked if she remembered anything unusual that might have happened to Meg on the set of *Black Sabbat*, the old colonial town in eastern Massachusetts.

"Oh, there was a lot of talk," she told him. Winningham reminded her that he was taping the conversation.

"I don't mind," she returned. "I'm only saying the truth. He might have been a great actor, and I'm sorry that he was murdered, but he was mighty strange, and if there's any way I can help that troubled girl, I'm glad to do it."

She said he should call the woman who was the head hairdresser on that shoot. "Barbara Lawrence," she said. "She was Barbara Blair then. I've worked with her quite a few times over the years, and I have her phone number. I think Barbara can tell you a thing or two, Mr. Winningham."

He checked the crew sheet. Barbara Blair, Hair Stylist. He called the number Shirley Horowitz gave him, which was different from the one listed on the sheet. An answering machine referred him to yet another number, one in Santa Fe, New Mexico. It turned out to be the location of a movie shoot in progress. He was transferred to the makeup trailer, and Barbara Lawrence came on the line.

Yes, she had some time, she said, and she told him that everyone on the Santa Fe set was talking about the shocking Meg Davis news this morning, and her bizarre ranting about witchcraft. She was particularly upset by it, she told him, because she had tried to take young Meg under her wing back then, from the day she walked in on the child and Nathanson in the actor's trailer.

"I felt at the time that I should tell her mother," Barbara Lawrence said, "but I was afraid she might pull Meg off the movie, and we were halfway through it. It was a very difficult shoot, and we were behind schedule. I knew that if I were responsible for losing Meg and stopping production, not to mention publicly embarrassing the star, I'd be fired, of course. And I was young. It was my first big picture. I'd probably never get another one—"

"What did you see when you walked in on them?"

"Well, they were pushing me to get Meg done and out there in place, and I was supposed to do her hair stringy and matted with dirt and blood, and I couldn't find her, so I was running from the lunch line to the rest rooms to wardrobe asking everybody where Meg was, and somebody said she was still in with Mr. Nathanson working on the afternoon scenes—"

"So you went to his trailer?"

"Yes, and by then I was frantic. I didn't even knock, I just pushed the door open. Well, there was Jack Nathanson down on all fours like a dog, in nothing but a pair of boxer shorts, and little Meg was standing over him with his belt in her hand, and he was saying, 'Hit me . . . hit me, Meg.' I was so shocked I just stood there with my mouth open, and he looked up and yelled 'Get the fuck out of here!' I don't know why he didn't have me fired that day. I guess he probably figured if he did, I'd talk. But that was the damnedest line-running I've ever seen in all my years in the business."

"*Did* you tell anybody?" Winningham asked.

"I started to," she said, "but everybody said 'Shhhh!' like it was some big, dark secret. And you know what? It *was*. Like I said, I wanted to keep my job, so I just went along to get along, and like everybody else, I didn't say a word. I don't know how Sally Davidson could miss it, but I guess she did, or maybe, and this is a terrible thing to say about a mother, maybe she knew about it too, but pretended she didn't. I mean, she was young herself, still in her twenties, and she was a single mother. . . ."

"Would you tell that story on camera?" he asked her.

"No," the woman said resolutely. "I can't go on the news; you know this business. These old-boy producers and directors would brand me a troublemaker, and I'd never get another job. Can't you just say that a person who worked on the picture told you? But please don't say a hairdresser—"

"Sure," Winningham said. "I understand your position."

"I'll tell you," Barbara Lawrence went on, "Nathanson was a sleaze, and everyone on his films knew it. But he's dead now, he won't be getting anybody hired or fired, and it's about time this came out. That poor girl needs to know that it wasn't her fault. These abused kids blame themselves, you know, and when I saw her on the news this morning it made me cry."

"How long did that behavior go on, do you know?" Winningham asked.

"Well, I can't say, because I never saw it happen again," she said, "and I'm sure he must have locked his door from that day on. But I *can* tell you that he had that little girl alone in his trailer just about every day, and the shoot lasted for almost a year."

Maxi came into the newsroom just as Richard was hanging up, and she leaned on the edge of his desk. "I changed clothes," she said.

"Good idea." He laughed. "The Yankee cap wouldn't really work for anchoring the news. How are you holding up, Maxi?" he asked, his eyes concerned.

"Aside from the fact that someone tried to kill me last night, okay, I guess," she said. "Yukon is struggling. Carlotta's funeral is this afternoon, and I need to get over there . . . for Ron."

"You must be exhausted," he said. "You didn't get much sleep."

"And you didn't get any at all. You know," she told him, "I've been thinking all morning about Meg Davis and her strange raving, and there's something wrong . . . something I'm missing . . ."

"Like what?"

"I don't know. Two days ago I met her, and I listened to her harangue. And last night, that . . . that *person* who was in my house, who took that cross and—" She shuddered.

"Go on," Richard said.

"Well, we know that Meg Davis bought that cross at the auction, and I actually saw her with it on Sunday, and I heard her eerie ranting that day, and the *world* heard it on the news this morning . . . but something is out of sync. Of course, I'm a frantic mess with all this. I'm probably just overwrought . . ."

"Let's go into your office," Richard said. "I just found out something about Meg Davis that's significant, I think." They walked across the noisy newsroom to Maxi's office, went inside, and sat on the couch. He told her what he had learned about the months of abuse that Meg Davis had probably endured on the set of *Black Sabbat* when she was ten years old.

Maxi's face darkened. She'd learned the hard way that Nathanson was lascivious, but she'd never known that she might have been married to a child molester. "Oh God, that poor little girl," she managed.

"Yes," Richard said. "If it's true, then Meg Davis was a victim—"

"Wait a minute. . . . That's it," Maxi cried. "That's what doesn't mesh!"

"What do you mean?"

Maxi was silent for a long moment before she went on. "The Meg Davis I met on Sunday was a *victim*—sad, clearly disoriented, like a disturbed child—I felt sorry for her," she said slowly. "The Meg Davis who was in my house last night, who tried to kill me, who almost killed Yukon . . . that person was violent, angry, cruel—"

Maxi abruptly got up and went over to her desk. "Richard,"

she said, "I want you to listen to something." She reached over to a rack and pulled out the audiotape of her conversation with Meg Davis on the beach. She explained what it was, and told Richard that she had given a copy to the detectives who were handling the Jack Nathanson murder investigation.

"Obviously, they can't use it, and neither can we," she said, "but I want you to listen to it." She popped the cassette into her playback machine.

. . . Tell me again what your mission is, Meg.

I have to save Gia. I must keep the evil spirits from permeating her soul. I have the cross now, and if I keep it near Gia, the witches will flee. God wants me to protect Gia so she won't be defiled like I am, so she can have a happy life. . . .

"You see," Maxi said, "Meg Davis talked about *protecting* Gia, *saving* her. She saw the cross as something sacred, an icon that would shield the girl, take care of her so she'd be safe. Meg Davis did not intend to kill people with that cross."

"And the intruder in your house last night?" Richard prompted.

"She . . . he . . . was a killer. Last night I told the police it was Meg Davis. It seemed so obvious. But now I feel sure it wasn't."

"But it doesn't make sense," Richard reasoned. "Who—?"

"I don't know," Maxi said. "I don't know . . . but it wasn't Meg Davis, I feel certain of that now. I was *this* close to both of them just a day apart, and I'm telling you, the person who was in my house last night was not Meg Davis."

"Would you go on the air with that?" Richard asked.

"I can't. I can't report on the story; you know that, Richard. I'm *part* of the story."

"I don't mean as a reporter," Richard said. "I mean as a witness. That same person probably killed Carlotta Ricco, and you're the only one alive who saw him. You think it was a man?"

"I don't know," she said. "The running shoes could have been either men's or women's, I didn't see them well enough, but the sheriff's crime-lab technicians took photos of footprints at my house this morning, so they'll know soon. The only thing I *do* know is that it was not Meg Davis. I'm sure of it."

"Come on, let's go talk to Pete," Richard said. "We've got to figure out what to do with this. Obviously, you have to let Mike Cabello know right away."

"I know," Maxi said. She was sitting at her desk, turning the tape cassette over in her hands. Her computer screen beeped, and she looked over at it. She had the wire services on line, and the word URGENT flashed on her screen. Idly, she watched for the story that would follow. The wires ran "urgents" frequently. As the story from the Associated Press scrolled down the screen, her eyes widened.

"Oh, God," she cried. "Oh, my God. Meg Davis has committed suicide!"

Maxi sat in front of Pete Capra's desk; Richard paced. Pete had Mike Cabello on the phone, telling him that Maxi Poole had been comparing in her mind the demeanor of Meg Davis to that of the attacker who was in her house last night, and she felt sure that they were *not* the same person.

"How the hell do I know why she'd commit suicide if she wasn't the killer? Yeah, yeah, Mike, she'll call you in five minutes," Capra said, and he slammed down the phone. "He needs to talk to you," Pete told Maxi. "But first, how are we gonna handle this? Richard, I think you should lead the early block with the update, 'Channel Six reporter Maxi Poole feels certain that actress Meg Davis, who jumped to her death this morning, was not the black-robed intruder who broke into her home,' et cetera, et cetera. Then back up the story to Carlotta Ricco, the cross, the auction, Jack Nathanson . . . pull a few frames of Meg Davis in *Black Sabbat* from Jensen's archives, and voice over the sidebar that the hairdresser on the picture says the kid was sexually abused. Then come out of the tape with an interview on set with Maxi about why she believes it wasn't the Davis woman, and so on. What do you two think?"

"Fine with me, if it's okay with Maxi," Richard said.

"Yes, I'll do it," Maxi told them. "I need to do it for Meg Davis. I think she only meant to do good. And for her family. They must be devastated. I want to vindicate her, for them.

"And I need to do it for myself," she went on. "I have to help any way I can. There's a killer out there who's alive, who's crazy, and who wants to kill *me!*"

37

Janet Orson was stunning in shimmering, clinging, white silk jersey—a floor-length Vera Wang gown that emphasized her long, sleek figure. Her golden hair was swept up in a twist and held by an oblong diamond clip. Diamond-and-pearl drop earrings accentuated her alabaster skin, and a pearl choker hugged her neck, fastened to one side with a wide diamond clasp.

"You are *breathtaking!*" Alan Bronstein proclaimed. "But you sure don't look like a grieving widow." His eyes twinkled. He had just arrived at the Beverly Hills Hotel to escort her to the big charity premiere of *Serial Killer*, her late husband's last movie.

"Don't start!" Janet smiled. She handed him her ermine jacket. He walked around behind her and placed it on her shoulders, then guided her to the door.

"The picture should only be half as good as you look," Alan said; "then we'd make a fortune with it." But they both knew that *Serial Killer* was *not* good. It was beautifully shot by a brilliant young French cinematographer, but the story was weak, and nothing could fix that in postproduction.

"Well, darling," Janet said with a sigh, "you didn't take this on to make money. You did it for Jack, remember?"

"Wrong!" he said. "I did it for *you*, Janet; let's make no mistake about that. Still, the old man wouldn't like to hear that I was running a philanthropic organization. It would be nice if we could make a few bucks with it." Bronstein thought to himself but didn't say, *The only thing this turkey's got going for it is that the famous sonofabitch who stars in it is dead.*

He handed Janet into the waiting limo for the short drive to the Century Plaza Cinemas, where Monogram had taken over all four screens to premiere *Serial Killer.* The black-tie gala afterward would benefit AmFAR, and many luminaries who worked for AIDS research would be there, as well as several of the stars of the movie.

As their limousine pulled off Santa Monica Boulevard onto the Avenue of the Stars in Century City, Janet looked up at the high-rise apartment buildings and shuddered. Her eyes traveled up the cluster of towers with their lighted windows, and she couldn't help thinking about actress Meg Davis, who had jumped off one of those terraces this morning, jumped nineteen floors to her death. That would be on everybody's mind tonight, she knew.

In fact, the suicide had been discussed that afternoon in a meeting at Monogram. It had happened in Century City, just yards from where tonight's premiere would be taking place. Would it put a damper on everybody's spirits? It would be an industry crowd, and Meg Davis was one of their own. The story had been all over the media since the actress's arrest last night, including her link to Jack Nathanson, and most of the 1,800 invitees would see the whole scenario played out again on the evening news before they arrived at the theater.

"Don't think I'm being crass," Alan Bronstein had said in the meeting, knowing, of course, that he was being crass, "but if anything, I think it just heightens the mood for this film. I mean, on the day of the premiere of Jack Nathanson's final film, which happens to be about a serial killer, *his* killer is arrested and commits suicide. I have to say, Jack himself would've loved the timing."

"Oh, are they saying that Meg Davis killed *him*, too?" studio chief Sid Levine had asked.

"No, not yet, but it's looking that way, Sid. CNN says she was obsessed with him, actually stalked him, followed him around for years, and of course she was bonkers. Probably had a crush on him way back when she was a vulnerable kid, doing *Black Sabbat*. Jack was in his early thirties then, a big star, and a charmer, not to mention successful, powerful, rich."

"Yeah, and didn't they say she was seen outside Debra Angelo's house on the day Nathanson was killed there?" put in Joe Austin, Monogram's head of marketing.

"Gee, it *is* kind of a nice circle, isn't it? But for chrissake, don't anybody quote me!" Sid Levine had said with a chuckle. The subject was closed.

The driver eased their stretch limo to a stop in front of the theater complex, and Janet and Alan stepped out into a barrage of minicams and flashbulbs, but abruptly the cameras stopped, and the army of press practically knocked the two of them down to get to the couple behind them. Michael Douglas and Catherine Zeta-Jones had just stepped out of their limousine and were making an entrance.

Bronstein laughed. The public was always more interested in the glittering faces they saw on the screen than the people behind the movies, and that was just fine with him. When one of his films scored big, he always walked away with the biggest chunk of the profits.

Bronstein had turned down reserved seats in one of the smaller upstairs theaters in favor of the largest theater in the complex, which accommodated eight hundred people. Even though just about everyone here tonight was connected to the movie business, after all the hoopla of the limos and the press and the fans waving autograph books, the celebrities, the colleagues, the air kisses, and the champagne in the lobby, when they took their seats and the lights went down, they turned into movie fans just like ordinary mortals, and Alan Bronstein wanted to hear their reactions. Later, at the dinner, they would all tell him they loved the movie, it was a winner, it couldn't miss, just as he would say at *their* screenings. But what they *really* thought of it would emerge inadvertently while they were sitting in the dark, immersed in the experience of the film. Alan would hear the gasps, the yelps of horror, the laughs, some in the wrong places—that's what would give him a true sense of how *Serial Killer* would do at the box office.

Chris Rock was on stage doing a welcoming monologue. The newly svelte Bette Midler was dressed totally in orange feathers—later she was going to perform. Streisand wouldn't sing, but she showed up, her husband James Brolin good-naturedly shielding her from the press. Actress Jennifer Lopez was in yet another dress that seemed glued to strategic parts of her body; actor Ed Burns was looking adorably confused, as he usually did. The massive Los Angeles Ballroom in the Century Plaza Hotel across the avenue from the theater complex was filled, and festive.

The lustrous crowd sat at tables set with peach-colored linens, fine china, and real crystal, and gracing each table were tall taper candles set in a lush centerpiece of lilies and peach roses. Tuxedoed waiters served an après-theater supper of crab and shrimp, cheeses and pâtés, lobster quiche, and baby grilled lamb chops, followed by lavish dessert trays with dozens of selections, along with wines, champagne, coffee, and liqueurs. Most of the participants, on stage and off, wore the AIDS red ribbons that were handed out at the doors.

For the silent auction to benefit AmFAR, Jean-Paul Gaultier had donated the famous pinstriped suit that Madonna made news in when she took the jacket off on the runway and displayed her perfect naked breasts; Bjork contributed the white froufrou swan dress that she sang in at the Oscars; Elizabeth Taylor had donated the pièce de résistance, the violet, chrome-bedecked Harley-

Davidson motorcycle Malcolm Forbes had given her. You could bid on a trip for two to Venice with a week at the fabulous Hotel Cipriani, or a week in Aspen with a suite at the Little Nell, along with ski outfits from the Aspen Mogul Shop. Artist David Hockney had donated a brilliant canvas; decorator to the stars Waldo Fernandez would completely redo a room in your house.

While Janet was chatting with friends, Alan wrote his name on the bidding sheet for a dazzling diamond-and-emerald necklace donated by a prominent Rodeo Drive jeweler. Its retail value, listed at the top of the sheet, was forty thousand dollars. Alan filled in his bid—fifteen thousand. He was pretty sure he would get it for that amount. He well knew the gentlemen's agreement at these celebrity-filled silent auctions. If a member of the "club" wanted a certain item and entered a reasonable bid, the rest would stay away from it and set their sights on something else. Unless, of course, someone who couldn't stand you wanted it. Or if someone who couldn't stand you didn't want it but enjoyed yanking your chain, they might bid higher and buy it just to piss you off, then, on their way out the door, clutching their purchase, smile and tell you it was a wonderful evening and let's do lunch. A small example of the civilized knife-twisting that went on all the time in this industry town. The jeweler stood to gain some quality publicity with potential customers in this rich and famous crowd, as well as a tax write-off for donating the piece. And Bronstein's own fifteen-thousand-dollar check would be made out to AmFAR, with a memo "for AIDS research" on the bottom, so he, too, could take a tax write-off. And not the least of it, he would be getting a terrific bargain on a fabulous piece of jewelry. It was a nice system where nobody lost, and everybody won. And he wanted to give that necklace to Janet.

"Do you mind if we stop for a nightcap on the way home?" Bronstein asked her now, as the star-studded benefit show was winding down. "Sid and the guys want to compare notes on how the picture played."

Outside the Century Plaza Hotel, the horseshoe drive was lined with limos. Alan waved for their driver, who pulled up and took them to Mortons, where they found the group from Monogram at a front table.

"So?" Alan asked, as he and Janet joined them.

"So, okay . . . it went okay, I thought," Sid Levine threw out. "And I got a not-too-bad feeling from the press. I mean, nobody looked away in embarrassment when I said hello."

"Yeah, me too," Alan responded. "Some nice laughs, no terrible gaffes . . . Shit, Sid, maybe we'll make our money back."

"You didn't get 'huge hit' vibes, huh?" Sid asked hopefully.

"Come on, buddy." Alan grinned. "We've both been in this business too long to kid ourselves. This one never smelled good, you know that." Suddenly, he became aware that Janet was looking uncomfortable. This was, after all, her late husband's picture, and he had been dead for less than three weeks.

"I'm sorry, Janet," he said to her. "We're being insensitive jerks. Maybe we should skip this—"

"No, no, no," she assured him, and smiled at the group around the table. "I'm okay. It's just all so hard to believe. . . . Would you order me an Armagnac?"

"You're a trouper," Alan said, signaling a waiter. "We won't stay long; one quick drink and I'll get you home."

A young man approached the table, one of the restaurant's parking attendants. He came over to Alan. "Mr. Bronstein," he said, "I have those tickets I told you about."

"Oh, great, Billy," Alan said, and extended his hand. Billy gave him an envelope, and left. "Wants to be an actor," Alan explained to the group. "Don't they all, huh? These are for a play his workshop is doing; I told him if I couldn't go, I'd give them to someone who counts."

The waiter arrived and they ordered drinks. The group chatted about the film's prospects, and congratulated themselves on throwing a very successful fundraiser—the morning publicity should get the movie launched in a climate of goodwill.

Later, as their limousine made its way toward the Beverly Hills Hotel, Janet felt suddenly drained. She longed to climb into bed and obliterate all thoughts of the murders, of Meg Davis, of Jack, the movie, the business, her future. Resting her head against the back of the car's plush upholstery, she closed her eyes and tried to relax.

The sound of a siren behind them jolted her alert, and she opened her eyes to the strobe of flashing lights bathing the interior of the limo. "What the hell—?" Alan muttered, and they both turned to see a squad car behind them. They were in a tony residential area on Canon Drive. A voice over a loudspeaker invaded the neighborhood stillness: "Pull over to the side of the road. Please pull your vehicle over to the curb and park, and roll down all your windows."

"I don't know what I did, Mr. Bronstein," the driver said, tossing back a nervous look to Alan as he pulled the cumbersome stretch limo over to the right and stopped. Quickly, he pressed the buttons to lower the windows, front and back.

An officer in the tan shirt, green pants, and helmet of the Los Angeles County Sheriff's Department, his gun drawn, stepped to the window on the driver's side and looked back into the interior of the car. "Mr. Alan Bronstein?" he asked.

"I'm Alan Bronstein—"

"Please step out of the vehicle, sir, and keep your hands above your head."

As Alan did so, another man approached from the radio car, a tall black man in street clothes. He produced a leather ID folder with a badge and credentials bearing his name, Jonathan Johnson, and the inscription of the Sheriff's Homicide Bureau, then he began with "You have the right to remain silent. . . ."

When he was finished quoting the Miranda rights, he took a

search warrant from his pocket, explained what it was, and presented it for Bronstein's inspection.

"What are you looking for?" Bronstein questioned.

"We want the envelope you received from William Randall James at Mortons restaurant tonight," Johnson said.

"I don't know what you're talking about," Alan protested, his arms raised.

Johnson nodded to the other deputy, who had his gun trained on Bronstein. With his free hand, he reached into Bronstein's top left inside coat pocket and retrieved the envelope. He handed it to Johnson. Janet recognized Johnson as one of the detectives who had been at her house the day Carlotta was found murdered. Johnson tore open the envelope and looked inside, then put it in his own coat pocket.

"You can take Ms. Orson home now," he told the driver. Then, looking at Alan, he said, "Mr. Bronstein, you're coming with us."

38

How many keys did you make for Bronstein?" Mike Cabello asked Billy James, who was shivering in the fluorescent glare of an interrogation room at the Los Angeles Hall of Justice.

"I don't remember," Billy said.

"Whose keys did you press? I want names."

"I don't remember—"

"Oh, yeah?" Cabello roared. "Well, you better fucking *start* remembering, or you'll be sitting in the slam with scumbags who are gonna love that pretty blond hair of yours. Whose keys did you give him tonight?"

"I'm not saying anything till I get a lawyer," Billy said.

"We told you to call your lawyer. You said you don't *have* a lawyer," Cabello snapped.

"You're supposed to get me one, aren't you?"

"Fucking TV movies," Cabello muttered. "You punks are so fucking smart. Okay, if we're done talking here, we'll get you booked. You know the charge: conspiracy to commit fraud."

The door opened, and Jon Johnson walked into the room with Alan Bronstein. "Ahh, together again, the dynamic duo," Mike Cabello jeered. "Nice of you to dress up for us," he said to Bronstein, eyeing his tuxedo.

"You can't hold me," Bronstein said coldly.

"You're keeping real intelligent company, Bronstein," Cabello said, cocking his head toward Billy James, who sat cowering in his chair.

"I've got some keys, Mike," Jon Johnson said, taking the yellow envelope out of his pocket and handing it to his partner.

"Thanks," Cabello said. He removed three keys from the envelope and turned them over in his hand. "Why don't you take Fred Astaire, here, and book him, Jon."

Jon Johnson led Bronstein out of the room. "See," Cabello explained to Billy, "your uptown friend is gonna call his high-priced lawyer, and his high-priced lawyer is gonna get him out of here in an hour. He'll be sleeping in his comfy bed in Beverly Hills tonight. Now, we're gonna get you a lawyer, yes, but it's gonna be a low-rent lawyer—we got some pips on the public-defender roster—we're gonna find you one, but your guy might not be able to get you outta here tonight. Or this year."

"When do I get a lawyer?" Billy asked.

"Oh, soon, soon," Cabello said, "but I hope you had enough paydays from Bronstein to hire yourself a big, expensive lawyer down the line, cuz you're goin' down, and Bronstein ain't goin' with you, I guarantee it. He'll be back eating shrimp at Mortons, and you'll be inside, eating macaroni with bugs in it."

"Can I have my lawyer now?" Billy asked. He had chills and he was sweating at the same time.

"In a minute, in a minute." Cabello waved him off. "I just want to paint a picture for you, Billy. I just want to tell you that I don't think Bronstein's gonna say 'Look, I ain't leavin' here till my little buddy Billy goes with me. I ain't goin' to Mortons till Billy James comes too, cuz nobody can park my fucking Porsche like Billy can.' I don't think he's gonna say that, do you?" Billy shrugged, and said nothing.

"I'll let you in on something," Cabello went on in measured tones. "We are searching Bronstein's house right now, and his office, and we will find every fucking key he's got. Now, if they're marked, and I'm guessing they are, we'll know the names I'm looking for. It'd just go down better for you if you tell us first. But if they're *not* marked," Cabello went on, "and my guys have to take that fucking pile of keys and go try every fucking door in L.A. County to find out where they fit, and it holds me up for-fucking-ever on my murder investigation—I said *murder*, Billy—then I'm going to be majorly pissed. Unless you want to cooperate and help me out, that is—then I might want to help *you* out, if you get my drift."

Billy was looking at him, weighing what he was hearing.

"Unless, of course, you think your pal Bronstein is such a prince he'll stick his neck out to get you out of this," Cabello added with a wicked smirk.

"Michael Eisner. Those keys are Michael Eisner's, the chairman of Disney," Billy said, pointing to the keys Cabello was holding out in the palm of his hand.

"Oh, yeah? Who else's did you do?"

"Jeffrey Katzenberg, Warren Beatty, Sam Breneman, Mike Ovitz . . ." Billy began singing.

Smiling, Cabello picked up the phone and put in an order for a public defender. Then he walked down the hall and entered the room where Jon Johnson and another deputy were sitting with Alan Bronstein.

"We're waiting for his attorney," Jon told Cabello. "Leo Greenwood. He'll be here any minute. Mr. Bronstein has asked Mr. Greenwood to also represent William James in this matter."

"Awww, too late," lamented Cabello. "The little asswipe already has a lawyer. And he volunteered a list of names, by the way. Jesus, Bronstein, you went big! Bob Zemeckis, Tom Hanks, Steven Soderbergh . . . "

While doing some checking in low places on Alan Bronstein, Cabello had unearthed the nuts and bolts of a scheme that Bronstein had been running for years. A source told him that Bronstein had a ringer who was duplicating keys belonging to the top people in the business; then he would send the guy, dressed as some kind of night janitor, into their offices with the keys at two, three in the morning on fishing expeditions with a tiny Minox.

"It's beautiful!" Cabello had told his partner. "A regular Tinseltown Watergate. It's how Bronstein always seems to know what scripts his marks are bidding on, what kind of numbers are in the contracts on their desks, things like that."

"What does he do with the information?" Johnson had asked.

"He uses it when he's negotiating, when he's chatting up deals. Nobody could figure out how Bronstein always seems to get the good scripts, the great packages, the right stars. Now we know—he has everybody's inside information."

"But you say the one thing he never got that he always wanted was Jack Nathanson's wife," Johnson countered.

"That's right. But he's got her now," Cabello said.

"But would he *kill* to get her?" Johnson asked.

"My opinion?" Cabello threw out. "This is a guy who'd kill his grandmother if it would get him a better split on a deal."

"Well, if you're right about this little scam of his, he won't have the widow for long. He won't have much of *anything* for long," Johnson declared.

Cabello had checked for twenty-four-hour key shops and found out that there were three in the city, one of them on the Westside, in the Rexall on La Cienega. He'd gone in and asked the man who ran the key service whether he had any repeat business that seemed like a lot, that seemed unusual for the average Joe who needed to get keys made. When Cabello flashed his badge, the clerk lifted the cash register drawer and showed a check for thirty-one dollars. Guy was in there every other week, he said, good-looking young blond dude. The check had no printed name or address on it, but it had a bank number, and it was signed *W. James*.

The detective put a trace on the account, which was in the name of one William Randall James. There were three men named William Randall James licensed to drive in the state of California, and one of them lived in West Los Angeles. A check on that one's Social Security number showed that he received regular paychecks from the parking concession at Mortons, the trendy restaurant at Melrose and Robertson that was frequented by showbiz folks. Bingo!

Cabello and Johnson set up a surveillance detail. The two plainclothes deputies who staked out Mortons had no trouble making William Randall James—he was the only blond guy parking cars there. On a hunch, one of the deputies went inside and asked the hostess what time Mr. Alan Bronstein was expected. She looked at her book and said she didn't have him down for that day, but next Tuesday there was a big movie premiere—Monogram Films had a table reserved for after-dinner drinks at 11:30, and Mr. Bronstein's name was on their list. Cabello and Johnson decided to show up for that party themselves. Johnson took Bronstein in, and Cabello nailed Billy James.

Now both detectives sat in an interrogation room talking to Bronstein and his lawyer, a well-known entertainment attorney. A few minutes after they got started, Paul Rossen and Andy Gomez, the deputies who had been conducting the search of Bronstein's house, burst in the door.

"Hey, Mike, merry Christmas a little early!" Gomez chucked a brown bag full of keys on the table.

"That was fast," Mike said appreciatively. "How'd you guys find 'em?"

"Easy," Rossen said. "We kicked in the door to his house. Excuse me, sir," he said to Bronstein, "you're gonna need a locksmith. And we had the board-up people secure your house with plywood and bolts, so probably a carpenter, too."

Bronstein groaned.

"Anyway, Mike," Rossen went on, "they were in a drawer in his den. You want me to check them in to the evidence room?"

"No, leave 'em here," Cabello said. "I wanna play with my Christmas present for a while."

Gomez and Rossen left, and Mike emptied the bag of keys out on the table. Each set was on a separate ring, and each was tagged with a name. Different keys had markings like HOME, OFFICE, CAR. Mike saw the attorney wince.

"Congratulations, Bronstein," Cabello said, rummaging through the keys. "You got the A-list here! I guess everybody eats at Mortons." Then he found the set he was looking for, on a ring marked J. NATHANSON. Cabello picked them up by the key that was labeled DEBRA, and dangled them in front of Bronstein and his attorney. "Marvin Samuels, he's Debra Angelo's lawyer, told us that her ex had a key to her house so he could bring the kid inside if he got there early and nobody was home," he said. "Now, it looks like Nathanson's killer slipped into Ms. Angelo's house with a key—there was no forced entry. And it was the middle of the afternoon, so the alarm wasn't set."

"What about Meg Davis?" Greenwood put in. "I thought *she* was your killer. She committed suicide—isn't that classic open and shut?"

"Oh, yeah, we hear all the geniuses in your business are saying Meg Davis was a witch, and she spirited herself in through the walls and killed Jack Nathanson for making her loony." Cabello laughed. "It might be hard for you to believe this, guys, but we don't think so. So we checked up on everybody we knew had a key to this front door," Cabello went on, twisting the key marked DEBRA between his thumb and his forefinger, "but we had no idea *you* had one, Bronstein!"

"Just because I had a key doesn't mean I killed the guy," Bronstein spat out. His attorney cautioned him to be quiet.

"Well, we'll see about that. But I'll tell you something it *does* mean," Cabello said, shuffling through the pile of keys. "When this little operation of yours hits the news, you ain't gonna get invited to any of these people's parties anymore!"

39

"Uh . . . do you want me to take you back to the hotel, Ms. Orson?" the limo driver asked.

"Yes, Zack, I guess." Janet Orson was in shock. She wasn't sure *what* to do. Maybe she should call her lawyer. Or Alan's lawyer. What in hell was *that* about?

At the premiere tonight, she'd felt uncomfortable. She sensed that people were telling each other it was rather soon after Jack was killed for her to be dressed in glitz and out on a date. And Alan didn't help. He'd hovered over her all evening, stroking her arm, kissing her cheek. No one could miss his proprietary behavior.

Yes, she'd slept with him on Sunday night. In fact, she'd slept with Alan Bronstein now and then, when she was between men, during all the years they'd known each other. They'd always had the most easygoing of relationships—they enjoyed each other, they were good friends, and each made no demands on the other. They used to dish together about their respective love interests, laugh about her quest for the perfect soul mate and his pursuit of this year's blonde. But since Jack's death and the resumption of their close friendship, Alan was different. Now he acted jealous if another man looked at her.

And he was full of anecdotes about how petty, how mean, how venal Jack was. He said there were times, like when he would hear Jack was cheating on her, that he wanted to kill the bastard. It seemed he couldn't keep his consuming hatred of Jack Nathanson from spilling out when she was with him.

Still, she needed him now. He had seen her through the harrowing aftermath of Jack's murder, and Carlotta's cruel death. But she was beginning to worry that she might be sending him the wrong message, that he might truly be getting serious about her. He'd acted like a lovesick puppy tonight in front of about two thousand of their most intimate friends. Hollywood people! She was sure they would all be clucking about it tomorrow.

And then he'd gifted her with this exquisite necklace, she mused, lifting a hand to her neck and running her fingers over the cool stones. He'd made a great show at the table at Mortons with this surprise, removing her pearl choker and placing the brilliant diamond-and-emerald piece around her neck, then tilting her chin up and kissing her on the lips. Later, he told her he'd planned to give it to her when they got back to the hotel, but when the whole Monogram gang started bad-mouthing Jack's picture like she wasn't even in the room, he decided to spring it on her then. She was embarrassed by the gesture, but she knew he meant well.

She couldn't imagine what kind of trouble Alan was in. She didn't want to think about the worst possible scenario. The terrible venom he'd always harbored for Jack, his penchant for getting what he wanted no matter what it took, and the fact that he'd made no secret of wanting Jack out of her life. Then there was the hoary reputation that clung to him, the rumors that he was connected to the underworld, that he could have someone killed, and probably had. He'd always laughed at those suggestions. Good for his tough-guy image, he'd say.

But he was *arrested* tonight—picked up by one of the detectives investigating Jack's murder. What did they have on him?

What did they *think* they had? Janet felt as if her world had shifted out of sync.

The driver pulled up to the canopied entrance to the Beverly Hills Hotel, and the doorman stepped over to help Janet out of the limo onto the gilt-edged red carpet that led to the massive glass and bronze front doors. It was after one in the morning—the lobby was quiet, just a few people coming out of the dining room, or wandering about, looking in the elegant shop windows. She stopped at the front desk for her messages. Maybe some light would be shed on what was going on with Alan. The night manager handed her the key to her bungalow and four telephone message slips. Nothing at all about Alan, she saw, glancing quickly through them. She walked past the celebrated Polo Lounge, which was humming with the usual show-business crowd. At the end of the corridor, past the lower-floor hotel rooms, she walked through the double doors to the rear grounds.

A maze of pathways led into the village of Mediterranean-style pink stucco bungalows nestling in the lush vegetation spread out over three acres. Tentatively, she started down a path that she was pretty sure led to bungalow 16, her home for the time being. As she made her way along the worn cobblestones that wound through the hedges of oleander and clumps of primroses, the many varieties of ancient, dripping ferns, the riot of hibiscus and birds of paradise, all of it overshadowed by towering trees a century old, Janet suddenly had the sense of being completely alone.

She hurried down the path. The cacophony of what seemed like a million crickets mingled with the splashing sounds of sprinklers over the hotel grounds, heightening her sense of isolation. Shivering, she pulled her ermine wrap tighter around her shoulders. She was being silly, just having a case of the jitters after this insane night, she knew. This was only her third day at the hotel, and she still had trouble picking out number 16, especially at night. She quickened her pace along the trail, aware of the echo of her high-heeled shoes click-clicking on the stones.

Finally spotting the aged brass numerals on the stucco and the lights that she'd left glowing inside, she hustled up the three front steps, her key and the message slips in one hand, her evening bag in the other. Stooping down, she turned the key in the lock and began to push open the door.

Abruptly penetrating the quiet, garbled sounds erupted behind her, filtered through the brush. Janet straightened and whirled around. Horror-stricken, she heard a distorted voice from behind the dense foliage that lined the path, intoning the words "*The ancient black art will rule. . . .*"

Before she could utter a scream, a black-robed figure lunged out of the shadowed thicket and leaped on top of her. Janet's head hit the door, knocking it open, and she fell backward to the floor inside the entry to the bungalow. The last thing she saw was the glint of a jagged metal cross in a black-gloved hand as it came down and slashed across her face, then her throat.

40

"No, you *can't* speak to her," Alexander Shine roared into the phone. "What the hell is wrong with you people? She's lost her only child!" He was about to slam the phone down when Maxi said, "Dr. Shine, somebody tried to kill me. I know it wasn't your daughter. I said so on the news last night, *before* Janet Orson was murdered."

"What did you say your name is?" he asked.

"Maxi Poole, from Channel Six. I'm the woman whose dog was slashed. I saw the killer, in my home, and I'm sure, now, that it *wasn't* Meg Davis—I told the detectives that yesterday. I need to talk to Meg's mother about it—no cameras, no story."

"Why?" he asked quietly. "They're saying that last night's murder was probably a copycat killing—and besides, it's too late for Meggie now."

"It's not too late to clear her name," Maxi said.

"Just a minute." Maxi could hear him talking in muffled tones. Then his wife came on the line.

"I'm sorry; the press keeps calling, and I—" Sally Shine began in an unsteady voice. "I saw your report last night, Ms. Poole, and I appreciate what you said about Meggie. I know my daughter could never have done those things."

Maxi could hear that the woman was close to tears. "Mrs. Shine," she said, "please let me come over there and talk to you about Meg, and I promise that nothing you say will go on the air, unless you want it to. I need your help."

"We're in the middle of moving. . . . I'm leaving this apartment—"

"I won't take more than a few minutes," Maxi pressed, "and this is important. You might save other lives."

When Sally Shine reluctantly agreed to a meeting, Maxi flew down to her car and headed for Century City, the teeming high-rise business and residential section of West Los Angeles that was once the old Twentieth Century Fox back lot. It was 9:20. Her clock-radio had gone off at seven, and Maxi woke to the stunning news of Janet Orson's brutal murder—Jack's widow, stabbed to death during the night on the grounds of the exclusive Beverly Hills Hotel. No witnesses, no murder weapon found, no motive known, just the enigmatic connection once again, as with Carlotta and herself, to Jack Nathanson.

Janet Orson's body was discovered just after six this morning by a room-service waiter bringing coffee and the newspapers to bungalow 16. The Associated Press quoted a preliminary statement from the detectives heading up the investigation, saying tracks of blood smeared across the threshold of the bungalow suggested the victim was killed on the portico, then dragged inside. Her body was found just inside the entryway; the front door had been closed and locked.

A key to bungalow 16 was found on the floorboards of the veranda outside. The night manager on duty told deputies that he had given Ms. Orson her key, along with her messages, when she had arrived back at the hotel at about 1:10 this morning. It was assumed the killer used that key to open the door to the bungalow, or perhaps Ms. Orson had opened it herself before she was attacked—the key was being tested for fingerprints.

Driving west on Sunset Boulevard, Maxi picked up her cell

phone and put in a call to her old friend Alison Pollock, the manager of the Beverly Hills Hotel. Alison told her to come by, of course she would make time for her. She turned up the sweeping drive that led to the hotel's lavish front entrance, where a green-uniformed parking attendant opened the door of her Corvette. "How long will you be, Ms. Poole?" he asked.

"No more than fifteen minutes," Maxi said. "Please leave the car up here instead of taking it down to the garage—I'm going to need it in a hurry." She handed him some bills, and hustled up the long red carpet into the lobby, then down the marble staircase to Alison Pollock's office.

Mrs. Pollock was a large, handsome woman in her fifties with a perennial tan and lustrous dark hair swept up in a loose chignon. She greeted Maxi with a hug, then guided her to one of the leather couches in her comfortable office. Frowning gravely, she asked Maxi what she knew about the terrible murder that had taken place on the grounds of her beloved hotel the night before.

"No more than you do, I'm afraid," Maxi responded. "But I don't think it was a copycat crime at all. Because I don't think it was Meg Davis who killed Jack Nathanson, or Carlotta Ricco, or attacked me."

"But everything points to that poor, unstable girl," Alison said. "The cross, the witchcraft business—"

"Ali, I'm the only person alive who has *seen* that killer, and even though he or she was in complete disguise, I'm betting my life that it wasn't Meg Davis. If it was, then I'd have nothing to fear," Maxi said. "But I believe the killer is still out there, and after *me* for some reason, something to do with my connection to Jack . . . and I'm scared."

"How can I help?" Alison asked.

"I know you can't let me into the bungalow; it's a crime scene," Maxi answered. "But let me have a copy of Janet Orson's phone records from the time she moved in here on Sunday. I'll take it back to the newsroom and check the numbers against the cross directory, see if anything looks unusual. I doubt this was a random strike—nobody's even suggesting robbery. I think the killer knew exactly where Janet was staying, and was waiting for her to come home."

Alison picked up her phone and buzzed the switchboard. She asked that the records of all calls that went out from bungalow 16 since Sunday be brought to her office.

"Can you get a copy of the messages that came *in* for her as well?" Maxi asked.

"No, I'm sorry," Alison said. "We're going to install voice mail, but the system's not in yet—for now, we still take messages the old-fashioned way, handwritten on message slips."

"No carbons?"

"No, it's never been our policy to log incoming messages," Alison said. "The switchboard puts calls through to the rooms, or the dining room, the beauty salon, the Polo Lounge, the gym, pool, wherever the guest leaves word to have calls forwarded. And when guests are out, they might call in to have their messages read to them, or they just pick up their written slips at the desk when they get back." Maxi made a mental note to find out whether the detectives had found any message slips in bungalow 16.

"Janet Orson did have her calls screened," Alison went on. "That's a service we offer. The switchboard operator asks who's calling, then plugs into the room to see if the guest is in and wants to take the call, then either puts the caller through or takes a message."

"But no records of those calls either?"

"No records," Alison confirmed.

Maxi could see anguish etched on Ali Pollock's face. She'd known Janet Orson for years. Janet had often breakfasted at the Polo Lounge with the industry crowd, and she'd hosted charity fundraisers at the hotel, as well as luncheons and dinners for friends and business associates. Alison had made it a point to come in to work on Sunday afternoon, she told Maxi, to welcome Janet, and to make sure that she was comfortably settled.

"Maxi, dear," she said, "until this horror is cleared up, I'd like to give you a suite here. I think it would be a good idea for you to stay with us until that killer is apprehended. You may not be safe in your house."

For a minute, both women reflected uneasily that Janet Orson hadn't even been safe at the world-famous, heavily staffed Beverly Hills Hotel. "I don't know," Maxi said. "I definitely don't want to stay alone at home tonight. I have a houseguest, Carlotta Ricco's son, but he's going back to school this afternoon. He's a star baseball player at his college, and he likes to keep a baseball bat with him to exercise his wrists. That's what saved me on Monday night. He scared the killer off, he and Yukon."

There was a knock on the office door, and Alison's assistant came in with the phone records. Maxi looked at the printout—thirty-four calls made from bungalow 16 on Sunday, Monday, and Tuesday.

"Thanks, Ali," she said. "And call me if you think of anything that might help—anything at all."

As Maxi drove the short distance to Century City, she pondered how to approach Meg Davis's mother to coax from her any clues that would point the way to the macabre *Black Sabbat* cross. Of course it was logical to assume that with all the publicity surrounding these crimes, anyone with information about the cross would contact authorities, but Maxi well knew that very often people, for their own reasons, were afraid to get involved.

It had occurred to her that perhaps more than one of those crosses had been made for *Black Sabbat*. Sometimes a film company will order an item in quantity for different purposes, like the seven pairs of ruby shoes made for Judy Garland in *The Wizard of Oz*, or the dozen identical pairs of sunglasses bought for Arnold Schwarzenegger for the *Terminator* movies. Consulting the *Black Sabbat* crew list that Richard was working from, Maxi reached

Tyler Scheibel, the property master on the film, who told her that only one cross was made for *Black Sabbat*, a one-of-a-kind art piece. He said the director had been specific about what he wanted the cross to look like and to feel like, and the prop master knew they'd never find such an item for sale. One of his assistants located an artist in Boston who worked in hammered metals, and the film company commissioned the cross—the artist was told to make it look solid, glitzy, and lethal. He fabricated the piece of silver-plated tempered steel, with luminous, multiple colors forged to the alloy. Because it was so distinctive, that cross made a very strong statement in *Black Sabbat*. Scheibel told Maxi that he was shocked to see the prop resurface in such horrendous circumstances.

At Sally Shine's apartment building, notorious now as the site where actress Meg Davis had committed suicide the day before, a moving van was parked at the curb, and a few curiosity seekers stood outside, looking up to the terrace on the nineteenth floor, some snapping pictures. *Poor Mrs. Shine*, Maxi thought. *How heartbroken she must be*.

Upstairs, the door to the apartment was ajar, and Maxi saw moving men busily packing dishes, sealing and marking boxes, hoisting furniture. Mrs. Shine came to the door and led her inside. "We'll go into Meggie's room where we can talk," she said. "The detectives won't allow us to move anything out of there yet." She closed the door behind them, and they settled on a white wicker settee.

"It's a beautiful room," Maxi said quietly, looking around at the queen-size bed with its pretty aqua comforter and multitude of pillows, the matching drapes, the overstuffed flower-print chair and ottoman, and the waxed-pine dresser, topped with a beautiful old Bible and a profusion of candles.

"I don't know what to do with her things," Sally said with a sigh.

"Mrs. Shine—"

"Please call me Sally," she said. Maxi sensed that the woman almost welcomed the distraction she was providing.

"Sally . . . Did you see the cross they're talking about, the one Meg bought at the auction?"

"Yes, I saw it on top of her dresser the morning after she bought it, and I think she took it with her when she went out that day. But I know she didn't—"

"I know that, too," Maxi interrupted gently. "But the cross is the key. Do you have any idea what happened to it?"

"No," she said. "I've been over and over that with the detectives. I just don't know. Meggie was reclusive, especially since that man's funeral—" Sally seemed to remember then that Maxi had been married to Jack Nathanson. "I'm sorry if—"

"Don't be," Maxi said, putting a reassuring hand on the woman's arm. "I'm more sorry for your pain. Can you tell me who some of Meg's friends were?"

"No. She never talked about any friends; no one ever called here for her. . . ."

Maxi could see that Sally Shine was about to weep. "I'm going to let you get back to your work," she said, "because the sooner you're out of here, the sooner you'll begin to heal, I think. I'm so sorry you have to go through this."

They walked out of the bedroom and through the living room, where Alex Shine was supervising the movers. He was a big man, good-looking, with salt-and-pepper hair and strong hands. He looked competent, Maxi noted, and caring, and comforting. She was glad that Meg's mother had him to lean on. At the door, she handed Sally one of her cards and asked her to call if she thought of anything that might be helpful.

"Ms. Poole . . . Maxi," Sally half whispered, "I'd like to ask you something."

"Of course," Maxi said, hesitating in the doorway.

"Last night on the news, your reporter said he'd talked to

some of the people who had worked on *Black Sabbat*, and they suggested that Meggie was . . . was *abused* by Jack Nathanson."

"Yes," Maxi said.

"Is he going to be following up on that? Talking to other members of the company?" she asked tremulously.

"I don't know," Maxi replied. "If the detectives find that Meg is no longer a posthumous suspect, and I feel certain that will happen as soon as their testing is completed, then there'll be much less interest in her."

"I hope so," Sally said. "It would be horrible if all that were dug up."

Maxi looked at her carefully. "Did you . . . know?"

The woman looked away. After a long moment, she directed her gaze back at Maxi. "No," she said. "But I should have known. I think if I'd wanted to, I *would* have known."

41

"No, I don't need a Luminol. . . . No, I don't need a DNA on the blood on the bungalow floor," Mike Cabello barked into the phone. "Of *course* it's the victim's blood!" He was talking to a serology technician at the crime lab. "Whatever happened to common sense?" he muttered, slamming down the phone.

Jon Johnson sat at the desk next to Cabello's in the noisy, cluttered, cavernous squad bay, scanning the latest report from the lab. "Meg Davis's shoes don't match the prints around the Nathanson house or outside Maxi Poole's house," he said. "But the prints show they were definitely *women's* shoes. Guess a lot of women have black Reeboks—my wife has two pairs, black *and* white."

"And none of the hairs or fibers from either house matched anything they swept up in the Davis woman's room or car," Cabello put in. "Also, Meg Davis was left-handed—"

"Yup," Johnson replied, "the dog was slashed in the left jugular and on the left side of the body. Maxi Poole said she's sure the intruder wielded the weapon in her right hand. *Can* we assume it was a she?"

"Not really—men committing crimes have been known to wear women's shoes, and this perp is evidently big on disguises."

"Well, can we rule out Meg Davis?" Johnson threw out.

"And release the body for burial? Let's wait on that," Cabello said. "Maybe we'll get a lead on the damn cross." He had found out that only one cross had been made for the *Black Sabbat* shoot. Wonder of wonders, Maxi Poole had actually called that one in—her priority had changed from working on the station's coverage of the murders to saving her own skin, he figured.

"What about Meg Davis's bedroom?" Johnson asked. "They've got movers there now, but we have an order in place that no one can touch that room. Can we lift it?"

"Might as well," Cabello mused. "Salinas and Brown raked that joint top to bottom. They defrosted the freezer. They pulled the *stove* apart."

"We'll tell the mother if she happens to find that cross in the move, give us a shout, huh?" Johnson grinned.

"Very funny," Cabello grunted. "If she finds the damn thing after our guys tore the place apart she can have my job."

"Who'd want it?" Johnson scoffed, his gaze scanning the Homicide section with its ninety-plus desks laden with dirty coffee mugs, stacks of newspapers, mountains of files, and the occasional picture of a spouse or kids whom the sweating men and women who worked there rarely saw.

"Yah, she'd love the overtime deal, huh?" Cabello laughed. Detectives in the bureau worked two weeks straight, then got three days off, which was a joke—most of the time they worked right through their scheduled days off. And their time sheets read nine to five, which was another joke—they often worked all night. It was regulation to list overtime on their weekly time sheets, along with the reasons why they felt the overtime was justified, but most of them didn't bother because they never got paid for it. Their overtime was routinely red-penciled, even if they wrote that they were working past five o'clock because a killer was holding them at gunpoint chained up in a cellar. Not good enough. The detectives would kid each other when they met in the squad room or in the field at two, three, four in the morning. "Working *pretend* overtime, huh?" they'd say.

Mike Cabello and Jon Johnson were pretend-overtime kings. They had been in the Hall until after three o'clock that morning, interrogating and processing Alan Bronstein and William James. They had both got home and logged a couple of hours' sleep when the calls came that Jack Nathanson's widow had been murdered at the Beverly Hills Hotel. They met at the crime scene to oversee the activity there, then came into the office to brainstorm the case. Over the department's bad coffee, they were trying to make sense out of what they knew, and how it fit together.

"So what have we got on the Orson woman?" Cabello asked.

"No struggle," Johnson said. "Nothing under her nails. Perfect uptown manicure. Probably didn't have a chance to put up a fight."

"And the key?"

"Her own fingerprints on it. Not even smudged. Looks like she opened the door herself, still had the key in her hand when she was attacked, then dropped it—"

"And the killer dragged her inside, then pulled the door closed and locked on the way out, to buy some time to get away," Cabello finished. "What about footprints around the bungalow?"

"They're photographing now, but Garcia says it's a swamp. The sprinklers drenched the area overnight, and they don't think they'll get anything useful. Some dust on the veranda. The techs are supergluing, but they're not optimistic."

"Our two lock-'n'-key boys are present and accounted for," Cabello noted. "Bronstein was released on bail at seven-fourteen this morning, and Billy-boy's still in the tank."

"If Bronstein was the mastermind behind these murders, Janet Orson would not have been on his kill sheet," Johnson observed. "He was in love with her. Boy, his whole world fell apart, big-time, in the space of a few hours."

"Yah, couldn't happen to a nicer guy," Cabello groused. "Christ, I'm beat."

"Well, get over it," Jon said. "It's gonna be a long day."

"Okay, moving down the checklist: No robbery—it didn't look like anything was disturbed in the bungalow, you agree?"

"Funny, the only one who would know for sure is Bronstein. The hotel people say he moved her into the place on Sunday; then they had dinner in the hotel dining room. On Monday he took her to the Sonora Cafe, a tony restaurant on La Brea, and last night they went to the movie premiere in Century City, then to Mortons for a nightcap," Johnson intoned, reading from his notes.

"And we know he slept with her in bungalow 16, at least on Sunday night," he went on. "We couldn't get any confirmation about Monday. But we're talking constant companion here. Do you want to haul him over to the bungalow to have a look?"

"Nah"—Cabello shook his head—"I don't want to look at his ugly face again today. Besides, you saw the body. Diamonds in her ears, diamonds in her hair, bracelet worth a zillion bucks—" The phone on his desk pealed, aggravating his throbbing head.

"Yah!" he rumbled into the mouthpiece. "Uh-huh . . . Okay, thanks." He put down the receiver.

"Big surprise," he deadpanned to Johnson. "Same blade, same wounds, same bloody fucking cross. So what have we got?"

"Same killer," Johnson said.

42

Maxi headed back toward Beverly Hills. Since she'd gotten no clues to the whereabouts of the cross from Sally Shine, she would start at the place where it had resurfaced in the public eye twenty years after the movie was made. Maybe the Sotheby's people could tell her something. It was a remote possibility, she knew, but she had no leads, no other avenues to pursue.

She entered through the ornately carved double doors and stepped into Sotheby's elegantly appointed lobby. A chic receptionist looked up over a pair of black-rimmed glasses and smiled. Maxi introduced herself, told her she was from Channel Six News and that she needed some information about the auction of Jack Nathanson's effects that they'd held on Saturday.

"Maxi Poole! I saw you there, and I saw the report you did on the auction that night," the woman said. "I'm Lenore Baines. If you tell me what information you need, I'll know who best to steer you to."

Maxi told her she wanted to find out anything she could about the cross that was a prop in *Black Sabbat*, the item she'd featured in her news story, which was purchased by the actress Meg Davis.

Lenore Baines nodded solemnly. Most of the city, in fact most of the country, was aware of the shocking, brutal killings and Meg Davis's suicide in the few days since the auction, that Meg Davis was the suspected killer, and her *Black Sabbat* cross was the suspected weapon. "Let me try Gabby in Decorative Arts," she said, picking up the phone and punching in a number. Almost immediately a cheerful young woman, tending a bit toward plump, with curly red-orange hair and a spattering of freckles, came through the inner door.

"This is Gabrielle Modine—Gabby," Lenore Baines said. "She processed that purchase for Ms. Davis." She introduced Maxi and explained what the reporter was after.

"Mmmm." Gabby's pretty face clouded. "Why don't you come to my office and I'll tell you what I can, although I'm afraid there isn't much to tell beyond what you had on the news."

She led the way back through a maze of corridors to a small, charming office. Maxi noticed the classic Louis XVI desk with the high-backed chair, the set of antique French cabinets, and the colorful Tibetan rug that partially covered the high-gloss hardwood floor. The two sat on a plush, damask-covered love seat, and Maxi's eyes gravitated to the canvas on the opposite wall. She gasped. It was an original Pierre Bonnard, a painting of a homey kitchen, a woman sitting with her needlework, a cat curled up on a chair, and a view out the open door of what looked like miles of glorious French countryside.

"Oh, don't be impressed." Gabby giggled, following Maxi's gaze. "That one goes on the block in January, with some really wonderful French Impressionist pieces we've taken on consignment. They like to hang some of the best ones here and there. If we ever did, God forbid, have a burglary, they figure the bandits would go right to the storerooms; it wouldn't occur to them to strip the stuff off the walls. Hide 'em under their noses, so to speak." Her hand suddenly flew to her mouth. "Oops! That's supposed to be a secret, and here I go telling the press!"

"Don't worry," Maxi said, laughing. "That information will never leave this room." She liked Gabby Modine immediately.

"Deal." Gabby smiled. "Now, how can I help you, Maxi?"

"Tell me everything you remember about Meg Davis, anything she might have said to you when she purchased that cross."

"To tell you the truth," Gabby said, "I thought she was on drugs. She didn't say much at all. As you know, her bid took the piece. Later, she came over to me to arrange to pick it up. I was concerned about the credit card she presented—it wasn't in her name—but when I checked with American Express it was valid, and she was listed as an authorized user."

"Did she chat at all, say why she wanted the cross, what she was going to do with it?" Maxi asked.

"You know, our typical auction patron is friendly, outgoing, *does* chat," Gabby remarked. "This woman was definitely not a schmoozer."

"Is there *anything* else you can tell me about her?"

"No . . . Wait, there *is* one thing that might help," Gabby said, brightening. "Remy Germain, the artist, came in after you'd left with your crew. She had done a few of the pieces in Nathanson's private collection, and she bought a couple of her paintings back that night. Anyway, I do remember that she had her sketch pad out, and she was sketching this and that. And I specifically remember her sketching Meg Davis while I was processing her purchase."

Maxi got up, thanked her, and took a last, loving look at the Bonnard. "What a treat, working in a room with *this* for inspiration," she said, her eyes lingering on the lush reds and oranges accenting the country scene. "The Channel Six concept of inspiring art on the newsroom walls is our courtroom artist's renditions of infamous killers," she remarked, as Gabby walked her back out to the front doors.

"You know," Gabby confided as she was leaving, "I get the chills every time I think that I held that cross in my hands, and now it's been used to kill people so savagely. I hope you find it, but please be careful."

Heading east down Wilshire Boulevard, Maxi called the Remy Germain Studio on Melrose Place in West Hollywood. Ms. Germain was in, a receptionist said, and she put the call through. Maxi asked about the sketches, and the artist graciously told her to come on over and she would get them out for her to look at. By the time Maxi clicked off her phone she was at the address.

Several of the artist's *avant* paintings were displayed in a small front showroom. The receptionist sat behind a desk, attending to customers and answering phones. She recognized Maxi, and took her back into the huge expanse of Remy Germain's working studio.

The artist was sitting on a stool in front of an easel, brushes in hand, dabbing at a canvas that depicted a man and a woman standing beside a jewel-like swimming pool, holding hands and unabashedly undressing each other with their eyes.

"You're way too fast for me," Remy exclaimed, glancing over her shoulder at Maxi in the doorway. She turned back to the work in progress, added a few touches that couldn't wait, then got up and extended a hand. "This is my heterosexual answer to Hockney," the artist offered with a mischievous grin, tilting her head toward the painting. Remy was slight, but the energy that was packed into her ninety-something pounds fired up the room. She was sunny, with finely chiseled features and fair skin framed by a wealth of ash brown hair. "You flew here by rocket?" she asked.

"I was just around the corner when I called." Maxi smiled, appreciating the profusion of warmth and cheer this woman exuded.

The small storefront showroom that Maxi had passed so many times along that short, artsy stretch of Melrose Place belied the enormous space within, where the artist worked. The walls were painted Grecian white, and were hung with a profusion of her colorful canvases. A couple of collectors were quietly browsing.

"Let me find those auction sketches for you," Remy said.

Maxi followed her to a bank of brightly colored file cases stacked in an alcove at the far end of the studio. Remy opened a drawer marked SKETCH PADS and pulled one of them out.

"You are really organized," Maxi marveled.

"Have to be," Remy said, laughing. "There's such chaos in my head that if I don't have order in my environment I can't work with any semblance of sanity."

She brought the eleven-by-fourteen-inch sketch pad over to a drafting table, pulled out a couple of tall stools, and switched on a panel of lights that lit up the space. She and Maxi settled on the stools, and Remy leafed through the pages.

"I have a few sketches of Meg Davis. Frankly, she was the most interesting subject at the auction, I thought. Poor woman"—she frowned—"you couldn't miss how troubled she was." She pointed to pencil drawings of Meg Davis in various poses, looking glazed, transfixed.

"Here she is with her friend," Remy said, showing a sketch of Meg doing business at a cloth-covered table, behind which sat a pleasant-looking young woman with a mop of curly hair, unmistakably Gabby Modine. Standing off to the side of Meg Davis was the figure of another woman, seeming to watch her intently.

"Who's the friend?" Maxi asked, studying the sketch.

"I don't know; someone she was with," Remy said. "What particularly struck me is how much alike they seemed. Alike, and both totally out of place there."

"What do you mean?"

"Well, look at the two of them in reference to each other," Remy responded, waving a hand from one to the other on the paper. "Both are tall, almost painfully thin, but more than thin, they're frail. Not healthy-looking. And decidedly out of place in this world of wealthy Westsiders, the usual types who frequent these high-end auctions. See how disoriented these two look?"

Remy showed her more sketches of both the women together. Maxi focused on the dark-haired woman in the cropped black leather jacket and torn jeans. Remy had captured the spacey demeanor she spoke of, but Maxi also saw anger and contempt in the angular face, the defiant tilt of the head.

"What did they do after Meg Davis paid for the cross, did you notice?" she asked the artist.

"Yes," Remy answered. "They both hustled out of there. And I must confess that my voyeuristic impulses compelled me to watch them out the door. Evidently they'd come separately, because Meg Davis's car was brought up first, and she waited until the other woman's car came. Then one followed the other out. There was something odd about their relationship."

Maxi perceived how Remy Germain's artist's eyes could see so much more than the ordinary observer. "Will you do anything with these sketches?" she asked her.

"I started a painting of Meg Davis," the artist responded. "I was moved to do it after I was so taken by her at the auction, and thanks to your news story that night, when I came to realize the significance to her of the piece she'd purchased, the cross that was a symbol in the movie she'd starred in as a child. I call my painting *Lost Girl*. I'll show you, if you'd like."

"I would, thanks," Maxi said. "Remy, would you let me take this sketch pad with me for just a day or two? I'd like to try to find out who this other woman is, find out if she has any idea what happened to that cross."

"How about if I make you copies of the sketches you want?"

"That'd be great," Maxi said.

Remy called her assistant into the studio and asked her to run off the copies, then she took Maxi over to a canvas leaning against a wall. It was an amplification of the sketch of Meg Davis claiming her purchase at the auction desk, her soulful eyes staring fixedly ahead.

"I doubt that I'll finish it now," Remy murmured, and she involuntarily shivered. "In light of all that's happened since, it seems exploitive. Maybe someday I'll fill in that tragic face," she said, "if those eyes are still haunting me."

43

It was the day before Halloween. Richard Winningham and his crew were on their way to The Carousel on Melrose, the largest and best-known costume shop in the city. It would be teeming with kids and their moms, dads, nannies, and pals, picking out costumes, trying them on, choosing accessories, buying trick-or-treat bags, makeup kits, wigs, glitter, glue, and what have you.

As a crime reporter, it sickened Richard to have to report after Halloween stories of youngsters biting into razor blades in cupcakes, or becoming ill from poisoned cookies, or being struck by cars. This season he decided to do a Halloween piece *before* the fact, to warn parents not to let their little ones go out alone, not to let them nibble on their goodies before adults had a chance to sort through them, and not to let them eat anything that wasn't prepackaged and properly sealed.

His cameraman, Greg Ross, was acting like a kid himself in the huge emporium, trying on masks, scaring little kids and getting them to giggle. The colorful, festive scene would make good visuals, Richard knew.

As Greg was laying out his shots, Richard was laying advice on some of the kids. To a little girl in an Olympic gymnast outfit, "You'll be cold in that costume tomorrow night, be sure you wear a sweater under it," and to a boy in an oversize bat mask, "Have your mom make the eye slits bigger so you'll be able to *see* in that."

"Hey, when are you going to have kids of your own?" Greg asked him. "You know, you're getting up there, old man."

"I have *you* to bring up," Richard countered. Greg was looking up at him through the eyes of a huge, hairy lion's head.

"Better get *on* it, buddy," Greg tossed back, "before you're so ancient you can't remember your little tykes' names." Richard took a swipe at him but missed, as Greg dropped to all fours and did his lion act for a couple of five-year-olds. He roared, and they shrieked.

Greg shot B-roll inside the shop, lots of little faces in scary masks, and cute kiddies modeling the gamut of costumes. Then he and Richard took the gear out front to do a stand-up. While Greg rolled, Richard stood on the sidewalk with a gang of kids around him, witches and Spidermen, princesses and ghosts, several Barney Rubbles, two kids dressed up as one horse. Looking straight into the camera, he ticked off his warnings, one by one, hoping parents would heed them.

As he was finishing, Maxi Poole pulled up to the curb in her black Corvette. "Hey, that looks like fun," she called out the window. Richard lit up. He told the kids to stay put on the sidewalk, and he walked around to the driver's side of her car.

"Hi. What brings you down here?" he asked.

Maxi was smiling, but he could see the strain of the past few harrowing days behind her eyes. "I just left Remy Germain's art studio down the street," she said. "I found out that she was at the auction of Jack's things, and she happened to make some sketches of Meg Davis buying that cross." She showed Richard the copies of Remy's sketches.

"Do they tell you anything?" he questioned, leafing through them.

"Only that Meg Davis was there with a friend." She pointed

out the sketches of the two women together. "I'm on my way back to Sotheby's now to see if they can identify this other woman. Maybe I can contact her and see if she knows anything." Richard looked dubious.

"Oh, I know it's probably a wild-goose chase," Maxi conceded, "but I can't just do nothing." Then she half whispered, "I'm so scared."

"Where are you staying tonight?" he asked.

"I don't know. I can't stay at home. Alison Pollock offered me a suite at the Beverly Hills Hotel, but with Janet Orson's murder there last night, that feels eerie. . . ."

"Stay at my place," Richard offered. "Hell, you almost know how to work the shower." He grinned, trying to lighten her mood.

"Thanks," she said. "Maybe I'll take you up on that, just for tonight, till I figure out what to do. I can't stay with Debra; she's not any safer than I am—"

The kids were jumping up and down on the sidewalk now, shouting, "Mr. Winningham, come on, Mr. Winningham, we want to be on television, Mr. Winningham!" Maxi looked toward the youngsters, and suddenly the color drained from her face. She was staring up at the shop window.

"What is it?" Richard demanded.

"That . . . that *costume!*" she said, pointing to a mannequin dressed as Dracula, its arms extended, displaying a wide black double cape. Richard followed her gaze to the black-clad figure. "That's what my intruder wore," Maxi whispered.

He turned back to face Maxi. He was afraid the accumulated stress of the last weeks might be wreaking havoc with her imagination. "What makes you think so?" he asked gently.

"The . . . the seams. The double-stitched seams in red thread," she breathed, her eyes still locked on the black costume. "I was closer to it than this, at home in my study. I'm sure—"

Richard turned to take another look. The long, wide sleeves, the mandarin neckline, the buttonholes, the seams, and the flowing hemline of the garment were all edged in thick, bright red stitching on the black fabric. The shop owner he interviewed told him that the new kids' movie about Dracula that had recently come out was making the costume his biggest seller this Halloween.

"I'll quiz the owner about his 'Dracula' customers, and I'll call some of the other costume shops in town, see if anything comes of it," he said to Maxi. "You're going back to the auction house?"

"Yes. And I'm going to look in on Yukon on the way. He's right around the corner on Robertson."

"I know, remember?" Richard smiled. "Tell him I'll come by on Saturday and watch the Laker game with him."

"Thanks, Richard—you cheer me up. Are you going back to the station when you're through here?"

"Yes—I have to edit this piece for the Four."

"Do me a favor? Take these phone records in and have one of the editorial assistants check them against the crisscross—they're all the calls Janet Orson made from the Beverly Hills Hotel." She handed Richard the printouts that Alison Pollock had given her.

"Sure thing—they'll be on your desk when you get in."

"Great. See you back in the newsroom."

"Don't forget, you can bunk at my place—I actually *like* sleeping on my leather couch." He smiled. "And Maxi? Be careful."

44

The surgery was just yesterday," Dr. Sullivan told Maxi. He was trying to be reassuring. He said her dog had come through his massive assault as well as could be expected, he seemed to be gaining a little strength, but the vet would not promise her that Yukon was going to make it. "Give it time. Don't be looking for miracles," he said.

But Maxi wanted miracles. She was thirty-two, she hadn't even had a date since her divorce from Jack Nathanson, she had no children, and her parents lived on the other side of the country. Five-year-old Yukon was her baby, her roommate, and the sum total of her family in California.

When she'd stopped in at the animal hospital to see him, she was horrified. Clinic staffers had been telling her on the phone that he was responding well. She had not been prepared for his terribly debilitated condition. She'd found Yukon still lying on the floor of his small kennel, his neck and chest bound up in blood-tinged bandages, his breaths coming in raspy, uneven gasps. His coat was dry and matted, and he'd lost an alarming amount of weight. It broke her heart.

"I guess I *was* expecting miracles, old boy," she said to him as she gently stroked his head. Beyond the fact that she loved him so much, it seemed that Yukon teetering on the edge of death symbolized the fragile state of her whole world as each new horror piled up upon the last. She wouldn't feel safe again until the killer was caught, and all her instincts told her that time was running out.

For the second time that morning, Maxi pulled into the parking lot at Sotheby's. At the reception desk, she asked for Gabby Modine.

"Go on in, Ms. Poole," Lenore Baines told her. "I'll let her know you're here."

Maxi found Gabby and told her what she'd learned, that Meg Davis had been with someone at the auction. She spread Remy Germain's sketches across her antique desk. Gabby put on her glasses and studied them, as Maxi pointed out Meg Davis's raven-haired friend. "Do you know who this woman is, Gabby?"

"Yes . . . I remember her, and somebody mentioned who she was. Let me think. . . ." After a long moment, she scooped up the sketches and took Maxi by the hand. "Come with me," she said.

Gabby led her into another office across the hall and introduced her to Justeen Luggio, who had worked the door on Saturday, she said. Gabby showed her the sketches. "Sure," Justeen said. "She's that disc jockey. Wait a sec; let me look at the patron list."

Justeen went over to a file cabinet and pulled out the guest register for the Nathanson auction. Running her finger down a ledger, she stopped at a name. "Here's your mystery woman," Justeen said. "Zahna Cole, KBIS Radio."

Maxi pulled her cell phone out of her purse and dialed Information for KBIS in Culver City. Connected to the disc jockey's line, she heard a recorded message: "Your call is being answered by Audix. Zahna Cole is not available. If you'd like to leave a message, please record at the tone."

Maxi punched the END button. A call from the press might

put the woman off. She'd probably think Channel Six was doing a story on Meg Davis and wanted a friend's comments on her suicide. She decided to drive over to the station.

On the way, she called Debra. She was sure that, like herself, Debra had to be panicked after hearing the news about Janet Orson's murder last night. Debra picked up immediately.

"God, Maxi," she shrieked into the phone, "what the hell is going on? Is some maniac after all the bastard's wives? Like it's *our* fault he was such a prick?"

"I have no idea, Debra, but I think you'd better get some security over there," Maxi responded.

"I've already done that. I had Gavin De Becker put a twenty-four-hour guard service in place. There's a huge bozo walking around my house right now with a gun. Jesus, Max, it's like being in prison."

"How's Gia?" Maxi asked. Debra told her about Gia getting expelled from school the day before. Bessie was in the kitchen right now carving Halloween pumpkins with her, she said, like she was on vacation. Debra didn't know whether to punish her or give her extra love and attention.

"Her shrink says just act normal, and enroll her in public school. Act normal!" Debra scoffed. "I don't *remember* normal."

"I don't either. How are you holding up?"

"I'm holding up. What choice do I have? I was offered a movie yesterday, a good part, in the new John Grisham film. The producer must have been living on the planet Jupiter for the last month—he didn't even express concern that it could be a slight production problem if I turned up dead or behind bars before we finished. God, I'm so broke, I would *love* to have that part."

"How did you leave it?"

"I told him to send the script over, give me a few days to read it. I'll stall him as long as I can. Maxi, what do you know? Anything?"

Maxi told her about her chase around town that morning to

try to find out something about the *Black Sabbat* cross and where it went.

"Good Lord, Maxi, that's *crazy!* You could get hurt. Stay out of it," Debra implored.

"I can't—I'm terrified, too. The worst thing I can do is sit around and wait."

"Are you getting some protection at *your* place?"

"No . . . but I'm not going to be staying there. You have Gia and Bessie, Deb. I'm totally alone. Yukon is still in the animal hospital, and when he gets home, he'll be ailing. Even with a guard patrolling outside, I'd be a wreck."

"Do you want to stay here?" Debra asked halfheartedly. Instinctively, they both knew that was a bad idea.

"I might stay at Richard Winningham's place tonight, then figure out what I should do from there. There's no point checking in to a hotel because Yuke will be getting out of the hospital soon. The vet says if there's no infection, maybe he'll release him on Friday." She didn't tell Debra that Yukon was fighting for his life. Maxi had always believed that if you expect the best, if you focus on the positive, you'll get it.

"Richard Winningham, your new crime reporter?" Debra asked. "He's a stud! What's *that* about?" Maxi had to laugh. That was Debra. Even in the most horrendous of circumstances, Debra was up for the dish. Maxi explained that Richard was just being a friend.

"Oh, *sure!* If he's just a friend, darling, send him over here. I could sure use a big, strong, gorgeous *friend* around!"

Maxi smiled. Debra practiced her own version of positive thinking. That's why she was a survivor. "You've got a guard outside, and I'm sure the neighbors are all looking out for you," Maxi said, trying to sound as cheerful as Debra did.

"Well, I'll be thinking about you with Mr. Fab tonight." Then, in a serious tone, she added, "Really, that's good, Maxi. At least I won't have to worry about you being alone."

"And it sounds like you've got things under control—I won't worry about you, either," Maxi ventured. But both friends knew they wouldn't stop worrying about the other until this insanity was resolved. They promised to talk later that night, and rang off just before Maxi reached the studios of KBIS-FM in Culver City.

A uniformed guard sat behind a counter in the lobby. Maxi told him she was there to see Zahna Cole, and she showed the guard her press pass. He looked at her picture, then up at Maxi. "Yeah, you *are* Maxi Poole." He grinned. "My wife and I watch your news every night—I get home just in time."

"Thank you, and thank your wife for me. Is Ms. Cole here?"

"I think she's on vacation," he told her. "But go in and see Edie, the program director's assistant—she's in charge of schedules. Down the hall, first right, and you'll see her office, marked *Edie Washington*." He buzzed Maxi through the security door.

Edie, a cheerful, rotund black woman of fifty-something, sat behind a desk that was heaped with what looked to be well-organized clutter. She looked up at Maxi and broke into a wide grin. "You're that newswoman, Maxi Poole." She beamed. "You coming to work here, honey? This joint could *use* some class!"

Maxi laughed. She told her she was looking for Zahna Cole. Zahna was on vacation, Edie said. Maxi asked if she knew where the disc jockey had gone.

"Oh, Zahna never goes anywhere," the woman offered. "I keep telling her she should, but she usually just stays home, kicks back, and gets lost for a while."

"How long will she be out?"

"All this week, and I think I've got her off next week, too. I've got a pile of mail to send out to her," the woman said, indicating a stack on her desk. "Zahna gets mail from all the late-night crazies. I'll check and see when she's due back."

Edie swiveled her chair around, and as Maxi watched, she brought up a screen on her computer with the header ARTISTS'

SCHEDULES. While Edie perused the file, Maxi glanced down at the stack of mail addressed to the DJ. Beside it was a large manila envelope with a typewritten address label in place:

Ms. Zahna Cole
6420 Sumac Drive
Sherman Oaks CA 91405

Maxi committed the address to memory. Sherman Oaks was in the San Fernando Valley, just east of the San Diego Freeway. It was on her way to work. On the drive back to Channel Six, she would stop by and see if she could catch Zahna Cole at home.

"Yup, she's off next week, too," Edie said. She turned back to Maxi. "Want me to give her a message for you?"

"No." Maxi smiled. "I won't bother her while she's on vacation. I'll call her when she gets back. Thanks, Edie."

Back in her car, Maxi checked her Thomas Guide and located Sumac Drive in Sherman Oaks. If she caught Zahna Cole at home, she could spare a few minutes to chat with her before she had to get to work.

45

Zahna stood in front of the glass cases displaying rings, watches, gold, diamonds, pearls. She had brought Janet Orson's pricey necklaces to the wholesale jewelry district, to a place called Estate Gems, one of hundreds of jewelry vendors in this busy section of downtown L.A. She'd pulled the name out of the Yellow Pages; the ad said they bought jewelry. She was the only customer in the small, shabby showroom on this Wednesday afternoon. A Mr. George Pasha had taken the pieces in the back, to appraise them, he said.

He could be calling the police, she knew, but the odds were with her. When news of the murder of Janet Orson broke, there had been no mention of jewelry missing. In fact, they reported that there was no indication of robbery. Still, you never knew. Often, the authorities concealed certain facts when they put a story out, she'd heard, to trip up the suspects—Mr. Pasha might know that.

Another man, slight, stooped, balding, in a shiny suit and wire-rimmed glasses, came out from the back and went over to one of the far showcases, took out a brooch and examined it with a jeweler's loupe, then put it back, but Zahna sensed that his real mission was to examine *her*. She could feel him surreptitiously looking her over. Her inclination was to flee, but that Pasha guy had the jewelry.

The man passed by her on the other side of the showcases and nodded somberly, then disappeared into the back. How the hell did they appraise jewelry, anyway—did they have machines that told how much gemstones were worth? And how could she trust them? Even as that thought occurred to her, Zahna caught the irony in it—who was *she* not to trust someone? Obviously they'd offer her much less than the pieces were worth, but she was hardly in a position to haggle.

She was cruising on cocaine and adrenaline, hadn't slept at all last night, never even went to bed. She'd spent every waking minute charting her own personal witness-protection program.

This would be her last errand before she skipped the country. By the time anyone figured out that the jewels had been taken, then maybe traced them to this small shop on the sixth floor of an old downtown building, she'd be in Mexico.

Her plan was all laid out. When she got back to her house she would burn her passport, her driver's license, and all other identification. She would carry only the new picture ID with her new name that she'd had made this morning at a local computer print shop. She would throw some things in a bag, then drive out to LAX, abandon her old, battered heap in one of the airport lots, grab a cab to the Greyhound bus station downtown, put her money on the counter, no questions asked, no names needed, and buy a bus ticket to San Diego. There, she would hop the light rail shuttle to the Mexican border and walk over the bridge into Tijuana, along with the hundreds of Americans and Mexicans who crossed back and forth every day, no papers needed, just a smile for the INS agents and the Mexican border patrol guards on the other side. In TJ, she'd take a cab to Generali Rodriguez Airport. At the Aeromexico counter, she'd buy a one-way ticket on the midnight flight to Mexico City under her new name, Carla Valdez.

Zahna could pass for Mexican, she figured—she had olive skin, dark eyes, dark hair. She'd get a room, find a job in that overcrowded, bustling city, perhaps in a shop, and reestablish herself under the identity of a Mexican woman. She spoke some Spanish—she would buy audiotapes and learn the language fluently, and she would become more proficient as she heard it spoken every day. She would apply for a Mexican driver's license, credit cards, insurance, everything in the name of Carla Valdez. In time she'd find a small apartment, and get a night job singing in one of the city's hundreds of clubs.

Mr. Pasha came out, carrying the pearl choker and the emerald-and-diamond necklace. He placed a black velvet tray on top of the glass case in front of her, then set the pieces on it. With his fingers still on the jewelry, he looked up at her intently. "Where did you say you got these, Miss . . . ?" he asked. She hadn't said, nor had she given him her name.

"Mrs. Williamson," she said. "Mrs. John Williamson. They were my mother's. She's passed away, and they're not something I would wear."

"But they're brand-new, hardly been worn."

"That's true," she told Pasha, forcing a smile. "My mother kept them in the safe and rarely wore them. It's time someone got some use out of them—I never would."

She had dressed conservatively in a gray light wool suit, a white blouse with a flared jabot tied primly at her throat, and black low-heeled pumps.

"Well, Mrs., ahh, Williamson," Pasha said, "I'm prepared to give you five thousand dollars for this one. . . ." He was fingering the diamond-and-emerald piece. "And twenty-two hundred for the other. Is that acceptable?"

"Oh, they're worth *much* more than that," Zahna said. Actually, she had no idea what they were worth, but her instincts told her not to pounce on the first deal he offered.

"Yes, they're worth more," Mr. Pasha said, "but these pieces won't be easy to sell, and we have to make a profit. It's up to you. Do you want to think about it and come back?"

"No," she said evenly, "I'll take it."

"Fine. I'll give you a receipt for the merchandise, and you can come by and pick up your check tomorrow."

"That's not possible," Zahna stated unequivocally. "I have to have the cash, now."

"But it's our policy to have a second appraisal made by a colleague outside the shop."

She wondered if it wasn't really their policy to clear such merchandise with the police, so the cops wouldn't come around confiscating it after the store had laid out the bread. She wouldn't mention that she was leaving town—that would certainly make him suspicious, if he wasn't already. She remembered a recent news story involving a ring of merchants operating here in the downtown jewelry district. A gang of them were sent to prison, convicted on multiple charges, including receiving stolen goods and laundering major drug money. The LAPD was now closely monitoring these operations for illegal activity, and the shop owners knew it. Pasha still said nothing; he looked to be sizing up the situation.

In an instant of resolve, she reached for the pieces. "I'll just take them somewhere else," she snapped.

"Wait just a moment," he checked her, again picking up the two necklaces. "I'll talk to my associate." He disappeared through the back door, carrying the goods.

Oh Jesus, she thought, *I've gotta get the fuck out of here*. But even though there were hundreds of jewelry shops in these several blocks, entire buildings filled with them, she didn't have time to run around peddling this stuff. And she knew that if she put them in her suitcase and tried to sell them in Mexico, they'd bring just a few hundred dollars. Or worse, they'd be stolen from her.

She resisted the urge to bolt and run. Then Pasha and his

goon would know for sure that the jewelry was stolen, and with the heat still on down here, they probably wouldn't take a chance on moving it. They'd call the cops immediately, and she'd probably get nailed before she made it out of the building. She shouldn't have tried this, but now it was too late.

Mr. Pasha came out front again, with the jewelry in hand. The weasel she'd seen earlier came out behind him and stood at his side. Pasha made no attempt to introduce him. To her surprise, he said, "We'll give you cash, right now. But under these circumstances, we can't give you the amount that we previously discussed." He took an envelope out of his pocket. "Here is fifty-five hundred dollars in hundred-dollar bills," he said, hanging on to the jewelry and placing the envelope on the velvet tray. And again he intoned, "It's up to you."

She snatched the envelope, and without pausing to count the money, she turned and left. *Jesus, they're on to me,* she thought. Bypassing the ancient elevator, she raced the six flights down the narrow stairwell, stuffing the envelope into her shoulder bag as she ran. She burst out the front doors of the building into the harsh sunlight of Hill Street, and hustled down the sidewalk toward Fifth Street where she'd parked her car.

Rounding the corner, she stopped in her tracks. An LAPD patrol car, lights flashing, was double-parked beside her beat-up Volkswagen Rabbit, blocking her exit, and two uniformed policemen were standing next to it on the sidewalk.

46

Alison Pollock sat at the ornate Georgian desk in her office at the Beverly Hills Hotel, trying to get a cup of tea down. She'd been able to think of little else but the heinous murder discovered that morning. Paul Farrento, the manager on duty last night, had called her at home at 6:15 after one of the room service waiters walked in on the body. Alison had dressed hurriedly and rushed to the hotel.

Farrento had already called the Beverly Hills police. They'd responded in minutes, and were at the bungalow when Alison got there. Investigators from the sheriff's department had been called in, Detectives Cabello and Johnson. They talked to her at length—they wanted to know if she'd been aware of any unusual behavior by any of her staff.

In fact, most of her employees were in shock, from the head chef to the pool attendants to the chambermaids—they were operating under a cloud of gloom today. Even the guests seemed to her a bit subdued when Alison walked through the lobby and promenade areas—the murder was all over the news.

Alison thought about Janet Orson. She couldn't shake the feeling there was something she was missing. They'd had a welcoming drink on Sunday afternoon, Janet, Alan Bronstein from

Monogram, who'd helped Janet with her move that day, and Alison, along with her fifteen-year-old granddaughter Davina who was spending the weekend with her. They all sat in a booth in the Polo Lounge, and Janet had mentioned how proud Ali must be of this venerable old hotel.

"Oh, yes, I'm proud," Alison had said. "These walls have seen the biggest and the best of Hollywood." She'd told them that the hotel was the very first structure built in Beverly Hills, and how back then it was the only building on Sunset Boulevard between there and the Pacific Ocean. And what had Janet responded? Something that Alison had thought was odd at the time, but she couldn't remember offhand.

The killer had clearly known exactly where to find Janet, so it had to be either someone she knew, or someone who had been able to find out what unit she was staying in. It weighed heavily on Alison's mind that an employee might have thoughtlessly given the killer Janet Orson's bungalow number.

She got up and went out to the switchboard. Treva Jones was working the day shift. The young woman looked up at Alison soberly, the murder on her mind, too. Alison asked her if she could remember anyone asking for Janet Orson's room number.

"You know we would never give out that information, Mrs. Pollock," Treva said.

"Of course I know you wouldn't," Alison assured her. "But by any chance, did anyone try to get the bungalow number from you? Can you remember?" she persisted.

Treva thought for a minute. "Yes," she said then. "There was a woman who was especially insistent. She said she had an appointment with Ms. Orson on Wednesday, and she needed to know what room to go to. I told her to just come to the front desk, and we'd call Ms. Orson, then direct her."

"Do you remember her name?" Alison asked.

"No, I'm sorry; we're answering these phones all day long—"

Alison made her promise to tell her immediately if she remembered anything more about that caller. Also, she asked Treva to question the other two women on the board to find out whether they had taken any calls for Janet Orson that were at all out of the ordinary.

The woman had an appointment with Janet on Wednesday? Alison thought as she left the room. *That's today.* The detectives had asked Alison to let them know if she thought of anything—she would tell them about that call that Treva took. In their search of the bungalow, they probably found Janet's datebook. Maybe her Wednesday appointments would provide a clue.

She headed up the stairs to the lobby to see if things were under control at the front desk, and whether the murder had caused many cancellations. She was sure there would be some. Up on the street level, the media were swarming everywhere. They were set up all over the grounds, they were congregating in the lobby with tons of equipment, and they were camped out behind the yellow crime-scene tape around bungalow 16. Usually, Alison had an excellent rapport with the press. She dealt with them often because of the many celebrities who stayed at the hotel. Today, they were a nightmare. She had declined to grant any interviews; she was bent on just staying out of their way.

Suddenly it hit her. *The media!* That was what Janet's reaction to Alison's pride in the hotel had been about. Janet had responded that everyone loved the Beverly Hills Hotel, and she mentioned that a woman who was going to interview her this week had begged to do it here instead of at Janet's office because she loved the Beverly Hills Hotel, she'd said. And now Alison remembered what had struck her as odd. The interview was to be for *radio*. Not television, where the setting mattered, not print, where there was a high priority on getting good photos. Radio! Where it would sound exactly the same, no matter *where* they did it. Yet she had insisted on doing the interview at the hotel, presumably in Janet Orson's bungalow.

Alison couldn't remember the woman's name, but she did remember that when Janet mentioned it, Davina piped up that she and her friends listened to her show all the time. "She's *bad!*" Davina had exclaimed. And when the adults looked at her for an explanation, she told them *bad* means *good*. "She disses everything," Davina offered by way of clarification, and everybody laughed when the teenager had to explain what *that* meant.

Alison hurried back downstairs to her office. She called Maxi at Channel Six, and got her voice mail. Rather than leave a message, she called back and asked for producer Wendy Harris. Wendy always knew where Maxi was, even if she was on the other side of the world.

Wendy came on the line. "Maxi's chasing around town trying to find out *anything* about Janet Orson's murder," she said. "She told me she was going to try to stop by and see you."

"Yes, she was here," Alison said. "And now I think I might have something for her. Will you tell her to call me as soon as she surfaces?"

"I sure will," Wendy said. "Meantime, I'll try her cell phone. If you don't hear from her, she'll be back here at the station at least by four for the Six O'clock News."

It was almost 3:30. Alison picked up Detective Mike Cabello's card on her desk and dialed the number.

"Cabello," he barked into the phone. She told him about the woman who had tried to get Janet Orson's room number from the hotel switchboard operator yesterday. And about Janet saying that a woman was going to interview her for a radio program today, and had insisted on doing it at the hotel instead of at Janet's office. She suggested that they look carefully at Janet Orson's appointment schedule for today. Maybe it was the same woman. And maybe the woman *did* find out which unit Janet was in. And waited for her to come back last night.

47

Zahna stopped on the sidewalk, clutching her shoulder bag with the fifty-five hundred-dollar bills inside. About twenty yards away, one of the LAPD officers was standing behind her car, examining her license plate and writing something down. Crack cocaine had her mind racing and her heart speeding. The cops hadn't seen her yet. *Be cool*, she told herself. Then she spied a tow truck hitching up to a car parked several vehicles behind hers.

Abruptly, she turned and started walking in the other direction. The traffic sign posted on the corner of Fifth Street read: NO PARKING AFTER 3:30 P.M. Zahna glanced at her watch; it was 3:39. She relaxed. The two policemen were among the corps ticketing vehicles parked on the downtown streets after the cutoff time, and the tow truck was one of many working the afternoon rush hour, hauling illegally parked cars out of the way of the oncoming traffic. It was an everyday happening at the start of the afternoon commute. She'd been caught in it once, and the ticket had cost her $85, plus another $160 to get her car out of hock from the garage they towed it to.

Zahna walked swiftly back down Hill Street, ducked through Pershing Square across to Olive, then doubled back to Fifth and approached her car from the opposite direction. Just as she'd hoped, the cops had moved ahead to the next offending vehicles, and the tow truck had moved off with its haul. She zipped down the street, her keys in hand, snatched the ticket off her windshield, jumped in her car, and peeled off.

The whole exercise exhilarated her. She felt empowered as she crumpled up the parking ticket and threw it on the floor. "So long, cops," she said out loud, as she rolled down Fifth Street toward the Hollywood Freeway. So long, L.A., and good riddance.

She had been knocking around this town for a lot of years, and she'd come to a stone-cold dead end. She had a nowhere job, she lived in a dump, she drove a wreck, she had no friends, no love life, no money, no prospects. That all could have changed, *should* have changed with Jack Nathanson. They were good together, had been from the start. She was the only woman who could give him what he needed—hadn't he told her that a hundred times? She was the one he kept coming back to. Yet she was the only one of his women who had ended up with nothing. Not even an acknowledgment that she existed.

She'd gone to his funeral, couldn't stay away. She used her station ID to get in, put on a hat and horn-rimmed glasses, pretended she was a reporter. The transparent casket freaked her out—for a minute she thought she was having a drug hallucination, seeing him lying there with that smug smirk on his face. How typical of him, even dead. Stifling the urge to scream at him, she turned away, and there stood the widow. She pulled out the pad and pencil she'd brought to pass herself off as press, and actually started to interview her. Zahna had no idea why she did that, or what she'd expected; she only knew that it made her feel . . . like *nothing*. Nobody.

They were all there, his wives, driving their expensive cars or riding in limos, dressed in their fancy clothes, talking to each other, taking their bows, sucking up everybody's sympathy. Janet Orson, the grieving widow; Debra Angelo, the madonna with child; Maxi Poole, the big-deal newswoman. His real love, his Zahna, was there, but not one person said hello, or said they were sorry, they hoped she was holding up all right. Nothing. That's what she had to show for giving him three years of her life: exactly nothing. At least Monica Lewinsky had her fifteen minutes and some bucks in the bank.

Saturday, she did some crack and went to the auction. She'd found herself in an alien world again. Nobody knew that she was Jack's real love. Janet Orson walked around with her nose in the air. Maxi Poole did a news story, acting like she owned the world. Debra Angelo didn't even bother to show up, even though all the money was going to her kid, according to the news reports. Everybody was talking about Jack Nathanson. But she, the woman he loved more than any of them and all of them, couldn't say a word.

She hooked up with that weirdo, the actress who bought the cross. God knows what *she* was on—the woman was out of it. But Zahna had sensed a kinship, had felt that she could talk to her, share Jack Nathanson stories. She'd connected with her, offered her pot, followed her out to the beach. And she was staggered when Meg Davis led her right to Debra Angelo's house, then proceeded to babble about saving the kid's soul. What the hell was *that* about? A nutcase.

She got stoned again on Sunday, with nothing to do and nobody to do it with, as usual, so she drove back out to the beach. And sure enough, there was Ms. Crazo again, just as she said she'd be, guarding the house, or casting a spell, or whatever the hell she thought she was doing.

Zahna got off watching *her* watch *them* for a while, then, to her amazement, Maxi Poole, wife number two, came over and took Meg Davis by the hand and brought her up to see Debra Angelo, wife number one. This was better than watching *Saturday Night Live*! Meantime, Zahna noticed, the ditso had left her bag, her books, and that bizarre cross on her blanket.

Zahna ambled over and snatched the cross, then dashed to her car and raced home. That's when she got the idea to go over to Jack's house and see if she could find some of the things she'd given him, expensive gifts that she couldn't afford and was still paying off on her credit cards, like the Sony CD player and the antique gold pocket watch. Or the exorbitant black leather jacket he had admired in Bijan's window—it actually looked terrific on *her*. Now that Jack was dead, why should Janet Orson have her things? She would take them back.

And maybe she'd snatch that twenty-carat diamond engagement ring *People* magazine said Jack gave Janet, or the white ermine jacket she read he gave her at the glitzy birthday party he threw for her at The Palm. And other pricey baubles, things he should have given Zahna. Janet Orson had everything, and Zahna had nothing. She hadn't meant to kill anybody that night at his house. She just wanted . . . *something*.

For Jack had never given her anything significant. Cheap, sexy underwear, a bottle of perfume, a teddy bear. Guess he thought his scintillating presence was enough for her. But he gave his wives *everything*. Cars, furs, jewelry, exciting nights on the town in limousines, first-class trips abroad. She would read about it in the columns. And he gave them marriage. Legitimacy. But Zahna wasn't even good enough to introduce to his ex-wife once removed.

She'd always believed that he would come around to her eventually. He had made her think he would. He'd only married Janet Orson to jump-start his career, get the acting jobs she could throw his way. Everybody knew that. Once he was back on his feet he would drop Janet and marry his Zahna. For keeps.

But now he was dead, and she had nothing, only his picture cut out of the newspaper to remember him by. Early in their relationship, her engineer had snapped a photo of the two of them in the KBIS studio while she was on the air. She'd had it enlarged, put it in a silver frame from Cartier, and gave it to him as a gift. He took it, but he told her he hated having his picture taken, she was never to let that happen again. He said he loathed being photographed because the paparazzi were always snapping away, invading his privacy. Later she'd realized that he simply didn't want to be photographed with *her*. She was sure he'd accepted the gift just to get rid of the photograph. Now some other woman's picture was probably ensconced in the expensive frame.

Since the day he was murdered, she'd been growing more and more enraged. She stayed stoned night and day, on the job and off, and now it took more stuff just to get high. That's when she started adding crack to the mix of powder, pot, and pills. Rocks were faster and more intense, made her feel powerful. And Sunday night, when she was coked up, gripped with obsession and seething with rage, she'd headed over to Jack's house to snag some things that should have been hers.

She'd had copies of his keys for a long time. He used to have her drive with him to the airport. It was precious time they could spend together, he'd tell her. Oh sure! He just wanted taxi and delivery service, with a quick feel thrown in. He liked to have his cars serviced while he was away, so he'd pick her up, she'd ride with him out to LAX, then drive his car back into town and drop it off at the shop, and his mechanic would have somebody run her home.

A couple of times, while driving his car, she had taken his key ring into a hardware store and had his keys duplicated, when he was living with Maxi, and then Janet. She liked having her secret keys. She knew his alarm code; he'd used the same combination of numbers for twenty years, he'd mentioned once, for his home alarm system, his PINs, his computer passwords, to retrieve messages on his answering machines, wherever he needed digits. It was always 25225. On a Touch-Tone phone, those numbers spelled out the word "black," for his biggest hit picture, *Black Sabbat*. He would never forget his codes, he'd said. Neither would she.

On Sunday night, back at her place, she'd put three tens in a pipe and went flying. She could do anything! She changed into a black sweater and black jeans to suit her mood; then, as an afterthought, she'd put that nutty costume on over her clothes. Every Halloween, the gang at the station dressed up and got crazy, and she had picked up this year's rage, a Dracula outfit. With it, she'd pulled on a black hooded mask she'd bought, which covered her entire face except for her eyes.

And the cross! The *Black Sabbat* prop was the capper to her disguise. When she'd got home from the beach the night before and flipped on the TV, she saw footage of Meg Davis and her precious cross all over the news. Now Zahna had that cross, she had the keys and the alarm code, she was ripped out of her mind, and she was ready to do the caper, ready to break into Jack's house. She'd seen in the trades that Janet Orson planned to move out of the mansion and take up residence at the Beverly Hills Hotel that weekend. So she figured the house would be vacant. If the house looked empty, Zahna was going in, and if anybody saw her, she would just wave the cross and spout some witchcraft gibberish and run like hell.

There was no way anyone could recognize her, and even better, they were sure to think she was that freaked-out Meg Davis. Everyone who watched the news or read the papers knew that this was Meg Davis's cross, and it wouldn't be hard for them to believe that this was the kind of thing Meg Davis would do, because she was obviously somewhere on the planet Blippo!

The house was dark. She had tried several of the keys until one of them fit, and she'd eased her way in. She pounced on the alarm box and punched in the code numbers, no problem. It was all working; it felt so right. She had no trouble finding the master bedroom on the ground floor. She'd switched on a light and was having a party, rummaging around grabbing cash, jewelry, and anything expensive-looking that she could carry.

She just hadn't figured on Carlotta. Carlotta had always worked for Jack; with Jack gone, it hadn't occurred to Zahna that

Carlotta might still be there. Carlotta had surprised her in the doorway of the bedroom suite. Still, she never would have killed her. She waved the cross and chanted some shit, and was about to power right past her and scram out the door. But Carlotta's eyes popped and she shrieked, "My God, it's Zahna!"

When Jack lived alone in the Stone Canyon house, Zahna would sleep over sometimes, and hang out by the pool after he went to work. Carlotta used to call her Miss Zahna and bring her iced tea. And often, when she was on the air at night, Jack told her he would keep the radio on, piped through the speakers in the house, to listen to her music and her sexy rap. Zahna Cole's whiskey voice was distinctive—low and raspy and sultry. A good chunk of Los Angeles knew that voice. And Carlotta knew that voice. So Zahna had no choice that night.

48

Mrs. Ziggy sat stiffly at the redwood table on Debra's deck, barely containing her fury. Mrs. Ziggy was married to the actor who played the lead in the popular CBS children's series *Ziggy & Me*. Debra could never remember the couple's name; she always thought of them as the Ziggys. They lived a few houses up the beach, and Gia occasionally played with their eight-year-old daughter. The mother had rung her doorbell this afternoon, she said, because she had a very serious complaint about Gia. Debra had to bite her tongue to keep from telling her she'd have to take a number.

Now the woman was sitting across from her and spitting out that Gia had made her daughter take her panties down in the cabana on the beach at their house. Debra didn't register surprise, didn't protest, didn't ask questions, she just listened. She was beyond being shocked at anything Gia did.

"Then Gia told Samantha she wanted to *touch* it," Mrs. Ziggy was hissing. "She told my daughter that she thought they could make a *baby!* She said, 'My mom says a girl can do anything a boy can do,' and—"

"I'm so sorry, Mrs., aah," Debra murmured. "Gia has been under tremendous strain—"

"I'm sure she has"—the woman cut her off brusquely—"but I have to look out for *my* child's welfare. I just came here to tell you that Gia is not welcome at our home again."

With that she stood up, marched down the steps off the veranda onto the sand, and headed up the beach. Debra watched her go. She didn't have the energy to even try to smooth this one over.

Debra slumped forward in her chair, leaned her elbows on the table, and put her head in her hands. She despaired of ever having any forward movement in her life again. It seemed there would be no break in the case, no work for her, no social life, no leaving town, and Gia would just keep on getting worse. She felt like Sisyphus pushing a ten-ton boulder up a hill, forever. It wouldn't budge, but she couldn't stop pushing or it would roll backward and kill her.

She got up and walked back through the living room to the kitchen where Gia sat with Bessie, carving pumpkins and having a great old time. She looked at her daughter, so sweet and adorable; she had Bessie laughing and chatting and totally charmed. So like her father. A budding "Bad Seed" child with the face of a Botticelli angel, and invisible horns growing out of that mop of curly dark hair. A preadolescent sociopath in the making if Debra didn't nip it, and soon. But how? Should she hire round-the-clock shrinks, like the rent-a-cops who were now guarding her house?

She sat down at the kitchen table, and Gia and Bessie started talking at once, excited about showing off their jack-o'-lanterns in progress. How to handle this? Debra pondered, then decided it was too late in the day for subtleties. Just lay it out there.

"Please listen to me," she began. "Mrs. Ziggy, whatever her name is, that woman who was just here, has told me something dreadful about Gia, and we have to discuss it."

The activity stopped, the babbling ceased, the two smiling faces sobered, and two pairs of apprehensive eyes fixed themselves on hers. *Yup,* Debra thought, *that's the thing I do best lately—cheer down a room.* She blurted the whole sorry story. Bessie pushed her chair back and made embarrassed noises to excuse herself; Gia started crying.

"Stop that, Gia," Debra snapped. "Tell me, what exactly did you do to Samantha?"

"Nothing," her daughter whimpered. Bessie walked over to the sink, as Debra lowered her eyes and counted to ten. *Not her fault; they are just so much clay*—the refrain echoed through her mind. Jack had always allowed Gia to sit up with him and watch movies with explicit sex scenes. Expose the child to everything, he'd say, and she will learn to discriminate. She won't have to look for smut in porno magazines, or get distorted information on the streets.

Debra knew that was ridiculous, it was dangerous, but beyond her strong objections there was nothing she could do. They had joint custody, Gia was with Jack exactly half the time, and Debra had no control over what went on at his house.

It was like the gun issue. Debra had never allowed Gia to play with toy guns. She'd talked it over with Maxi when she was her stepmom, and Maxi said she definitely agreed. Later, Maxi told Debra that Jack did *not* agree, and try as she might, she couldn't persuade him otherwise. Jack not only bought Gia toy guns, he would take her to the firing range and let her shoot *real* guns. Of course it was against the law to let minors handle firearms, but Jack was a major movie star, the owner of the gun club was his pal, and a clique of the good-old-boy members who hung out there got a kick out of his angelic little girl actually shooting a Colt .45. So they cheered her on, and Gia loved the attention, and she developed a huge fascination for guns.

And now she had turned into a ten-year-old pervert, Debra fumed. She had to find the key that would turn it all off, that would halt the decline and fall of the soul of Gia Nathanson.

She'd thought it would get easier after she was no longer in the grip of her father's magnetic influence, but for reasons she couldn't fathom, Gia had become even more difficult since Jack's death. Her daughter was out of control, and escalating.

"All right, Gia," she said, with as much composure as she could muster. "What went on in the pool house over at Samantha's this morning?" No answer.

"Gia, I have never slapped you—don't make me do it now," Debra said evenly, not taking her eyes off the child. Still no answer, just more tears. Bessie stood at the sink, fidgeting with her apron.

"Young lady," Debra tried again. "Did you tell Samantha to take off her panties?"

"No," Gia sniffled. "She just did."

"And did you take your panties down?"

"No," she squeaked.

"Tell me, and don't you dare lie to me. . . . Did you touch Samantha?" Bessie visibly flinched. "*Did you?*" Debra demanded.

"Yes . . ."

"And precisely what did you then say to Samantha?" she demanded, leaning in to Gia. "Look at me. *What did you say to her?*"

"I *hate* you," Gia shrieked. "I *hate* you," she screamed again, and her mother realized that this was meant for her. Sobbing uncontrollably now, she slid off the chair and ran over to Bessie, threw her arms around the woman's ample middle, and clung to her. Bessie resisted putting her arms around the girl. She held them out at her sides, pained and embarrassed to be in this position.

Debra got up and went over to Gia, knelt down beside her, took her by the shoulders and shook her. "No, you don't," she reproached sternly. "Don't try to play me against Bessie. It won't work, do you understand? Look at me, Gia. You tell me you're sorry, immediately!"

Gia was screaming now, pulling away from her mother, trying to bury her face in Bessie's skirts. Debra saw tears streaming over

Bessie's cheeks. She wrenched Gia away and slapped her hands to break the hold she had on her nanny. She took her daughter's face in her two hands, and would not allow her to back away. Gia's nose was running, her eyes were red and swelling, she was gasping for breath. She lifted a hand to wipe her eyes and Debra yanked it away from her face.

"No, you are *not* going to get away with this," she said fervidly. "A tantrum will get you nowhere. Don't you ever, ever say 'I hate you' to me again. Tell me that you are sorry, young lady. And then I want to hear exactly what you said and exactly what you did to that child."

Gia's slender body was racked with spasms. She was bawling and hyperventilating. Bessie was weeping silently. The grinning jack-o'-lanterns on the table seemed to be mocking them now. But Debra was adamant. If Gia were allowed to get by with this, she would do it again, she knew, and again, and again. And worse. Much as she wanted to fold her troubled little girl in her arms, to comfort and soothe her and dry her tears, she would not back down.

"I saw Daddy," Gia gasped now, between tortured sobs. "I saw Daddy—"

"You saw Daddy *what?*" Debra demanded, not about to let her use her father's death as an excuse for her outrageous behavior.

"I saw Daddy *dead,*" she wailed.

"What do you mean?" Debra exacted. *She's going to tell me she's having nightmares*, Debra thought, *try to get my sympathy*.

"*Shh*, Gia," Bessie admonished.

"When Daddy got shot—" Gia was screaming, sobbing hysterically now. Suddenly, she tore herself from Debra's grasp and ran out of the kitchen. The two women could hear Gia's violent wailing until the door to her room slammed shut.

Debra, still kneeling on the floor, looked up at Bessie. "Why did you shush her?" she demanded. "What was she saying?"

"Nothing," Bessie answered, and when Debra's face told her

she wasn't satisfied with that response, she added, "I wanted her to calm down before she made herself sick."

Debra's eyes never left the woman's face. Bessie was by nature open and forthright; dissembling was not easy for her. On the few occasions when she had tried to hide something from Debra, that Gia had eaten a bag of cookies and that's why she wasn't hungry for dinner, that her daughter had knocked over the expensive vase in the living room when she'd been careless with a softball, Bessie's discomfort had been patently obvious. Now Debra could read plainly on the woman's darkened countenance that she most certainly knew what this was about, and she was shielding Gia again. This time, though, Debra sensed that it was about much more than cookies and softballs.

She put a hand on the other woman's arm. Both of them were badly shaken. "Please, Bessie, I need you to tell me what's going on here," she said gently, tears forming in her eyes, too.

Bessie broke down. "Oh, Miss Debra, she's gone through so much—"

"What is it you're not telling me?" Debra persisted. "Why did she run to you for reassurance? What do you know that I don't know? I'm appealing to you as this child's mother—you must tell me, Bessie, or I'll lose her."

Bessie extracted a handkerchief from the pocket of her apron and blew her nose. Debra guided the older woman over to the table, and the two sat down.

"I . . . It's about the day Mr. Nathanson was shot," Bessie began, wiping her eyes with the crumpled handkerchief.

"Go on, Bessie," Debra urged, her heart clutching with fear. Bessie proceeded then to stammer through a story that made Debra's eyes widen with incredulity and horror. The first part was familiar. Mr. Nathanson had come into the kitchen on that Saturday afternoon, she said, and he told Bessie that they'd be going up to the cabin at Lake Arrowhead for the weekend, so Gia would need her down jacket. Since Gia was just about to have her lunch, he said that he would go into the girl's room to get it.

Bessie told Debra that she had offered to run in and get the jacket out of Gia's closet, but Mr. Nathanson said no, he'd go, maybe he would see something else they should take with them. Bessie told him that Gia's wool gloves were in the bottom drawer of her dresser, and there were some warm hats and scarves in there too. Mr. Nathanson went into Gia's room.

"Gia took a couple of bites of her sandwich," Bessie went on. "Then she jumped up and ran after her father. She said she wanted to bring that new red sweater that you'd just bought her, Miss Debra. A few minutes later I heard the gunshots, two of them. And Gia came flying back into the kitchen and she clutched me the way she just did, and told me her daddy got shot."

Bessie paused, catching her breath, sniffling and dabbing at her eyes. Debra felt as if the bottom had fallen out of her stomach. "*. . . her daddy got shot.*" That phrase echoed another one her daughter had told her: "*. . . one of the kids got bit.*" It turned out, of course, that Gia had done the biting. Barely breathing, Debra whispered, "Bessie, where did she get the gun?"

"Gia told me she found your gun in the nightstand beside your bed, and she was showing it to her father."

"But her fingerprints weren't on it, only *mine*—"

"I don't know," Bessie said. "I don't know about any fingerprints," she repeated, shrugging her shoulders.

"What else did she tell you?"

"Nothing," the woman said simply. "I told her she must never tell anyone anything at all about it again, not ever, not even me."

"You told her to *lie!*" Debra threw out.

"No, I told her not to tell."

"That's the same as lying," Debra shouted.

Bessie nodded. She knew that now. "It's not the child's fault," she cried. "It's my fault. I thought it was the best thing to do, but now I know I made a terrible mistake. Some days she'd be bright and cheerful for a while, like she was today carving pumpkins. Then I'd think she was over it. But soon she'd turn mean again, and I know it's because that day is on her mind all the time. She never talked about it again, until now. I knew I had to tell you, Miss Debra, but I didn't know how."

"Bessie, you told the detectives that Gia never left the kitchen," Debra breathed, still unwilling to believe what she was hearing.

"I know." Bessie began to sob now. "But I knew if those men put Gia through all that terror again and again, if they made her tell, and made her tell, she would *never* get over it. She would always be the little girl who killed her own father, for the rest of her life." Bessie's words were muffled in the drenched handkerchief. "She's so fragile as it is. . . ."

Debra grasped the woman's arm. "Bessie," she said in strangled tones, "you know that they've charged *me* with murder—what were you *thinking?* Were you going to let me go to *prison?*"

"No," Bessie said mournfully. "I knew they could never prove that you killed Mr. Nathanson. You were in your room. If it came to that, I would have told. You can fire me," she went on disconsolately. "I can pack tonight. . . ."

"Oh, my God," Debra was murmuring. "Oh, my God." Getting up, she walked over to the wall phone and punched in the number for Marvin Samuels.

49

Zahna—that's her name, Zahna Cole," Jon Johnson told his partner, looking at Janet Orson's appointments for today.

"And what was her business with the deceased?" Mike Cabello asked. "I mean, this is pretty flimsy."

"She's a disc jockey at an FM station, and she was scheduled to interview Orson at the Beverly Hills Hotel this afternoon at three o'clock," Jon read from the daybook notes.

"And tell me why we should care?" Mike threw out. He was cranky. His head ached and his stomach was queasy. He hadn't slept more than a couple of hours at a time in days, and he hadn't eaten two decent meals in a row in years. And he was sneezing and sniffling and he had a sore throat. It was 52 degrees and fiercely windy, the Santa Anas were rattling the windows in their casings, but the department had cut back on heat at the Hall. "Christ, it's cold enough to hang meat in here," he grumbled.

"Well," Jon forged ahead, ignoring his partner's foul mood, "the manager of the Beverly Hills Hotel says that one of her switchboard operators remembers taking a call from a woman who insisted on having Janet Orson's room number. This woman said she had to know what room Ms. Orson was in because she was going to interview her at the hotel."

"So?" Mike shot back. "Did she say she had to know Orson's room number because she was going to *kill* her at the hotel?"

"God, I hate it when you have PMS," Jon moaned. "Why don't you get a life, Mike? Find a nice, intelligent woman who can turn you into a human being, for both our sakes." Johnson continued studying Janet Orson's agenda book.

"Yeah, right," Mike groused. "How'd you ever get Cicily? She's a saint."

"Mike"—his partner looked at him now—"Cicily is not a saint. She's a loving woman, she's a fabulous babe, she's my helpmate, and the mother of my children, but she doesn't have to be a saint to put up with me. That's because I'm a normal guy. You're a train wreck."

"No lectures; I feel rotten," Mike said, managing to look wounded. "But for your information, I'm having dinner with Lyn on Friday."

"You should be so lucky to get Lyn back," his partner scolded. "She still seeing that plastic surgeon?"

"Nah—she says he doesn't make her knees weak. She wants to get married again, though—says her biological clock is ticking and she wants to have a baby. Guess she wouldn't be able to conceive with strong knees," he tossed out with a smirk.

"How come you two never had children? You were married, what? Seven, eight years?"

"I wanted to wait till I made enough money, till we could buy a house. Joke's on me."

"Did Lyn want to wait?"

"Nope, it was me who knew all the answers."

"What else is new?"

"Nothing new with this damn case," Mike lamented, "except the bodies keep stacking up. Tell me more about the radio chick."

"Okay, the hotel manager says Orson had mentioned she was going to be interviewed by this DJ about some rock star who was her client. And the woman specifically wanted to do the interview at the hotel. Because she loved the famous Beverly Hills Hotel, she said."

"Disc jockeys are nuts," Mike said. "Especially *women* disc jockeys."

Jon shook his head. "No wonder Lyn divorced you. Why is she having dinner with you, anyway? She can't be that hungry."

"We always have dinner on our anniversary. It's Friday. Would have been thirteen years."

"You really need a shrink." Jonathan shrugged. "And when she gets married again, and has those kids she wants, are you still going to take her to dinner on the anniversary of your failed marriage?"

"If she'll go with me. So what about the interview?"

"The interview was supposed to be today. Alison Pollock, the hotel manager, remembered Orson talking about this interview, but she couldn't remember the disc jockey's name. But she says her granddaughter knew who she was. The kid is fifteen, and she's a big rock fan. When Mrs. Pollock asked me about Janet Orson's appointments for today, she recognized the name Zahna Cole right away."

"And the granddaughter is the kid who said this Zahna woman is on vacation this week," Mike finished for him.

"Exactly. Why would someone book an interview during their vacation? And if she scheduled the vacation after she'd set the interview, why didn't she cancel?"

"Rock 'n' roll DJs are notorious cokeheads—"

"There you go again," Johnson said, clipping him. "How the hell did you get to be so cynical?"

"Been on the street too long," Mike threw back. "So you're saying she probably never intended to interview Orson at all. You think maybe she just wanted to find out what unit she was in so she could waste her? Damn, we are grasping at straws here. But that's all we got," he said. "Straws."

"Think we should take a ride out to see her boss, nose around?" Jon asked.

"Yeah, at least the car's got heat. Lemme see that thing," Mike said, reaching for the daybook. "I'll call Pete Capra first. He mixes with a lot of these media people. See if he knows her." Cabello picked up the phone and dialed Channel Six.

"Why don't you call Maxi Poole?" his partner asked. "She's a reporter—she probably knows who this DJ is."

"We don't need to be buddies with Maxi Poole," Cabello said. "She's a suspect."

50

Twenty minutes to four. Maxi was pushing it. She should really go directly to the station so she'd have time to check the wires, be briefed by reporters on their stories, write some of the readers and lead-ins, and get properly made up and ready for the Six O'clock News.

The northbound San Diego Freeway was already jammed with rush-hour traffic heading for the bedroom communities of the San Fernando Valley. Strong Santa Ana winds had kicked up so ferociously that her small sports car was swaying against the shifting blasts. These fierce, dry, dangerous winds, a Southern California phenomenon, whipped up off the desert and came screeching down through the canyons with stunning force. *Santana* winds, old-timers called them—devil winds. Maxi shivered. If she could make fair time through Sepulveda Pass and down into the Valley, she would detour over to the address on Sumac Drive and see if Zahna Cole was home. It would be just a few minutes out of her way.

The wind flung sand and pebbles against the windshield, and cold air forced its way through every seam along the doors and windows of the low-slung Corvette, causing frigid drafts that cut through the warmth emanating from the heater, and sending more shivers through Maxi's slender frame. Why couldn't she shake the profound feeling of foreboding that accompanied the chill?

Why, indeed? With the horror that had been going on around her, it was little wonder that the roar of the devil winds seemed to presage impending evil. She longed for warmth and light back in her world, for order to replace the chaos.

Thanksgiving was coming, and she was planning a trip back home. This year would be really special—the whole family would be in New York. Maxi's father was a pharmacist who owned a successful chain of drugstores, and her mother ran a well-patronized ballet studio and still taught dance. Her sister and brother-in-law and the kids were coming in from Jeddah—Bucky was with the diplomatic corps based in the Middle East, and Ellie taught English to Saudi children. Maxi didn't see enough of any of them, and she'd been looking forward to being home for Thanksgiving.

Normalcy, she thought. She needed a heavy dose of everyday, family stuff—turkey smells, kids yelling, and football games on television, news of each of their absorbing lives, and Mom's little Maltese, Anita, skidding on the marble floors of the old brownstone on East Seventy-first where Maxi grew up. She yearned to be where she would feel safe.

Daddy hadn't liked Jack Nathanson. He'd never said as much, but he didn't have to. Her mother had adored him. Most women did. On family visits, her mother would fairly hover over Jack, bringing him his favorite Kir over ice with the afternoon newspapers, and a pâté with truffles she'd buy especially for him because she knew he liked it. And Jack would take all of them out on the town in a limousine, to dinner at La Côte Basque or Le Cirque, to the theater, where he would always manage to get the best house seats, and for drinks with New York's literary elite at Elaine's. But Daddy saw something else in Jack. He used to ask Maxi, "Are you happy, honey?" She'd assure him she was, but she felt he was never quite convinced. Maxi was his baby, and he made it his business to look beyond the man's charm and urbanity.

Still, nobody really saw all of Jack. During their marriage, Maxi came to realize that her husband was the classic "riddle wrapped in a mystery inside an enigma." Even now that he was dead, she found herself trying to understand what motivated him, and what it said about her. Had she loved him? Yes, she did, until she didn't anymore. Was she happy with him? Yes, she was, until she wasn't anymore. And could she put it behind her now? She'd have to, but she knew that Jack Nathanson had changed her life irrevocably. Never again would she blithely trust what she heard and what she saw.

And now her heretofore ordered world was upside down and wrenched with violence. People who had been closest to Jack Nathanson were being attacked or killed. Even his innocent little girl seemed tormented. Maxi had to keep searching for an answer to this madness.

Ten to four. She had made good time to the Valley. She'd be cutting it close, she knew, as she drove east on Ventura Boulevard across Sherman Oaks. She would have a quick chat with Zahna Cole, if the woman was at home and available, see if she had any insights into what happened to Meg Davis's cross.

Once on Sumac Drive, she studied the numbers; 6420 was a small, dilapidated house badly in need of paint, with a rusted iron gate set in an iron wall of lethal-looking upright arrows. Still mindful that if the woman saw her coming, if she had time to think about it for a minute she might not want to talk to her, Maxi continued on past the house, made a U-turn, and parked at the curb on the other side of the street, a few doors away.

She left her purse, locked her car, and slipped the keys into the pocket of her blazer as she approached the house. She pressed the bell on the stanchion beside the gate, and waited. Looking up at the windows, Maxi got the feeling that nobody was home. She rang again, longer this time. No answer.

Well, it was worth a try, she thought. She would come back and try again after the show. Maxi turned away from the forlorn gate and walked back to her car.

Seated behind the wheel, she was just about to turn on the ignition when a dented black Volkswagen Rabbit roared up the quiet street and screeched to a halt in front of Zahna Cole's weathered little house with the peeling paint. Maxi watched as a tall, gangly woman, dressed in a conservative business suit that looked like it didn't belong to her, got out of the car and slammed the door. Maxi knew from Remy Germain's sketches that it was Zahna Cole. In her rush, the woman hadn't noticed Maxi sitting in her car across the street. Maxi watched her quickly unlock the gate, turn and lock it again behind her, then stride across the tamped-down dirt fringed with straggly weeds that once was lawn, and disappear inside.

Five past four. Maxi had very little time, but it was an opportunity she couldn't pass up. She'd wait a couple of minutes, give the woman a chance to catch her breath before she rang her doorbell.

51

Zahna slammed into the house, dropped her shoulder bag on the nearest chair, and glanced around the living room at the battered furniture, the clutter, the take-out cartons crusted with stale food that littered the floor and tabletops. "Fucking pigsty," she grumbled, and bounded for the bookcase next to the inoperable old fireplace that was stuffed with trash. Removing a copy of Jack Kerouac's *Desolation Angels*, she reached back into the empty slot for the small Ziplock bag with the jewels. Her beautiful rocks. Carefully, she poured out one, then another of the little beauties, and dropped them into the glass pipe that she'd fished out of her purse. Might as well blast off, she thought, flick her Bic and light her fire, do what she had to do, then get the hell out of there.

She wasn't going to miss this dump. Funny, she thought, back when she would be expecting Jack to drop by at any time, she really kept the place nice. It was actually cozy, kind of shabby-chic, with the slipcovered couch and chairs in the small living room, the down comforter and fluffy pillows on the king-size bed. Now she never bothered to make the bed, and she hadn't washed the sheets since Jack was killed.

Nice thing about rocks, they're so clean, she mused, holding her breath on a huge drag that almost immediately took the edge off, calmed her nerves, then began to stoke her up in an exquisite way. Wonderful! No needles, no tourniquets, no cooking, straining, no messing with ether, no collapsed veins or spongy nose cartilage, no feeling sick half the time. No clumsy paraphernalia, just her little glass pipe and a bag of pearls. And you could pick them up anywhere.

She would have to stock up on the way to the airport, pack a good-size stash for the trip. She had no doubt that she would find all she wanted in Mexico City, but it might take her a few days to scope out the terrain, and she would have to be careful for a while. She would cruise Century Boulevard tonight, where she knew she'd have her pick of dealers working both sides of the street from Hollywood Park all the way to the airport. They were easy to spot, hanging out singly or in groups, leaning against storefronts, sitting on bus benches, smoking cigarettes, not talking much. Wearing hats. They all wore hats—pimp-style fedoras, knit pulldowns, or baseball caps slapped on backwards. Some of them were even known to bring chairs out on the sidewalk, set up a damn office. Now and then the cops would sweep them up, but they would be back on the street doing business in an hour.

Easy business, too, both ways. "Hey, got a few twenties for me tonight?" she would glide by and ask. "Sure, babe, how many ya need?" "Three dozen," she'd say, and the dude's eyes would light up. That was a big score. Big score for a big trip. "Can I see whatcha got?" he'd probably ask her on a buy that size, and she'd have six hundreds ready to flash at him. "Let me see what *you* got," she'd say, and she would inspect his merchandise.

He would count them out into a glassine bag, and she would put her nose about a foot away and count right along with him or he'd short her, figure she was a rich white chick from the Westside, and easy. Then, seeing she was watching and she was sharp, he would probably throw in a couple extra as a bonus, let her know about it, cultivate her business. The whole transaction would take about ninety seconds.

Nice, neat, and portable. You could tuck the little bag in a zippered pocket of your purse, or throw it in a pouch with your lighter and pipe, and it looked like a makeup kit. You could do crack anywhere, in your car, in a ladies' room, behind a tree if you were careful. She was sure she'd have no problem knocking down a few in the airplane john on the late-night flight to Mexico City.

Had to pack. That would take no time at the rate she was flying. No big deal, cram a few things in a bag and kiss off the rest. The important stuff was the money and the jewelry, thank you Janet Orson.

She had the fifty-five hundred bucks in her purse, her windfall from the afternoon outing. And about fourteen hundred in the little leather box that she'd snatched from Jack's house on Sunday night. And she'd cleaned out her savings account, thirty-one hundred, and there was another thousand or so from the bungalow at the Beverly Hills Hotel. A lot of people keep cash in their bedroom dresser drawers, Zahna knew. She was in grab-and-run mode last night, moving at a million miles an hour, but on a hunch, she'd quickly opened up the bureau drawers and found the bills, stacked under the paper lining. And while she was at it, she nailed two more nice watches and a few other trinkets. Back home, she had thrown them into a plastic grocery sack with her haul from the big house; those goodies she would sell as needed in Mexico.

The two necklaces were truly an afterthought. Opening up Janet Orson's silver beaded handbag, she'd pulled out a loose bunch of bills. Then she saw the pearl-and-diamond choker. What was it doing in her purse? she wondered, and her eyes shot to the dead woman's neck. Another one! Emeralds, she guessed. Emeralds and diamonds! With one black-gloved hand holding the body to the floor, she'd planted her other hand firmly around the necklace and gave it a mighty yank. The clasp flew apart, and she had them both.

Janet Orson. Zahna hadn't given any thought to what made her swoop down and whack Janet Orson last night. She hadn't had time. She'd been on a rocket ride since Sunday, from the minute she'd snatched the cross and gone over to Jack's house. And killed Carlotta. A three-day rampage, and it was like she wasn't even in her own body, she was standing off to the side in a drug-induced haze, watching her bloody trip on television. Emotionally detached, but she couldn't turn the program off because she was the star.

After fleeing from Jack's mansion on Sunday night, she was totally wired, couldn't sleep, couldn't go to work the next day. She *did* have the presence of mind to call the station and tell them she needed to take some time off. A family matter, she'd told the program director. Hah! A family she'd never been included in. Jack Nathanson's serial family, the wives, always in the light and the warmth, always in the news, always in the money. Janet Orson, Maxi Poole, Debra Angelo. All three of them together never gave Jack Nathanson as much of what he needed as Zahna did, she was sure.

She'd seen a notice in the trades that recently widowed top agent Janet Orson had just signed the lead singer from Minefield, who was starring in a movie. That gave Zahna the idea to call Orson's office and request an interview about the singer for her radio show. She'd never use it, of course—her fans didn't want to hear some woman talk about a rock star, they just wanted to get stoned and listen to the music. But that would get her into Janet Orson's orbit again—she still wanted that huge diamond ring, the one Jack *should* have given Zahna.

She was amazed that Orson accepted—after all, she was supposed to be *grieving,* wasn't she? Coldhearted bitch, business as usual, she didn't care that Jack was dead. Zahna scheduled the interview at the Beverly Hills Hotel because she'd probably have her good stuff there. She figured Janet wouldn't be ready when she came to the door to do the interview—that kind of woman never is. She'd be fussing with her hair and makeup in the bathroom, and while Zahna was waiting, she'd poke around and snatch things, whatever she saw lying around. Maybe that ring would be on the dresser. She would carry her tape equipment in a big tote bag, and toss some nice expensive goodies into it.

Not a bad plan. The only problem was that Janet Orson might recognize her from the funeral. So she came up with an even better plan. On the night before the scheduled interview, they showed live coverage of the arrivals at the premiere of Jack Nathanson's last movie, *Serial Killer,* on the news. And there she was, Janet Orson, the star's beautiful widow, entering the theater on the arm of the man Zahna had seen her with at the auction. The glittering scene added more fuel to Zahna's fury. Her rage, and the vodka, the crack, and the pills, turned up Superwoman again, and the caped crusader found herself gearing up for another mission.

She'd tried to get Janet Orson's room number from the hotel operator that afternoon, but the woman was snippy. Turns out she didn't need it—Orson actually returned her call and gave her the number herself. "Just come to bungalow 16," she'd said in her message, and she added that she looked forward to meeting Zahna the next day.

Why wait? Zahna decided to go over to the hotel that night, get to the bungalows the back way, off Crescent Drive, find number 16, and maybe break a window—those units wouldn't be wired for alarms, and they were pretty secluded. She would prowl around the place, filch a few pricey little presents for herself while the lady was at the party.

When she got there, there were too many waiters, bellmen, security guards, guests, and strollers around the grounds for her to break in without being noticed. So she hid in the bushes and smoked some rocks, and lost track of time. When she became aware that the activity had died down and there was no one around, she was about to make her move when she heard the click-click-click of high heels coming along the quiet walk.

Peering out through thick oleander hedges, she saw a vision. In her cracked-out, light-sensitive haze, her eyes adjusted to see a gleaming goddess moving toward her in slow motion, floating in a shimmering, silver-white floor-length gown and a white fur wrap, and glistening, dripping in diamonds.

Suddenly, the picture snapped into focus. It was that damn Janet Orson, in the dress she'd seen her in on the news earlier, coming back to the bungalow before Zahna had a chance to break a window and get in and out of the place with some booty. It infuriated her, sent her into a frenzy. *She's spoiling my life again*, she thought, and she pounced on the silver goddess and ripped at her with the death cross, again and again.

Why did she kill Janet Orson? Because it felt right. In that final few seconds, it wasn't about jewelry and furs anymore; she was evening the score. Janet Orson had it all, and Zahna had nothing. After spending every waking minute over the last three years obsessing about one or the other of Jack's damn wives, it was payback time.

It was supposed to be Zahna's turn, she'd told the woman, and Janet Orson stole her turn. Jack was never meant to marry her, he was supposed to marry his Zahna. If Ms. Superagent hadn't gone sucking around him, seducing him and promising him movie projects, none of this would have happened, she told the eyes of Janet Orson staring up from the floor. Thinking back on it now, getting angry all over again, she was glad she killed her.

And she'd wanted to kill Debra Angelo, who had Jack's kid. And Maxi Poole, that smug little bitch, on the news every night and everybody thinking she was the quintessential L.A. Woman. That was how Los Angeles regarded his wife, Jack had told Zahna once, and ever since then she'd refused to play that Doors song on her show. But Jack loved Zahna more; he told her so. Still, he wouldn't leave Maxi. And even when Maxi Poole was begging him to move out, he wouldn't go. He would come over to Zahna's house at night and drink Scotch and smoke a couple of joints and ball her brains out, and then have the fucking nerve to cry over Maxi, and ramble on that he had to win his wife back.

She had fully intended to kill Maxi Poole. She still had the key to Maxi's house, copied during one of those airport runs, and people never bothered to change their alarm codes. She was going to steal some of Maxi's nice things, too, things that should have been Zahna's, and make it look like a robbery. But Maxi had managed to escape her wrath. She'd just killed her goddamned dog. Too bad. She'd go back and do it tonight if she didn't have to get the hell out of Dodge.

She finished off the double whammy, and she was soaring. Ready to burn all her identification, toss some things in a bag, and clear out of there. She would buy some clothes in Mexico City, start fresh.

At that instant, her doorbell rang. She froze. Her heart felt like it was exploding as she shuffled over to the front window and peered out from behind the tattered curtains.

She couldn't believe who was standing on the other side of her gate. *Maxi Poole!*

52

Hey, buddy, I'd like to help, but to answer your question, *everybody* bought a Dracula costume this year, and if you ask me, *all* of them were odd," the manager of Westside Masquerade yelled into the phone.

Richard sat at his desk and checked off another costume shop in the L.A. Yellow Pages. Tomorrow was Halloween, and most of the salespeople blew him off—they were busy.

His second line lit up. It was Pete Capra, wanting to see him. Richard got up and walked across the newsroom to the glass-enclosed office where Pete sat barking orders into the phone. The early block was on the air. The Four, Five, and Six O'clock News shows ran back to back, two and a half hours of live broadcasting where anything could go wrong, and usually did.

Richard's Halloween warning report was running on the Four, slated at forty-two minutes into the hour. He had finished writing the script, tracking the narration, editing the tape, and hammering out the ins and outs, and the piece was ready to go. The anchors would throw to him for the lead-in, live from the newsroom camera, in about fifteen minutes.

It was almost 4:30. He'd been using the time while waiting to go on the air to try to find a merchant in the L.A. area who might have observed anything strange while selling the costume that Maxi thought she saw on the killer. A long shot, but you never knew.

Pete cocked his head toward a chair in front of his desk, indicating that Richard should sit down, while he continued chewing out the director in the control booth for taking a three-shot when it should have been a close-up on the political editor.

"Fucking idiot belongs in Boise!" Pete muttered, slamming down the phone. "Richard, you're a big music fan. . . . Ever heard of a disc jockey named Zahna Cole?"

"Nope." Richard shook his head.

"I thought you were hip," Pete carped, flicking the ash of his cigar into an empty coffee cup on his desk. Though he was off cigarettes, he figured cigars didn't count.

"I'm new in town, remember?" Richard pointed out. "I'm still trying to wean myself off Don Imus."

"I need you to do some legwork," Pete said. "Find out what you can about this Zahna Cole that Cabello is investigating. He says it's not much of a lead, but she made an appointment to interview Janet Orson today, and insisted on doing it at the Beverly Hills Hotel where Orson was staying, but it turns out she happens to be on vacation this week, so maybe she just wanted to find out which unit the victim was staying in."

Mike Cabello and his partner were on their way over to KBIS in Culver City right now, Pete said, to find out what they could about the lady. In the meantime, the detectives wanted to know if Pete had ever heard anything about her inside the industry.

"So if you come up with something in the next twenty, thirty minutes, call Cabello," Pete said, ripping half a page off a yellow legal pad with the detective's cell phone number scribbled on it.

Richard walked back through the newsroom with the number. Where to begin? Might as well continue on the tack he'd taken, but in the vicinity of that radio station. He went behind the assignment desk to a set of shelves filled with area phone books and pulled out the Culver City Yellow Pages.

The third shop he dialed was Culver Costumes, owned by a Mr. Oscar Pepys. Richard identified himself, and Mr. Pepys happened to recognize his name. "Oh, you're that crime guy on the news," he said, and Richard acknowledged that he was. "But this isn't a crime story, Mr. Pepys," he said, "it's a piece on zany disc jockeys who dress up on Halloween. You know, they're on radio, and the listeners can't see them, so we're going to show what they look like in their wacky costumes, that kind of thing."

"Uh-huh," Pepys said.

"Yah, well, we're told the disc jockey Zahna Cole bought her costume from you, and we want to know what it was," Richard said. "Do you know Zahna Cole, Mr. Pepys?"

"Oh, yes. She's quite a character. Her station is right down the street. She bought her costume here, but maybe she wants to keep it a secret. Why don't you ask *her?*"

"We can't," Richard responded. "She's off today, and her station doesn't know where to reach her. But she's very popular, and we wouldn't want to leave her out of the story."

Pepys hesitated, so Richard jumped in again. "And we'll mention the name of your shop," he lied, "if that's okay with you."

"Well, all right, sure," Oscar Pepys replied. "She's gonna be Dracula this year."

The words sent a chill through Richard's body. The warning lights came on in the newsroom then, blazing incandescent key lights that flooded the set where the newsroom camera was mounted, signaling that the next reporter's piece was up in two minutes. It was 4:40—these lights were for him.

He grabbed his script, skidded over to the set, jumped into the seat, jammed his telex in his ear, adjusted his tie, and looked straight into the lens, just in time to hear the anchorman in the studio say, "Tomorrow is Halloween. Our crime-watch reporter,

Richard Winningham, has some tips to protect the trick-or-treaters in your family. . . ." Richard did his lead-in and watched his tape roll, then tagged the piece off and answered a couple of anchor questions. When he was finished the lights went off, and he raced back to his desk.

He dialed the number that Pete had given him for Mike Cabello and caught him in his squad car. He told Cabello what Maxi had said this afternoon, that her attacker had worn a Dracula costume. And he had just learned that Culver Costumes had sold a Dracula costume to the woman they were asking about, Zahna Cole.

"Yeah, well," Cabello yelled into the phone, "the whole country is probably buying Dracula costumes this week with that movie out, but thanks for the tip, Winningham. We're pulling up at the station now. Call if you hear anything else."

He looked up to see Pete Capra lumbering toward him. "Maxi's not in yet," Capra blustered. "She's never late. The assignment editors don't have her out on a story—"

"I ran into her on Melrose a couple of hours ago," Richard offered. "She was chasing down an ID on a woman who was with Meg Davis at that auction where she bought the cross." As he heard himself say those words, his blood ran cold. He grabbed the phone and asked Information for the number for Sotheby's in Beverly Hills.

Yes, Maxi Poole had been in some time ago, the receptionist said. Richard told her he knew that Maxi had gone to Sotheby's to identify a woman who was portrayed in some sketches she had with her, and he needed to know if she'd been successful.

The receptionist told him that Gabrielle Modine had helped Ms. Poole, but she was gone for the day. She couldn't give out Gabby's phone number, she said, but she would try to reach her in her car, and if she wasn't able to get her there, she would leave a message on her answering machine at home. She took Richard's number, and promised she would ask Gabby to call him ASAP.

Pete Capra was standing over him. "What's Maxi's cell phone number?" Richard asked him. Pete yelled the question in the direction of the assignment desk, and one of the editors consulted his computer files and yelled back the number. Richard was dialing before he'd finished. He punched up the speaker phone so Pete could hear. A recording blared: "Thank you for calling. The mobile customer you are trying to reach is away from the phone, or beyond our service area. Please try your call again later."

Richard told Pete then that Maxi said the assailant was wearing a Dracula costume, black with red stitching—she'd realized it when she happened to spot that same costume at the shop where he was doing his Halloween story. And that he'd just found out that this disc jockey the detectives were running down, Zahna Cole, had recently bought one.

His phone lit up. He punched up the line, leaving the speaker on. It was Gabby Modine. She was in her car and had just got his message, she said.

"Were you able to identify the woman in Maxi Poole's sketches?" he asked.

"Sure," Gabby told him. "She's a radio personality called Zahna Cole."

Richard and Pete both pounced on the assignment desk at once. "You check Information for L.A., the Westside, and the Valley," Pete thundered. "I'll take the cross-reference directories, see what they have on radio personnel."

When they had no luck, Pete dialed one of his tipsters at Los Angeles traffic court. The clerk paused to consult his computer. Yes, a Zahna Cole had been issued an eighty-five-dollar parking ticket in downtown Los Angeles—the address listed on the citation was 6420 Sumac Drive in Sherman Oaks. Slamming down the phone, Pete scrawled it on his legal pad. "But who the hell knows if she still lives there?" he growled to Richard. "She got the damn ticket six years ago."

An EA approached the assignment desk and handed Richard

a sheaf of papers—Maxi's crisscross list of names and addresses corresponding to the phone numbers Janet Orson had called from the Beverly Hills Hotel. Glancing quickly through the pages, the name jumped out at him: Zahna Cole. Orson had called her twice yesterday, probably to confirm the interview set for today, he figured, holding up the sheet for Pete to see—the address listed for Zahna Cole was 6420 Sumac Drive in Sherman Oaks!

Pete grabbed a Thomas Guide. "Bring Cabello's cell phone number," he barked. "We'll take one of the news vans. Let's go!"

53

Debra Angelo sat on the comfortable, canvas-covered couch with her arm around Gia, who looked scared and small among the big down cushions. Bessie perched stiffly on a straight-backed chair, facing her adopted family. Marvin Samuels was settled into an overstuffed club chair on the other side of a wide coffee table, on which rested a gin and tonic he was working on. And Dr. Bob Jamieson was pacing. Debra had summoned the lawyer and the therapist, and assembled the group in her living room to go over the horror story, and to try to figure out what they should do for her daughter on every level.

"I think," Debra said soberly, "we should begin by having Bessie tell the story that she told me an hour ago." The nanny had a fresh cotton handkerchief at the ready. All eyes turned to her, including Gia's, who looked relieved that she wasn't being asked to speak.

"I lied to the detectives," Bessie began, and Gia looked startled at her admission. "I told them Gia did not leave the kitchen the whole time Mr. Nathanson was here the afternoon he was . . . was shot, and that isn't true." Marvin Samuels shifted in his chair and watched her intently.

The woman went on to tell what really happened, how Gia

followed her father into her bedroom, how Bessie had heard a shot but wasn't sure what it was, then heard another. And how Gia had come running back into the kitchen then, crying and gasping and saying her daddy got shot with her mom's gun.

"Tell them what you told Gia," Debra said sternly, and Bessie began to weep.

"I did wrong," the housekeeper whimpered forlornly. "I told her not to tell anybody, not to ever talk about it again, and that I would say she'd stayed right there in the kitchen with me the whole time, and I asked her if she understood."

"Evidently she did," Debra said dryly, directing her words at Marvin. "Gia never said another word about it."

The attorney was the only one in the group who looked comfortable, Debra noted, and that was reassuring to her. Of course, she knew in her heart that it didn't necessarily mean anything. She was sure Marvin Samuels would be comfortable in a burning building. He would probably sit and have a drink, and maybe some crackers and pâté, while he considered which route would provide the most efficient egress.

"What should we do, Marvin?" she asked. He had come out to the beach as soon as he got her frantic call telling him that the person who killed Jack was actually Gia. By accident, of course. She explained how the girl had found her gun and wanted to show it to her father.

"Are you *sure* it was an accident?" he'd asked her.

"For God's sake, Marvin!" she'd exclaimed. "Could that even be an *issue* with a ten-year-old?"

"In today's world, yes," he'd said. It had been Marvin's idea to get the psychologist over there, too. Meanwhile, he'd told her on the phone, she should hold all thoughts and comments until they got there, and they'd go through it together.

"Can we freshen your drink?" Debra asked him now, taking his cue to stay civilized, stay cool.

"That would be great." Marvin smiled, and Bessie jumped to her feet, grateful for the diversion.

"And Bessie, bring some cheese, would you, and whatever else you can put together . . . some of those lovely green grapes. Who else would like a drink?" she asked. Gia wanted lemonade; Debra would have a glass of wine.

It was amazing what interjecting small amenities into the most horrendous of crises could do to put a better face on things, she reflected. Even wonderful, concerned Dr. Jamieson, who still wouldn't sit down, whose veins pulsated at his temples as he paced—even *he* visibly relaxed a bit and asked Bessie for a glass of juice.

Bessie escaped into the kitchen, and Marvin addressed Debra's question. "What to do? I'm going to have to call Mike Cabello and tell him, of course, right away," he said.

"Well, what would the procedure be in a case like this?" Debra asked with a hint of exasperation. "Surely they'll just dismiss everything and close the book on it—it was a tragic accident involving a youngster; you read about this kind of thing all the time."

"Debra," Marvin said quietly, "it's not going to be that simple. They are not going to just accept this scenario at face value, thank you very much, case closed. They are going to tear the stories apart, second by second, Bessie's, and Gia's, too—"

"Oh, Marvin," Debra wailed, giving Gia a supportive squeeze, "can't they at least spare *her?*"

"No," Marvin said. "Time for a reality check, Debra. For all they know, you might have cooked this story up to get yourself off the hook. *They* know that *you* know they can't throw a ten-year-old in prison. They'll be all over the kid's story, and so will the press—count on it."

"There'll be more publicity?" she asked with a sinking heart.

"Debra, the *hordes of hell* will be on your doorstep. Starting tomorrow. Maybe even today, after I tell Mike Cabello. It'll leak right away, trust me on that—those guys need to close this case."

Dr. Jamieson had dropped into a chair. "The best thing would be to get Gia out of here for a while," he said. "Take her to the mountains or somewhere—she's out of school anyway, and *you* could use a change of scenery, too," he told Debra.

Catching the glint of hope that sprang into Debra's eyes, Marvin pronounced resolutely, "Nice idea, but they won't let either of you go out of town, so don't even think about it."

"Well, then, we'll just have to help Gia through this, won't we?" Jamieson said, smiling kindly at the girl.

"Gia," Marvin said, "we want to hear from *you*, now. Tell us everything that happened on the day your daddy got shot. From the beginning, Gia," he said when the girl hesitated, looking up at her mother for reassurance.

Bessie had come back into the room with a tray of drinks and snacks, which she set on the coffee table. Once again, Gia was temporarily spared by the distraction presented by the refreshments, and she jumped up and made a great production of building herself a sandwich with meat and cheese, spreading the bread carefully with mustard, arranging pickles and olives just so on her plate. Debra gave her a minute to play with her food before she yanked her back on the spot.

"Well, uhh," Gia stammered, licking mustard off her fingers, "I went in my room to get my red sweater?" She made it a question, looking for approval.

"Yes," Marvin encouraged her. He already knew the opening text; he'd heard it from both Debra and Bessie. But only Gia knew exactly what had gone on inside that bedroom, and that's what he had come to hear. He'd told Debra not to press the child for details until he got there, that handling it would have to be delicate. Everyone in the small group was facing Gia now, paying her rapt attention.

"And we found my jacket," Gia went on. "And my boots

with the fur inside? And I showed Daddy Debra's gun," she said, lowering her voice, reddening, dropping her head. She used "Debra" instead of "Mom" sometimes, when she was trying to detach from her. Gia knew that taking that gun out of the drawer was strictly forbidden, and now that the secret was out, she'd be punished for it.

"Go on," Marvin said gently. Gia started to cry, her tears splashing onto the plate of food she was holding with both hands on her lap.

"Then Daddy got shot," she sobbed, not looking at anyone, her eyes riveted to her soggy sandwich.

Debra couldn't bring herself to ask the question. Dr. Jamieson did. "Did you shoot your daddy, Gia?" he asked.

"No," Gia wailed.

"Don't lie, young lady," Debra pressed, all too aware of her daughter's usual tactic when in a tight spot—it was her father's tactic as well, she knew.

"I didn't shoot him," Gia cried, and the plate slid off her lap onto the floor, spilling its contents onto the Kashan carpet. Bessie leaped to clean up the mess.

Debra knew that Gia actually could handle a gun—her father had taught her, she'd told Marvin that. And she knew that it would be natural for her daughter to want to show off the firearm to her dad, just as she knew Gia would have had every intention of spiriting it back into her nightstand drawer without letting her mother find out. Debra wondered now how many times she'd had it out, examined it, maybe even played with it—a loaded gun! She'd been a fool to leave it in that drawer, but she'd wanted it readily accessible in the middle of the night if she ever needed it, and it had never occurred to her that Gia would ever see it, let alone handle it. And it had a hair trigger! Tony Morano at the gun club had recommended that, for Debra's protection. She had been meticulously instructed, and he'd trusted that she was coolheaded enough never to aim the weapon unless she feared for her life. If she ever *were* in danger, he didn't want her having to struggle with the trigger and risk being overpowered. Yes, Gia definitely *could* handle that Smith & Wesson .38.

"Well, then, *who* shot him?" Marvin asked, never expecting to hear what came next.

"Zahna," Gia said. Bessie let out a gasp.

"And who is Zahna?" Debra demanded incredulously.

"Daddy's girlfriend," Gia whimpered.

54

Maxi stood outside the warped, rusted-out gate and waited. She sensed that the woman was observing her from behind the curtain at the front window. So much for the element of surprise. She'd wanted to catch her off guard; that would have made it harder for Zahna Cole to say no to a quick interview. Now she would be deciding whether or not to open the door.

There was a nearly imperceptible change in the configuration of light and shadow behind the window, and seconds later, the front door opened. The woman in the sketches stepped out onto the stoop and down the trampled path, and stood facing Maxi on the other side of the locked gate.

"Hello," Maxi offered, smiling. "I'm Maxi Poole from Channel Six News."

"I know who you are," Zahna responded in a guttural voice. Her eyes were red, her pupils dilated, her demeanor spacey. Drugs, Maxi knew immediately.

"Can we talk for just a few minutes?" Maxi began. "About Meg Davis. I understand she was a friend of yours."

"What do you want to talk about?" Zahna asked. Maxi could feel hostility emanating from this woman. Paranoia was a major side effect of drug abuse, she knew.

"The people at Sotheby's told me you were with her at the auction," Maxi returned. "I'd like to talk to you about what kind of woman she was, and what she might have done with the cross she purchased that night."

"If we knew *that,* we'd know who's doing all these killings, wouldn't we?" the woman snarled. Then she surprised Maxi with a complete about-face. "Wanna come in?" she asked sweetly.

Zahna took a key out of her jacket pocket and opened the gate from the inside. "This used to be electric," she muttered, "but it doesn't work anymore."

She pulled the creaking gate inward a couple of feet and stood aside for Maxi to walk through, then slammed it shut and locked it again with the key. Maxi was uncomfortable with that, but she figured the woman probably locked it out of habit, for security reasons.

Zahna ushered her into the cluttered living room, and Maxi was assaulted with the stench of acrid perspiration and rotting food. Trash littered the floor and tabletops, and rays of sunshine streaming in through soiled lace curtains revealed a thick coat of dust over every surface.

Pushing some newspapers, a sweatshirt, some socks, and tennis shoes off a tattered canvas-backed director's chair onto the floor, Zahna gestured to Maxi to have a seat. Dropping cross-legged on the floor, Zahna leaned back against a faded flowered couch and looked up at Maxi with a vacant smile.

Inhaling the rancid odors and the dust-laden air, Maxi stifled a wave of nausea. She experienced an ominous sense of dread, looking down at the drugged-out woman who sat at her feet with a self-satisfied smile on her face. Her instincts told her to ask a few questions and get out of there fast.

What's to be scared of? She's just a junkie, Maxi thought. The tennis shoes, she flashed, eyeing them on the floor by her chair—*black Reeboks*. But lots of women wore black Reeboks—Maxi owned a pair herself. Maybe it was the fact that she felt trapped, that she was dependent on this whacked-out woman to unlock the gate and let her out. Whatever was provoking it, Maxi had the sensation that hell was just beneath the floorboards.

"Did you know Meg Davis well?" she asked now, trying to conceal her apprehension.

"Nope, didn't know her at all," Zahna said without changing her vacuous expression.

"Oh. The women at Sotheby's said you were at the auction together, so I hoped you could tell me something about her," Maxi said, fixing her gaze steadily on the woman's face, trying not to look around her at the squalid quarters. "Her mother didn't know of any other friends she might have had."

"Is it fun playing detective?" Zahna asked, with an edge of sarcasm.

"No, not fun," Maxi returned, "but it's part of my job. You went to the auction with her?" she persisted, not wanting to get sucked in to some druggie head game with this woman.

"No," Zahna shot back. "I met her there."

Maxi decided to attempt a couple more questions, then leave. She was getting nowhere, her trepidation was mounting, and she was due at the station. "Well, I was told you left together," she tried. "Did she tell you anything about that cross?"

"Yup, it was a prop in a movie she was in with Jack Nathanson. You know, *Black Sabbat*," she said. "I was in one of his movies, too."

"Really," Maxi replied. "Which one?"

"*Internet Crypto*. You see that one?"

Maxi didn't know if this woman was aware that she had been married to Jack Nathanson, in fact during the time that he shot *Internet Crypto*. "Yes," she said. "Which character did you play?"

"I was the disc jockey he listened to when he couldn't sleep at night," Zahna Cole answered. Maxi remembered that sultry voice now.

"I have something of Jack Nathanson's, too. Wanna see it?" the woman asked, almost mischievously.

"Uhh, okay, sure," Maxi responded, curious despite the impulse that told her to flee.

"C'mon, I'll show you," Zahna said, and she got up and walked toward a door that led to a darkened hall, beckoning Maxi to follow.

She led Maxi into a bedroom that exuded the stench of dirty laundry. Zahna snapped on a switch that illuminated a dim lamp with a broken lampshade listing on a table beside the bed, revealing a room so filthy and disheveled it was hard to believe a woman lived there. On the king-size bed was a wrinkled, stained sheet, oily and threadbare in the center. Soiled blankets lay in a heap on the floor. Clothes were strewn everywhere, and a bentwood chair with a broken cane seat was lying on its side.

"Here's what I have of Jack Nathanson's," Zahna tossed back over her shoulder, heading for a scarred pine bedside table on which stood, among other things, a half-empty two-quart bottle of a grocery-store-label vodka. "Come over here, Maxi Poole," she said, "and I'll show you what I have of Jack Nathanson's."

Expecting to see some object on the nightstand, Maxi moved closer, and suddenly Zahna grabbed her arm. In one fierce motion, almost jerking her off her feet, she pulled her toward the black iron bars of the headboard, and Maxi felt sharp steel scrape across her skin and clamp shut around her wrist. She let out a gasp of horror, and tugged at the handcuffs that had her lashed to the bed. "What is this, a joke?" she shrieked.

"Nope, no joke," Zahna hissed, glowering at her, and Maxi saw hatred blazing in the woman's black, sunken eyes. "Those handcuffs belonged to Jack Nathanson. Now get on the bed."

"I'm not getting on the bed," Maxi said evenly. "Unlock these handcuffs, Zahna, before you find yourself in big trouble."

"Oh, you really *scare* me, bitch." Zahna laughed menacingly, and she knelt down and reached under the bed. She was feeling around on the floor, her head lowered, and Maxi had the urge to kick her as hard as she could, knock her over. But she knew that would only enrage her, and she was helpless, shackled to the bed. Better to try talking this woman out of whatever madness she was intent on.

Zahna loomed up before her now, brandishing something that glinted in the lamplight. "Is this the cross you're looking for?" she asked with a leer. Maxi felt her heart stop and her knees crumple beneath her as she caught sight of the *Black Sabbat* cross in Zahna Cole's hand. She collapsed onto the bed, fighting desperately to keep from blacking out.

"Good girl," Zahna said, and she loped around the bed and reached for a second set of handcuffs that was fastened to another one of the iron slats of the headboard. She lunged for Maxi's left arm and cinched on the cuff.

"These were Jack's too," she said. "Didn't he ever handcuff you to the bed for sex, Maxi Poole?"

Maxi heard a low groan escape her. She had to rally her wits, try to keep the woman talking, give someone time to get to them. But who? When she didn't show up for the six o'clock show, Pete would be looking for her. Richard would remember that she'd been on her way to Sotheby's, but the auction house closed at five. They wouldn't find out about Zahna Cole.

She felt a stinging slap across her face, and her eyes flew open. "Hey, I'm *talking* to you," Zahna jeered, looming over her now. "I *said*, didn't your husband ever chain you to the bed and fuck your brains out? He loved that—"

"Who are you?" Maxi interrupted weakly.

"No you don't, Miss Hot-Shot Newsbitch; *I'm* asking the questions here," Zahna rasped. "Did he cuff you to the bed?" she demanded, and she slapped her again.

"No. Is that what he did with you?" Maxi asked, knowing that keeping this crazed woman talking amounted to the only slim hope she had.

"Oh, yeah," Zahna purred, "that and a lot of other things too. Wanna hear some of them, Miss Frigid?"

"Sure," Maxi ventured. "This S-and-M stuff is actually very erotic." She hoped that would sound convincing to Zahna, who was now stuffing something into a small glass pipe. Crack, Maxi surmised. Crystalline rocks, which were known to turn users violent, sometimes give them superhuman strength. Maxi shuddered to realize that this was probably what had given Zahna Cole the force and the bravado to kill the way she had with that cross.

Zahna was smoking her pipe now, and babbling on about lewd acts that Jack had supposedly performed with her. Maxi hoped she appeared interested, but her mind kept wandering. To death, and dying, she realized.

Funny, she thought, how her mind was skittering over trivial things. She was sorry she wouldn't get to try the new Vera Brown jade moisture cream she'd just bought. She regretted that she wouldn't see her family at Thanksgiving. Where were the deep, profound concepts that should come when death was imminent? Probably eluding her because she was generally comfortable with the concept of death, and with the way she'd lived her life. Oh, she had her venal moments, her human failings, actions she regretted. *Dear God,* she prayed, *don't let me start dredging all of them up now. Forgive me, okay?*

"Ever smoke this shit?" Zahna was asking her.

"N-no," Maxi stammered.

"Well, here, take a hit," the woman cajoled, bringing the pipe up to Maxi's lips.

Maxi turned her head to the side. "No, please," she pleaded. "I don't want to."

"Hey, Newsbitch, *this just in!* I don't give a shit *what* you don't want," Zahna bellowed, and she slapped her hard again, leaving a reddened imprint of her hand on Maxi's cheek. "You probably don't want me to *kill* you, either, but I'm going to. Smoke it," she ordered, and she jammed the pipe stem into Maxi's mouth.

"Suck it up, dammit!" Zahna roared, and Maxi inhaled the fiery smoke. Almost immediately she felt her head swimming, her blood beating a cacophonous rush through distended arteries, and she saw sharp, blinking lights whirling kaleidoscopically before her eyes. Zahna saw the effects taking place and smiled. She took two more drags herself.

"Nice, huh?" she taunted, and shoved the pipe into Maxi's mouth again, forcing her captive to inhale more, then more. Maxi squeezed her eyes shut to keep the room from spinning.

She felt a hand on her breast, rubbing, tweaking her nipple. The cocaine was making her hallucinate. The hand moved over to her other breast. She opened her eyes to see Zahna Cole in the half-light, fondling her, moving her free hand down her body now and between her legs, while Maxi writhed in repulsion.

"Jack loved to watch two women together," Zahna murmured in a husky voice. "He taught me to like it. He brought me women. Didn't he ever bring chicks home for you?"

Maxi's mind was racing. She felt a surge of strength, and she jolted her body to shake Zahna off.

"Oh, no, you don't, baby," Zahna snapped. She laid the cross down on the bed, grabbed the front of Maxi's blouse, and furiously ripped it open. Then she picked up the cross, and with the sharp, jagged point, she pierced through the flesh just below Maxi's throat, and cut a deep line straight down between her breasts, almost to her waist. Maxi felt her warm blood spilling over her body. Tears streamed down her face.

Zahna lowered her head and licked the blood, then moved to Maxi's face and licked her tears. Maxi turned her face away, feeling sharp pain at her wrists where she'd been straining at the handcuffs. Putting a hand on Maxi's face and savagely tilting it toward her, Zahna bent down and kissed her hard on the mouth, running one hand through Maxi's disheveled hair, and with the other, squeezing Maxi's breast, her tongue hungrily exploring the inside of her mouth.

Suddenly she released her. "I have to pack. I'm going to Mexico, where they'll never find me," she said in a rush, taking another hit from the pipe. "You can watch me pack, Maxi Poole; it won't take long. And then I'm going to have you. And then I'm going to kill you."

Zahna clutched a handful of Maxi's hair and yanked her head up. She stuffed an oily, fetid pillow behind her, propping her up so Maxi could watch her move about in the foul-smelling room. Maxi yearned for unconsciousness now, but the drug had sent her speeding. She felt bile rise up into her throat. She tasted it, gagged on it. She was going to throw up. She swallowed it.

Zahna threw a dirty canvas duffel bag on the foot of the bed and started tossing things into it. "You know that I killed Jack, don't you?" she threw at Maxi. "I didn't mean to, really. But he pissed me off. I just went to Debra's house to *talk* to him. I knew he picked the brat up at two on Saturdays."

She pulled a black garter belt out of a dresser drawer and held it up. "What do you think, Maxi Poole? Jack bought me this." She laughed. "He liked to undo it with his teeth." She threw it in the bag. "Might need it down there. Might have to sell my bod for a while." She drew on the pipe again, several times, until she determined that it was finished.

"He didn't call for a couple of weeks, and I saw a picture of him and the Orson broad in the paper, dressed to kill for some frigging society bash. And I was rattling around all by myself on a Saturday afternoon, obsessing about him as usual, and I decided to take a drive to the beach and tell him I missed him.

"He saw me there when he pulled up. He saw me standing right across the street. I smiled. I waved. I expected him to come over and say something. Anything. Like, 'Hi, what're *you* doing here?' Know what he did?"

Maxi didn't respond. She wasn't listening anymore. Zahna

leaped to the head of the bed and yanked her upright by the hair again. *"Do you know what he did, Maxi Poole?"* she shrieked.

Maxi let out a low moan, which Zahna took for a response.

"He ignored me. He never even acknowledged that I was standing there. He looked right through me. Like I was invisible. That's what I always was to him. Invisible.

"Not you! And not the fucking mother of his only child. Not Janet Orson, the ice queen. You're all larger than life and in living color. *I'm* the invisible woman. Do you have any idea how that feels, Maxi Poole?" This time she didn't bother looking to Maxi for a response.

"I had a key," she went on, as she sorted clothes and threw her choices into the bag. "Had yours, too, you know. I decided to power right into the house after him, and if the freaking spaghetti movie star saw me, I'd just tell her to get the hell out of my way. I wasn't good enough to introduce to her. Same with the kid. The fucking kid knew me, and treated me like I was dirt, and Jack let her. A junior prig. I'd swat her outta my way if I saw her."

Maxi was crying softly, in pain, humiliation, anger, and despair. She wanted it to be over. All the pieces fit, made sense in a macabre way.

"I got in easy; the alarm wasn't set," Zahna rattled on. "Heard some voices coming from the kitchen, so I ducked into the kid's room off the hall to figure out what I was gonna do, when who the hell walks in? *Himself!*"

Zahna was relishing telling the tale, but it was lost on Maxi, who was light-headed now. She wondered if she was dying. She wondered why her life wasn't flashing before her eyes. She used to joke that when she died, Barbara Walters' life would flash before her eyes. She thought about that now, and managed a feeble smile. That's how Debra would handle it, she reflected foggily. Laugh to the end.

"And he sees me, and he says what the hell are you doing here? And I tell him I missed him and I was hurt that he didn't call me, and he grabs my arm and tells me he's calling the Malibu sheriffs, they're gonna come and arrest me for breaking and entering. I told him I'd tell about us, and he said, 'Yeah, right; who's gonna believe you?' He said, 'I'm through with you; you're nothing. Nothing but a dumb slut.' He was furious—you know how he gets, Maxi Poole?" Maxi vaguely heard her name from far away.

"Then, would you believe, I thought I must be totally fried, the *kid* walks in and she's holding a *gun*. A *real* gun! Jack was reaching for the phone. He said he was calling the sheriffs. So I grabbed the kid and snatched the gun away from her, aimed it at Jack, and shot him. Just like that. Like in the movies. I put the gun to the kid's head then, and said if she told anyone I'd come back and kill her, too. Then I wiped the fingerprints off on my shirt, dropped the gun, and I just waltzed out the same door I came in.

"I saw you, you know," Zahna went on. "I was driving like a maniac down the street, and I saw you going past me in your fucking big-deal black Corvette toward the house, Maxi Poole. *Maxi Poole!*" she screeched, getting no response from the sweating, bleeding figure on the bed. Maxi had passed out. Zahna went over and shook her.

"Wake up, Maxi Poole!" Zahna spat out. "We're gonna have a party!"

55

Richard was driving; Pete was navigating. Doing 90 on the Ventura Freeway, the address on Sumac was fifteen minutes from the station, tops. Richard was fervently hoping to pick up a Highway Patrol escort.

"Get off at the Van Nuys off-ramp," Pete barked, "and for chrissake, try not to get us killed, okay?"

"Can't find a cop when you need one," Richard muttered.

"Now, south on Van Nuys, across Ventura Boulevard to something called Roblar Place, then hang a left. Got it?"

"Yeah, I got it," Richard said, careening around corners at speeds the unwieldy news van was definitely not meant to travel, with its bulky microwave mast jutting in the air.

"Okay, down Roblar one block to Knobhill Drive, go south till you round a bend, and . . . yes! There's Sumac Drive! Go *right*, go *right*, to 6420 . . ." They both scanned the numbers on the small clapboard and stucco houses.

"There's Maxi's car!" Richard shouted. He screeched to a stop opposite the black Corvette, and he and Pete jumped out of the van. The address was on the other side of the street, three houses down.

The gate was locked. Richard put his right hand on the top

crossrail, hoisted himself up and over the sharp, rusty iron spikes, and dropped to the ground on the other side.

"Open it for me," Pete yelped, and Richard tried.

"Can't," he said, rattling the handle. "It's locked from the inside—need a key."

Richard left Pete standing on the dirt sidewalk eyeing the gate and the iron fence, while he sprinted up the path to the front door. He rang the bell; no response. He tried the knob; the door was locked. He backed off and scoured the parched front yard, mostly dirt and weeds, with a few persistent blades of grass. There was a small pile of rocks in a corner, probably used for some kind of decorative garden at one time. He hefted the biggest boulder, about the size of a watermelon. Maxi was in there, and she wasn't having tea. She hadn't shown up for work, and she hadn't called in, so something was up, and Richard wasn't about to be polite.

Pete was laboriously trying to climb up the outside of the iron wall, not easy at 220 pounds in slippery Italian loafers. He stopped and watched as Richard held the rock in front of him, dug in his Nikes, and made a fast run toward the house. Just before he hit the front door, he shifted his hands behind the rock and slammed it through the hardwood, just inches from the doorknob. The rock splintered the aged wood and opened a wide gash in the door as it fell inside.

Richard quickly reached in and grabbed the doorknob. He was relieved to feel it give, unlike the setup on the front gate. The door pushed open. He barged into the living room bellowing, "Maxi! Maxi, where are you?"

Suddenly, from behind the door, someone grabbed him by the shoulder, and he heard his jacket being slashed down the back. He whirled around to face a tall, thin, frenzied woman with glazed dark eyes. She'd reared back and was ready to strike again with what Richard knew immediately was the *Black Sabbat* cross.

With both his hands, he landed a mighty shove at her midsection, knocking her backward off her feet onto a cluttered glass-topped coffee table that shattered when she landed. With four long strides Richard vaulted out of the dingy living room to the back of the house.

Stumbling into the bedroom, he gasped to see Maxi shackled to the bedposts, her head to one side, her eyes closed, and her clothes ripped apart, revealing a gaping, bleeding wound that looked like it had rent her torso in two.

Was he too late? He leaped to the bedside and reached for the base of her neck to find a pulse. It was weak, but steady. "Maxi," he said. "Can you hear me, Maxi? It's Richard. I'm going to get you out of here."

He reached into his inside coat pocket where he always kept a few oversize paper clips to clamp scripts together in the field, and he twisted one of them straight. Grasping the handcuffs on Maxi's right hand, he inserted the aluminum tip into the lock. Deftly moving it back and forth, he listened until the tumblers released, then opened the cuffs and gently removed Maxi's bruised wrist. He leaped around the bed and did the same with the other set of handcuffs.

He stripped off his jacket, revealing the bulletproof vest that had saved him from a vicious gash down his back. Before they left, Pete and Richard had fastened on Kevlar vests—they were kept stored in the backs of all Channel Six vans.

Richard propped Maxi up and slipped his jacket behind her. Its silk lining would be safer against her skin than the filthy bedding, he reasoned. He pulled her torn blouse back over her wounds, and buttoned his slashed coat across her chest.

Carefully picking Maxi up, he wondered if the deranged lady of the house had been knocked out. He'd been so intent on finding Maxi that he'd left her there in the living room, sprawled in shattered glass. He didn't hear any sounds now in the small house.

Quickly, he loped out into the hallway, carrying Maxi. He

peered around the corner into the living room. Zahna Cole wasn't there. The front door was still open, and he could see Pete outside, standing in the middle of the street. Pete had evidently abandoned his attempt to scale the wall.

Richard ran to the door with Maxi in his arms, yelling, "Pete, quick, I'm going to hand Maxi over the gate to you; she's hurt—"

In midstride, he was about to hit the stoop when Zahna flew at him with an unearthly shriek from behind the door. He shifted Maxi's weight to his left arm, ducked down, and with his right hand he lunged for the woman's legs, getting a grip on one of them and yanking it up from under her body.

She dropped to the floor, but immediately began pulling herself up. She was gaunt and frail-looking, but from somewhere she was able to summon an uncanny strength. Richard darted back into the living room, quickly swooped Maxi down onto the couch, and was about to turn and go for Zahna, but in the seconds that he'd been turned away, the woman had jumped onto his back with tremendous force and was poised to deal him a strike to the neck with the deadly cross that was still clenched in her fist.

In that instant, a blast ripped through the room, and her grasp on the weapon released. Richard threw himself over Maxi to shield her, and watched the cross fall to the grimy carpet, to be anointed with a stream of blood that splattered off its painted colors. He lunged for it, picked it up, and whirled around to see Zahna Cole clutching her bleeding wrist, and Mike Cabello standing in the doorway holding a smoking gun.

56

Katie Anderson, the nurse in charge of 5-South at St. Joseph's Medical Center in Burbank, figuratively looked the other way as visitors entered room 518. Hospital rules mandated that no more than two people could be at a patient's bedside at one time, but she couldn't keep people from streaming in to see Maxi Poole, the Channel Six reporter. Maxi was one of her favorites on the news. Katie had ordered extra chairs brought into the private room. They seemed to be a pretty well behaved group, she noted, as she walked past 518 and glanced inside to make sure they weren't getting into party mode.

"Pete waved us down and flagged the house," Mike Cabello was saying, "and we shimmied over the wall and saw the Cole woman just about to do a guillotine number on the crime dog, here," he said, cocking his head at Richard, who was sitting on a chair at the foot of Maxi's bed.

"It was quite marvelous the way you were able to shoot that dreadful cross right out of her hand," Maxi's mother, Brigitte, said to Mike Cabello. "You did that so you could take her alive, isn't that right? So she'll have to stand trial, and it'll clear the name of that poor young actress, Meg Davis."

Cabello beamed at the commendation. Jon Johnson jumped

in. "Ma'am"—he addressed Maxi's mother—"it's only in the movies that lawmen aim for the legs, or the hand, or the gun. Actually, we're trained in life-threatening situations to aim for the largest area of the suspect's body. My partner's just a bad shot." Mike cuffed him hard on the shoulder.

"Just trying to keep you humble so I can live with you, buddy," Jon protested.

"How did you two manage to get there in time?" Maxi asked the detectives. She was propped up on her own extra-large down pillows from home. Her mother had brought them, along with a couple of pretty nightgowns and a robe, some personal articles and books, and her comfy sheepskin slippers.

Pete Capra related how Cabello had asked him for an industry check on Zahna Cole yesterday afternoon because of the suspicious way she'd set up an interview with Janet Orson. At the same time, he said, Richard was in the newsroom running down Maxi's lead on the Dracula costume, talking to merchants who'd recently sold them. "And I was up to my ass in alligators," he said, "so I asked Richard—"

"Pete, you're not in the newsroom," Richard interrupted. "Please excuse his language, Mrs. Poole—we can't take him anywhere." Richard went on to explain about the costume shop selling a Dracula outfit to Zahna Cole.

"Nobody was terribly concerned about this woman until you didn't show up for the Six O'clock, Maxi, and we tried to track you down. I checked with Sotheby's then, and found out that the woman in the sketches was Zahna Cole," Richard said. "Between Pete and your crisscross list we knocked down her address, and we jumped out there."

"Jumped out there?" Pete echoed. "If you ever get the urge to ride a roller coaster, just have Winningham drive you around town in one of our rickety news vans. Same sensation."

Richard went on: "Anyway, while I drove, Pete was calling everybody in town—the cops, the sheriffs, nine-one-one, the highway patrol; I think he also ordered pizza," he said with a grin, looking sideways at Pete. "And he reached Mike and Jon at KBIS, and told them to get over to Zahna Cole's house ASAP."

"Yeah." Pete laughed, pointing at Richard. "If anyone needs backup, it's this guy and me."

"Speak for yourself, Mr. Capra," Richard piped up. "You're the one who couldn't make it over the fence."

"I planned it that way," Pete offered as an alibi. "I stayed outside to wave Mike and Jon down, be sure they got to the right place. Good thing, huh?"

"As it turns out, yes," Richard conceded, "but thirty pounds less and you could have helped me overpower the she-devil."

"Yeah, Pete!" chimed Wendy Harris, who was committed to vigorous daily workouts. "At *least* thirty pounds."

"Okay, Winn, I concede you're the big hero here," Pete tossed out good-naturedly, eager to change the subject from the state of his physique. "You were *wounded*," he said with mock concern. "In the Brooks Brothers jacket!" Everybody laughed.

"Hey, that was an Armani," Richard groused. "Cost me a week's pay. Is the station going to buy me a new one?"

Pete's turn to laugh. "Check your contract, crime dog," he shot back. "Channel Six doesn't provide wardrobe for newsies."

"*I'll* buy you an Armani jacket," Maxi's dad put in. "I'll buy you *six* of them, with pants to go with them!" Maxwell Poole was very grateful to Richard for saving his daughter's life.

He and Brigitte had got the call from Pete Capra at their home in Manhattan at about 8:40 the night before, telling them that Maxi had just been brought into the ER at St. Joseph's—the two managed to make the ten o'clock red-eye to Los Angeles. On the drive to JFK, Max put in a call to Dr. Rick Gold in Los Angeles, an old family friend and Maxi's doctor in California. Rick met them in the hospital lobby, and they went up to Maxi's room. It was after one in the morning; Maxi was sleeping fitfully. Brigitte sat down on the bed, put her hand on her daughter's forehead, and kissed her gently. Maxi's eyes fluttered open, and in the dim illumination of the night-light she saw her mother bending over her, and her father standing by her side.

"Mom, Dad, you're here," she'd said weakly. Then, "Oh my God, am I dying?"

"No, darling." Her mother smiled, dabbing at a couple of tears. "You're going to be fine. Daddy and I just wanted to be here. Dr. Rick is with us." She drew the doctor into Maxi's view. "He's been conferring with the staff here."

"Hi, Maxi," Dr. Gold said. "Everything's fine. You'll be good as new, I promise." Maxi attempted a smile. If Dr. Gold said she was going to be okay, she could count on it.

"Daddy!" she said then, and held an unsteady hand out to her father.

He bent and kissed her protectively on the cheek. "I love you, little girl," he murmured. Maxi drifted back to sleep.

Today, they'd found her heavily bandaged from her neck to her waist, but awake and alert, and eager to talk. She'd shuddered as she filled her parents in on the details she could remember of the previous day's events. Brigitte was horrified. Max was proud of his girl, and tremendously relieved.

"Mom," Maxi had whispered to her mother then, looking down at her bandaged body. "What am I going to *look* like? For the rest of my life I'll have to wear turtlenecks, even on swimsuits."

"I'm way ahead of you," her mother said. "I've already had this discussion with Rick. He's lining up the best plastic surgeon in the country, who happens to be right here in Beverly Hills. Rick says name any Hollywood beauty, and Dr. Frank Kamer has probably worked on her."

Maxi sighed. She was lucky to have Brigitte and Max for parents. She was lucky to be alive. She was going to be released from the hospital tomorrow, and so was Yukon. They would both be hobbling around the house together, all bandaged up. But they would both recover fully, the experts said. Maxi wondered idly if she could get the plastic-surgeon-to-the-stars to fix Yukon up too. Guess not, she thought, smiling to herself. Dr. Sullivan had done a great job. Besides, Yukon had loads of hair to hide his scars.

She couldn't wait to be home. Dr. Rick had said she could probably go back to work in a couple of weeks. And she'd be fine to fly east for Thanksgiving.

A nurse's aide brought in another basket of flowers. She handed Maxi the card, along with a large, flat package. The flowers were from Alison Pollock, a huge arrangement of pink and purple cabbage roses. The card read simply: *Maxi, thank heaven you're okay!* The story had been all over the news that morning. Pete told Maxi that the switchboard at the station was swamped by viewers calling to find out how she was.

The aide took a small pair of scissors out of her pouch and helped Maxi open the package that had arrived. Maxi gasped. It was one of the sketches Remy Germain had made at the auction. It pictured Meg Davis purchasing the *Black Sabbat* cross from Gabby Modine, with Zahna Cole in profile standing prominently in the foreground. Signed by the artist, it was floated on a white matte board and set in a black acrylic frame. On a card accompanying the sketch, Remy had written: *Maxi, there was no way you or I could have known. Your planets must be aligned perfectly. Your guardian angel must be on your shoulder. Here's a memento for your trophy wall. Call me—let's do lunch. xx RG*

Maxi smiled. "An original Remy Germain—I'll put this up in my office." Remy Germain was a very interesting woman. Maxi had a feeling they were going to be friends.

There was a bustle out in the hall, and Debra Angelo swept into the room, carrying an enormous pink-cellophane-wrapped basket of fruit, chocolates, magazines, and, as Debra pointed out, three bottles of Amstel Light, Maxi's favorite beer, embedded surreptitiously beneath a bunch of grapes, along with a jeweled bottle opener. Attached to the top of the basket was a silver box tied with black ribbon, from Theodore on Rodeo Drive.

"That's a go-silk gown and robe, and some undies," Debra said, indicating the box on top. "I didn't know Brigitte was going to be here, so I brought you some survival gear." She went over and hugged Max and Brigitte, and introduced herself to Pete, Wendy, and Richard.

"And, of course, *we've* had the pleasure," she said, flashing a disparaging smile at Mike Cabello and Jon Johnson. "May I leave the frigging country now, gentlemen?" Maxi giggled.

"Well, actually, no," Mike Cabello said with a big grin. He had jumped to his feet when Debra entered and helped her wrestle the giant basket to a side table. "You'll get an official release from the sheriff's department through your attorney," he told her, "probably by the end of the week."

"*Really*," Debra said sweetly. "Well, try and find me, guys," she said. "Tomorrow I'll be in Europe."

Debra had decided, after everything broke, to take Gia to Italy the next morning for a short vacation. She would enroll her in a Malibu school in two weeks, but right now she felt they both sorely needed a change of scene. Her mother and dad were there, the Abruzzi was home, and it would nourish her soul. Walking over to the bed, she regarded Maxi critically. "Good Lord," she said, lightly fingering Maxi's bandages. "What the hell is under there?" She had heard accounts of Maxi's jagged injuries on the morning news. "This looks like a job for Frank Kamer, miracle man!"

"Got it covered. Love your priorities, Deb," Maxi said, laughing, and she meant it.

"I'm a satisfied customer—this is his nose," Debra countered with a grin.

Cabello was still standing. "Jon and I have to go," he said. "We have to get back to work."

"No, Mike has to go buy a new suit," his partner clarified. "He's got a date with his ex-wife tomorrow night and he doesn't have a thing to wear." Cabello cuffed him again, and the two headed for the door.

"Before you leave," Debra said to the detectives, "would you please explain to me how come my fingerprints were on the damn gun? Instead of Zahna Cole's, or even Gia's? Which is what got me in all the trouble to begin with, right?"

"Yes, we had a lengthy conversation with Ms. Cole about that, among other things," Jon Johnson offered.

"Lengthy?" Mike jumped on the word. "It was lengthy, all right—like from seven o'clock last night after they stitched up her arm, till about five this morning. She confessed everything."

"My *mother* would confess after ten hours in a room with *you*," Jon remarked. "Anyway," he said to Debra, "she said she wiped her prints off the gun with her shirt. That would have taken your daughter's prints off it too, and left only yours on other parts of the gun, from loading and handling it."

"Wonderful," Debra said. "Can I sue you guys for false arrest? I'll ask Marvin about that."

"Nope. We were within our rights," Cabello returned. "By the way," he said, addressing Richard now, "where the hell did you learn how to pick locks like that? You were a second-story man before you got into television?"

"I did a series showing viewers how to protect their homes against crime," Richard told him. "I used Wee Willy Wade as my expert. He showed how easy it is for a burglar to get into any lock. You fellas heard of him?"

"Oh, yeah," Cabello said admiringly. "New York guy. He could get into anything. Ed Koch made an unpopular joke once—said he was gonna give Wee Willy a key to the city. Said he might as well; he could get in anywhere he wanted anyway." Cabello chuckled. "Isn't Wade doing time?"

"Three to five," Richard said. "He writes to me. Nothing better to do, I guess. Anyway, Willy taught me how to pick locks."

"We saw that series," Brigitte said brightly. "It was excellent! I made Max put dead bolts on all the outside doors. We miss you in New York, Richard."

Cabello and Johnson had moved to the door. They said their good-byes, Jon thanked Maxi for breaking their case, Mike shot a parting look at Debra in her skintight knit dress, and they left.

"He's actually cute," Debra said, grinning after Mike Cabello.

"Don't even *think* about it, Deb," Maxi warned. "He's trying to get back with his ex-wife."

"Fine, fine," Debra said. "There are lots of other fish out there. There's an absolutely gorgeous fish in my new film. Coincidentally, he plays the detective."

"Great—you took the part!" Maxi beamed.

Maxi's folks wanted to know about the movie. Debra explained how she had been offered the role last week, and she was dying to grab it, but while she was out on bail on murder charges she couldn't negotiate any work, and the producer thought that she was holding out for more money, so he made a fabulous deal with her agent this morning. She would be starting the picture after she got back from Italy. It would be shot mostly here in the Los Angeles area, she told them.

"And what about Bessie?" Maxi asked. "Is she going to survive this?"

"Oh, Bessie will be fine," Debra said. "Bessie is hardy British stock. She was doing what she thought was right for Gia. Misguided though it was, how can I fault her for that? I couldn't replace Bessie in a million years."

Pete Capra got up to leave. "The early block is going on the air—I have to go bash some heads," he said, and he was out the door, with Wendy in tow. Richard and Maxi laughed. They knew he wasn't kidding.

"I'm going too," Debra said. "Gotta pack. When are you getting out of here, Max?"

"Tomorrow," Maxi responded, looking over at Debra's whopping basket of goodies. She laughed. "As usual, you overdid."

"Oh, you'll have fun with that stuff at home," Debra tossed off. "You'll find a great little edition of the *Kama Sutra* buried in there." She smiled wickedly, glancing pointedly at Richard.

Brigitte laughed. She always got a kick out of Debra. Maxi looked up at her dad to see how *he* had taken that remark. He was usually an unmitigated prude where his daughter was concerned. Not bad, she observed, not too bad at all. He was actually smiling. *Mom has done a great job of liberating Pop*, she mused.

Max got up too. "We'll walk out with you," he said to Debra. "We're going back to the hotel to freshen up for dinner. I'm taking Brigitte to Spago."

"We left so fast I don't have a *thing* to wear," Brigitte lamented.

"I know, darling." Max looked at her affectionately. "Only a suitcaseful. It's amazing what your mother was able to pack in twelve minutes flat," he said to Maxi.

"Still, I'm staying until Maxi can go back to work, so I'll have to shop."

"That's the spirit, Brigitte!" Debra applauded, as they crowded around the hospital bed to kiss Maxi good-bye.

"We'll pick you up in the morning," Maxi's father told her, "and your mother will get you settled in at home while I go get Yukon."

Maxi felt very blessed. Richard was going to sit with her for a while, until she got tired. She felt as if the two of them had been through the Blitz together.

At the doorway, her father paused and turned to them.

"Honey, invite Richard for Thanksgiving," he said, completely astonishing both Maxi and her mother. "You know we have plenty of rooms to accommodate your sister and Bucky, the kids, *and* him," he went on. "Because Richard and I have a date on the morning after Thanksgiving."

"A date? Where?" Maxi asked him.

"On Madison Avenue," he said, winking at Richard. "At Giorgio Armani."

Acknowledgments

MAXI POOLE AND I WANT TO THANK SOME VERY IMPORTANT FRIENDS OF OURS WHO HELPED GET *THE REPORTER* "BANGED OUT AND ON THE AIR," AS THE HARDWORKING FOLKS IN THE SWEATY NEWSROOM AT FICTIONAL CHANNEL SIX NEWS WOULD SAY:

My thanks to dynamic NBC-4 News producer ***Wendy Harris***, the soul of the newsroom and my longtime friend, who plays herself in all my books.

And to my former news director ***Tom Capra***, who would jump on the desk in the newsroom and point and scream, "*You, get a vest on and scout the riot area; you, get downtown and smoke out the mayor!*" (and who would get severely cranky every time he gave up smoking); and my former managing editor ***Pete Noyes***, who was known to punch out a reporter for burying the lead (before they put you in jail for that). Together these two inspired my character, Maxi's boss, Pete Capra. Thanks, guys, and don't get mad.

I owe *The Reporter* and Maxi Poole's very life to my editor ***Sara Ann Freed***, the sage of the Mysterious Press, who never let up on me for one single minute and still made me love her madly.

Special thanks to the irrepressible ***Susan Richman***, the patrician of New York PR people; and ***Kim Dower*** of "Kim from L.A.," Susan's counterpart in La-La Land.

And to these wonderful women of Warner Books: ***Maureen Egen***, the mother of us all; ***Jamie Raab***, the first to read *The Reporter* and run with it; ***Heather Kilpatrick***, who's every bit as good with plot points as she is with legalese; ***Penina Sacks***, who went to the mat with me on the minutiae of grammatical correctness (she won); and the astute and exacting ***Anne Montague***, who dazzled me with her canny input.

To my literary agent ***Robin Rue***, who insisted that *The Reporter* must have a home with the crème de la crème, Warner Books.

To my super-readers: author/screenwriter ***Linda Palmer***, social conscience of *The Reporter* ("You *cannot* let Maxi drink wine before driving off to a story!"); brilliant comedy writer ***Gail Parent***, my friend, neighbor, and partner on the TV show *Kelly & Gail*, who inspires the humor in everything I write; filmmaker ***Verna Harrah***, owner of Middle Fork Productions, whose mantra is "Story! Story! Story!"; and gorgeous ***Gale Hayman***, cofounder of Giorgio, Beverly Hills, Maxi's arbiter of fashion, beauty, and taste.

Hugs to playwright ***Marvin Braverman***, who feeds me ideas, along with Maxi's (and my) favorite "mushroom pizza with very thin crust."

My eternal gratitude to ***Shawn Kendrick*** of Borders, who walks behind me with a wheelbarrow full of my books at all manner of outlandish events (on the Santa Monica Pier during an afternoon cloudburst, on the pitcher's mound at Dodger Stadium during seventh inning stretch) and has managed to hang on to his aplomb and his cash box.

I am indebted to actor/screenwriter ***Bob Factor*** for helping me out of some deadline jams; ***Jim Alvarez***, head of NBC Wardrobe, for suitably dressing both Maxi and me; NBC-4 News editor ***Bart Cannistra***, my savior-in-chief from computer crashes; ***Mark Gray*** in NBC Reprographics for churning out *The Reporter* in its every phase; ***Terry Beebe*** and the gang at the NBC Credit Union for letting me monopolize their copy machine; and ***Patti Hansen***, head of NBC Travel, for keeping Maxi and me flying between the palms of Los Angeles and the publishing canyons of New York.

I'm grateful to attorney ***Neil Papiano***, who keeps me and my characters out of prison; to restaurateur ***Ron Salisbury***, who throws me book parties and feeds me besides; and to ***Barbara Jean Thomas***, who keeps me reasonably sane at home.

And what would I do without my treasured friends, ***Dr. David Walker*** of the Los Angeles Church of Religious Sciences, who teaches Maxi and me our metaphysical philosophy of life, and ***Vera Brown***, skin specialist to L.A.'s most glamorous movie stars, and the grande dame of TV's *Shop NBC*, for providing me with a soft landing at life and literature's many crises.

My profound adoration to my fascinating sister ***Ellie Poole***, the spiritual sister of Maxi Poole.

And always and forever, eternal love and gratitude to my sturdy bookends, ***Alice Scafard***, my incredible mom, and ***Kelly Lansford***, my princess daughter.

IF YOU LIKED *THE REPORTER*, AND YOU'D LIKE TO SPEAK TO ME OR MAXI (WE'RE VERY CLOSE), VISIT OUR WEB SITE—WWW.KELLY-LANGE.COM. BOTH OF US WOULD LOVE YOUR COMMENTS AND INPUT FOR OUR ONGOING "MAXI POOLE" SERIES. (IF YOU *DIDN'T* LIKE *THE REPORTER*, IN THE WORDS OF THAT GREAT NEWSWOMAN ROSANNE ROSANNADANA, "*NEVER MIND.*")